ONE-HUNDRED-AND-ONE MORE
READ-ALOUD CLASSICS

One-Hundred-and-One More
Read-Aloud Classics

EDITED BY PAMELA HORN

Tess
Press

J808.3
ONE

This edition published by Tess Press, an imprint of
Black Dog & Leventhal Publishers, Inc.
151 West 19th Street
New York, New York 10011

Book design by Alleycat Design, Inc.

Editorial Readers: Nicole Burman and Joanna Lehan

ISBN: 1-57912-532-8

Manufactured in the United States of America

b d f h g e c a

TABLE OF CONTENTS

INTRODUCTION

ne-Hundred-and-One More Read-Aloud Classics was compiled in response to the enthusiastic reception that the first volume, *One-Hundred-and-One Read-Aloud Classics* has received. Volume one was created on the premise that there is great value and significance in reading stories aloud to children. The demand for volume two confirms that children love the sound of language and benefit from being read to.

We all remember being read to as children. These memories are indelible for many reasons. The escape of exploring new adventures through these stories, the companionship and security of being read to by someone else, and the priceless excitement of learning to love books are all poignant moments for a child. Reading aloud together is an activity that not only bonds reader and listener, but teaches and reinforces patience, attentiveness, and curiousity—not to mention whetting the child's appetite for reading on his or her own.

The selections in *One-Hundred-and-One More Read-Aloud Classics* may appeal to children ranging from ages four through nine. The younger children learn to listen and develop a love for the stories, and as they get older they want to practice their own reading skills. When they are old enough to meet the challenge of reading themselves, the children use this collection as a springboard for reading, on their own, those entire books excerpted here.

Many of the stories in this collection may be beyond your child's reading level, but not beyond his or her listening level. Reading to children builds not only their listening skills, but also their vocabulary. Hearing the words, following the storyline, and creating a whole picture allows the child to contextualize the words, and become accustomed to using them in complete sentences. If your child's language development skills are already beyond simple word recognition, then reading to your child will compel his or her imagination in a plethora of directions.

More and more studies have proven that home reinforcement of concepts learned in school is an invaluable and effective educational step. Parents and readers of these stories can give children the attention and guidance that a teacher in a classroom cannot give. Most importantly, children learn to look forward to these moments of reading together and ultimately anticipate reading for themselves.

ABOUT THE SELECTIONS

ne-Hundred-and-One More Read-Aloud Classics contains traditional fairy tales, myths, and fables, as well as contemporary works. You will find talking animals, curious kids, and wild creatures experiencing adventure, humor, hardship, and mystery. The stories follow friendships, families, growing up, and going to school. We tried to include international and multicultural stories that come from various eras through time. This broad spectrum of genres, themes, and settings all aim to capture a read-aloud audience for approximately ten-minutes per piece. Some run shorter and some longer, but most will satisfy the attention span of both reader and listener.

Amazing Adventures

THE ADVENTURES OF HUCKLEBERRY FINN

THE ADVENTURES OF TOM SAWYER

ALICE'S ADVENTURES IN WONDERLAND

TREASURE ISLAND

CHARLIE AND THE CHOCOLATE FACTORY

THE WONDERFUL WIZARD OF OZ

THE PHANTOM TOLLBOOTH

ROBINSON CRUSOE

JAMES AND THE GIANT PEACH

MARY POPPINS

THE LION, THE WITCH AND THE WARDROBE

INCREDIBLE JOURNEY

Samuel Langhorne Clemens was born in 1835 and spent his boyhood in Hannibal, Missouri. In his twenties, he worked on riverboats on the Mississippi; in fact, the name he assumed as an author, "Mark Twain," is what boatmen called out when they measured the depths of the river.

His experience on the Mississippi is reflected in The Adventures of Tom Sawyer, which was published in 1876. The Mississippi plays an even more notable role in the exploits of Tom's footloose comrade, who comes into his own in The Adventures of Huckleberry Finn, published in 1884. A selection from each of these classics follows.

THE ADVENTURES OF HUCKLEBERRY FINN

MARK TWAIN

Huck fakes his death to ellude his dangerous father and heads down the Mississippi in a canoe to set up camp on an island a few miles away. Believing his body was in the river, the whole town comes out on a ferry, firing a canon regularly to make the body rise to the top. Huck lays low and observes the whole thing.

I made two mile and half, and then stuck out a quarter of a mile or more towards the middle of the river, because pretty soon I would be passing the ferry landing, and people might see me and hail me. I go out amongst the drift wood and then laid down in the bottom of the canoe and let her float. I laid there and had a good rest and a smoke out of my pipe, looking away into the sky, not a cloud in it. The sky looks ever so deep when you lay down on your back in the moonshine; I never knowed it before.

I was away below the ferry now. I rose up and there was Jackson's Island, about two mile and a half downstream, heavy-timbered and standing up out of the middle of the river, big and dark and solid, like a steamboat without any light.

I run the canoe into a deep dent in the bank that I knowed about; I had to part the willow branches to get in; and when I made fast nobody could a seen the canoe from the outside.

I went up and set down on a log at the head of the island and looked out on the big river and black driftwood, and away over to the town, three mile away, where there was three or four lights twinkling. A monsterous big lumber raft was about a mile upstream, coming along down, with a lantern in the middle of it. I watched it come creeping down, and when it was most abreast of where I stood I heard a man say, "Stern oars, there! Heave her head to stabboard!" I heard that just as plain as if the man was by my side.

There was a little gray in the sky, now; so I stepped into the woods and laid down for a nap before breakfast.

The sun was up so high when I waked, that I judged it was after eight o'clock. I laid there in the grass and the cool shade, thinking about things and feeling rested and rather comfortable and satisfied. I could see the sun out at one or two holes, but mostly it was big trees all about, and gloomy in there amongst them. There was freckled places on the ground where the light sifted down through the leaves, and the freckled places swapped about a little, showing there was a little breeze up there. A couple of squirrels set on a limb and jabbered at me very friendly.

I was powerful lazy and comfortable—didn't want to get up and cook breakfast. Well, I was dozing off again, when I thinks I hears a deep sound of "boom" away up the river. I rouses up and rests on my elbow and listens; pretty soon, I hears it again. I hopped up and went and looked out at a hole in the leaves, and I see a bunch of smoke laying on the water a long ways up—about abreast the ferry. And there was the ferryboat full of people, floating along down. I knowed what was the matter, now. "Boom!" I see the white smoke squirt out of the ferryboat's side. You see, they was firing cannon over the water, trying to make my carcass come to the top.

I was pretty hungry, but it warn't going to do for me to start a fire, because they might see the smoke. So I set there and watched the cannonsmoke and listen to the boom. The river was a mile wide, there, and it always looks pretty on a summer morning—so I was having a good enough time seeing them hunt for my remainders, if I only had a bit to eat. Well, then I happened to think how they always put quicksiver in loaves of bread and float them off because they always go right to the drownded carcass and stop there. So says I, I'll keep a lookout, and if any of them's floating around after me, I'll give them a show. I changed to the Illinois edge of the island to see what luck I could have, and I warn't disappointed. A big double loaf come along, and I most got it, with a long stick, but my foot slipped and she floated out further. But by-and-by along comes another one, and this time I won. I took out the plug and shook out the little dab of quicksilver, and set my teeth in. It was "baker's bread"—what the quality eat—none of your low-down corn pone.

I got a good place amongst the leaves, and set there on a log, munching the bread and watching the ferry boat, and very well satisfied. And then something struck me. I says, now I reckon the widow or the parson or somebody prayed that this bread would find me, and here it has gone and done it. So there ain't no doubt but there is something in that thing. That is, there's something in it when a body like the widow or the parson prays, but don't work for me, and I reckon it don't work for only just the right kind.

I lit a pipe and had a good long smoke and went on watching. The ferryboat was floating with the current, and I allowed I'd have a chance to see who was aboard when she come along, because she would come in close, where the bread did. When she'd got pretty well along down towards me, I put out my pipe and went to where I fished out the bread, and laid down behind a log on the bank in a little open place. Where the log forked I could peep through.

By-and-by she come along, and she drifted in so close that they could a run out a plank and walked ashore. Most everybody was on the boat. Pap, and Judge Thatcher, and Bessie Thatcher, and Jo Harper, and Tom Sawyer, and his old Aunt Polly, and Sid and Mary, and plenty more. Everybody was talking about the murder, but the captain broke in and says: "Look sharp, now; the current sets in the closest here, and maybe he's washed ashore and got tangled amongst the brush at the water's edge. I hope so, anyway."

I didn't hope so. They all crowded up and leaned over the rails, nearly in my face, and kept still, watching with all their might. I could see them first-rate, but they couldn't see me. Then the captain sung out:

"Stand away!" and the cannon let off such a blast right before me that it made me deaf with the noise and pretty near blind with the smoke, and I judged I was gone. If they'd a had some bullets in, I reckon they'd a got the corpse they was after. Well, I see I warn't hurt, thanks to goodness. The boat floated on and went out of sight around the shoulder of the island. I could hear the booming, now and then, further and further off, and by-and-by after an hour, I didn't hear it no more. The island was three mile long. I judged they had got to the foot and was giving it up. But they didn't yet a while. They turned around the foot of the island and started up the channel on the Missouri side, under steam, and booming once in a while as they went. I crossed over to that side and watched them. When they got abreast the head of the island they quit shooting and dropped over to the Missouri shore and went home to the town.

I knowed I was all right now. Nobody else would come a-hunting after me. I got my traps out of the canoe and made me a nice camp in the thick woods. I made a kind of tent out of my blankets to put my things under so the rain couldn't get at them. I catched a cat-fish and haggled him open with my saw, and towards sundown I started my campfire and had supper. Then I set out a line to catch some fish for breakfast.

When it was dark I set by my campfire smoking, and feeling pretty satisfied; but by-and-by it got sort of lonesome, and so I went and set on the bank and listened to the currents washing along, and counted the stars and driftlogs and rafts that come down, and then went to bed; there ain't no better way to put in time when you are lonesome; you can't stay so, you soon get over it

Twain, Mark. *Mark Twain.* New York: Crown Publishers, Inc., 1982.

THE ADVENTURES OF TOM SAWYER

MARK TWAIN

In this famous episode, Tom Sawyer has to paint his Aunt Polly's fence on a beautiful Saturday after-noon, but rascal that he is, he soon finds a clever way to get his friends to do his work for him.

CHAPTER II

Saturday morning was come, and all the summer world was bright and fresh, and brimming with life. There was a song in every heart; and if the heart was young the music issued at the lips. There was cheer in every face and a spring in every step. The locust trees were in bloom, and the fragrance of the blossoms filled the air. Cardiff Hill, beyond the village and above it, was green with vegetation, and it lay just far enough away to seem a Delectable Land, dreamy, reposeful, and inviting.

Tom appeared on the sidewalk with a bucket of whitewash and a long-handled brush. He surveyed the fence, and all gladness left him, and a deep melancholy settled down upon his spirit. Thirty yards of board fence nine feet high. Life to him seemed hollow, and existence but a burden. Sighing he dipped his brush and passed it along the topmost plank; repeated the operation; did it again; compared the insignificant white-washed streak with the far-reaching continent of unwhitewashed fence and sat down on a tree-box discouraged.

He began to think of the fun he had planned for this day, and his sorrows multiplied. Soon the free boys would come tripping along on all sorts of delicious expeditions, and they would make a world of fun of him for having to work; the very thought of it burnt him like fire. He got out his worldly wealth and examined it—bits of toys, marbles, and trash; enough to buy an exchange of work, maybe, but not half enough to buy so much as half an hour of pure freedom. So he returned his straightened means to his pocket and gave up the idea of trying to buy the boys. At this dark and hopeless moment an inspiration burst upon him! Nothing less than a great, magnificent inspiration.

He took up his brush and went tranquilly to work. Ben Rogers hove in sight presently —the very boy, of all boys, whose ridicule he had been dreading. Ben's gait was the hop-skip-and-jump—proof enough that his heart was light and his anticipations high. He was eating an apple, and giving a long, melodious whoop at intervals, followed by a deep-toned ding-dong-dong, ding-dong-dong, for he was personating a steamboat. As he drew near, he slackened speed, took the middle of the street, leaned far over to starboard and rounded to ponderously and with laborious pomp and circumstance—for he was personating the "Big Missouri," boat, and captain, and engine bells combined, so he had to imagine himself standing on his own hurricane deck giving the orders and executing them:

"Stop her, sir! Ting-a-ling!" The headway ran almost out and drew up slowly toward the side walk.

"Hi-yi! You're up a stump, ain't you!"

No answer. Tom surveyed his last touch with the eye of an artist; then he gave his brush another gentle sweep and surveyed the result, as before. Ben ranged up alongside of him. Tom's mouth watered for the apple, but he stuck to his work. Ben said:

"Hello, old chap, you got to work, hey?"

Tom wheeled suddenly and said:

"Why it's you Ben! I warn't noticing."

"Say—I'm going in a swimming, I am. Don't you wish you could? But of course you'd druther work—wouldn't you? Course you would!"

Tom contemplated the boy a bit, and said:

"What do you call work?"

"Why ain't that work?"

Tom resumed his whitewashing, and answered carelessly:

"Well, maybe it is, and maybe it ain't. All I know is, it suits Tom Sawyer."

"Oh come, now, you don't mean to let on that you like it?"

The brush continued to move.

"Like it? Well I don't see why I oughtn't to like it. Does a boy get a chance to white-wash a fence every day?"

That put the thing in a new light. Ben stopped nibbling his apple. Tom swept his brush daintily back and forth—stepped back to note the effect—added a touch here and there—criticised the effect again—Ben watching every move and getting more and more interested, more and more absorbed. Presently he said:

"Say, Tom, let me whitewash a little."

Tom considered, was about to consent; but he altered his mind:

"No—no—I reckon it wouldn't hardly do, Ben. You see, Aunt Polly's awful particular about this fence—right here on the street, you know—but if it was the back fence I wouldn't mind and she wouldn't.

"Yes, she's awful particular about this fence; it's got to be done very careful; I reckon there ain't one boy in a thousand, maybe two thousand, that can do it the way it's got to be done."

"No—is that so? Oh come, now—lemme just try. Only just a little—I'd let you, if you was me, Tom."

"Ben, I'd like to, honest injun' but Aunt Polly—well Jim wanted to do it, but she wouldn't let him; Sid wanted to do it, and she wouldn't let Sid. Now don't you see how I'm fixed? If you was to tackle this fence and anything was to happen to it—"

"Oh, shucks, I'll be just as careful. Now lemme try. Say—I'll give you the core of my apple."

"Well, here— No, Ben, now don't. I'm afeard—"

"I'll give you all of it!"

Tom gave up the brush with reluctance in his face but alacrity in his heart. And while the late steamer "Big Missouri" worked and sweated in the sun, the retired artist sat on a barrel in the shade close by, dangled his legs, munched his apple, and planned the slaughter of more innocents. There was no lack of material; boys happened along every little while; they came to jeer, but remained to whitewash. By the time Ben was fagged out, Tom had traded the next chance to Billy Fisher for a kite, in good repair; and when he played out, Johnny Miller bought in for a dead rat and a string to swing it with—and so on, and so on, hour after hour. and when the middle of the afternoon came, from being a poor poverty-stricken boy in morning, Tom was literally rolling in wealth. He had beside the things before mentioned, twelve marbles, part of a jews-harp, a piece of blue bottle glass to look through, a key that wouldn't unlock anything, a fragment of chalk, a glass stopper of a decanter, a tin soldier, a couple of tadpoles, six firecrackers, a kitten with only one eye, a brass doorknob, a dog-collar—but no dog—the handle of a knife, four pieces of orange peel, and a dilapidated old window-sash.

He had had a nice, good, idle time all the while—plenty of company—and the fence had three coats of whitewash on it!

Twain, Mark. *Mark Twain*. New York: Crown Publishers, Inc., 1982.

ALICE'S ADVENTURES IN WONDERLAND

Lewis Carroll

On an otherwise unremarkable day, young Alice follows a white rabbit down a rabbit hole and begins a day of magical adventures. In the following passage, she meets a cruel and bizarre Duchess who has a very unusual baby.

Chapter VI PIG AND PEPPER

The door led right into a large kitchen, which was full of smoke from one end to the other: the Duchess was sitting on a three-legged stool in the middle, nursing a baby; the cook was leaning over the fire stirring a large cauldron which seemed to be full of soup.

"There's certainly too much pepper in that soup!" Alice said to herself, as well as she could for sneezing.

There was certainly too much of it in the air. Even the Duchess sneezed occasionally; and as for the baby, it was sneezing and howling alternately without a moment's pause. The only two creatures in the kitchen that did not sneeze were the cook and a large cat which was lying on the hearth and grinning from ear to ear.

"Please would you tell me," said Alice, a little timidly, for she was not quite sure whether it was good manners for her to speak first, "why you cat grins like that?"

"It's a Cheshire Cat," said the Duchess, "and that's why. Pig!"

She said the last word with such sudden violence that Alice quite jumped; but she saw in another moment that it was addressed to the baby, and not to her, so she took courage, and went on again—:

"I didn't know that Cheshire Cats always grinned; in fact, I didn't know that cats could grin."

"They all can," said the Duchess; "and most of 'em do."

"I don't know of any that do," Alice said very politely, feeling quite pleased to have got into a conversation.

"You don't know much," said the Duchess; "and that's a fact."

Alice did not at all like the tone of this remark, and thought it would be as well to introduce some other subject of conversation. While she was trying to fix on one, the cook took the cauldron of soup off the fire, and at once, set to work throwing everything within her reach at the Duchess and the baby—the fire irons came first, then followed a shower of saucepans, plates, and dishes. The Duchess took no notice of them even when they hit her; and the baby was howling so much already, that it was quite impossible to say whether the blows hurt it or not.

"Oh, please mind what you're doing!" cried Alice, jumping up and down in an agony of terror. "Oh, there goes his precious nose!," as an unusually large saucepan flew close by it, and very nearly carried it off.

"If everybody minded their own business," the Duchess said, in a hoarse growl, "the world would go round a deal faster than it does."

"Which would not be an advantage," said Alice who felt very glad to get an opportunity of showing off a little of her knowledge. "Just think what work it would make with the day and night! You see the earth takes twenty-four hours to turn round on its axis—"

"Talking of axes," said the Duchess, "chop off her head!"

Alice glanced rather anxiously at the cook, to see if she meant to take the hint; but the cook was busily stirring the soup and seemed not to be listening, so she went on again: "Twenty-four hours, I think, or is it twelve? I—"

"Oh, don't bother me!" said the Duchess. "I never could abide figures!" and with that she began nursing her child again, singing a sort of lullaby to it as she did so, and giving it a violent shake at the end of every line:

> *"Speak roughly to your little boy,*
> *And beat him when he sneezes:*
> *He only does it to annoy,*
> *Because he knows it teases."*

> Chorus
> (in which the cook and the baby joined):
> *"Wow! wow! wow!"*

While the Duchess sang the second verse of the song, she kept tossing the baby violently up and down, and the poor little thing howled so, that Alice could hardly hear the words:

> *"I speak severely to my boy,*
> *I beat him when he sneezes;*
> *For he can thoroughly enjoy*
> *The pepper when he pleases!"*

> Chorus:
> *"Wow! wow! wow!"*

"Here! You may nurse it a bit, if you like!" the Duchess said to Alice, flinging the baby at her as she spoke. "I must go and get ready to play croquet with the Queen," and she hurried out of the room. The cook threw a frying pan after her as she went, but it just missed her.

Alice caught the baby with some difficulty, as it was a queer-shaped little creature, and held out its arms and legs in all directions, "just like a starish," thought Alice. The poor little thing was snorting like a steam engine when she caught it, and kept doubling itself up and straightening itself out again, so that altogether, for the first minute or two, it was as much as she could do to hold it.

As soon as she had made out the proper way of nursing it (which was to twist it up into a sort of knot, and then keep tight hold of its right ear and left foot, so as to prevent its undoing itself), she carried it out into the open air. "If I don't take this child away with me," thought Alice, "they're sure to kill it in a day or two. Wouldn't it be murder to leave it behind?" She said the last words out loud, and the little thing grunted in reply (it had left off sneezing by this time). "Don't grunt," said Alice; "that's not at all a proper way of expressing yourself."

The baby grunted again, and Alice looked very anxiously into its face to see what was the matter with it. There could be no doubt that it had a very turn up nose, much more like a snout than a real nose; also, its eyes were getting extremely small for a baby: altogether, Alice did not like the look of the thing at all. "But perhaps, it was only sobbing," she thought, and looked into its eyes again, to see if there were any tears.

No, there were no tears. "If you're going to turn into a pig, my dear," said Alice seriously, "I'll have nothing more to do with you. Mind now!" The poor little thing sobbed again (or grunted, it was impossible to say which), and they went on for some while in silence.

Alice was just beginning to think to herself, "Now, what am I to do with this creature, when I get it home?" When it grunted again, so violently, that she looked down into its face in some alarm. This time there could be no mistake about it: it was neither more nor less than a pig, and she felt that it would be quite absurd for her to carry it any further.

So she set the little creature down, and felt quite relieved to see it trot away quietly into the wood.

Carroll, Lewis. *Alice's Adventures in Wonderland and Through the Looking-Glass.* New York: Dell Publishing, a division of Bantam Doubleday Dell, 1992.

TREASURE ISLAND

Robert Louis Stevenson

Jim Hawkins's family runs an inn which has lately been the residence of a dangerous and disreputable old sea captain, known as Bones. After Bones dies at the inn, Jim finds a strange book and a packet; after a run-in with some scoundrels who were obviously after these things, he brings them to the trustworthy Doctor Livesey and the squire, Mr. Trelawney. The Doctor knows that Bones had once sailed with an infamous pirate named Flint, and they discover that they now hold the map to Flint's hidden treasure.

Chapter VI THE CAPTAIN'S PAPERS

And so, Jim," said the doctor, "you have the thing that they were after, have you?"

"Here it is, sir," said I and gave him the oilskin packet.

The doctor looked it all over, as if his fingers were itching to open it; but instead of doing that, he put it quietly in the pocket of his coat.

"And now, squire," said the doctor.

"And now, Livesey," said the squire in the same breath.

"One at a time, one at a time," laughed Dr. Livesey. "You have heard of this Flint, I suppose?"

"Heard of him!" cried the squire. "Heard of him, you say! He was the bloodthirstiest buccaneer that sailed. Blackbeard was a child to Flint. The Spaniards were so prodigiously afraid of him, that, I tell you sir, I was sometimes proud he was an Englishman. I've seen his topsails with these eyes, off Trinidad, and the cowardly son of rumpucheon that I sailed with put back—put back, sir, into Port of Spain."

"Well, I've heard of him myself, in England," said the doctor. "But the point is, had he money?"

"Money!" cried the squire. "Have you heard the story? What were these villains after but money? What do they care for but money? For what would they risk their rascal carcasses but money?"

"That we shall soon know," replied the doctor. "But you are so confoundedly hot-headed and exclamatory that I cannot get a word in. What I want to know is this: supposing that I have here in my pocket some clue to where Flint buried his treasure, will that treasure amount to much?"

"Amount, sir!" cried the squire. "It will amount to this: if we have the clue you talk about, I fit out a ship in Bristol dock, and take you and Hawkins here along, and I'll have that treasure if I search a year."

"Very well," said the doctor. "Now, then, if Jim is agreeable, we'll open the packet"; and he laid it before him on the table.

The bundle was sewn together, and the doctor had to get out his instrument case, and cut the stitches with his medical scissors. It contained two things—a book and a sealed paper.

"First of all, we'll try the book," observed the doctor.

The squire and I were both peering over his shoulder as he opened it, for Dr. Livesey had kindly motioned me to come round from the side table, where I had been eating, to enjoy the sport of the search. On the first page there were only some scraps of writing, such as a man with a pen in his hand might make for idleness of practice. One was the same as the tattoo mark, "Billy Bones his fancy"; then there was "Mr. W. Bones, mate." "No more rum." "Off Palm Key he got itt" and some other snatches, mostly single words and unintelligible. I could not help wondering who it was that had "got itt," and what "itt" was that he got, a knife in his back as like as not.

"Not much instruction there," said Dr. Livesey, as he passed on.

The next ten or twelve pages were filled with a curious series of entries. There was a date at one end of the line and at the other, a sum of money, as in common account books; but instead of explanatory writing, only a varying number of crosses between the two. On the 12th of June, 1745, for instance, a sum of seventy pounds had plainly become due to some one, and there was nothing but six crosses to explain the cause. In a few cases, to be sure, the name of a place would be added, as "Offe Caraccas"; or a mere entry of latitude and longitude, as "62° 17' 20", 19° 2' 40".

The record lasted over nearly twenty years, the amount of the separate entries growing larger as time went on, and at the end, a grand total had been made out after five or six wrong additions, and these words appended, "Bones, his pile."

"I can't make head or tail of this," said Dr. Livesey.

"The thing is as clear as noonday," cried the squire. "This is the black-hearted hound's account book. These crosses stand for the names of ships or towns that they sank or plundered. The sums are the scoundrel's share, and where he feared an ambiguity, you see he added something clearer. 'Offe Caraccas' now; you see here was some unhappy vessel boarded off that coast. God help the poor souls that manned her."

"Thrifty man!" cried the doctor. "He wasn't the one to be cheated."

"And now," said the squire, "for the other."

The paper had been sealed in several places. The doctor opened the seals with great care, and there fell out the map of an island, with latitude and longitude soundings, names of hills, and bays and inlets, and every particular that would be needed to bring a ship to a safe anchorage upon its shores. It was about nine miles long and five across, shaped you might say, like a fat dragon standing up, and had two fine land-locked harbors, and a hill in the center part marked "The Spy-glass." There were several additions of a later date; but, above all, three crosses of red ink—two on the north part of the island, one in the southwest, and, beside this last, in the same red ink, and in a small, neat hand, very different from the captain's tottery characters, these words: "Bulk of treasure here."

That was all; but brief as it was, and to me, incomprehensible, it filled the squire and Dr. Livesey with delight.

"Livesey," said the squire, "you will give up his wretched practice at once. Tomorrow I start for Bristol. In three weeks' time—three weeks!—two weeks—ten days—we'll have the best ship, sir, and the choicest crew in England. Hawkins shall come as cabin boy. You'll make a famous cabin boy, Hawkins. You, Livesey, are ship's doctor; I am admiral. We'll take Redruth, Joyce, and Hunter. We'll have favorable winds, a quick passage, and not the least difficulty in finding the spot, and money to eat—to roll in—ever after."

Stevenson, Robert Louis. *Treasure Island.* New York: Charles Scribner's Sons, 1911.

CHARLIE AND THE CHOCOLATE FACTORY

ROALD DAHL

Willie Wonka is giving a tour of his chocolate factory when Veruca Salt decides she must have one of the squirrels that have been specially trained to pry walnuts from their shells. In these two excerpts find out what happens when she won't take No for an answer.

PART I

Chapter 24 VERUCA IN THE NUT ROOM

Mr. Wonka rushed on down the corridor. THE NUT ROOM, it said on the next door they came to.

"All right," said Mr. Wonka, "stop here for a moment and catch your breath, and take a peek through the glass panel of this door. But don't go in! Whatever you do, don't go into THE NUT ROOM! If you go in, you'll disturb the squirrels!"

Everyone crowded around the door.

"Oh look, Grandpa, look!" cried Charlie.

"Squirrels!" shouted Veruca Salt.

"Jeepers!" said Mike Teavee.

It was an amazing sight. One hundred squirrels were seated upon high stools around a large table. On the table, there were mounds and mounds of walnuts, and the squirrels were all working away like mad, shelling the walnuts at a tremendous speed.

"These squirrels are specially trained for getting the nuts out of walnuts," Mr. Wonka explained.

"Why use squirrels?" Mike Teavee asked. "Why not use Oompa-Loompas?"

"Because," said Mr. Wonka, "Oompa-Loompas can't get walnuts out of walnut shells in one piece. They always break them in two. Nobody except squirrels can get walnuts whole out of walnut shells every time. It is extremely difficult. But in my factory, I insist upon using only whole walnuts. Therefore I have to have squirrels to do the job. Aren't they wonderful, the way they get those nuts out! And see how they first tap each walnut with their knuckles to be sure it's not a bad one! If it's bad, it makes a hollow sound, and they don't bother to open it. They just throw it down the garbage chute. There! Look! Watch that squirrel nearest to us! I think he's got a bad one now!"

28

They watched the little squirrel as he tapped the walnut shell with his knuckles. He cocked his head to one side, listening intently, then suddenly he threw the nut over his shoulder into a large hole in the floor.

"Hey, Mummy!" shouted Veruca Salt suddenly, "I've decided I want a squirrel! Get me one of those squirrels!"

"Don't be silly, sweetheart," said Mrs. Salt. "These all belong to Mr. Wonka."

"I don't care about that!" shouted Veruca. "I want one. All I've got at home is two dogs and four cats and six bunny rabbits and two parakeets and three canaries and a green parrot and a turtle and a bowl of goldfish and a cage of white mice and a silly old hamster! I want a squirrel!"

"All right, my pet," Mrs. Salt said soothingly. "Mummy'll get you a squirrel just as soon as she possibly can."

"But I don't want any old squirrel!" Veruca shouted. "I want a trained squirrel!"

At this point, Mr. Salt, Veruca's father, stepped forward. "Very well, Wonka," he said importantly, taking out a wallet full of money, "how much d'you want for one of these crazy squirrels? Name your price."

"They're not for sale," Mr. Wonka answered. "She can't have one."

"Who says I can't!" shouted Veruca. "I'm going in to grab me a squirrel this very minute!"

"Don't!" said Mr. Wonka quickly, but he was too late. The girl had already thrown open the door and rushed in.

The moment she entered the room, one hundred squirrels stopped what they were doing and turned their heads and stared at her with small black beady eyes.

Veruca Salt stopped also and stared back at them. Then her gaze fell upon a pretty little squirrel sitting nearest to her at the end of the table. The squirrel was holding a walnut in its paws.

"All right," Veruca said, "I'll have you!"

She reached out her hands to grab the squirrel . . . but as she did so . . . in that first split second when her hands started to go forward, there was a sudden flash of movement in the room, like a flash of brown lightning, and every single squirrel around the table took a flying leap towards her and landed on her body.

Twenty-five of them caught hold of her right arm and pinned it down.

Twenty-five more caught hold of her left arm and pinned that down.

Twenty-five caught hold of her right leg and anchored it to the ground.

Twenty-four caught hold of her left leg.

And the one remaining squirrel (obviously, the leader of them all) climbed up on to her shoulder and started tap-tap-tapping the wretched girl's head with its knuckles.

"Save her!" screamed Mrs. Salt. "Veruca! Come back! What are they doing to her?"

"They're testing her to see if she's a bad nut," said Mr. Wonka. "You watch."

Veruca struggled furiously, but the squirrels held her tight, and she couldn't move. The squirrel on her shoulder went tap-tap-tapping the side of her head with his knuckles.

Then all at once, the squirrels pulled Veruca to the ground and started carrying her across the floor.

"My goodness, she is a bad nut after all," said Mr. Wonka. "Her head must have sounded quite hollow."

Veruca kicked and screamed, but it was no use. The tiny strong paws held her tightly, and she couldn't escape.

"Where are they taking her?" shrieked Mrs. Salt.

"She's going where all the other bad nuts go," said Mr. Willy Wonka. "Down the garbage chute."

"By golly, she is going down the chute!" said Mr. Salt, staring through the glass door at his daughter.

"Then save her!" cried Mrs. Salt.

"Too late," said Mr. Wonka. "She's gone!" And indeed she had.

PART II

But where?" shrieked Mrs. Salt, flapping her arms. "What happens to the bad nuts? Where does the chute go to?"

"That particular chute," Mr. Wonka told her, "runs directly into the great big main garbage pipe which carries away all the rubbish from every part of the factory—all the floor sweepings and potato peelings and rotten cabbages and fish heads and stuff like that."

"Who eats fish and cabbage and potatoes in this factory, I'd like to know?" said Mike Teavee.

"I do, of course," answered Mr. Wonka. "You don't think I live on cacao beans, do you?"

"But. . .but. . .but. . ." shrieked Mrs. Salt, "where does the great big pipe go to in the end?"

"Why, to the furnace, of course," Mr. Wonka said calmly. "To the incinerator."

Mrs. Salt opened her huge red mouth and started to scream.

"Don't worry," said Mr. Wonka, "there's always a chance that they've decided not to light it today."

"A chance!" yelled Mrs. Salt. "My darling Veruca! she'll . . . she'll. . . she'll be sizzled like a sausage!"

"Quite right, my dear," said Mr. Salt. "Now see here, Wonka," he added, "I think you've gone just a shade too far this time, I do indeed. My daughter may be a bit of a frump—I don't mind admitting it—but that doesn't mean you can roast her to a crisp. I'll have you know I'm extremely cross about this, I really am."

"Oh, don't be cross, my dear sir!" said Mr. Wonka. "I expect she'll turn up again sooner or later. She may not even have gone down at all. She may be stuck in the chute just below the entrance hole, and if that's the case, all you'll have to do is go in and pull her up again."

Hearing this, both Mr. and Mrs. Salt dashed into the Nut Room and ran over to the hole in the floor and peered in.

"Veruca!" shouted Mrs. Salt. "Are you down there!"

There was no answer.

Mrs. Salt bent further forward to get a closer look. She was kneeling right on the edge of the hole with her head down and her enormous behind sticking up in the air like a giant mushroom. It was a dangerous position to be in. She needed only one tiny little push . . . one gentle nudge in the right place . . . and that is exactly what the squirrels gave her!

Over she toppled, into the hole head first, screeching like a parrot. "Good gracious me!" said Mr. Salt, as he watched his fat wife go tumbling down the hole, "what a lot of garbage there's going to be today!" He saw her disappearing into the darkness. "What's it like down there, Angina?" he called out. He leaned further forward.

The squirrels rushed up behind him. . . .

"Help!" he shouted.

But he was already toppling forward, and down the chute he went, just as his wife had done before him—and his daughter.

"Oh dear!" cried Charlie, who was watching with the others through the door, "what on earth's going to happen to them now?"

"I expect someone will catch them at the bottom of the chute," said Mr. Wonka.

"But what about the great fiery incinerator?" asked Charlie.

"They only light it every other day," said Mr. Wonka. "Perhaps this is one of the days when they let it go out. You never know . . . they might be lucky. . . ."

"Ssshh!" said Grandpa Joe. "Listen! Here comes another song!"

From far away down the corridor came the beating drums. Then the singing began.

> *"Veruca Salt!" sang the Oompa-Loompas.*
> *"Veruca Salt, the little brute,*
> *Has just gone down the garbage chute,*
> *(And as we very rightly thought*
> *That in a case like this we ought*
> *To see the thing completely through,*
> *We've polished off her parents, too.)*
> *Down goes Veruca! Down the drain!*
> *And here, perhaps, we should explain*
> *That she will meet, as she descends,*
> *A rather different set of friends*
> *To those that she has left behind—*
> *These won't be nearly so refined.*
> *A fish head, for example, cut*
> *This morning from a halibut.*
> *"Hello! Good morning! How d'you do?*
> *How nice to meet you! How are you?"*
> *And then a little further down*

A mass of others gather round:
A bacon rind, some rancid lard,
A loaf of bread gone stale and hard,
A steak that nobody could chew,
An oyster from an oyster stew,
Some liverwurst so old and gray
One smelled it from a mile away,
A rotten nut, a reeky pear,
A thing the cat left on the stair,
And lots of other things as well,
Each with a rather horrid smell.
These are Veruca's new found friends
That she will meet as she descends,
And this the price she has to pay
For going so very far astray.
But now, my dears, we think you might
Be wondering—is it really right
That every single bit of blame
And all the scolding and the shame

Should fall upon Veruca Salt?
Is she the only one at fault?
For though she's spoiled, and dreadfully so
A girl can't spoil herself, you know.
Who spoiled her, then? Ah, who indeed?
Who pandered to her every need?
Who turned her into such a brat?
Who are the culprits? Who did that?
Alas! You needn't look so far
To find out who these sinners are.
They are (and this is very sad)
Her loving parents, MUM and DAD.
And that is why we're glad they fell
Into the garbage chute as well.

Dahl, Roald. *Charlie and the Chocolate Factory.* New York: Penguin Books USA, Inc., 1964.

THE WONDERFUL WIZARD OF OZ

L. FRANK BAUM

Dorothy, the Scarecrow, the Cowardly Lion, and the Tin Woodman embark on a journey down the yellow brick road through the Land of Oz. Knowing that the great Wizard is the only one who can help Dorothy get back home to Kansas, they brave the perils that lurk in the woods.

Chapter VII THE JOURNEY TO THE GREAT OZ

They were obliged to camp out that night under a large tree in the forest, for there were no houses near. The tree made a good, thick covering to protect them from the dew, and the Tin Woodman chopped a great pile of wood with his ax, and Dorothy built a splendid fire that warmed her and made her feel less lonely.

When it was daylight the girl bathed her face in a little rippling brook, and soon after, they all started toward the Emerald City.

This was to be an eventful day for the travelers. They had hardly been walking an hour when they saw before them a great ditch that crossed the road and divided the forest as far as they could see on either side. It was a very wide ditch, and when they crept up to the edge and looked into it, they could see it was also very deep, and there were many big, jagged rocks at the bottom. The sides were so steep that none of them could climb down, and for a moment, it seemed that their journey must end.

"What shall we do?" asked Dorothy, despairingly.

"I haven't the faintest idea," said the Tin Woodman; and the Lion shook his shaggy mane and looked thougthful.

But the Scarecrow said: "We cannot fly, that is certain; neither can we climb down into this great ditch. Therefore, if we cannot jump over it, we must stop where we are."

"I think I could jump over it," said the Cowardly Lion, after measuring the distance carefully in his mind.

"Then we are all right," answered the Scarecrow, "for you can carry us all over on you back, one at a time."

"Well, I'll try it," said the Lion. "Who will go first?"

"I will," declared the Scarecrow, "for, if you found that you could not jump over the gulf, Dorothy would be killed, or the Tin Woodman badly dented on the rocks below. But if I am on your back, it will not matter so much, for the fall would not hurt me at all."

"I am terribly afraid of falling, myself," said the Cowardly Lion, "but I suppose there is nothing to do but try it. So get on my back and we will make the attempt."

The Scarecrow sat upon the Lion's back, and the big beast walked to the edge of the gulf and crouched down.

"Why don't you run and jump?" asked the Scarecrow.

"Because that isn't the way we lions do these things," he replied. Then giving a great spring, he shot through the air and landed safely on the other side. They were all greatly pleased to see how easily he did it, and after the Scarecrow had got down from his back, the Lion sprang across the ditch again.

Dorothy thought she would go next; so she took Toto in her arms and climbed on the Lion's back, holding tightly to his mane with one hand. The next moment it seemed as if she was flying through the air; and then, before she had time to think about it, she was safe on the other side. The Lion went back a third time and got the Tin Woodman, and then they all sat down for a few moments to give the beast a chance to rest, for his great leaps had made his breath short, and he panted like a big dog that has been running too long.

They found the forest very thick on this side, and it looked dark and gloomy. After the Lion had rested, they started along the road of yellow brick, silently wondering, each in his own mind, if ever they would come to the end of the woods and reach the bright sunshine again. To add to their discomfort, they soon heard strange noises in the depths of the forest, and the Lion whispered to them that it was in this part of he country that the Kalidahs lived.

"What are the Kalidahs?" asked the girl.

"They are monstrous beasts with bodies like bears and heads like tigers, replied the Lion, "and with claws so long and sharp that they could tear me in two as easily as I could kill Toto. I'm terribly afraid of the Kalidahs."

"I'm not surprised that you are," returned Dorothy. "They must be dreadful beasts."

The Lion was about to reply when suddenly they came to another gulf across the road; but this one was so broad and deep that the Lion knew at once he could not leap across it.

So they sat down to consider what they should do, and after serious thought, the Scarecrow said, "Here is a great tree, standing close to the ditch. If the Tin Woodman can chop it down, so that it will fall to the other side, we can walk across it easily."

"That is a first-rate idea," said the Lion. "One would almost suspect you had brains in your head, instead of straw."

The Woodman set to work at once, and so sharp was his ax that the tree was soon chopped nearly through. Then the Lion put his strong front legs against the tree and pushed with all his might, and slowly, the big tree tipped and fell with a crash across the ditch, with its top branches on the other side.

They had just started to cross this queer bridge when a sharp growl made them all look up, and to their horror, they saw running toward them two great beasts with bodies like bears and heads like tigers.

"They are the Kalidahs!" said the Cowardly Lion, beginning to tremble.

"Quick!" cried the Scarecrow, "let us cross over."

So Dorothy went first, holding Toto in her arms; the Tin Woodman followed, and the Scarecrow came next. The Lion, although he was certainly afraid, turned to face the Kalidahs, and then he gave so loud and terrible a roar that Dorothy screamed and the Scarecrow fell over backwards, while even the fierce beasts stopped short and looked at him in surprise.

But, seeing they were bigger than the Lion, and remembering that there were two of them and only one of him, the Kalidahs again rushed forward, and the Lion crossed over the tree and turned to see what they would do next. Without stopping an instant, the fierce beasts also began to cross the tree, and the Lion said to Dorothy,

"We are lost, for they will surely tear us to pieces with their sharp claws. But stand close behind me, and I will fight them as long as I am alive."

"Wait a minute!" called the Scarecrow. He had been thinking what was best to be done, and now he asked the Woodman to chop away the end of the tree that rested on their side of the ditch. The Tin Woodman began to use his ax at once, and just as the two Kalidahs were nearly across, the tree fell with a crash into the gulf, carrying the ugly, snarling brutes with it, and both were dashed to pieces on the sharp rocks at the bottom.

"Well," said the Cowardly Lion, drawing a long breath of relief, "I see we are going to live a little while longer, and I am glad of it, for it must be a very uncomfortable thing not to be alive. Those creatures fought me so badly that my heart is beating yet."

"Ah" said the Tin Woodman, sadly, "I wish I had a heart to beat."

This adventure made the travelers more anxious than ever to get out of the forest, and they walked so fast that Dorothy became tired, and had to ride on the Lion's back. To their great joy, the trees became thinner the further they advanced, and in the afternoon, they suddenly came upon a broad river, flowing swiftly just before them. On the other side of the water, they could see the road of yellow brick running through a beautiful country, with green meadows dotted with bright flowers and all the road bordered with trees hanging full of delicious fruits. They were greatly pleased to see this delightful country before them.

"How shall we cross the river?" asked Dorothy.

"That is easily done," replied the Scarecrow. "The Tin Woodman must build us a raft, so we can float to the other side."

So the Woodman took his ax and began to chop down small trees to make a raft, and while he was busy at this the Scarecrow found on the river bank a tree full of fine fruit. This pleased Dorothy, who had eaten nothing but nuts all day, and she made a hearty meal of the ripe fruit.

But it takes time to make a raft, even when one is as industrious and untiring as the Tin Woodman, and when night came the work was not done. So they found a cozy place under the trees where they slept well until the morning; and Dorothy dreamed of the Emerald City, and of the good Wizard of Oz, who soon would send her back home again.

Baum, L. Frank. *The Wonderful Wizard of Oz.* New York: Books of Wonder, William Morrow and Co., Inc., 1987.

THE PHANTOM TOLLBOOTH

Norton Juster

When Milo visits the island of Conclusions, life takes off. He meets Tock, a watchdog who teaches him about time, the Lethargarians, who live in the Doldrums, and King Azaz, the Unabridged, who rules over Dictionopolis, a book-shaped kingdom. When Milo and Tock arrive in Dictionopolis, King Azaz, the Humbug, and the rest of the court are finishing a huge banquet.

Chapter 8 THE HUMBUG VOLUNTEERS

"I couldn't eat another thing," puffed the duke, clutching his stomach.

"Oh my, oh dear," agreed the minister, breathing with great difficulty.

"M-m-m-m-f-f-m-m," mumbled the earl, desperately trying to swallow another mouthful.

"Thoroughly stuffed," sighed the count, loosening his belt.

"Full up," grunted the undersecretary, reaching for the last cake.

As everyone finished, the only sounds to be heard were the creaking of chairs, the pushing of plates, the licking of spoons, and, of course, a few words from the Humbug.

"A delightful repast, delicately prepared and elegantly served," he announced to no one in particular. "A feast of rare bouquet. My compliments to the chef, by all means; my compliments to the chef." Then, with a most distressed look on his face, he turned to Milo and gasped, "Would you kindly fetch me a glass of water? I seem to have a touch of indigestion."

"Perhaps you've eaten too much too quickly," Milo remarked sympathetically.

"Too much too quickly, too much too quickly," wheezed the uncomfortable bug, between gulps. "To be sure, too much too quickly. I most certainly should have eaten too little too slowly, or too much too slowly, or too little too quickly, or taken all day to eat nothing, or eaten everything in no time at all, or occasionally eaten something any time, or perhaps I should have—" And he toppled back, exhausted, into his chair and continued to mumble indistinctly.

"Attention! Let me have your attention!" insisted the king, leaping to his feet and pounding the table. The command was entirely unnecessary, for the moment he began to speak everyone but Milo, Tock, and the distraught bug rushed from the hall, down the stairs, and out of the palace.

"Loyal subjects and friends," continued Azaz, his voice echoing in the almost empty room, "once again on this gala occasion we have—"

"Pardon me," coughed Milo as politely as possible, "but everyone has gone."

"I was hoping no one would notice," said the king sadly. "It happens every time."

"They've all gone to dinner," announced the Humbug weakly, "and just as soon as I catch my breath I shall join them."

"That's ridiculous. How can they eat dinner right after a banquet?" asked Milo.

"SCANDALOUS!" shouted the king. "We'll put a stop to it at once. From now on, by royal command, everyone must eat dinner before the banquet."

"But that's just as bad," protested Milo.

"You mean just as good," corrected the Humbug. "Things which are equally bad are also equally good. Try to look at the bright side of things."

"I don't know which side of anything to look at," protested Milo. "Everything is so confusing, and all your words only make things worse."

"How true," said the unhappy king, resting his regal chin on his royal fist as he thought fondly of the old days. "There must be something we can do about it."

"Pass a law," the Humbug suggested brightly.

"We have almost as many laws as words," grumbled the king.

"Offer a reward," offered the bug again.

The king shook his head and looked sadder and sadder.

"Send for help.

"Drive a bargain.

"Pull the switch.

"File a brief.

"Lower the boom.

"Toe the line.

"Raise the bridge.

"Bar the door," shouted the bug, jumping up and down and waving his arms. Then he promptly sat down as the king glanced furiously in his direction.

"Perhaps you might allow Rhyme and Reason to return," said Milo softly, for he had been waiting for just such an opportunity to suggest it.

"How nice that would be," said Azaz, straightening up and adjusting his crown. "Even if they were a bother at times, things always went so well when they were here." As he spoke he leaned back on the throne, clasped his hands behind his head, and stared thoughtfully at the ceiling. "But I'm afraid it can't be done."

"Certainly not; it can't be done," repeated the Humbug.

"Why not?" asked Milo.

"Why not indeed?" exclaimed the bug, who seemed equally at home on either side of an argument.

"Much too difficult," replied the king.

"Of course," emphasized the bug, "much too difficult."

"You could if you really wanted to," insisted Milo.

"By all means, if you really wanted to, you could," the Humbug agreed.

"How?" asked Azaz, glaring at the bug.

"How?" inquired Milo, looking the same way.

"A simple task," began the Humbug, suddenly wishing he were somewhere else, "for a brave lad with a stout heart, a steadfast dog, and a serviceable small automobile."

"Go on," commanded the king.

"Yes, please," seconded Milo.

"All that he would have to do," continued the worried bug, "is travel through miles of harrowing and hazardous countryside, into unknown valleys and uncharted forests, past yawning chasms and trackless wastes, until he reached Digitopolis (if, of course, he ever reached there). Then he would have to persuade the Mathemagician to agree to release the little princesses—and, of course, he'd never agree to agree to anything that you agreed with. And, anyway, if he did you certainly wouldn't agree to it.

"From there it's a simple matter of entering the Mountains of Ignorance, full of perilous pitfalls and ominous overtones—a land to which many venture but few return, and whose evil demons slither slowly from peak to peak in search of prey. Then an effortless climb up a two-thousand-step circular stairway without railings in a high wind at night (for in those mountains it is always night) to the Castle in the Air."

He paused momentarily for breath, then began again.

"After a pleasant chat with the princesses, all that remains is a leisurely ride back through those chaotic crags whose frightening fiends have sworn to tear any intruder limb from limb and devour him down to his belt buckle.

"And, finally, after the long ride back, a triumphal parade (if, of course, there is anything left to parade) followed by hot chocolate and cookies for everyone." The Humbug bowed low and sat down once again, very pleased with himself.

"I never realized it would be so simple," said the king, stroking his beard and smiling broadly.

"Quite simple indeed," concurred the bug.

"It sounds dangerous to me," said Milo.

"Most dangerous, most dangerous," mumbled the Humbug, still trying to be in agreement with everybody.

"Who will make the journey?" asked Tock, who had been listening very carefully to the Humbug's description.

"A very good question," replied the king. "But there is one far more serious problem."

"What is it?" asked Milo, who was rather unhappy at the turn the conversation had taken.

"I'm afraid I can tell you that only when you return," cried the king, clapping his hands three times. As he did so, the waiters rushed back into the room and quickly cleared away the dishes, the silver, the tablecloth, the table, the chairs, the banquet hall, and the palace, leaving them all suddenly standing in the market place.

"Of course you realize that I would like to make the trip myself," continued Azaz, striding across the square as if nothing had happened; "but, since it was your idea, you shall have all the honor and fame."

"But you see—" began Milo.

"Dictionopolis will always be grateful, my boy," interrupted the king, throwing one arm around Milo and patting Tock with the other. "You will face many dangers on your journey, but fear not, for I have brought you this for your protection."

He drew from inside his cape a small heavy box about the size of a schoolbook and handed it ceremoniously to Milo.

"In this box are all the words I know," he said. "Most of them you will never need, some you will use constantly, but with them you may ask all the questions which have never been answered and answer all the questions which have never been asked. All the great books of the past and all the ones yet to come are made with these words. With them there is no obstacle you cannot overcome. All you must learn to do is use them well and in the right places."

Milo accepted the gift with thanks, and the little group walked to the car, still parked at the edge of the square.

"You will, of course, need a guide," said the king, "and, since he knows the obstacles so well, the Humbug has cheerfully volunteered to accompany you."

"Now see here," cried the startled bug, for that was the last thing in the world he wanted to do.

"You will find him dependable, brave, resourceful, and loyal," continued Azaz, and the Humbug was so overcome by the flattery that he quite forgot to object again.

"I'm sure he'll be a great help," cried Milo as they drove across the square.

"I hope so," thought Tock to himself, for he was far less sure.

"Good luck, good luck; do be careful," shouted the king, and down the road they went.

Milo and Tock wondered what strange adventures lay ahead. The Humbug speculated on how he'd ever become involved in such a hazardous undertaking. And the crowd waved and cheered wildly, for, while they didn't care at all about anyone arriving, they were always pleased to see someone go.

Chapter 9 IT'S ALL HOW YOU LOOK AT THINGS

Soon all traces of Dictionopolis had vanished in the distance and all those strange and unknown lands that lay between the kingdom of words and the kingdom of numbers stretched before them. It was late afternoon and the dark-orange sun floated heavily over the distant mountains. A friendly, cool breeze slapped playfully at the car, and the long shadows stretched out lazily from the trees and bushes.

"Ah, the open road!" exclaimed the Humbug, breathing deeply, for he now seemed happily resigned to the trip. "The spirit of adventure, the lure of the unknown, the thrill of a gallant quest. How very grand indeed." Then, pleased with himself, he folded his arms, sat back, and left it at that.

In a few more minutes they had left the open countryside and driven into a dense forest.

"THIS IS THE SCENIC ROUTE:
STRAIGHT AHEAD TO POINT OF VIEW"

announced a rather large road sign; but, contrary to its statement, all that could be seen were more trees. As the car rushed along, the trees grew thicker and taller and leafier until, just as they'd hidden the sky completely, the forest abruptly ended, and the road bent itself around a broad promontory. Stretching below, to the left, the right, and straight ahead, as far as anyone could see, lay the rich green landscape through which they had been traveling.

"Remarkable view," announced the Humbug, bouncing from the car as if he were responsible for the whole thing.

"Isn't it beautiful?" gasped Milo.

"Oh, I don't know," answered a strange voice. "It's all in the way you look at things."

Juster, Norton. *The Phantom Tollbooth*. New York: Random House, 1961.

ROBINSON CRUSOE

Daniel Defoe

First published in 1719, Robinson Crusoe is a classic tale of a sailor who becomes stranded on an uninhabited island for many years. The following excerpt tells of Crusoe's very first misshap at sea, when he realizes he should have listened to his father and chosen a more conventional profession.

Never any young adventurer's misfortunes, I believe, began sooner, or continued longer, than mine. The ship was no sooner gotten out of the Humber, but the wind began to blow and the waves to rise in a most frightful manner; and as I had never been at sea before, I was most inexpressibly sick in body and terrified in mind. I began now seriously to reflect upon what I had done, and how justly I was overtaken by the judgment of Heaven for my wicked leaving my father's house, and abandoning my duty; all the good counsel of my parents, my father's tears and my mother's entreaties, came now fresh into my mind; and my conscience reproached me with the contempt of advice, and the breach of my duty to God and my father.

All this while the storm increased, and the sea, which I had never been upon before, went very high, though nothing like what I have seen many times since; no, nor like what I saw a few days after: but it was enough to affect me then, who was but a young sailor, and had never known anything of the matter. I expected every wave would have swallowed us up, and that every time the ship fell down, as I thought, in the trough or hollow of the sea, we should never rise more; and in this agony of mind I made many vows and resolutions, that if it would please God here to spare my life this one voyage, if ever I got my foot upon dry land again, I would go directly home to my father, and never set it into a ship again while I live; that I would take this advice, and never run myself into such miseries as these anymore. Now I saw plainly the goodness of his observations about the middle station of life, how easy, how comfortably he had lived all his days and never had been exposed to tempests at sea or troubles on shore; and I resolved that I would, like a true repenting prodigal, go home to my father.

These wise and sober thoughts continued all the while the storm continued, and indeed some time after; but the next day the wind was abated and sea calmer; towards night the weather cleared up, the wind was quite over, and a charming fine evening followed; the sun went down perfectly clear and rose so the next morning; and having little or no wind and a smooth sea, the sun shining upon it, the sight was, as I thought, the most delightful that ever I saw.

I had slept well in the night, and was now no more seasick but very cheerful, looking with wonder upon the sea that was so rough and terrible the day before, and could be so calm and so pleasant in so little time after. And now, lest my good resolutions should continue, my companion, who had indeed enticed me away, comes to me. "Well, Bob," says he, clapping me on the shoulder, "how do you after it? I warrant you were frightened, weren't you, last night, when it blew but a cap full of wind?" "A cap full d'you call it?" said I, "twas a terrible storm." "A storm, you fool, you," replies he, "do you call that a storm? Why, it was nothing at all; give us but a good ship and sea room, and we think nothing of such a squall of wind as that; but you're but a freshwater sailor, Bob; come, let us make a bowl of punch and we'll forget all that; d'ye see what charming weather 'tis now?" To make short this sad part of my story, we went the old way of all sailors, the punch was made, and I was made drunk with it, and in that one night's wickedness I drowned all my repentance, and my reflections upon my past conduct, and all my resolutions for my future.

The sixth day of our being at sea we came into Yarmouth bay; the wind having been contrary and weather calm, we had made but little way since the storm. Here we were obliged to come to since the storm. Here we were obliged to come to anchor, and here we lay, the wind continuing contrary, for seven or eight days. On the eighth day it blew a terrible storm indeed, and now I began to see terror and amazement in the faces even of the seamen themselves. The master, though vigilant to the business of preserving the ship, yet as he went in and out of his cabin by me, I could hear him softly to himself say several times. 'Lord, be merciful to us, we shall be all lost, we shall be all undone'; and the like.

I was dreadfully frightened. I got up out of my cabin, and looked out; but such a dismal sight I had never seen: the sea went mountains high, and broke upon us every three or four minutes; when I could look about, I could see nothing but distress round us. Two ships that lay near us we found had cut their masts by the board, being deep laden; and our men cried out that a ship which lay about a mile ahead of us was foundered. Two more ships, being driven from their anchors, were run out to sea, and that with not a mast standing. The light ships fared the best, as not so much labouring in the sea.

Anyone may judge what condition I must be in at all this, who was but a young sailor, and who had been in such a fright before at but a little. But the worst was not come yet; the storm continued with such fury, that the seamen themselves acknowledged they had never known a worse. We had a good ship, but she was deep laden, and wallowed in the sea, so that the seamen every now and then cried out she would founder. It was my advantage in one respect, that I did not know what they meant by 'founder' till I inquired. However, the storm was so violent, that I saw what is not often seen, the master, the boatswain, and some others more sensible than the rest, at their prayers, and expecting every moment that the ship would go to the bottom. In the middle of the night, and under all the rest of our distresses, one of the men cried out we had sprung a leak; another said there was four-foot water in the hold. Then all hands were called to the pump. At that very word my heart, as I thought, did within me, and I fell backwards upon the side of my bed where I sat, into the cabin. However, the men roused me, and told me that I that was able to do nothing before, was as well able to pump as another; at which I stirred up and went to the pump, and worked very heartily. While this was doing, the master, seeing some light colliers, who, not able to ride out the storm, were obliged to slip and run away to sea and would come near us, ordered to fire a gun as a signal of distress. I, who knew nothing what that meant, was so surprised that I thought the ship had broke, or some dreadful thing had happened.

We worked on, but the water increasing in the hold, it was apparent that the ship would founder, and though the storm began to abate a little, yet as it was not possible she could swim till we might run into a port, so the master continued firing guns for help; and a light ship just ahead of us ventured a boat out to help us. It was with the utmost hazard the boat came near us, but it was impossible for us to get on board, or for the boat to lie near the ship's side, till at last, the men rowing very heartily and venturing their lives to save ours, our men cast them a rope over the stern with a buoy to it, which they after great labor and hazard took hold of, and we hauled them close under our stern and got all into their boat. It was to no purpose for them or us after we were in the boat to think of reaching to their own ship, so all agreed to let her drive and only to pull her towards shore as much as we could, and our master promised them that if the boat was staved upon shore, he would make it good to their master; so partly rowing and partly driving, our boat bent away to the norward, sloping towards the shore almost as far as Winterton Ness.

We were not much more than a quarter of an hour out of our ship but we saw her sink, and then I understood for the first time what was meant by a ship foundering in the sea.

Defoe, Daniel. *The Life and Adventures of Robinson Crusoe.* New York: Riffin Books, a division Penguin Books USA Inc., 1719, 1986.

JAMES AND THE GIANT PEACH

ROALD DAHL

One day James meets a very odd little man who bequeaths to him a handful of green, glistening crystals. James accidentally spills them on the old peach tree in his mean aunts' yard. The peach at the top of the tree starts to grow at an alarming rate. Soon James's aunts are charging admission to all the people who come to see it. Then one day James crawls inside the giant peach and his adventures with giant Grasshopper, Ladybug, Centipede, and the others who live inside begins.

CHAPTER 14

We're off!" someone was shouting. "We're off at last!"

James woke up with a jump and looked about him. The creatures were all out of their hammocks and moving excitedly around the room. Suddenly the floor gave a great heave, as though an earthquake were taking place.

"Here we go!" shouted the Old-Green-Grasshopper, hopping up and down with excitement. "Hold on tight!"

"What's happening?" cried James, leaping out of his hammock. "What's going on?"

The Ladybug, who was obviously a kind and gentle creature, came over and stood beside him. "In case you don't know it," she said, "we are about to depart forever from the top of this ghastly hill that we've all been living on for so long. We are about to roll away inside this great big beautiful peach to a land of . . . of . . . of . . . to a land of—"

"Of what?" asked James.

"Never you mind," said the Ladybug. "But nothing could be worse than this desolate hilltop and those two repulsive aunts of yours—"

"Hear, hear!" they all shouted. "Hear, hear!"

"You may not have noticed it," the Ladybug went on, "but the whole garden, even before it reaches the steep edge of the hill, happens to be on a steep slope. And therefore the only thing that has been stopping this peach from rolling away right from the beginning is the thick stem attaching it to the tree. Break the stem, and off we go!"

"Watch it!" cried Miss Spider, as the room gave another violent lurch. "Here we go!"

"Not quite! Not quite!"

"At this moment," continued the Ladybug, "our Centipede, who has a pair of jaws as sharp as razors, is up there on top of the peach nibbling away at that stem. In fact, he must be nearly through it, as you can tell from the way we're lurching about. Would you like me to take you under my wing so that you won't fall over when we start rolling?"

"That's very kind of you," said James, "but I think I'll be all right."

Just then, the Centipede stuck his grinning face through a hole in the ceiling and shouted, "I've done it! We're off!"

"We're off!" the others cried. "We're off!"

"The journey begins!" shouted the Centipede.

"And who knows where it will end," muttered the Earthworm, "If you have anything to do with it. It can only mean trouble."

"Nonsense," said the Ladybug. "We are now about to visit the most marvelous places and see the most wonderful things! Isn't that so, Centipede?"

"There is no knowing what we shall see!" cried the Centipede.

"We may see a Creature with forty-nine heads
Who lives in the desolate snow,
And whenever he catches a cold (which he dreads)
He has forty-nine noses to blow.

"We may see the venomous Pink-Spotted Scrunch
Who can chew up a man with one bite.
It likes to eat five of them roasted for lunch
And eighteen for its supper at night.

"We may see a Dragon, and nobody knows
That we won't see a Unicorn there.
We may see a terrible Monster with toes
Growing out of the tufts of his hair.

"We may see the sweet little Biddy-Bright Hen
So playful, so kind and well-bred;
And such beautiful eggs! You just boil them and then
They explode and they blow off your head.

"A Gnu and a Gnocerous surely you'll see
And that gnormous and gnorrible Gnat
Whose sting when it stings you goes in at the knee
And comes out through the top of your hat.

"We may even get lost and be frozen by frost.
We may die in an earthquake or tremor.

49

Or nastier still, we may even be tossed
On the horns of a furious Dilemna.

"But who cares! Let us go from this horrible hill!
Let us roll! Let us bowl! Let us plunge!
Let's go rolling and bowling and spinning until
We're away from old Spiker and Sponge!"

One second later . . . slowly, insidiously, oh most gently, the great peach started to lean forward and steal into motion. The whole room began to tilt over and all the furniture went sliding across the floor and crashed against the far wall. So did James and the Ladybug and the Old-Green-Grasshopper and Miss Spider and the Earthworm, also the Centipede, who had just come slithering quickly down the wall.

CHAPTER 15

Outside in the garden, at that very moment, Aunt Sponge and Aunt Spiker had just taken their places at the front gate, each with a bunch of tickets in her hand, and the first stream of early morning sightseers was visible in the distance climbing up the hill to view the peach.

"We shall make a fortune today," Aunt Spiker was saying. "Just look at all those people!"

"I wonder what became of that horrid little boy of ours last night," Aunt Sponge said. "He never did come back in, did he?"

"He probably fell down in the dark and broke his leg," Aunt Spiker said.

"Or his neck, maybe," Aunt Sponge said hopefully.

"Just wait till I get my hands on him," Aunt Spiker said, waving her cane. "He'll never want to stay out all night again by the time I've finished with him. Good gracious me! What's that awful noise?"

Both women swung around to look.

The noise, of course, had been caused by the giant peach crashing through the fence that surrounded it, and now, gathering speed every second, it came rolling across the garden toward the place where Aunt Sponge and Aunt Spiker were standing.

They gaped. They screamed. They started to run. They panicked. They both got in each other's way. They began pushing and jostling, and each one of them was thinking only about saving herself. Aunt Sponge, the fat one, tripped over a box that she'd brought along to keep the money in and fell flat on her face. Aunt Spiker immediately tripped over Aunt Sponge and came down on top of her. They both lay on the ground, fighting and clawing and yelling and struggling frantically to get up again, but before they could do this, the mighty peach was upon them.

There was a crunch.

And then there was silence.

The peach rolled on. And behind it, Aunt Sponge and Aunt Spiker lay ironed out upon the grass as flat and thin and lifeless as a couple of paper dolls cut out of a picture book.

CHAPTER 16

And now the peach had broken out of the garden and was over the edge of the hill, rolling and bouncing down the steep slope at a terrific pace. Faster and faster and faster it went, and the crowds of people who were climbing up the hill suddenly caught sight of this terrible monster plunging down upon them, and they screamed and scattered to right and left as it went hurtling by.

At the bottom of the hill it charged across the road, knocking over a telegraph pole and flattening two parked automobiles as it went by.

Then it rushed madly across about twenty fields, breaking down all the fences and hedges in its path. It went right through a flock of sheep, and then through a paddock full of horses, and then through a yard full of pigs, and soon the whole countryside was a seething mass of panic-stricken animals stampeding in all directions.

The peach was still going at a tremendous speed with no sign of slowing down, and about a mile farther on it came to a village.

Down the main street of the village it rolled, with people leaping frantically out of its path right and left, and at the end of the street it went crashing right through the wall of an enormous building and out the other side, leaving two gaping holes in the brickwork.

This building happened to be a famous factory where they made chocolate, and almost at once a great river of warm, melted chocolate came pouring out of the holes in the factory wall. A minute later, this brown sticky mess was flowing through every street in the village, oozing under the doors of houses and into people's shops and gardens.

Children were wading in it up to their knees, and some were even trying to swim in it, and all of them were sucking it into their mouths in great greedy gulps and shrieking with joy.

But the peach rushed on across the countryside—on and on and on, leaving a trail of destruction in its wake. Cowsheds, stables, pigsties, barns, bungalows, hayricks, anything that got in its way went toppling over like a ninepin. An old man sitting quietly beside a stream had his fishing rod whisked out of his hands as it went dashing by, and a woman called Daisy Entwistle was standing so close to it as it passed that she had the skin taken off the tip of her long nose.

Would it ever stop?

Why should it? A round object will always keep on rolling as long as it is on a down-hill slope, and, in this case, the land sloped downhill all the way until it reached the ocean—the same ocean that James had begged his aunts to be allowed to visit the day before.

Well, perhaps he was going to visit it now. The peach was rushing closer and closer to it every second, and closer also to the towering white cliffs that came first.

These cliffs are the most famous in the whole of England, and they are hundreds of feet high. Below them, the sea is deep and cold and hungry. Many ships have been swallowed up and lost forever on this part of the coast and all the men who were in them as well. The peach was now only a hundred yards away from the cliff—now fifty— now twenty—now ten—now five—and when it reached the edge of the cliff it seemed to leap up into the sky and hang there suspended for a few seconds, still turning over and over in the air . . .

Then it began to fall . . .
Down . . .
Down . . .
Down . . .
Down . . .
Down . . .
SMACK! It hit the water like a colossal splash and sank like a stone.

But a few seconds later, up it came again, and this time, up it stayed, floating serenely upon the surface of the water.

Dahl, Roald. *James and the Giant Peach*. New York: Puffin Books, A Division of Penguin Books USA, Inc., 1961.

MARY POPPINS

P.L. TRAVERS

You may have heard of Mary Poppins, the British nanny who brings her charges on marvelous, magical adventures. But what does this mysterious nanny do on her day off?

PART I

Mary Poppins walked down the garden path and opened the gate. Once outside in the Lane, she set off walking very quickly as if she were afraid the afternoon would run away from her if she didn't keep up with it. At the corner she turned to the right and then to the left, nodded haughtily to the Policeman, who said it was nice day, and by that time, she felt that her Day Out had begun.

She stopped beside an empty motor-car in order to put her hat straight with the help of the wind-screen, in which it was reflected, then she smoothed down her frock and tucked her umbrella more securely under her arm so that the handle, or rather the parrot, could be seen by everybody. After these preparations, she went forward to meet the Match-Man.

Now, the Match-Man had two professions. He not only sold matches like any ordinary match-man, but he drew pavement pictures as well. If it was wet, he sold matches because the rain would have washed away his pictures if he had painted them. If it was fine, he was on his knees all day, making pictures in colored chalks on the sidewalks, and doing them so quickly that often you would find he had painted up one side of a street and down the other almost before you'd had time to come round the corner.

On this particular day, which was fine but cold, he was painting. He was in the act of adding a picture of two bananas, an apple, and a head of Queen Elizabeth to a long string of others, when Mary Poppins walked up to him, tip-toeing so as to surprise him.

"Hey!" called Mary Poppins softly.

He went on putting brown stripes on a banana and brown curls on Queen Elizabeth's head.

"Ahem!" said Mary Poppins, with a ladylike cough.

He turned with a start and saw her.

"Mary!" he cried, and you could tell by the way he cried it that Mary Poppins was a very important person in his life.

Mary Poppins looked down at her feet and rubbed the toe of one shoe along the pavement two or three times. Then she smiled at the shoe in such a way that the shoe knew quite well that the smile wasn't meant for it.

"It's my Day, Bert," she said. "Didn't you remember?" Bert was the Match-Man's name — Herbert Alfred for Sundays.

"Of course I remembered, Mary," he said, "but—" and he stopped and looked sadly into his cap. It lay on the ground beside his last picture, and there was tuppence in it. He picked it up and jingled the pennies.

"That all you got, Bert?" said Mary Poppins, and she said it so brightly you could hardly tell she was disappointed at all.

"That's the lot," he said. "Business is bad today. You'd think anybody'd be glad to pay to see that, wouldn't you?" And he nodded his head at Queen Elizabeth. "Well—that's how it is, Mary," he sighed. "Can't take you to tea today, I'm afraid."

Mary Poppins thought of the raspberry-jam-cakes they always had on her Day Out, and she was just going to sigh, when she saw the Match-Man's face. So, very cleverly, she turned the sigh into a smile—a good one with both ends turned up—and said: "That's all right, Bert. Don't you mind. I'd much rather not go to tea. A stodgy meal, I call it—really."

And that, when you think how very much she liked raspberry-jam-cakes, was rather nice of Mary Poppins.

The Match-Man apparently thought so too, for he took her white-gloved hand in his and squeezed it hard. Then together they walked down the row of pictures.

"Now, there's one you've never seen before!" said the Match-Man proudly, pointing to a pointing of a mountain covered with snow and its slopes simply littered with grasshoppers sitting on gigantic roses.

This time Mary Poppins could indulge in a sigh without hurting his feelings.

"Oh, Bert," she said, "that's a fair treat!"

The next picture Mary Poppins and the Match-Man came to was even better. It was the country — all trees and grass and a little bit of blue sea in the distance, and something that looked like Margate in the background.

"My word!" said Mary Poppins admiringly, stooping so that she could see it better. "Why, Bert, whatever is the matter?"

For the Match-Man had caught hold of her other hand now and was looking very excited.

"Mary," he said, "I got an idea! A real idea. Why don't we go there–right now–this very day? Both together, into the picture. Eh, Mary?" And still holding her hands he drew her right out of the street, away from the iron railings and the lampposts, into the very middle of the picture. Pff! There they were, right inside it!

How green it was there and how quiet, and what soft crisp grass under their feet! They could hardly believe it was true, and yet here were green branches huskily rattling on their hats as they bent beneath them, and little colored flowers curling round their shoes. They stared at each other, and each noticed that the other had changed. To Mary Poppins the Match-Man seemed to have bought himself an entirely new suit of clothes, for he was now wearing a bright green-and-red striped coat and white flannel trousers and, best of all, a new straw hat. He looked unusually clean, as though he had been polished.

"Why, Bert, you look fine!" she cried in an admiring voice.

Bert could not say anything for a moment, for his mouth had fallen open, and he was staring at her with round eyes. Then he gulped and said: "Golly!"

That was all. But he said it in such a way and stared so steadily and so delightedly at her that she took a little mirror out of her bag and looked at herself in it.

She too, she discovered, had changed. Round her shoulders hung a cloak of lovely artificial silk with watery patterns all over it, and the tickling feeling at the back of her neck came, the mirror told her, from a long, curly feather that swept down from the brim of her hat. Her best shoes had disappeared, and in their place were others much finer and with large diamond buckles shining upon them. She was still wearing the white gloves and carrying the umbrella.

"My goodness," said Mary Poppins, "I am having a Day Out!"

"I'm the Waiter, you know!"

So, still admiring themselves and each other, they moved on together through the little wood, till presently they came upon a little open space filled with sunlight. And there on a green table was Afternoon-Tea!

PART II

A pile of raspberry-jam-cakes as high as Mary Poppins's waist stood in the center, and beside it tea was boiling in a big brass urn. Best of all, there were two plates of whelks and two pins to pick them out with.

"Strike me pink!" said Mary Poppins. That was what she always said when she was pleased.

"Golly!" said the Match-Man. And that was his particular phrase.

"Won't you sit down, Moddom?" enquired a voice, and they turned to find a tall man in a black coat coming out of the wood with a table-napkin over his arm.

Mary Poppins, thoroughly surprised, sat down with a plop upon one of the little green chairs that stood round the table. The Match-Man, staring, collapsed on to another.

"I'm the Waiter, you know!" explained the man in the black coat.

"Oh! But I didn't see you in the picture," said Mary Poppins.

"Ah, I was behind the tree," explained the Waiter.

"Won't you sit down?" said Mary Poppins, politely.

"Waiters never sit down, Moddom," said the man, but he seemed pleased at being asked.

"Your whelks Mister!" he said, pushing a plate of them over to the Match-Man. "And your Pin!"

He dusted the pin on his napkin and handed it to the Match-Man.

They began upon the afternoon-tea, and the Waiter stood beside them to see they had everything they needed.

"We're having them after all," said Mary Poppins in a loud whisper, as she began on the heap of raspberry-jam-cakes.

"Golly!" agreed the Match-Man, helping himself to two of the largest.

"Tea?" said the Waiter, filling a large cup for each of them from the urn.

They drank it and had two cups more each, and then, for luck, they finished the pile of raspberry-jam-cakes. After that, they got up and brushed the crumbs off.

"There is Nothing to Pay," said the Waiter, before they had time to ask for the bill. "It is a Pleasure. You will find the Merry-go-Round just over there!" And he waved his hand to a little gap in the trees, where Mary Poppins and the Match-Man could see several wooden horses whirling round on a stand.

"That's funny," said she. "I don't remember seeing that in the picture, either."

56

"Ah," said the Match-Man, who hadn't remembered it himself, "it was in the Background, you see!"

The Merry-go-Round was just slowing down as they approached it. They leapt upon it, Mary Poppins on a black horse and the Match-Man on a grey. And when the music started again and they began to move, they rode all the way to Yarmouth and back, because that was the place they both wanted most to see.

When they returned it was nearly dark and the Waiter was watching for them.

"I'm very sorry, Moddom and Mister," he said politely, "but we close at Seven. Rules, you know. May I show you the Way Out?"

They nodded as he flourished his table-napkin and walked on in front of them through the wood.

"It's a wonderful picture you've drawn this time, Bert," said Mary Poppins, putting her hand through the Match-Man's arm and drawing her cloak about her.

"Well, I did my best, Mary," said the Match-Man modestly. But you could see he was really very pleased with himself indeed.

Just then the Waiter stopped in front of them, beside a large white doorway that looked as though it were made of thick chalk lines.

"Here you are!" he said. "This is the Way Out."

"Good-bye, and thank you," said Mary Poppins, shaking his hand.

"Moddom, goodbye!" said the Waiter, bowing so low that his head knocked against his knees.

He nodded to the Match-Man, who cocked his head on one side and closed one eye at the Waiter, which was his way of bidding him farewell. Then Mary Poppins stepped through the white doorway and the Match-Man followed her.

And as they went, the feather dropped from her hat, and the silk cloak from her shoulders, and the diamonds from her shoes. The bright clothes of the Match-Man faded, and his straw hat turned into his old ragged cap again. Mary Poppins turned and looked at him, and she knew at once what had happened. Standing on the pavement, she gazed at him for a long minute, and then her glance explored the wood behind him for the Waiter. But the Waiter was nowhere to be seen. There was nobody in the picture. Nothing moved there. Even the Merry-go-Round had disappeared. Only the still trees and the grass and the unmoving little patch of sea remained.

But Mary Poppins and the Match-Man smiled at one another. They knew you see, what lay behind the trees. . . .

Travers, P.L. *Mary Poppins.* New York: Bantam Doubleday Dell, 1981

THE LION, THE WITCH AND THE WARDROBE

C.S. LEWIS

Lucy, Peter, Edmund, and Susan are on holiday in a big old house that belongs to a professor. Part I of this excerpt begins one rainy morning when the children decide to do some exploring. The first room in the house that they investigate seems empty except for a large wardrobe. They all move on except for Lucy, who opens the wardrobe, climbs inside. Part II follows Lucy as she enters a strange country called Narnia. After what seems like hours there, she suddenly finds herself back in the wardrobe and hears Susan, Peter, and Edmund talking.

EDMUND AND THE WARDROBE

PART 1

ucy ran out of the empty room into the passage and found the other three. "It's all right," she repeated, "I've come back."

"What on earth are you talking about, Lucy?" asked Susan.

"Why," said Lucy in amazement, "haven't you all been wondering where I was?"

"So you've been hiding, have you?" said Peter. "Poor old Lu, hiding and nobody noticed! You'll have to hide longer than that if you want people to start looking for you."

"But I've been away for hours and hours," said Lucy.

The others all stared at one another.

"Batty!" said Edmund, tapping his head. "Quite batty."

"What do you mean, Lu?" asked Peter.

"What I said," answered Lucy. "It was just after breakfast when I went into the wardrobe, and I've been away for hours and hours, and had tea, and all sorts of things have happened."

"Don't be silly, Lucy," said Susan. "We've only just come out of that room a moment ago, and you were there then."

"She's not being silly at all," said Peter, "she's just making up a story for fun, aren't you, Lu? And why shouldn't she?"

"No, Peter, I'm not," she said. "It's—it's a magic wardrobe. There's a wood inside it, and it's snowing, and there's a Faun and a Witch and it's called Narnia; come and see."

The others did not know what to think, but Lucy was so excited that they all went back with her into the room. She rushed ahead of them, flung open the door of the wardrobe and cried, "Now! go in and see for yourselves."

"Why, you goose," said Susan, putting her head inside and pulling the fur coats apart, "it's just an ordinary wardrobe; look! there's the back of it."

Then everyone looked in and pulled the coats apart; and they all saw—Lucy herself saw—a perfectly ordinary wardrobe. There was no wood and no snow, only the back of the wardrobe, with hooks on it. Peter went in and rapped his knuckles on it to make sure that it was solid.

"A jolly good hoax, Lu," he said as he came out again, "you have really taken us in, I must admit. We half-believed you."

"But it wasn't a hoax at all," said Lucy, "really and truly. It was all different a moment ago. Honestly it was. I promise."

"Come, Lu," said Peter, "that's going a bit far. You've had your joke. Hadn't you better drop it now?"

Lucy grew very red in the face and tried to say something, though she hardly knew what she was trying to say, and burst into tears.

For the next few days she was very miserable. She could have made it up with the others quite easily at any moment if she could have brought herself to say that the whole thing was only a story made up for fun. But Lucy was a very truthful girl, and she knew that she was really in the right; and she could not bring herself to say this. The others who thought she was telling a lie, and a silly lie too, made her very unhappy. The two elder ones did this without meaning to do it, but Edmund could be spiteful, and on this occasion he was spiteful. He sneered and jeered at Lucy and kept on asking her if she'd found any other new countries in other cupboards all over the house. What made it worse was that these days ought to have been delightful. The weather was fine, and they were out of doors from morning to night, bathing, fishing, climbing trees, and lying in the heather. But Lucy could not properly enjoy any of it. And so things went on until the next wet day.

That day, when it came to the afternoon and there was still no sign of a break in the weather, they decided to play hide-and-seek. Susan was "It" and as soon as the others scattered to hide, Lucy went to the room where the wardrobe was. She did not mean to hide in the wardrobe, because she knew that would only set the others talking again about the whole wretched business. But she did want to have one more look inside it; for by this time she was beginning to wonder herself whether Narnia and the Faun had not been a dream. The house was so large and complicated and full of hiding places that she thought she would have time to have one look into the wardrobe and then hide somewhere else. But as soon as she reached it she heard steps in the passage outside, and then there was nothing for it but to jump into the wardrobe and hold the door closed behind her. She did not shut it properly because she knew it is very silly to shut oneself into a wardrobe, even if it is a magic one.

Now the steps she had heard were those of Edmund, and he came into the room just in time to see Lucy vanishing into the wardrobe. He at once decided to get into it himself —not because he thought it was a particularly good place to hide but because he wanted to go on teasing her about her imaginary country. He opened the door. There were the coats hanging up as usual, and a smell of mothballs, and darkness and silence, and no sign of Lucy. "She thinks I'm Susan come to catch her," said Edmund to himself, "and so she's keeping very quiet in at the back."

He jumped in and shut the door, forgetting what a very foolish thing this is to do. Then he began feeling about for Lucy in the dark. He had expected to find her in a few seconds and was very surprised when he did not. He decided to open the door again and let in some light. But he could not find the door either. He didn't like this at all and began groping wildly in every direction; he even shouted out, "Lucy! Lu! Where are you? I know you're here."

PART II

There was no answer and Edmund noticed that his own voice had a curious sound—not the sound you expect in a cupboard, but a kind of open-air sound. He also noticed that he was unexpectedly cold, and then he saw a light.

"Thank goodness," said Edmund, "the door must have swung open of its own accord." He forgot all about Lucy and went toward the light, which he thought was the open door of the wardrobe. But instead of finding himself stepping out into the spare room he found himself stepping out from the shadow of some thick, dark fir trees into an open place in the middle of a wood.

There was crisp, dry snow under his feet and more snow lying on the branches of the trees. Overhead there was a pale blue sky, the sort of sky one sees on a fine winter day in the morning. Straight ahead of him he saw between the tree trunks the sun, just rising, very red and clear. Everything was perfectly still, as if he were the only living creature in that country. There was not even a robin or a squirrel among the trees, and the wood stretched as far as he could see in every direction. He shivered.

He now remembered that he had been looking for Lucy; and also how unpleasant he had been to her about her "imaginary country" which now turned out not to have been imaginary at all. He thought that she must be somewhere quite close and so he shouted, "Lucy! Lucy! I'm here too—Edmund."

There was no answer.

"She's angry about all the things I've been saying lately," thought Edmund. And though he did not like to admit that he had been wrong, he also did not much like being alone in this strange, cold, quiet place, so he shouted again.

"I say, Lu! I'm sorry I didn't believe you. I see now you were right all along. Do come out. Make it Pax."

Still there was no answer.

"Just like a girl," said Edmund to himself, "sulking somewhere, and won't accept an apology." He looked round him again and decided he did not much like this place, and had almost made up his mind to go home, when he heard, very far off in the wood, a sound of bells. He listened and the sound came nearer and nearer and at last there swept into sight a sledge drawn by two reindeer.

The reindeer were about the size of Shetland ponies, and their hair was so white that even the snow hardly looked white compared with them; their branching horns were gilded and shone like something on fire when the sunrise caught them. Their harness was of scarlet leather and covered with bells. On the sledge, driving the reindeer, sat a fat dwarf who would have been about three feet high if he had been standing. He was dressed in polar bear's fur, and on his head he wore a red hood with a long, gold tassel hanging down from its point; his huge beard covered his knees and served him instead of a rug. But behind him, on a much higher seat in the middle of the sledge sat a very different person—a great lady, taller than any woman that Edmund had ever seen. She also was covered in white fur up to her throat and held a long, straight. golden wand in her right hand and wore a golden crown on her head. Her face was white—not merely pale, but white like snow or paper or icing-sugar, except for her very red mouth. It was a beautiful face in other respects, but proud and cold and stern.

The sledge was a fine sight as it came sweeping toward Edmund with the bells jingling, and the dwarf cracking his whip, and the snow flying up on each side of it.

"Stop!" said the Lady, and the dwarf pulled the reindeer up so sharp that they almost sat down. Then they recovered themselves and stood champing their bits and blowing. In the frosty air the breath coming out of their nostrils looked like smoke.

"And what, pray, are you?" said the Lady, looking hard at Edmund.

"I'm . . . I'm . . . my name's Edmund," said Edmund rather awkwardly. He did not like the way she looked at him.

The Lady frowned. "Is that how you address a Queen?" she asked, looking sterner than ever.

"I beg your pardon, your Majesty, I didn't know," said Edmund.

"Not know the Queen of Narnia?" cried she. "Ha! You shall know us better hereafter. But I repeat—what are you?"

"Please, your Majesty," said Edmund, "I don't know what you mean. I'm at school—at least I was—it's the holidays now."

Lewis, C.S. *The Chronicles of Narnia: The Lion, the Witch and the Wardrobe.* New York: HarperCollins Publishers, Inc., 1950.

INCREDIBLE JOURNEY

SHEILA BURNFORD

Jim Hunter gives his two dogs and cat to his friend John Longridge before he goes to England with his family. The old bull terrier, young Labrador retreiver and Siamese cat become accustomed to their new home and show affection towards Longridge, but they still pine for their old master. When Longridge leaves for a vacation, the animals set out on a very difficult journey of their own through the Canadian wilderness to get back to their owner and family.

CHAPTER 2

ongridge started the car and waved to them out of the window as he drove slowly down the drive, feeling foolish as he did so. "What do I expect them to do in return?" he asked himself with a smile. "Wave back? Or shout 'Good-by'? The trouble is I've lived too long alone with them and I'm becoming far too attached to them."

The car turned around the bend at the end of the long tree-lined drive and the animals heard the sound of the engine receding in the distance. The cat transferred his attention to a hind leg; the old dog stopped panting and lay down; the young dog remained stretched out, only his eyes moving and an occasional twitch of the nose.

Twenty minutes passed by and no move was made; then suddenly the young dog rose, stretched himself, and stood looking intently down the drive. He remained like this for several minutes, while the cat watched closely, one leg still pointing upwards; then slowly the Labrador walked down the driveway and stood at the curve, looking back as though inviting the others to come. The old dog rose too, now, somewhat stiffly, and followed. Together they turned the corner, out of sight.

The cat remained utterly still for a full minute, blue eyes blazing in the dark mask. Then, with a curious hesitating run, he set off in pursuit. The dogs were waiting by the gate when he turned the corner, the old dog peering wistfully back, as though he hoped to see his friend Mrs. Oakes materialize with a juicy bone; but when the Labrador started up the road he followed. The cat still paused by the gate, one paw lifted delicately in the air—undecided, questioning, hesitant; until suddenly, some inner decision reached, he followed the dogs. Presently all three disappeared from sight down the dusty road, trotting briskly and with purpose.

About an hour later Mrs. Oakes walked up the driveway from her cottage, carrying a string bag with her working shoes and apron, and a little parcel of tidbits for the animals. Her placid, gentle face wore a rather disappointed look, because the dogs usually spied her long before she got to the house and would rush to greet her.

"I expect Mr. Longridge left them shut inside the house if he was leaving early," she consoled herself. But when she pushed open the kitchen door and walked inside, everything seemed very silent and still. She stood at the foot of the stairs and called them, but there was no answering patter of running feet, only the steady tick-tock of the old clock in the hallway. She walked through the silent house and out into the front garden and stood there calling with a puzzled frown.

"Oh, well," she spoke her thoughts aloud to the empty, sunny garden, "perhaps they've gone up to the school. . . . It's a funny thing, though," she continued, sitting on a kitchen chair a few minutes later and tying her shoelaces, "that Puss isn't here—he's usually sitting on the window sill at this time of the day. Oh, well, he's probably out hunting —I've never known a cat like that for hunting, doesn't seem natural somehow!"

She washed and put away the few dishes, then took her cleaning materials into the sitting room. There her eye was caught by a sparkle on the floor by the desk, and she found the glass paperweight, and after that the remaining sheet of the note on the desk. She read it through to where it said: "I will be taking the dogs (and Tao too of course!) . . .", then looked for the remainder. "That's odd," she thought, "now where would he take them? That cat must have knocked the paperweight off last night—the rest of the note must be somewhere in the room."

She searched the room but it was not until she was emptying an ash tray into the fireplace that she noticed the charred curl of paper in the hearth. She bent down and picked it up carefully, for it was obviously very brittle, but even then most of it crumbled away and she was left with a fragment which bore the initials J.R.L.

"Now, isn't that the queerest thing," she said to the fireplace, rubbing vigorously at the black marks on the tile. "He must mean he's taking them all to Heron Lake with him. But why would he suddenly do that, after all the arrangements we made? He never said a word about it on the telephone—but wait a minute, I remember now—he was just going to say something about them when the line went dead; perhaps he was just going to tell me."

While Mrs. Oakes was amazed that Longridge would take the animals on his vacation, it did not occur to her to be astonished that a cat should go along too, for she was aware that the cat loved the car and always went with the dogs when Longridge drove them anywhere or took them farther afield for walks. Like many Siamese cats, he was as obedient and as trained to go on walks as most dogs, and would always return to a whistle.

Mrs. Oakes swept and dusted and talked to the house, locked it and returned home to her cottage. She would have been horrified to the depths of her kindly, well-ordered soul if she had known the truth. Far from sitting sedately in the back of a car traveling north with John Longridge, as she so fondly visualized, the animals were by now many miles away on a deserted country road that ran westward.

They had kept a fairly steady pace for the first hour or so, falling into an order which was not to vary for many miles or days; the Labrador ran always by the left shoulder of the old dog, for the bull terrier was very nearly blind in the left eye, and they jogged along fairly steadily together—the bull terrier with his odd, rolling, sailorlike gait, and the Labrador in a slow lope. Some ten yards behind came the cat, whose attention was frequently distracted, when he would stop for a few minutes and then catch up again. But, in between these halts, he ran swiftly and steadily, his long slim body and tail low to the ground.

When it was obvious that the old dog was flagging, the Labrador turned off the quiet, graveled road and into the shade of a pinewood beside a clear, fast-running creek. The old dog drank deeply, standing up to his chest in the cold water; the cat picked his way delicatley to the edge of an overhanging rock. Afterwards they rested in the deep pine needles under the trees, the terrier panting heavily with his eyes half closed, and the cat busy with his eternal washing. They lay there for nearly an hour, until the sun struck through the branches above them. The young dog rose and stretched, then walked towards the road. The old dog rose too, stifflegged, his head low. He walked toward the waiting Labrador, limping slightly and wagging his tail at the cat, who suddenly danced into a patch of sunlight, struck at a drifting leaf, than ran straight at the dogs, swerving at the last moment, and as suddenly sitting down again.

They trotted steadily on, all that afternoon—mostly traveling on the grassy verge at the side of the quiet country road; sometimes in the low overgrown ditch that ran alongside, if the acute hearing of the young dog warned them of an approaching car.

By the time the afternoon sun lay in long, barred shadows across the road, the cat was still traveling in smooth, swift bursts, and the young dog was comparatively fresh. But the old dog was very weary, and his pace had dropped to a limping walk. They turned off the road into the bush at the side, and walked slowly through a clearing in the trees, pushing their way through the tangled undergrowth at the far end. They came out upon a small open place where a giant spruce had crashed to the ground and left a hollow where the roots had been, filled now with drifted dry leaves and spruce needles.

The late afternoon sun slanted through the branches overhead, and it looked invitingly snug and secure. The old dog stood for a minute, his heavy head hanging, and his tired body swaying slightly, then lay down on his side in the hollow. The cat, after a good deal of wary observation, made a little hollow among the spruce needles and curled around in it, purring softly. The young dog disappeared into the undergrowth and reappeared presently, his smooth coat dripping water, to lie down a little away apart from the others.

The old dog continued to pant exhaustedly for a long time, one hind leg shaking badly, until his eyes closed at last, the labored breaths came further and further apart, and he was sleeping—still, save for an occasional long shudder.

Later on, when darkness fell, the young dog moved over and stretched out closely at his side and the cat stalked over to lie between his paws; and so, warmed and comforted by their closeness, the old dog slept, momentarily unconscious of his aching, tired body or his hunger.

In the nearby hills a timber wolf howled mournfully; owls called and answered and glided silently by with great outspread wings; and there were faint whispers of movement and small rustling noises around all through the night. Once an eerie wail like a baby's crying woke the old dog and brought him shivering and whining to his feet; but it was only a porcupine, who scrambled noisily and clumsily down a nearby tree trunk and waddled away, still crying softly. When he lay down again the cat was gone from his side—another small night hunter slipping through the unquiet shadows that froze to stillness at his passing.

The young dog slept in fitful, uneasy starts, his muscles twitching, constantly lifting his head and growling softly. Once he sprang to his feet with a full-throated roar which brought a sudden splash in the distance, then silence—and who knows what else unknown, unseen or unheard passed through his mind to disturb him further? Only one thing was clear and certain—that at all costs he was going home, home to his own beloved master. Home lay to the west, his instinct told him; but he could not leave the other two—so somehow he must take them with him, all the way.

Burnford, Sheila. *Incredible Journey*. New York: Atlantic-Little, Brown, 1961.

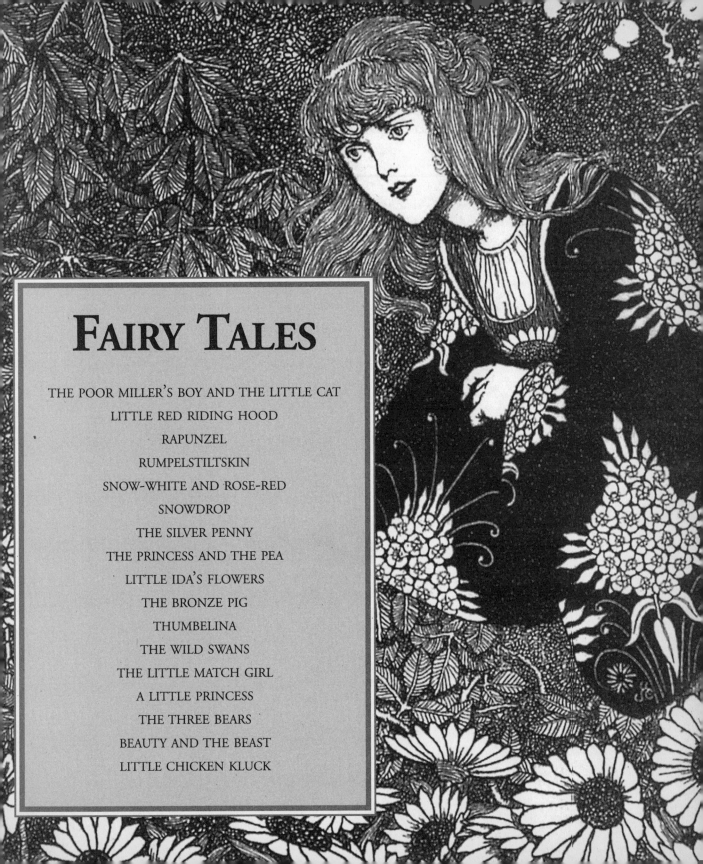

FAIRY TALES

GRIMM'S FAIRY TALES

Grimm's Fairy Tales are stories that were told through the generations in various Northern European countries and then were compiled by Jacob and Wilhelm Grimm in the early 1800s. They remain a classic in the canon of Western children's literature. Here are some of the tales collected for you to enjoy

The Brothers Grimm Fairy Tales. New York: Puffin Books, a division of Penguin Books USA, 1981

THE POOR MILLER'S BOY AND THE LITTLE CAT

THE BROTHERS GRIMM

This is the tale of a man who was called "simple," and everyone thought he would never achieve anything, but he ended up surprising everyone.

In a mill lived an old miller who had neither wife nor children, and three young fellows worked for him. One day when they had been with him for some years, he said, "I am getting old; I want to sit behind the oven and take my ease. Go out into the world, and whichever one brings home the best horse shall have the mill and in return he must take care of me until I die."

Now the third young boy was only an apprentice. The two others took him for a simpleton and begrudged him the mill, so the three of them set out, and as they were leaving the village, the two said to simple John, "You might just as well stay here; you'll never get a horse as long as you live." But John went along anyway, and at nightfall they came to a cave and went in and lay down to sleep. The two smart ones waited till John had fallen asleep, then they got up and made off and left Johnny lying there and thought they had done something very clever.

When the sun came up, John woke and there he lay deep in a cave. He peered all around and cried, "Dear God! Where am I!" and he rose and scrambled out of the cave and went into the forest and thought, Here I am, alone and forsaken. How shall I ever get a horse! And as he was walking along deep in thought, he met a little speckled cat that spoke kindly to him and said, "Where are you off to, John?"

"Oh, it's nothing you can help me with."

"I know very well what it is you want," said the little cat. "You want a pretty horse. Come with me and be my faithful servant for seven years, and I will give you one more handsome than anything you've seen in your whole life."

What a strange cat, thought John, but I might as well go along and see if she is telling the truth. And so she took him with her to her bewitched little palace where she had nothing

71

but cats to wait on her. They leaped nimbly up and down the stairs, happy and full of fun. In the evening, when they sat down to supper, there were three who made music; one played the double bass, another the violin, and third put the trumpet to her mouth and blew up her cheeks for all she was worth. When they had eaten, the table was removed and the cat said, "Come, John, dance with me."

John himself had to wait on the cat. Every day he had to chop firewood and had a silver ax to do it with, and the wedges and the saw were all made of silver and the mallet was of copper. He chopped and chopped and stayed in that house, had plenty of food and drink, but never saw a soul except the speckled cat and her household. One day she said, "Go and mow the meadow, and dry the hay," and she gave him a golden whetstone and told him to be sure to bring everything back, and so John went and did as he was told, and when he was finished he brought scythe, whetstone, and hay back home and said wasn't she going to give him his earnings.

"No," said the cat, "first you must do one more thing. Here is silver lumber, and the carpenter's ax, the square, and everything you need, all made of silver. Build me a little house with it."

John built the little house, and when it was finished he said now he had done everything and still he didn't have a horse. And yet the seven years had passed as if they were six months. The cat asked him if he wouldn't like to see her horses. "Yes," said John, so she opened the little house, and as she is opening up the door, there are twelve horses standing there and oh, weren't they proud-looking, and didn't they shine and gleam like mirrors, it made his heart leap for joy. So then she gave him food and drink and said, "Go home. I won't give you your horse to take with you. In three days I will come and bring it after you." So then John got ready to leave and she showed him the way to the mill. But she hadn't even given him a new suit of clothes, and he had to wear the old ragged smock he came in that had grown too short and tight for him those seven years.

Now when he got home, the two others were back as well, and though they had each brought a horse, the horse of one was blind and the other's horse was lame. They asked "John, where's your horse?" "It's being sent after me in three days." They laughed and said, "Yes, John, sure, John! Where would you get a horse? This is going to be something!" John came inside but the miller said they couldn't have him sitting at the table, he was so torn and ragged one would be ashamed if somebody dropped in, so they gave him a little bit of food to take outside; and in the evening, when they lay down to sleep, the two others would not let him in the bed, and he had to crawl into the goose pen and lie down on a little hard straw. And in the morning he wakes up and the three days have already passed, and here comes a carriage drawn by six horses; my, it was a pleasure to see how they gleamed, and there's a servant and he's brought yet a seventh horse, which is for the poor miller's apprentice. But out of the carriage there stepped this magnificent princess and she came into the mill, and the princess was the little speckled cat that poor John had served for seven years.

She asked the miller where's the boy, the miller's apprentice? So then the miller says, "We couldn't have him in the mill, he's so ragged, he's lying outside in the goose pen." So then the princess said they should go and get him at once.

They went and got him out, and he had to hold his little smock together to cover himself. And the servant unpacked magnificent clothes and washed him and dressed him, and when he was ready no king could have been more handsome. After that the lady asked to see the horses which the others had brought, and one horse was blind and the other lame. So then she had the servant bring the seventh horse. When the miller saw it, he said that nothing like it had even entered his yard. "Well, this is for the apprentice," said she.

"Then he shall have the mill," said the miller, but the princess said he could have the horse, and he could keep his mill, and takes her faithful John and puts him in the carriage and drives off with him. And they drive to the little house he built with the silver tools, and it is a great palace and everything in it is silver and gold, and she married him and he is rich—so rich he had plenty of everything as long as he lived. And that is why nobody should say that a simple person can never amount to anything.

LITTLE RED RIDING HOOD

THE BROTHERS GRIMM

This fairy tale has been a favorite for generations and tells the story of a young girl whose grandmother loves her very much and makes her a red-velvet hooded cape. The girl goes to visit her grandmother one day with some treats and runs into a wolf while walking in the forest. The wolf is extremely hungry and decides to trick Little Red Riding Hood.

There was once a sweet little maid, much beloved by everybody, but most of all by her grandmother, who never knew how to make enough of her. Once she sent her a little riding hood of red velvet, and as it was very becoming to her, and she never wore anything else, people called her Little Red Riding Hood.

One day her mother said to her, "Come, Little Red Riding Hood, here are some cakes and a flask of wine for you to take to grandmother; she is weak and ill, and they will do her good. Make haste and start before it grows hot, and walk properly and nicely, and don't run, or you might fall and break the flask of wine, and there would be none left for grandmother. And when you go into her room, don't forget to say good morning, instead of staring about you." "I will be sure to take care," said Little Red Riding Hood to her mother and gave her hand upon it.

Now the grandmother lived away in the wood, half an hour's walk from the village; and when Little Red Riding Hood had reached the wood, she met the wolf; but as she did not know what a bad sort of animal he was, she did not feel frightened.

"Good day, Little Red Riding Hood," said he. "Thank you kindly, wolf," answered she. "Where are you going so early, Little Red Riding Hood?" "To my grandmother's." "What are you carrying under your apron?" "Cakes and wine; we baked yesterday; and my grandmother is very weak and ill, so they will do her good and strengthen her."

"Where does your grandmother live, Little Red Riding Hood?" "A quarter of an hour's walk from here; her house stands beneath the three oak trees, and you may know it by the hazel bushes," said Little Red Riding Hood.

The wolf thought to himself, "That tender young thing would be a delicious morsel and would taste better than the old one; I must manage somehow to get both of them."

Then he walked by Little Red Riding Hood a little while, and said, "Little Red Riding Hood, just look at the pretty flowers that are growing all round you; and I don't think you are listening to the song of the birds; you are posting along just as if you were going to school, and it is so delightful out here in the wood."

Little Red Riding Hood glanced round her, and when she saw the sunbeams darting here and there through the trees, and lovely flowers everywhere, she thought to herself, "if I were to take a fresh nosegay to my grandmother, she would be very pleased, and it is so early in the day that I shall reach her in plenty of time"; and so she ran about in the wood, looking for flowers. And as she picked one, she saw a still prettier one a little farther off, and so she went farther and farther into the wood.

But the wolf went straight to the grandmother's house and knocked at the door. "Who is there?" cried the grandmother. "Little Red Riding Hood," he answered, "and I have brought you some cake and wine. Please open the door." "Lift the latch," cried the grandmother; "I am too feeble to get up."

So the wolf lifted the latch, and the door flew open, and he fell on the grandmother, and ate her up without saying one word. Then he drew on her clothes, put on her cap, lay down in her bed, and drew the curtains.

Little Red Riding Hood was all this time running about among the flowers, and when she had gathered as many as she could hold, she remembered her grandmother, and set off to go to her. She was surprised to find the door standing open, and when she came inside she felt very strange and thought to herself, "Oh dear, how uncomfortable I feel, and I was so glad this morning to go to my grandmother!"

And when she said, "Good morning," there was no answer. Then she went up to the bed and drew back the curtains there lay the grandmother with her cap pulled over her eyes, so that she looked very odd.

"O grandmother, what large ears you have!" "The better to hear with."

"O grandmother, what great eyes you have!" "The better to see with."

"O grandmother, what large hands you have!" "The better to take hold of you with."

"But, grandmother, what a terrible large mouth you have!" "The better to devour you!" And no sooner had the wolf said it than he made one bound from the bed, and swallowed up poor Little Red Riding Hood.

Then the wolf, having satisfied his hunger, lay down again in the bed, went to sleep, and began to snore loudly. The huntsman heard him as he was passing by the house, and thought, "How the old woman snores—I had better see if there is anything the matter with her."

Then he went into the room, and walked up to the bed, and saw the wolf lying there. "At last I find you, you old sinner!" said he; "I have been looking for you a long time."

And he made up his mind that the wolf had swallowed the grandmother whole, and that she might yet be saved. So he did not fire, but took a pair of shears and began to snip up the wolf's body. When he made a few snips Little Red Riding Hood appeared, and after a few more snips, she jumped out and cried, "Oh dear, how frightened I have been! It is so dark inside the wolf." And then out came the old grandmother, still living and breathing. But Little Red Riding Hood went and quickly fetched some large stones, with which she filled the wolf's body, so that when he woke up, and was going to rush away, the stones were so heavy that he sank down and fell dead.

They were all three very pleased. The huntsman took off the wolf's skin, and carried it home. The grandmother ate the cakes, and drank the wine, and held up her head again, and Little Red Riding Hood said to herself that she would never more stray about in the wood alone, but would mind what her mother told her.

It must also be related how a few days afterwards, when Little Red Riding Hood was again taking cakes to her grandmother, another wolf spoke to her and wanted to tempt her to leave the path; but she was on her guard, and went straight on her way, and told her grandmother how the wolf had met her, and wished her good day, but had looked so wicked about the eyes that she thought if it had not been on the high road, he would have devoured her.

"Come," said the grandmother, "we will shut the door, so that he may not get in."

RAPUNZEL

THE BROTHERS GRIMM

This classic fairy tale concerns a young girl named Rapuzel who is raised by a very mean old witch. The witch keeps Rapunzel locked up all alone in a tower. But Rapunzel loves to sing and one day while she is singing a prince hears her and discovers a way of getting into the tower.

There once lived a man and his wife who had long wished for a child but in vain. Now there was at the back of their house a little window which overlooked a beautiful garden full of the finest vegetables and flowers, but there was a high wall all round it, and no one ventured into it, for it belonged to a witch of great might, and of whom all the world was afraid. One day, when the wife was standing at the window, and looking into the garden, she saw a bed filled with the finest rampion; and it looked so fresh and green that she began to wish for some; and at length she longed for it greatly. This went on for days, and as she knew she could not get the rampion, she pined away and grew pale and miserable.

Then the man was uneasy and asked, "What is the matter, dear wife?" "Oh," answered she, "I shall die unless I can have some of that rampion to eat that grows in the garden at the back of our house." The man, who loved her very much, thought to himself, "Rather than lose my wife, I will get some rampion, cost what it will."

So in the twilight he climbed over the wall into the witch's garden, plucked hastily a handful of rampion and brought it to his wife. She made a salad of it at once, and ate of it to her heart's content. But she liked it so much, and it tasted so good that the next day she longed for it thrice as much as she had done before; if she was to have any rest, the man must climb over the wall once more. So he went in the twilight again; and as he was climbing back, he saw, all at once, the witch standing before him, and was terribly frightened, as she cried, with angry eyes, "How dare you climb over into my garden like a thief, and steal my rampion! It shall be the worse for you!"

"Oh," answered he, "be merciful rather that just; I have only done it through necessity; for my wife saw your rampion out of the window, and became possessed with so great a longing that she would have died if she could not have had some to eat!"

Then the witch said, "If it is all as you say, you may have as much rampion as you like, on one condition—the child that will come into the world must be given to me. It shall go well with the child, and I will care for it like a mother."

In his distress of mind, the man promised everything; and when the time came when the child was born, the witch appeared, and giving the child the name of Rapunzel (which is the same as rampion), she took it away with her.

Rapunzel was the most beautiful child in the world. When she was twelve years old the witch shut her up in a tower in the midst of a wood, and it had neither steps nor door, only a small window above. When the witch wished to be let in, she would stand below and would cry, "Rapunzel, Rapunzel! Let down your hair!"

Rapunzel had beautiful long hair that shone like gold. When she heard the voice of the witch she would undo the fastening of the upper window, unbind the plaits of her hair, and let it down twenty ells below, and the witch would climb up by it.

After they had lived thus a few years, it happened that as the king's son was riding through the wood, he came to the tower; and as he drew near, he heard a voice singing so sweetly that he stood still and listened. It was Rapunzel in her loneliness trying to pass away the time with sweet songs. The king's son wished to go in to her, and sought to find a door in the tower, but there was none. So he rode home, but the song had entered into his heart, and every day he went into the wood and listened to it.

Once, as he was standing there under a tree, he saw the witch come up, and listened while she called out, "Oh Rapunzel, Rapunzel! Let down your hair."

Then he saw how Rapunzel let down her long tresses, and how the witch climbed up by them and went in to her, and he said to himself, "Since that is the ladder, I will climb it, and seek my fortune." And the next day, as soon as it began to grow dusk, he went to the tower and cried, "Oh Rapunzel, Rapunzel! Let down your hair." And she let down her hair, and the king's son climbed up by it.

Rapunzel was greatly terrified when she saw that a man had come in to her, for she had never seen one before; but the king's son began speaking so kindly to her, and told her how her singing had entered into his heart, so that he could have no peace until he had seen her himself. Then Rapunzel forgot her terror, and when she saw that he was young and beautiful, she thought to herself, "I certainly like him much better than old mother Gothel," and she put her hand into his hand, saying, "I would willingly go with you, but I do not know how I shall get out. When you come, bring each time a silken rope, and I will make a ladder, and when it is quite ready I will get down by it out of the tower, and you shall take me away on your horse."

They agreed that he should come to her every evening, as the old woman came in the daytime. So the witch knew nothing of all this until once Rapunzel said to her unwittingly, "Mother Gothel, how is it that you climb up here so slowly, and the king's son is with me in a moment?"

"O wicked child," cried the witch, "what is this I hear! I thought I had hidden you from all the world, and you have betrayed me!"

In her anger she seized Rapunzel by her beautiful hair, struck her several times with her left hand, and then grasping a pair of shears in her right—snip, snap—the beautiful locks lay on the ground. And she was so hardhearted that she took Rapunzel and put her in a waste and desert place, where she lived in woe and misery.

The same day on which she took Rapunzel away, she went back to the tower in the evening and made fast the severed locks of hair to the window hasp, and the king's son came and cried, "Rapunzel, Rapunzel! Let down your hair."

Then she let the hair down, and the king's son climbed up, but instead of his dearest Rapunzel, he found the witch looking at him with wicked, glittering eyes.

RUMPELSTILTSKIN

THE BROTHERS GRIMM

Rumplestilskin is a tale about greed and the value of material objects versus good will.

There was once a miller who was poor, but he had a beautiful daughter. It happened one day that he came to speak with the King, and, to give himself more consequence, he told him that he had a daughter who could spin gold out of straw. The King said to the miller, "That is an art that pleases me well; if your daughter is as clever as you say, bring her to my castle tomorrow, that I may put her to the proof."

When the girl was brought to him, he led her into a room that was quite full of straw, and gave her a wheel and spindle, and said, "Now set to work, and if by the early morning you have not spun this staw to gold you shall die." And he shut the door himself, and left her there alone.

And so the poor miller's daughter was left there sitting, and could not think what to do for her life; she had no notion how to set to work to spin gold from straw, and her distress gew so great that she began to weep. Then all at once the door opened, and in came a little man, who said, "Good evening, miller's daughter; why are you crying?" "Oh!" answered the girl, "I have got to spin gold out of straw, and I don't understand the business."

Then the little man said, "What will you give me if I spin it for you?" "My necklace," said the girl.

The little man took the necklace, seated himself before the wheel, and whirr, whirr, whirr! three times round and the bobbin was full; then he took up another, and whirr, whirr, whirr! three times round, and that was full; and so he went on till the morning, when all the straw had been spun, and all the bobbins were full of gold. At sunrise came the King, and when he saw the gold he was astonished and very much rejoiced, for he was very avaricious. He had the miller's daughter taken into another room filled with straw, much bigger than the last, and told her that as she valued her life she must spin it all in one night.

The girl did not know what to do, so she began to cry, and then the door opened, and the little man appeared and said, "What will you give me if I spin all this straw into gold?" "The ring from my finger," answered the girl.

So the little man took the ring, and began again to send the wheel whirring round, and by the next morning all the straw was spun into glistening gold. The King was rejoiced beyond measure at the sight, but as he could never have enough of gold, he had the miller's daughter taken into a still larger room full of straw, and said, "This, too, must be spun in one one night, and if you accomplish it you shall be my wife." For he thought, "Although she is but a miller's daughter, I am not likely to find any one richer in the whole world."

As soon as the girl was left alone, the little man appeared for the third time and said, "What will you give me if I spin the straw for you this time?" "I have nothing left to give," answered the girl. "Then you must promise me the first child you have after you are Queen," said the little man.

"But who knows whether that will happen?" thought the girl; but as she did not know what else to do in her necessity, she promised the little man what he desired, upon which he began to spin, until all the straw was gold. And when in the morning the King came and found all done according to his wish, he caused the wedding to be held at once, and the miller's pretty daughter became a Queen.

In a year's time she brought a fine child into the world, and thought no more of the little man; but one day he came suddenly into her roon, and said "Now give me what you promised me."

The Queen was terrified greatly, and offered the little man all the riches of the kingdom if he would only leave the child; but the little man said, "No, I would rather have something living than all the treasures of the world."

Then the Queen began to lament and to weep, so that the little man had pity upon her. "I will give you three days," said he, "and if at the end of that time you cannot tell my name, you must give up the child to me."

Then the Queen spent the whole night in thinking over all the names that she had ever heard, and sent a messenger through the land to ask far and wide for all the names that could be found. And when the little man came next day, beginning with Caspar, Melchior, Balthazar, she repeated all she knew, and went through the whole list, but after each the little man said, "That is not my name."

The second day the Queen sent to inquire of all the neighbors what the servants were called, and told the little man all the most unusual and singular names, saying, "Perhaps you are Roast-ribs, or Sheepshanks, or Spindleshanks?" But he answered nothing but "That is not my name."

The third day the messenger came back again, and said, "I have not been able to find one single new name; but as I passed through the woods I came to a high hill, and near it was a little house, and before the house burned a fire, and round the fire danced a comical little man, and he hopped on one leg and cried,

"Today do I bake, tomorrow I brew,
The day after that the Queen's child comes in;
And Oh! I am glad that nobody knew
That the name I am called is Rumpelstiltskin!"

You cannot think how pleased the Queen was to hear the name, and soon afterwards, when the little man walked in and said, "Now, Mrs. Queen, what is my name?" she said at first, "Are you called Jack?" "No," answered he. "Are you called Harry?" she asked again. "No," answered he. And then she said, "Then perhaps your name is Rumpelstiltskin!"

"The devil told you that! the devil told you that!" cried the little man, and in his anger he stamped with his right foot so hard that it went into the ground above his knee; then he seized his left foot with both hands in such a fury that he split in two, and there was an end of him.

SNOW-WHITE AND ROSE-RED

FROM THE BLUE FAIRY BOOK
COLLECTED BY ANDREW LANG

In these two stories you will learn about two sisters who are so good and trusting that they befriend a big black bear and even help an ugly, ungrateful old troll. Their generous nature serves them well, as the bear turns out to be a prince whose been cursed by the troll.

PART I

A poor widow once lived in a little cottage with a garden in front of it, in which grew two rose trees, one bearing white roses and the other red. She had two children, who were just like the two rose trees; one was called Snow-white and the other Rose-red, and they were the sweetest and best children in the world. The two children loved each other so dearly that they always walked hand-in-hand whenever they went out together, and when Snow-white said: "We will never desert each other," Rose-red answered, "No, not as long as we live;" and the mother added: "Whatever one gets she shall share with the other." They often roamed about in the woods gathering berries, and none of the animals tried to hurt them; on the contrary, they came up to them all trustingly; the little hare would eat a cabbage leaf from their hands, the deer would graze beside them, the stag would bound past them merrily, and the birds remained on the branches and sang with all their might. No evil ever befell them, if they tarried late in the wood and slept till morning, and their mother knew they were quite safe and never felt anxious about them.

Snow-white and Rose-red kept their mother's cottage so beautifully clean and neat that it was a pleasure to go into it. In summer Rose-red looked after the house, and every morning before her mother awoke she placed a bunch of flowers before the bed, from each tree a rose. In winter Snow-white lit the fire and put on a kettle, which was made of brass, but so beautifully polished that it shone like gold. In the evening when the snowflakes fell their mother said: "Snow-white, go and close the shutters"; and they drew round the fire, while the mother put on her spectacles and read aloud from a big book and the two girls listened and sat and spun. Beside them on the ground lay a lamb, and behind them perched a little white dove with its head tucked under its wing.

One evening as they sat thus cosily together someone knocked at the door as though he wanted to be let in. The mother said: "Rose-red, open the door quickly; it must be some traveler seeking shelter." Rose-red hastened to unbar the door and thought she saw a poor man standing in the darkness outside; but it was no such thing, only a bear, who poked his thick black head through the door. Rose-red screamed aloud and sprang back in terror, the lamb began to bleat, the dove flapped its wings, and Snow-white ran and hid behind her mother's bed. But the bear began to speak, and said: "Don't be afraid: I won't hurt you. I am half frozen and only wish to warm myself a little." "My poor bear," said the mother, "lie down by the fire, only take care you don't burn your fur." Then she called out: "Snow-white and Rose-red, come out; the bear will do you no harm: he is a good, honest creature." So they both came out their hiding places, and gradually the lamb and dove drew near too, and they all forgot their fear The bear asked the children to beat the snow a little out of his fur, and they fetched a brush and scrubbed him till he was dry. Then the beast stretched himself in front of the fire and growled quite happily and comfortably. The children soon grew quite at their ease with him and led their helpless friend around. They tugged his fur with their hands, put their small feet on his back, and rolled him about here and there, or took a hazel wand and beat him with it; and if he growled, they only laughed. The bear submitted to everything with the best possible good nature, only when they went too far he cried,

> *'Oh! children, spare my life!*
> *Snow-white and Rose-red,*
> *Don't beat your lover dead.'*

When it was time to retire for the night, and the others went to bed, the mother said to the bear, "You can lie there on the hearth with God's blessing; it will be shelter for you from the cold and wet." As soon as day dawned the children let him out, and he trotted over the snow into the wood.

From this time on the bear came every evening at the same hour, and lay down by the hearth, and let the children play what pranks they liked with him; and they got so accustomed to this that the door was never shut till their black friend had made his appearance.

When spring came, and all outside was green, the bear said one morning to Snow-white, "Now I must go away and not return again the whole summer." "Where are you going to, dear bear?" asked Snow-white. "I must go to the wood and protect my treasure from the wicked dwarfs. In winter, when the earth is frozen hard, they are obliged to remain underground for they can't work their way through; but now, when the sun has thawed and warmed the ground, they break through and come up above to spy the land and steal what they can: what once falls into their hands and into their caves is not easily brought back to light." Snow-white was quite sad over their friend's departure, and when

85

she unbarred the door for him, the bear, stepping out, caught a piece of his fur in the door latch, and Snow-white thought she caught sight of glittering gold beneath it, but she couldn't be certain of it; and the bear ran hastily away and soon disappeared behind the trees.

A short time after this the mother sent the children into the wood to collect firewood. They came in their wanderings upon a big tree which lay felled on the ground, and on the trunk among the long grass they noticed something jumping up and down, but they couldn't make out what it was. When they approached nearer they saw it to be a dwarf with a wizened face and a snow-white beard a yard long. The end of this beard was jammed into a cleft of the tree, and the little man sprang about like a dog on a chain and didn't seem to know what else to do. He glared at the girls with his fiery red eyes, and screamed out: "What are you standing there for? Can't you come and help me?" "What were you doing, little man?" asked Rose-red. "You stupid, inquisitive goose!" replied the dwarf; "I wanted to split the tree, to get some little chips of wood for our kitchen fire; those thick logs that serve to make fires for coarse, greedy people like yourselves quite burn up all the little food we need. I had driven the wedge in nicely, and all was going well, but the cursed wood was so slippery that it suddenly sprang out, and the tree closed up so quickly that I had no time to take my beautiful white beard out, so here I am stuck fast, and I can't get away; and you silly, smooth-faced, milk-and-water girls just stand and laugh! Ugh! what wretches you are!"

The children did all in their power, but they couldn't get his beard out; it was wedged in far too firmly. "I will run and fetch somebody," said Rose-red. "Crazy blockheads!" snapped the dwarf, "What's the good of calling anyone else? You're already two too many for me. Can't you think of anything better than that?" "Don't be so impatient," said Snow-white, "I'll see you get help"; and taking her scissors out of her pocket, she cut the end off his beard. As soon as the dwarf felt himself free he seized a bag full of gold which was hidden among the roots of the tree, lifted it up, and muttered aloud: "Curse these boorish wretches, cutting off a piece of my splendid beard!" With these words he swung the bag over his back, and disappeared without so much as looking at the children again.

PART II

hortly after this Snow-white and Rose-red went out to get some fish for supper. As they approached the stream they saw something which looked like an enormous grasshopper, springing towards the water as if it were going to jump in. They ran forward and recognized their old friend the dwarf. "Where are you going to?" asked Rose-red, "You're surely not going to jump into the water?" "I'm not such a fool," screamed the dwarf. "Don't you see that cursed fish is trying to drag me in?" The little man had been sitting on the bank fishing, when unfortunately the wind had entangled his beard in the line; and when immediately afterwards a big fish bit, the feeble little creature had not strength to pull it out. The fish had the upper fin and dragged the dwarf toward him. He clung on with all his might to every rush and blade of grass, but it didn't help much; he had to follow every movement of the fish and was in great danger of being drawn into the water. The girls came up just at the right moment, held him firm, and did all they could to disentangle his beard from the line; but in vain, beard and line were in hopeless muddle. Nothing remained but to produce the scissors and cut the beard, thus removing yet another small part of it.

When the dwarf saw what they were about he yelled at them: "Do you call that manners, you toadstools! to disfigure a fellow's face? It wasn't enough that you shortened my beard before, but you must now need cut off the best bit of it." Then he fetched a sack of pearls that lay among the rushes, and without saying another word, he dragged it away and disappeared behind a stone.

It happened that soon after this their mother sent the two girls to the town to buy needles, thread, laces, and ribbons. While trudging along they saw a big bird hovering in the air, circling slowly above them, but always descending lower, till at last it settled on a rock not far from them. Immediately afterwards they heard a sharp, piercing cry. They ran forward, and saw with horror that the eagle had pounced on their old friend, the dwarf, and was about to carry him off. The tender-hearted children seized a hold of the little man and struggled so long with the bird that at last he let go his prey.

When the dwarf had recovered from the first shock he screamed in his screeching voice: "Couldn't you have treated me more carefully? you have torn my poor old coat all to shreds, useless, awkward hussies that you are!" Then he took a bag of precious stones and vanished under the rocks into his cave. The girls were accustomed to his ingratitude and went on their way and did their business in town. On their way home, as they were again passing the heath, they surprised the dwarf pouring out his precious stones in a little clearing for he had thought no one would pass by at so late an hour. The evening sun shone on the glittering stones, and they gleamed so beautifully that the children stood still and gazed on them. "What are you standing there gaping for?" screamed the dwarf, and his ashen-grey face became scarlet with rage. He was about to go off with these angry words when a sudden growl was heard, and a black bear trotted out of the wood. The dwarf jumped up in a great fight, but he hadn't time to reach his place of retreat for the bear was already close to him. Then he cried in terror: "Dear Mr. Bear, spare me! I'll give you all my treasure. Look at those beautiful precious stones lying there. Spare my life! what pleasure would you get from a poor feeble little fellow like me? You won't feel me between your teeth. There, lay hold of these two wicked girls, they will be a tender morsel for you, as fat as young quails; eat them up, for heaven's sake." But the bear, paying no attention to his words, gave the evil little creature one blow with his paw, and he never moved again.

The girls had run away, but the bear called after them: "Snow-white and Rose-red, don't be afraid; wait, and I'll come with you," Then they recognized his voice and stood still, and when the bear was quite close to them his skin suddenly fell off, and a splendid man stood beside them, all dressed in gold. "I am a king's son," he said, "and have been cursed by that unholy little dwarf, who had stolen my treasure, to roam about the woods as a wild bear till his death should set me free. Now he has got the punishment he deserved.'

Snow-white married the prince and Rose-red his brother, and they divided the great treasure the dwarf had collected in his cave between them. The old mother lived for many years peacefully with her children; and she carried the two rose trees with her, and they stood in front of her window, and every year they bore her the finest roses, both white and red.

Lang, Andrew, comp. *Blue Fairy Book*. New York: Penguin Books Ltd., 1975.

SNOWDROP

This is a favorite fairy tale about a beautiful young woman, seven very concerned and caring dwarfs, and a mean stepmother.

It was the middle of winter when a certain queen sat working at a window, the frame of which was made of fine black ebony; and as she was looking out upon the snow, she pricked her finger, and three drops of blood fell upon it. Then she gazed upon the red drops which sprinkled the white snow, and said: "Would that my little daughter may be as white as snow, as red as blood, and as black as ebony!" And so the little girl grew up; her skin was white as snow, her cheeks as rosy as the blood, and her hair as black as ebony; and she was called Snowdrop.

But this queen died; and the king married another wife, who had a magical looking-glass, to which she used to go and gaze upon herself and say:

"Tell me, glass, tell me true! Of all the ladies in the land, Who is the fairest? Tell me who?"

And the glass answered:

"Thou, queen, art fairest in the land."

But when Snowdrop was seven years old, the glass one day answered the Queen:

"Thou, queen, may'st fair and beauteous be, but Snowdrop is lovelier far than thee!"

When she heard this she turned pale with rage and envy, and called to one of her servants and said:

"Take Snowdrop into the wide wood, that I may never see her more."

Then the servant led her away; but his heart melted when she begged him to spare her life, and he said:

"I will not hurt thee, thou pretty child."

So he left her by herself; and he felt as if a great weight were taken off his heart when he made up his mind not to kill her.

Then poor Snowdrop wandered through the wood in fear. In the evening she came to a cottage, and went in to rest herself, for her little feet would carry her no farther. Everything was neat: on the table was spread a white cloth, and there were seven little plates with seven little loaves, and seven little glasses with wine in them; and knives and forks lay in order; and by the wall stood seven little beds. Then, as she was very hungry, she picked a little piece off each loaf, and drank a very little wine out of each glass; and after that she thought she would lie down and rest. So she tried all the little beds; one was too long, another was too short, till at last the seventh suited her; and there she laid herself down and went to sleep. Presently in came the masters of the cottage, seven little dwarfs who lived among the mountians, and dug and searched for gold. They lighted their seven lamps, and saw directly that all was not right.

The first said:

"Who has been sitting on my stool?"

The second:

"Who has been eating off my plate?"

The third:

"Who has been picking my bread?"

The fourth:

"Who has been meddling with my spoon?"

The fifth:

"Who has been handling my fork?"

The sixth:

"Who has been cutting with my knife?"

The seventh:

"Who has been drinking my wine?"

Then the first looked round and said:

"Who has been lying on my bed?"

And the rest came running to him, and everyone cried out that somebody had been upon his bed. But the seventh saw Snowdrop, and called to his brethren to come and see her; and they cried out with wonder and astonishment, and brought their lamps to look at her, and said:

"Good heavens! What a lovely child she is!"

And they were delighted to see her, and took care not to wake her; and the seventh dwarf slept an hour with each of the other dwarfs in turn, till the night was gone.

In the morning Snowdrop told them her story; and they pitied her, and said if she would keep all things in order, and cook, and wash, and knit, and spin for them, she might stay where she was and they would take care of her. Then they went out all day long to work, seeking for gold and silver in the mountians; and Snowdrop remained at home.

The Queen, now that she thought Snowdrop was dead, believed that she was certianly the handsomest lady in the land; and she went to the glass and said:

"Tell me, glass, tell me true! Of all the ladies in the land, Who is fairest? Tell me who?"

And the glass answered:

> *"Thou, queen, art the fairest in all this land;*
> *But over the hills, in greenwood shade,*
> *Where the seven dwarfs their dwelling have made,*

There Snowdrop is hiding her head; and she
Is lovelier far, O queen! than thee."

Then the Queen was alarmed; for she knew that the glass always spoke the truth, and was sure that the servant had betrayed her. She could not bear to think that anyone lived more beautiful than she was; so she disguised herself as an old peddler, and went to the place where the dwarfs dwelt. There she knocked at the door, and cried:

"Fine wares to sell!"

Snowdrop looked out at the window, and said:

"Good day, good woman; what have you to sell?"

"Good wares, fine wares," said she; "laces and bobbins of all colors."

"I will let the old lady in; she seems to be a very good sort of body," thought Snowdrop, so she ran down, and unbolted the door.

"Bless me!" said the old woman. "how badly your stays are laced! Let me lace them up with one of my nice new laces."

Snowdrop did not dream of any mischief; so she stood up before the old woman; but she set to work so nimbly, and pulled the lace so tight, that Snowdrop lost her breath, and fell down as if dead.

"There's an end of all that beauty," said the spiteful Queen and went away home.

In the evening the seven dwarfs returned, and were grieved to see their faithful Snowdrop stretched upon the ground motionless, as if dead. However, they lifted her up, and when they found what was the matter, they cut the lace; and in a little time she began to breathe, and soon came to life again. Then they said:

"The old woman was the Queen herself; take care another time, and let no one in when we are away."

When the Queen got home, she went straight to her glass, and spoke to it as usual; but still it said:

"Thou, queen, art the fairest in all this land,
But over the hills, in the greenwood shade,
Where the seven dwarfs their dwelling have made,
There Snowdrop is hiding her head;
And she is loveier far, O queen! than thee."

Then the blood ran cold in her heart with spite and malice to see that Snowdrop still lived; and she dressed herself again in a very different disguise, and took with her a poisened comb. When she reached the dwarf's cottage, she knocked at the door, and cried:

"Fine wares to sell!"

But Snowdrop said:

91

"I dare not let anyone in."

Then the Queen said:

"Only look at my beautiful combs," and gave her the poisoned one. And it looked so pretty that she took it up and put it into her hair to try it, but the moment it touched her head the poison was so powerful that she fell down senseless.

"There you may lie," said the Queen, and went her way. By good luck the dwarfs returned early that evening, and when they saw Snowdrop lying on the ground, they thought what had happened, and soon found the poisoned comb. And when they took it away, she recovered; and they warned her once more not to open the door to anyone.

Meantime the Queen went home to her glass, and trembled with rage when she received the same answer as before. She went secretly into a chamber, and prepared a poisoned apple: the outside looked rosy and tempting, but whoever tasted it was sure to die. Then she dressed herself up as a peasant's wife, and travelled over the hills to the dwarfs' cottage, and knocked at the door; but Snowdrop put her head out of the window and said:

"I dare not let anyone in."

"Do as you please," said the old woman, "but at any rate take this pretty apple; I will make you a present of it."

"No," said Snowdrop, "I dare not take it."

"You silly girl!" answered the other, "what are you afraid of? do you think it is poisoned? Come! you eat one part, and I will eat the other."

Now the apple was so prepared that one side was good, though the other side was poisoned. Then Snowdrop was very much tempted to taste, for the apple looked exceedingly nice; and when she saw the old woman eat, she could refrain no longer. But she had scarcely put the piece in her mouth, when she fell down dead upon the ground.

"This time nothing will save thee," said the queen; and she went home to her glass, and at last it said:

"Thou, queen, art the fairest of all the fair."

And her envious heart was glad, and as happy as such a heart could be.

When evening came and the dwarfs returned home they found Snowdrop lying on the ground: no breath passed her lips, and they were afraid that she was dead. They lifted her up and combed her hair, and washed her face with wine and water; but all was in vain, the little girl seemed quite dead. So they laid her upon a bier, and watched and bewailed her three whole days; then they proposed to bury her: but her cheeks were still rosy and her face looked as it did while she was alive. So they made a coffin of glass that they might still look at her, and wrote her name upon it, in gold letters, and that she was the king's daughter. And the coffin was placed upon the hill, and one of the dwarfs sat by and watched.

And thus Snowdrop layed for a long time, and still only looked as though she were asleep; for she was even now as white as snow, and as red as blood, and as black as ebony.

At last a prince came and called at the dwarfs' house; and he saw Snowdrop, and read what was written in gold letters. Then he offered the dwarfs money, and earnestly prayed them to let him take her away; but they said:

"We will not part with her for all the gold in the world."

At last, however, they had pity on him, and gave him the coffin: but the moment he lifted it up to carry it home with him, the piece of apple fell from between her lips, and Snowdrop awoke, and said:

"Where am I?"

And the Prince answered:

"Thou art safe with me."

Then he told her all that had happened, and said:

"I love you better than all the world: come with me to my father's palace, and you shall be my wife."

And Snowdrop consented, and went home with the Prince: and everything was prepared with pomp and splendor for their wedding.

To the feast was invited, among the rest, Snowdrop's old enemy, the Queen; and as she was dressing herself in fine rich clothes, she looked in the glass and said:

> *"Tell me, glass, tell me true!*
> *Of all the ladies in the land,*
> *Who is fairest? tell me who?"*

And the glass answered:

> *"Thou, lady, art lovliest here, I ween;*
> *But lovelier far is the new made queen."*

When she heard this, she started with rage; but her envy and curiosity were so great, that she could not help setting out to see the bride. And when she arrived, and saw that it was no other than Snowdrop, who, as she thought, had been dead a long while, she choked with passion, and fell ill and died; but Snowdrop and the Prince lived and reigned happily over that land many years.

Jerrold, Walter, ed. *The Big Book of Fairy Tales.* London: Blackie and Son Ltd., 1911.

HANS CHRISTIAN ANDERSEN

Hans Christian Andersen was born in Denmark in 1805. He was the son of a poor shoemaker who read to his son, took him to see plays, and built him toy theaters. The young boy had a natural gift for expression, and was awarded a scholarship to study at a high school in Copenhagen. He had a difficult time as he was teased for his strange appearance and the fact that he was older than the other boys in his class.

Hans grew to become a master of the fairy tale—writing stories based on the Danish and European tales his father told him when he was young. He was a man who lived very much through his own imagination and used it as a means to escape the awkwardness and solitude of his own childhood.

His fairy tales are windows into a fantasy world that include children, animals, and flowers—all special in some way. The characters may be extraordinarily small like Thumbelina, or have a missing leg like the Tin Soldier (see "Fantasies and Folk Tales" Chapter). They may be a nuisance to the adults around them, like Elise and her brothers, or they may be extremely imaginative like Ida. Andersen's themes are timeless and his stories resonate for their richness, brilliance, and acute sense of the world.

Andersen, Hans C. *Andersen's Fairy Tales.* Illustrated by Troy Howell. Stamford: Longmeadow Press, 1988.

Other Editions:

_____. *Andersen's Fairy Tales: Classic Fairy Tales.* New York: Crown Publishers, 1989.

_____. *Complete Hans Christian Anderson Fairy Tales.* New York: Random House, 1993.

THE SILVER PENNY

HANS CHRISTIAN ANDERSEN

When a perfectly good silver penny goes abroad, everyone calls it bad and worthless. It takes a fellow countryman to recognize its value.

There was a penny that had come bright from the mint, skipping and clinking. "Hurrah!" it cried. "I'm off into the wide world!" And it was.

The child held on to it tightly with warm hands and the miser with cold and clammy hands; old people turned it over and over many times, while the young sent it rolling on at once. The penny was a silver one with just a little copper in it; and it had been a whole year in the world—that is to say, in the country where it had been minted—when, one day, it went on a journey abroad. It was the last of the country's coins that were left in the purse of its traveling master, and he had no idea that he had it till it got between his fingers.

"Why, I've still got a penny from home!" he said. "It can travel along with me." And the penny clinked and skipped for joy as he put it back into the purse. It lay there with foreign companions who came and went; one would make way for the next, but always the penny from home stayed behind. That was a distinction.

Several weeks had now gone by, and the penny was far out in the world, without exactly knowing where; it heard from the other coins that they were French and Italian, and one would say that now they were in this town, and another would say that now they were in that; but of all this the penny could have no idea, for you don't see the world when you're always in a bag, which is where it was. But noticing one day that the purse wasn't shut, it crept to the opening in order to peep out. Now this it should never have done, but then it was inquisitive, and you have to pay for that: it fell out into the trouser pocket, and when the purse was laid aside in the evening, the penny was left where it was and went with the clothes into the corridor; there it dropped straight onto the floor, and nobody heard it, nobody saw it.

In the morning the clothes were brought in, and the gentleman put them on and went away. And the penny didn't go with him, but was found, put into service again, and went out with three other coins.

Well, it's nice to see the world! thought the penny. To know other people, other customs!

"What sort of a penny's this?" somebody said all at once. "This isn't our money! It's false! No good!"

95

And here begins the penny's story, as it afterwards told it.

"False! No good! It cut me," said the penny. "I knew I was of good silver and good ring, and of good mint. Surely they were mistaken and couldn't mean me! But they did mean me! It was me they were calling false! Me that was no good! 'I'll have to pass this in the dark!' said the man who had me. And so I was passed in the dark and abused in broad daylight. "False! No good! We must get rid of this."

And the penny would tremble in the fingers every time it was to be secretly passed off as lawful coin.

"Miserable me!" said the penny, "What was the use of silver, my stamp, my mint, when they didn't mean anything? Your worth to the world is the value the world puts on you. How awful to have a guilty conscience and slink along paths of wickedness when I, though I was perfectly innocent, could feel as I did by only seeming to! Every time I was taken out I dreaded the eyes that would look at me, for I knew that I should be thrust back and flung on the counter, as if I were a cheat and a liar.

"Once I was passed to a poor penniless woman who got me in payment for her daily labor, and she was unable to get rid of me. Nobody would have me; I was a real trouble to her.

"'I can't help it, I shall have to cheat somebody with it,' she said. 'I can't afford to hold on to a bad penny. The rich baker shall have it; he can best afford it. But I shall still be doing wrong.'

"So now I'm going to trouble the woman's conscience!" I sighed. "Can I really have changed so very much in my old age?"

"And so the woman went to the rich baker's; but he knew, only too well, what coins were lawful. I didn't stay long where I was laid, but was flung in the woman's face; she got no bread for me, and I was made thoroughly miserable by having been thus minted for others' misfortune; I who in my younger days had been so cheerful and so confident, so conscious of my value and my goodness. I grew as melancholy as a poor penny can when nobody will have it. But taking me back home the woman looked at me very gently and with great kindness and friendliness. 'No,' she said, 'I shan't cheat anybody with you! I'll punch a hole in you so everybody can see you're a bad one. And yet, come to think of it, you may be a lucky penny. Yes, I do believe! It's an idea! I'll punch a hole, thread a string through it, and then give the penny to the neighbor's little girl to hang round her neck for luck!'

"And so she punched a hole in me. It's never very nice to have a hole punched in you, but when the intention's good, you can put up with a good deal. I was threaded and so became a sort of medal to be worn. I was hung round the little child's neck; and the child smiled at me and kissed me, and for a whole night I rested on her warm and innocent breast.

"In the morning her mother took me between her fingers and looked at me, thinking to herself as she did so, as I soon realized. Getting out a pair of scissors she cut the thread.

"'Lucky penny!' she said. 'Well, we'll soon see!' And so saying she put me in acid, and made me turn green; whereupon she sealed up the hole, rubbed me a little, and went off in the dark to the lottery agent for a lottery ticket that would bring good luck.

"How miserable I felt! I was so crushed that I could have snapped in two. I knew I should be called bad and flung back, and, what's more, in the sight of all those pennies and shillings with inscriptions and faces they could be proud of. But I escaped. There were so many people at the agent's, and he was so busy, that I fell clinking into the till with all the other coins. Whether the ticket ever won a prize I cannot say, but I do know that I was recognized as a bad penny the very next day, put on one side, and sent out to cheat, always cheat. It's unbearable when you're an honest character as I declare I am.

"Year by year I thus passed from hand to hand and from house to house, always being abused and always looked down on; nobody believed in me, and I didn't even believe in myself or in the world. It was a hard time.

"Then one day a traveller came and, of course, I was made to cheat him, and he was innocent enough to take me for good money; but he was just about to spend me when once more I heard the cries of 'No good! False!'

"'I took it for a good one,' said the man, taking a closer look at me. Then all at once his face lit up, as no other face had ever done on giving me a closer look, as he said: 'Why, what's this? If it isn't one of our own coins; a good honest penny from home with a hole punched in it, and they're calling it bad. Well, this is funny! I shall keep you and take you back home with me!'

"I was thrilled with joy: I had been called a good, honest penny and was going back home where everybody would know me and tell that I was of good silver and true coin. I could have sparked for joy, only it isn't my nature to spark: that's for steel to do, not silver.

"I was wrapped up in fine white paper so that I shouldn't get mixed up with the other coins and be lost, and was only taken out on special occasions when fellow countrymen got together, and then was extremely well spoken of. They said I was interesting; and it's a pleasant thought that you can be interesting without saying a word.

"And so I came home! My troubles were all over, and my joys were beginning; for I was of good silver, and I had the right stamp, and it didn't do the slightest harm having a hole punched in me for being bad because it doesn't matter when you aren't. You have to hold out, for everything will come right in the end! Well, that's my belief!" said the penny.

THE PRINCESS
AND THE PEA

HANS CHRISTIAN ANDERSEN

A very short tale about how to test a true princess.

Once upon a time, there was a prince and he wanted to marry a princess, only she had to be a real princess. So he went all over the world looking for one. But every time there was something the matter: princesses there were in plenty, but whether they were real princesses or not, he could never really make out, there was always something not quite real about them. So he came home again and was so very sad because he did so want a real princess.

Now, one night there was a terrible storm. It thundered and lightened, and the rain poured down—it was frightful! All at once, there was a knock at the city gate, and the old king went out to open it.

There, standing outside, was a princess. But dear me, what a sight she looked, in the wind and the rain. The water was running down her hair and her clothes, and it was running in at the toes of her shoes and out again at the heels. And then she said she was a real princess.

"We'll see about that!" thought the old queen. But she didn't say anything; she went into the bedroom, took off all the bedclothes, and put a pea in the bottom of the bed. Then she took twenty mattresses and put them on top of the pea, and then again twenty feather-beds on top of the mattresses.

That was to be the princess's bed for the night.

In the morning they asked her how she had slept.

"Dreadfully!" said the princess, "I hardly got a wink of sleep all night. Goodness knows what can have been in the bed! There was something hard in it, and now I'm just black and blue all over. It's really dreadful!"

So now they were able to see that she was a real princess, because she had felt the pea right through the twenty mattresses and the twenty feather-beds. Only a real princess could be so tender as that.

So the prince took her for his wife, now he knew he had a real princess. And the pea was placed in the museum, where it may still be seen—if nobody has taken it.

There, now that was a real story!

LITTLE IDA'S FLOWERS

Hans Christian Andersen

Ida wonders why all of her flowers are so withered, and so her friend, the Student, tells her all about the flowers and what they do for fun while everyone is asleep.

y poor flowers are quite dead!" said little Ida. "They were so pretty last night, and now all the leaves hang faded and withered! Why do they do that?" she asked the Student, who was sitting on the sofa. She liked the Student very much, for he could tell her the most wonderful stories and cut such comical figures out of paper-hearts, in the center of which were little ladies who danced, flowers, and great castles, the doors of which could open and shut. He was a jolly Student indeed! "Why do the flowers look so bad today?" she asked again, and showed him a bunch of flowers that was quite withered.

"Do you know what is the matter with those flowers?" said the Student. "They were at a ball last night, and that is why they hang their heads so!"

"But the flowers cannot dance!" said little Ida.

"Yes, indeed, they can," said the Student. "When it is dark and we others are asleep, they jump merrily about. They have a ball almost every night!"

"May any children go to that ball?"

"Oh, yes," said the Student, "the tiny daisies and the lilies of the valley!"

"Where do the most beautiful flowers go to dance?" asked little Ida.

"You have often been outside the town gate near the great castle, have you not, there where the king lives during the summer, and where the beautiful garden is with its many flowers? And you have seen the swans which swam toward you when you give them bread crumbs? You may be quite sure that out there some very wonderful balls take place."

"I was out in that garden yesterday with my mother," said Ida. "But there were no leaves on the trees, and there was not a single flower left! Where are they? Last summer I saw so many!"

"They are inside the castle," said the Student. "You must know that as soon as the king and all court ladies and gentlemen move to the city, the flowers immediately run up out of the garden and into the castle, and there they have such merry times! You just ought to see! The two most beautiful roses seat themselves on the throne. They are the king and queen. All the red cockscombs arrange themselves on each side, and bow. They are the chamberlains. Then all the most beautiful flowers come in, and the ball begins. The blue violets make believe they are naval cadets, and dance with the hyacinths and crocuses, which they call young ladies! The tulips and the large yellow lilies are elderly ladies, who watch over the younger set and take care that they conduct themselves properly!"

"But," asked little Ida, "does not anyone punish the flowers for dancing in the king's castle?"

"No one really knows anything about it!" said the Student. "Sometimes, of course, the old steward of the castle, who has to keep watch there, comes in during the night. He carries a great bunch of keys with him, but as soon as the flowers hear the rattling of the keys they all become very quiet, hiding behind the long curtains and putting their heads out to peep around. 'It smells like flowers here!' says the old steward of the castle. But he cannot see a single one of them."

"That is fine!" said little Ida, clapping her hands, "but should not I be able to see the flowers, either?"

"Oh, yes," said the Student, "when you go out there again just be sure to remember to look through the window, and you will certainly see them. That is what I did today. A long yellow Easter lily lay on the sofa stretching herself. She was one of the court ladies!"

"Can the flowers in the botanical gardens also go out there? Are they able to travel that long distance?"

"Of course they can!" said the Student. "They can fly, if they want to! Have you not seen the beautiful butterflies, some red, some yellow, and some white, that look so much like flowers? That is what they once were; but they leaped from their stalks high in the air, and beat with their leaves as though they were little wings–and away they flew! And because they behaved themselves nicely, they were given permission to fly about in the daytime, too; They did not have to go home again and sit quiet on their stalks. And thus the leaves at last became real wings. That you have seen for yourself! It might be, however, that the flowers in the botanical gardens have never been outside the king's castle, or do not even know that there is such merriment there during the night. So now I am going to tell you something that will astonish the Professor of Botany next door very much. You know him, of course. When you go into his garden you must tell one of the flowers that a grand ball takes place at the castle. Then it will tell the news to all the others, and away they will fly. When the Professor goes to walk in his garden, there will not be a single flower, and he will not be able to understand where they are."

"But how can the flower tell it to the others? The flowers cannot talk!"

"No, of course they can't," answered the Student, "but they can make signs. Have you not seen how the flowers nod when the wind blows a little, and move all their green leaves? That is just as plain as if they talked!"

"Can the Professor understand the sign language?" asked Ida.

"Certainly he can! One morning he went down into his garden and saw a great stinging nettle make signs with its leaves to a pretty red carnation. 'You are so beautiful,' it said, 'and I love you very much!' But the Professor does not like such things and struck the leaves off the nettle, for you see they are its fingers. But the thorny leaves stung him, and since that time he never dares touch a nettle."

"That is very amusing!" said little Ida, laughing.

"What nonsense to put into a child's head!" said the tiresome Councilor, who had come to pay a visit and was sitting on the sofa. He did not like the Student, and always grumbled when he saw him cutting out the queer, comical figures. Sometimes it was a man hanging on a gibbet and holding a heart in his hand, for he was a heart stealer; sometimes an old witch riding on a broomstick and carrying her husband on her nose. Such things the Councilor could not bear to see, and he would always say, as he did now, "What nonsense to put in a child's head! Nothing but stupid fancies!"

But, to little Ida, the things the Student told her about her flowers were very amusing, and she thought about them a great deal.

THE BRONZE PIG

HANS CHRISTIAN ANDERSEN

One magical winter evening in Italy, a statue takes a poor little boy on a tour of all the great art in Florence; and all of it has come to life!

In the town of Florence, not far from the Piazza del Granduca, there is a little street called Porta Rossa, and there across from a small market place, where vegetables are sold, stands a fountain cast in the shape of a pig. Clear, fresh water spouts from its snout, which shines brightly as bronze can, while the rest of the body is green with age. The snout is polished daily by schoolboys and beggars who rest their hands upon it, while leaning over to drink.

It was late on a winter evening. The tops of the hills that surround the city were covered with snow. But it was not dark, for the moon was out; and the moon in Italy gives as much light as the sun does on a northern winter day.

In the ducal gardens, where thousands of flowers bloom in winter, a ragged little boy had sat all day under a large pine tree. He was hungry and thirsty: and though he had held out his little hand all day, no one had dropped anything into it. Night fell, and the watchman who came to close the gardens drove him away. On a bridge over the Arno, the boy stood for a long time, staring into the water and dreaming, as he watched the reflections of the many stars, the beautiful marble bridge called Santa Trinita, and himself, shimmering in the river.

He walked back to the fountain and, putting his arms around the bronze pig's neck, he drank water from its shining spout. Nearby he found some lettuce leaves and a few chestnuts, and they were his dinner. It was cold and the streets were deserted. He was alone. He climbed up on the pig's back and, leaning his curly head forward so that it rested on the pig's head, he fell asleep.

It was midnight. The metal animal beneath him moved and said very distinctly, "Little boy, hold on tight, for I am going to run!"

And it did run. And thus began the strangest ride that anyone has ever taken. The pig went first to the Piazza del Granduca. The bronze horse, on which the duke was mounted, neighed loudly when it saw them. All the colored coats of arms of the old town hall shone brilliantly; Michelangelo's David swung his sling. Every statue was alive.

In the arcade of the Palazzo degli Uffizi, where the nobles of Florence gathered for their masquerades, the bronze pig stopped.

"Hold tight," the bronze pig warned, "for now we are going up the stairs." The little boy did not answer; half joyfully, half fearfully, he clutched the neck of the pig.

They entered the long gallery. The boy knew it well, he had been there before: the walls were covered with paintings and here were the loveliest statues. But now the gallery was more brilliantly lighted than during the day; and every painting seemed more colorful, every bust and figure more beautiful. But the most magnificent moment—and the one the boy never would forget—was when the door to one of the smaller rooms opened. Here was the sculpture of a woman: beauty as only nature, marble and the greatest of all artists can create it. She moved her lovely limbs, and the dolphins at her feet arched their backs and leaped about. This sculpture is known to the world as the Medici Venus.

What beauty! What loveliness! The little boy saw it all, for the bronze pig walked slowly through every room of the palace.

"Thank you!" whispered the boy as the pig went bumpity, bumpity down the stairs with him on his back.

"Thank yourself!" replied the metal animal. "I have helped you and you have helped me, for only when an innocent child sits on my back, do I become alive and have the strength to run as I have tonight. It is only into the church that I am not allowed to go; but with you on my back I can peep through the door. But don't try to get down, for if you do, then I shall be dead, as I am in the daylight, when you see me in the Via Porta Rossa."

"I will stay with you," the child promised; and away they ran, through the streets of the town, till they came to the Church of Santa Croce.

The portals of the church opened by themselves. All the candles on the great altar were lit, and the light shone all the way out to the deserted square, where stood the bronze pig with a boy mounted on his back.

Down the right aisle, all the marble figures on the richly decorated sarcophagi had come alive. Dante with laurel leaves on his head, Michelangelo, Machiavelli, Alfieri: here they were, side by side, the glory of Italy! The Church of Santa Croce is not as large as Florence's cathedral, but it is much more beautiful.

The marble clothes of the statues seemed to move, while the great men's heads appeared to have turned so that they could look out into the night. From the altar came the sweet voices of white-clad choir boys, who swung censers, from which the strong smell of incense pervaded the air, even as far as the square.

Then the boy heard the wind whistling in his ears, and heard a loud bang as the big doors of the church closed. He lost consciousness. He felt cold; then he opened his eyes, he was awake.

It was morning, he was sitting—almost falling off—the bronze pig, which stood as immobile as ever in the Via Porta Rossa.

THUMBELINA

HANS CHRISTIAN ANDERSEN

Thumbelina is no bigger than half a thumb, which is how she got her name. She sleeps in a walnut shell and has a blanket made of a rose leaf. One night she is kidnapped by an old toad. This is the beginning of Thumbelina's many adventures.

There was once a woman who wished very much for a little tiny child. But she did not know where she could get one, and so she went to an old witch.

"I would so love to have a little child!" she said to the witch. "Will you please tell me where I can get one?"

"Oh yes, that can easily be managed," said the witch. "There is a barleycorn; but it is not at all the kind that grows in the farmer's field or is fed to the chickens. Plant it in a flowerpot, and see what happens!"

"Thank you," said the woman, and she gave the witch twelve bright shillings.

Then she went home and planted the barleycorn, and immediately up sprang a great, beautiful flower which looked exactly like a tulip; but the petals were tightly closed, as though the flower were still a bud.

"That is a lovely flower," said the woman; and she kissed its beautiful red and yellow cup. Just as she kissed it the flower opened with a loud pop! It was a real tulip, as one could see; but in the middle of the flower upon the green stamens sat a tiny little maiden, wonderfully delicate and beautiful. She was not over half a thumb's length in height, and so she was called Thumbelina.

She was given a beautifully polished walnut shell for a cradle, with blue-violet leaves for mattresses, and a rose leaf for a coverlet. There she slept at night; but in the daytime she played about on the table, where the woman had set a plate with a wreath of flowers all around it, their stalks standing in water. On the water in this plate floated a great tulip leaf, and on this the little maiden could sail from one side of the plate to the other. She had two white horse hairs with which to row, and a very pretty sight it all made, indeed! She could sing also, and so delicately and sweetly that nothing like it had ever before been heard in this world.

One night, as she lay in her pretty bed, an old Toad came hopping in through the window, where a pane had been broken out. The Toad was very ugly, big, and damp, and it hopped right down on the table where Thumbelina lay sleeping under the red rose leaf.

"That would be a lovely wife for my son!" said the Toad, and without more ado she seized the walnut shell in which Thumbelina slept, and hopped away with it through the broken window pane down into the garden.

There flowed a great, broad brook; the ground at the edge of the water was swampy and soft, and here lived the Toad and her son. Ugh! he was ugly and repulsive; he looked just like his mother.

"Croak! croak! brek-ke-ke-kex!" That was all he could say when he saw the pretty little maiden in the walnut shell.

"Don't talk so loud, or she will wake up!" said the old Toad. "She could run away from us yet, for she is as light as a bit of swan's down! We must put her out in the brook on one of the broad water lily leaves. It will seem just like an island to her, she is so small and light. Then she cannot run away while we are getting the parlor in order under the soft mud, where you two are to keep house together."

Out in the brook grew many water lilies. Their broad green leaves looked as if they were floating on top of the water. The leaf farthest out in the brook was the largest. So the old Toad swam out and on it laid the walnut shell with Thumbelina still asleep.

Early in the morning the poor little maid awoke, and when she saw where she was she began to cry bitterly, for there was water on all sides of the great green leaf, and she could not get to land.

The old Toad sat in the marsh, decking out her room with marsh grasses and yellow weeds–it was to be made very pretty for the new daughter-in-law; then she swam out, with her ugly son, to the leaf where Thumbelina stood. They had come to fetch her pretty bed, which was to be placed in the bridal chamber before she herself entered it. The old Toad bowed low in the water before her and said:

"This is my son; he is to be your husband, and you shall live splendidly together down in the mud.'

"Croak! croak! brek-ke-ke-kex!" was all the son could say.

Then they took the dainty little bed and swam away with it, leaving Thumbelina all alone on the great leaf. She wept, for she did not want to live with the nasty Toad or have her ugly son for a husband. The little fishes swimming in the water below had seen the Toad and heard what she had said; so they put their heads out of the water, for they wanted to get a look at the little girl. When they saw how wonderfully pretty she was, they felt very sorry that she should have to go down to live with the ugly Toad. No, that must never be! They crowded round the green stalk which held the leaf on which the little maiden stood, and gnawed it off with their teeth. Away floated the leaf, far down the stream, with Thumbelina–far away, where the Toad could not get her.

Thumbelina sailed on and on; the little birds that sat in the bushes saw her, and sang, "What a lovely little maiden!" Farther and farther floated the leaf, and thus out of the country traveled Thumbelina.

A beautiful little white Butterfly kept fluttering round her, and at last, alighted on the leaf, for it liked Thumbelina very much; she, too, was pleased and happy, for now the Toad could not get her, and everything was so beautiful about her as she floated along. The sun shone upon the water, which glistened like the brightest gold. Then she took her girdle and bound one end of it round the Butterfly, fastening the other end of the ribbon to the leaf. The leaf now glided onward much faster, and Thumbelina, too, for she was standing on the leaf, you know.

Just then a big Beetle came flying along; he saw her and immediately clasped his claw round her slender waist and flew with her up into a tree. The green leaf went floating away down the brook, and the Butterfly with it, for you know he was fastened to the leaf, and could not get loose.

My! how frightened poor little Thumbelina was when the Beetle carried her off into the tree! But she was most sorry for the beautiful white Butterfly that she had bound to the leaf; if he could not free himself, he would have to starve to death.

THE WILD SWANS

HANS CHRISTIAN ANDERSEN

Elise and her eleven brothers are very happy indeed, until one day when their father, the king, marries a wicked queen. She sends Elise away to live with a poor peasant family and turns her eleven brothers into swans.

ar away, there where the swallows fly in winter, lived a king who had eleven sons and one daughter, Elise. The eleven brothers, the princes, went to school wearing stars on their breasts and swords at their sides. They wrote on golden slates with diamond pencils, and could recite just as well by heart as they could read from the book. Anyone hearing them knew immediately that they were princes. Their sister, Elise, sat upon a little footstool made of looking glass, and she had a picture book which had cost half the kingdom to buy.

Oh, these children were very, very happy! But thus it was not always to be.

Their father, who was king over all the land, married a wicked queen who was not at all kind to the poor children; they felt that on the very first day. There were great festivities at the castle, and the children played at visiting and having company. But instead of letting them have all the cakes and baked apples they could eat, as they were used to having, the queen gave them only some sand in a teacup, telling them they could make believe that it was something to eat.

The following week she sent Elise into the country to live with some peasant people, and it did not take her long to make the king believe so many bad things of the boys that he cared no more about them.

"You shall fly out into the world and look after yourselves," said the wicked queen; "fly away as great voiceless birds!"

But she could not make things as bad for them as she would have liked, for they turned into eleven beautiful wild swans. With strange cries they flew out of the palace window, away over the park and the forest.

It was still very early in the morning when they reached the peasants' cottage where their sister Elise lay asleep. They hovered above the roof, turning and twisting their long necks, and flapping their wings; but no one heard or saw them, and they had to fly on. They soared up toward the clouds and far out into the wide world. They flew away over a great dark forest, which stretched to the shore of the sea.

Poor little Elise stood in the peasants' room, playing with a green leaf, for she had no other toys. She made a little hole in the leaf and looked through it at the sun, and it seemed to her as if she saw her brothers' bright eyes. And every time the warm sunbeams shone upon her cheek, it reminded her of their kisses.

The days went by, one just like the other. When the wind blew through the hedges outside the house, it whispered to the roses, "Who could be more beautiful than you?" The roses shook their heads and answered, "Elise!" And when the old woman sat in the doorway on a Sunday reading in her psalm book, the wind turned the pages and said to the book, "Who could be more devout than you?" "Elise!" answered the book. And both knew the roses and the book of psalms spoke the exact truth.

When she was fifteen Elise had to go back home, but when the queen saw how pretty she was, she was filled with anger and hatred toward her. She would willingly have turned her into a wild swan, too, like her brothers, but she did not dare do it at once, for the king wanted to see his daughter.

In the early morning the queen always went to her bath, which was built of marble and adorned with soft cushions and beautiful carpets.

There she took three toads, kissed them, and said to the first, "Sit upon Elise's head when she comes to bathe, that she may become stupid and sluggish like you. Sit on her forehead," she said to the second, "that she may become homely like you, so that her father won't know her! Rest near her heart," she whispered to the third. "Let an evil spirit come over her, that will make her suffer." Then she put the toads into the clear water, which immediately took on a tinge of green. She called Elise, undressed her, and made her go into the bath. As she dipped under, one of the toads got into her hair, another on her forehead, and the third on her breast, but Elise seemed not to notice them at all. When she stood up three scarlet poppies floated on the water; had the creatures not been made poisonous from having been kissed by the sorceress, they would have been changed into crimson roses. Nonetheless, flowers they became from merely having rested a moment on the good girl's head and near her heart. She was too pure and innocent for the enchantment to have any power over her.

When the wicked queen saw this she rubbed walnut juice on Elise's skin, so that she became brown. Then she smeared her face with some evil-smelling ointment, and tangled up her beautiful hair; it would have been quite impossible to recognize the pretty Elise.

When her father saw her he was quite horrified and said that she could not be his daughter. Nobody would have anything to say to her, except the watch dog, and the swallows, but they were poor animals whose opinion went for nothing.

Poor Elise wept, and thought of her eleven brothers, who were all far away. She crept sadly out of the palace and wandered all day over fields and marshes, into the great forest. She did not know in the least where she was going, but she felt very sad, and longed for her brothers. No doubt, they too, like herself, had been driven out into the world; and she made up her mind to seek and find them.

THE : WILD : SWANS

She had been in the wood only a short while when night fell. She had quite lost her way; so she said her evening prayer, lay down on the soft moss, and leaned her head against a stump. It was very still and the air was mild, and round about in the grass and on the moss, hundreds of glow worms shone like green fire. When she touched one of the branches above her gently the glowing insects fell down to her like a shower of stars. All night long she dreamed about her brothers. Again they were children playing together; they wrote upon golden slates with diamond pencils and looked at the wonderful picture book that had cost half a kingdom. But they no longer wrote just lines and circles on their slates as they used to do; no, they wrote down all their bravest deeds and everything that they had seen and experienced.

THE LITTLE MATCH GIRL

HANS CHRISTIAN ANDERSEN

In this fairy tale you get a brief glimpse of a poor child's dreams and fears, all at once illuminated by the glow of her matches.

It was the last evening of the year. In the cold and darkness a poor little girl, with bare head and feet, was wandering about the streets, her feet were quite red and blue with the cold. In her tattered apron she carried a bundle of matches, and there were a good many more in her hand. No one had bought any of them the livelong day—no one had given her a single penny. Trembling with cold and hunger, she crept on, the picture of sorrow.

The snowflakes settled on her long fair hair, which fell in ringlets over her shoulders; but she thought neither of her own beauty, nor of the cold. Lights shone from every window, and the smell of roast goose reached her, for it was New Year's eve, and it was of that she thought.

In a corner formed by two houses, one which came a little farther forward than the other, she sat down, drawing her feet close under her, but in vain—she could not warm them. She dared not go home—she had sold no matches, earned not a single penny, and her father would certainly beat her; besides, her home was almost as cold as the street—it was an attic; and although the larger of many holes in the roof were stopped up with straw and rags, the cold wind came whistling through. Her hands were nearly frozen. A match would warm them, perhaps, if she dared to light it. She drew one out, and struck it against the wall. It was a bright, warm light, like a little candle, and she held her hands over it. It was quite a wonderful light. It seemed to that poor little girl as though she were sitting before a large iron stove with polished brass feet and brass ornaments. So beautifully did the fire within burn that the child stretched out her feet to warm them also. Alas! in an instant the flame had died away, the stove vanished, and the little girl sat cold and comfortless, with the remains of the burnt match in her hand.

A second match was struck; it kindled and blazed, and wherever its light fell the wall became transparent as a veil, and the little girl could see into the room. She saw the table spread with a snowy white tablecloth and set with shining china dinner dishes. A roast goose, stuffed with apples and dried plums, stood at one end, smoking hot, and—pleasantest of all

113

to see—the goose, with knife and fork still in her breast, jumped down from the dish, and waddled along the floor right up to the poor child. The match was burnt out, and only the thick, hard wall was beside her.

She lighted a third match. Again the flame shot up, and now she was sitting under a most beautiful Christmas tree, far larger, and far more prettily decked out than the last one she had seen last Christmas-eve through the glass doors of the rich merchant's house. Thousands of wax tapers lighted up the branches, and tiny painted figures, such as she had seen in the shop windows, looked down from the tree upon her. The child stretched out her hands towards them and the match went out. Still, however, the Christmas candles burned higher and higher, till they looked to her like the stars in the sky. One of them fell, the light streaming behind it like a long, fiery tail.

"Now someone is dying," said the little girl softly, for she had been told by her old grandmother, the only person who had been kind to her—but she was now dead—that whenever a star falls a soul flies up to God. She struck another match against the wall and the light shone round her, and in its brightness she saw her dear dead grandmother, gentle and loving as always, but bright and happy as she had never looked during her lifetime.

"Grandmother!" said the child, "oh, take me with you! I know you will leave me as soon as the match goes out—you will vanish like the warm stove, like the New Year's feast, and like the beautiful Christmas tree." And she hastily lighted all the remaining matches in the bundle, lest her grandmother should disappear. And the matches burned with such a splender, that noonday could scarcely have been brighter. Never had the good old grandmother looked so tall and stately, so beautiful and kind. She took the little girl in her arms, and they both flew away together radiant with happiness. They flew far above the earth, higher and higher, till they were in that place where neither cold, nor hunger, nor pain is ever known—in the presence of God.

But in the cold morning hour, crouching in the corner of the wall, the poor little girl was found—her cheeks glowing, her lips smiling—frozen to death on the last night of the Old Year. The New Year's sun shone on the lifeless child; motionless she sat there with the matches in her lap, one bundle of them quite burnt out.

"She had been trying to warm herself, poor thing!" some people said; but no one knew of the sweet visions she had beheld, or how gloriously she and her grandmother were celebrating their New Year's festival.

Jerrold, Walter, ed. *The Big Book of Fairy Tales*. London: Blackie and Son Ltd., 1911.

A LITTLE PRINCESS

FRANCES HODGSON BURNETT

Sara's wealthy father, Captain Crewe, sends his beloved daughter to Miss Minchin's school in England when she is seven years old. She is afforded every luxury imaginable by her generous father; a maid, a pony, and beautiful clothes, and this causes a few of Miss Minchin's jealous students, especially Livinia, to be cruel to her. Through it all Sara is always kind and generous with all the girls; she even takes one of the younger girls, Lottie, under her wing as her "adopted daughter." In this section we see how Sara got to be known as a princess.

essons for the day were over, and they were sitting before the schoolroom fire, enjoying the time they liked best. It was the time when Miss Minchin and Miss Amelia were taking their tea in the sitting room sacred to themselves. At this hour a great deal of talking was done, and a great many secrets changed hands, particularly if the younger pupils behaved themselves well, and did not squabble or run about noisily, which it must be confessed they usually did. When they made an uproar the older girls usually interfered with scolding and shakes. They were expected to keep order, and there was danger that if they did not, Miss Minchin or Miss Amelia would appear and put an end to festivities. Even as Lavinia spoke the door opened and Sara entered with Lottie, whose habit was to trot everywhere after her like a little dog.

"There she is, with that horrid child!" exclaimed Lavinia in a whisper. "If she's so fond of her, why doesn't she keep her in her own room? She will begin howling about something in five minutes."

It happened that Lottie had been seized with a sudden desire to play in the schoolroom and had begged her adopted parent to come with her. She joined a group of little ones who were playing in a corner. Sara curled herself up in the window seat, opened a book, and began to read.

She was so far away from the schoolroom that it was not agreeable to be dragged back suddenly by a howl from Lottie. Never did she find anything so difficult as to keep herself from losing her temper when she was suddenly disturbed while absorbed in a book. People who are fond of books know the feeling of irritation which sweeps over them at such a moment. The temptation to be unreasonable and snappish is one not easy to manage.

"It makes me feel as if someone had hit me," Sara had told Ermengarde once in confidence. "And as if I want to hit back. I have to remember things quickly to keep from saying something ill-tempered."

She had to remember things quickly when she laid her book on the window seat and jumped down from her comfortable corner.

Lottie had been sliding across the schoolroom floor and, having first irritated Lavinia and Jessie by making a noise, had ended by falling down and hurting her fat knee. She was screaming and dancing up and down in the midst of a group of friends and enemies, who were alternately coaxing and scolding her.

"Stop this minute, you cry baby! Stop this minute!" Lavinia commanded.

"I'm not a cry baby . . . I'm not!" wailed Lottie. "Sara, Sa—ra!"

"If she doesn't stop, Miss Minchin will hear her," cried Jessie. "Lottie darling, I'll give you a penny!"

"I don't want your penny," sobbed Lottie; and she looked down at the fat knee, and seeing a drop of blood on it, burst forth again.

Sara flew across the room and, kneeling down, put her arms round her.

"Now, Lottie," she said. "Now, Lottie, you promised Sara."

"Come and sit in the window seat with me," Sara went on, "and I'll whisper a story to you."

"Will you?" whimpered Lottie. "Will you—tell me—about the diamond mines?"

"The diamond mines?" broke out Lavinia. "Nasty, little spoiled thing, I should like to slap her!"

Sara got up quickly on her feet. It must be remembered that she had been very deeply absorbed in the book about the Bastille and had had to recall several things rapidly when she realized that she must go and take care of her adopted child. She was not an angel, and she was not fond of Lavinia.

"Well," she said, with some fire, "I should like to slap you—but I don't want to slap you!" restraining herself. "At least I both want to slap you—and I should like to slap you—but I won't slap you. We are not little gutter children. We are both old enough to know better."

Here was Lavinia's opportunity.

"Ah, yes your royal highness," she said. "We are princesses I believe. At least one of us is. The school ought to be very fashionable now Miss Minchin has a princess for a pupil."

Sara started toward her. She looked as if she were going to box her ears. Perhaps she was. Her trick of pretending things was the joy of her life. She never spoke of it to girls she was not fond of. Her new "pretend" about being a princess was very near to her heart, and she was shy and sensitive about it. She had meant it to be rather a secret, and here was Lavinia deriding it before nearly all the school. She felt the blood rush up into her face and tingle in her ears. She only just saved herself. If you were a princess, you did not fly into rages. Her hand dropped, and she stood quite still a moment. When she spoke it was in a quiet, steady voice; she held her head up, and everybody listened to her. "It's true," she said. "Sometimes I do pretend I am a princess. I pretend I am a princess, so that I can try and behave like one."

Lavinia could not think of exactly the right thing to say. Several times she had found that she could not think of a satisfactory reply when she was dealing with Sara. The reason for this was that, somehow, the rest always seemed to be vaguely in sympathy with her opponent. She saw now that they were pricking up their ears interestedly. The truth was, they liked princesses, and they all hoped they might hear something more definite about this one, and drew nearer Sara accordingly.

Lavinia could only invent one remark, and it fell rather flat.

"Dear me," she said, "I hope, when you ascend the throne, you won't forget us!"

"I won't" said Sara, and she did not utter another word, but stood quite still and stared at her steadily as she saw her take Jessie's arm and turn away.

After this, the girls who were jealous of her used to speak of her as "Princess Sara" whenever they wished to be particularly disdainful, and those who were fond of her gave her the name among themselves as a term of affection. No one called her "princess" instead of "Sara," but her adorers were much pleased with the picturequesness and grandeur of the title and Miss Minchin, hearing of it, mentioned it more than once to visiting parents, feeling that it rather suggested a sort of royal boarding school.

Burnett, Frances Hodgson. *A Little Princess.* New York: Harper Collins Publishers, 1905.

THE THREE BEARS

ROBERT SOUTHEY

This is the tale of a dishonest little old woman who enters the home of three unsuspecting bears.
Read on to see what takes place in this cabin in the woods.

here were once upon a time Three Bears, who lived in a wood. One of them was a Little, Small, Wee Bear; one was a Middle-sized Bear; and the other was a Great, Huge Bear. Each had a pot for its porridge: a little pot for the Little, Small, Wee Bear; a middle–sized pot for the Middle Bear; and a great pot for the Great, Huge Bear. Each had a chair to sit in: a little chair for the Little, Small, Wee Bear; a middle-sized chair for the Middle Bear; and a great chair for the Great, Huge Bear. Each had a bed to sleep in: a little bed for the Little, Small, Wee Bear; a middle-sized bed for the Middle Bear; and a great bed for the Great, Huge Bear.

One day, after they had made the porridge for their breakfast, they walked out into the wood while the porridge was cooling. While they were walking, a little old Woman came to the house. She could not have been a good, honest old Woman; for first she looked in at the window, and then she peeped in at the keyhole; and, seeing nobody in the house, she lifted the latch. So the little old Woman went in, and well pleased she was when she saw the porridge on the table. If she had been a good, little old Woman she would have waited till the Bears came home, and then, perhaps they would have asked her to breakfast; for they were good Bears—a little rough or so, as the manner of Bears is, but for all that very good-natured and hospitable. But she was an impudent, bad old Woman and set about helping herself.

First she tasted the porridge of the Great, Huge Bear; but that was too hot, and she said a bad word about that. Then she tasted the porridge of the Middle Bear; but that was too cold, and she said a bad word about that. Then she went to the porridge of the Little, Small, Wee Bear, and tasted that; and that was neither too hot nor too cold, but just right; and she liked it so well that she ate it all up: but the naughty old Woman said a bad word about the little porridge pot, because it did not hold enough for her.

Then the little old Woman sat down in the chair of the Great, Huge Bear, and that was too hard. Then she sat down in the chair of the Middle Bear; that was too soft for her. Then she sat down in the chair of the Little, Small, Wee Bear, and that was neither too hard nor too soft, but just right. So she seated herself in it, and there she sat till the bottom of the chair came out, and down she came, plump on the ground; and the naughty old woman said a wicked word about that too.

Then the little old Woman went upstairs to the bed-chamber in which the Three Bears slept. First she lay down in the bed of the Great, Huge Bear; that was too high at the head for her. Next she lay down upon the bed of the Middle Bear; that was too high at the foot for her. Then she lay down upon the bed of the Little, Small, Wee Bear; and that was just right. So she covered herself up and lay there till she fell fast asleep.

By this time the Three Bears came home to breakfast. Now the little old Woman had left the spoon of the Great, Huge Bear standing in his porridge.

"Somebody has been at my porridge!" said the Great, Huge Bear in his great, rough, gruff voice. When the Middle Bear looked at his, he saw the spoon was standing in it too.

"Somebody has been at my porridge!" said the Middle Bear in his middle voice.

Then the Little, Small, Wee Bear looked at his, and there was the spoon in the porridge-pot, but the porridge was all gone.

"Somebody has been at my porridge, and has eaten it all up!" said the Little, Small, Wee Bear in his little, small, wee voice.

Upon this the Three Bears, seeing that someone had entered their house, and eaten up the Little, Small, Wee Bear's breakfast, began to look about them. Now the little old

"So she covered herself up"

119

Woman had not put the hard cushion straight when she rose from the chair of the Great, Huge Bear.

"Somebody has been sitting in my chair!" said the Great, Huge Bear in his great, rough, gruff voice.

And the little old Woman had squatted down on the soft cushion of the Middle Bear.

"Somebody has been sitting in my chair!" said the Middle Bear in his middle voice.

And you know what the little old Woman had done to the third chair.

"Somebody has been sitting in my chair, and has sat the bottom of it out!" said the Little, Small, Wee Bear in his little, small, wee voice.

Then the Three Bears went upstairs. Now the little old woman had pulled the pillow of the Great, Huge Bear out of its place.

"Somebody has been lying in my bed!" said the Great, Huge Bear in his great, rough, gruff voice.

And the little old Woman had pulled the bolster of the Middle Bear out of its place.

"Somebody has been lying in my bed!" said the Middle Bear in his middle voice.

And when the Little, Small, Wee Bear came to look at his bed, there was the bolster in its place, and the pillow in its place upon the bolster, and upon the pillow was the little old Woman's ugly, dirty head–which was not in its place, for she had no business there.

"Somebody has been lying in my bed, and here she is!" said the Little, Small, Wee Bear in his little, small, wee voice.

The little old Woman had heard in her sleep the great, rough, gruff voice of the Great, Huge Bear; but she was so fast asleep that it was no more to her than the roaring of wind, or the rumbling of thunder. And she had heard the middle voice of the Middle Bear, but it was only as if she had heard someone speaking in a dream. But when she heard the little, small, wee voice of the Little, Small, Wee Bear, it was so sharp and so shrill, that it awakened her at once. Up she started; and when she saw the Three Bears on one side of the bed, she tumbled herself out at the other, and ran to the window. Now the window was open, because the Bears, like good, tidy Bears, as they were, always opened their bed-chamber window when they got up in the morning. Out the little old Woman jumped; and whether she broke her neck in the fall, or ran into the wood and was lost there, or found her way out of the wood, I cannot tell. But the Three Bears never saw anything more of her.

Jerrold, Walter, ed. *The Big Book of Fairy Tales.* London: Blackie and Son Ltd., 1911

BEAUTY AND THE BEAST

CHARLES PERRAULT

In these two excerpts, you will learn the tale of a woman who prefers goodness to beauty and is therefore rewarded for this virtue.

PART 1

There was once a merchant who had six children, three boys and three girls. The three daughters were all handsome but particularly the youngest; so very beautiful indeed was she that everyone, during her childhood, called her the Little Beauty, and being called still the same when she was grown up, nobody called her by any other name; this made her sisters extremely jealous. This youngest daughter was not only handsomer than her sisters, but was better tempered also.

Owing to some accident, the merchant suddenly lost his fortune, having nothing left but a small cottage in the country. He said to his daughters, the tears all the time running down his cheeks:

"My children, we must go and live in the cottage, and try to get a subsistence by labor, for we have no other means of support left!"

When they had removed to their cottage, the merchant and his three sons employed themselves in the fields and garden, that they might have corn and vegetables for their support. Beauty rose by four o'clock, lighted the house, and got breakfast for the whole family. When she had done her work she amused herself with reading, playing on the harpsichord, or singing as she spun. Her sisters were at a loss what to do to pass the time away! They breakfasted in bed, and did not rise till ten, when they walked out, but finding themselves very soon tired, would frequently sit down under a shady tree and lament the loss of their carriage and fine clothes.

The family had lived in this manner about a year, when the merchant received a letter which informed him that one of his richest vessels, which he thought lost, had arrived in port. This made the two sisters almost mad with joy. When they found it necessary for their father to take a journey to the ship they begged he would bring them on his return some new gowns, caps, rings, and all sorts of trinkets. Beauty asked for nothing; for she thought that the ship's cargo would scarcely purchase all that her sisters wished for.

"You, Beauty," said the merchant, "ask for nothing; what can I bring you?"

"Since you are so kind to think of me, dear father," answered she, "I should be obliged to you to bring me a rose, for we have none in our garden."

It was not that Beauty wished for a rose, but she was unwilling to condemn, by her example, the conduct of her sisters, who would have said she refused only to be praised. The merchant took his leave, and set out on his journey; but, on arriving at the port, some dishonest persons went to law with him about the merchandise; so after a great deal of trouble he returned to his cottage as poor as he had left it. When he was within thirty miles of his home, and thinking of the happiness he should enjoy in again embracing his children, his road lay through a thick forest, and he lost himself. All at once, happening to look down a long avenue, he discovered a light, but it seemed at great distance. He pursued his way towards it, and found it proceeded from a splendid palace brilliantly illuminated. He quicked his pace, and was surprised to find not a single creature in any of the outer yards. His horse, which followed him, finding a stable with the door open, entered, and, being nearly starved, helped himself to a plentiful meal of oats and hay. His master then tied him up, and walked toward the house, which he entered, without, to his great astonishment, seeing a living creature: pursued his way to a large hall, in which was a good fire, and a table provided with the most delicate dishes, on which was laid a single cover.

As snow and rain had wetted him to the skin, he approached the fire.

"I hope," says he, "the master of the house or his servants will excuse the liberty I take, for it surely will not be long before they make their appearance."

He waited a considerable time, and still nobody came: at length the clock struck eleven; and the merchant, overcome with hunger and thirst, helped himself to a chicken, of which he made but two mouthfuls, and then to a few glasses of wine, all the time trembling with fear. He sat until the clock struck twelve and not a creature had he seen. He now took courage, and began to think of looking a little farther about him: accordingly, he opened a door at the end of the hall, and entered an apartment magnificently furnished, which opened into another, in which there was an excellent bed; and finding himself quite overcome by fatigue, he resolved to shut the door, undress and get into it. It was ten o'clock the next morning before he thought of rising; when, what was his astonishment at seeing a handsome suit of clothes entirely new, in the place of his own, which were quite spoiled!

"No doubt," said he to himself, "this palace belongs to some good fairy, who has taken pity on my unfortunate situation."

He looked out of the window; and instead of snow, he saw the most delightful flowers. He returned to the hall where he had supped, and found a breakfast table, with chocolate ready prepared.

"Truly, my good fairy," said the merchant aloud, "I am extremely indebted to you for your kind care of me."

Having made a hearty breakfast, he took his hat and was going toward the stable to pay his horse a visit. As he passed under one of the arbors, which was loaded with roses, he recollected Beauty's request, and gathered a bunch of them to carry home. At the same instant he heard a most horrible noise, and saw such a hideous Beast approaching him, that he was ready to sink with fear!

"Ungrateful man!" said the Beast in a terrible voice; "I have saved your life by receiving you in my palace, and in return you steal my roses, which I value more than all my other possessions. With your life you shall atone for your fault: you shall die in a quarter of an hour!'

The merchant fell on his knees, and, clasping his hands, said:

"My lord, I humbly entreat your pardon: I did not think it could offend you to gather a rose for one of my daughters."

"I am not a lord, but a beast," replied the monster; "I do not like compliments, but that people should say what they think; so do not imagine you can move me with your flattery. You say, however, that you have daughters; I will pardon you, on the condition that one of them shall come hither and die in your place: do not attempt to argue with me, but go; and if your daughters should refuse, swear to me that you will return in three months."

The merchant had no intention to let one of his daughters die in his stead; but thought that, by seeming to accept the Beast's condition, he should have satisfaction of once again embracing them. He accordingly swore, and the Beast told him he might set off as soon as he pleased: "But," added he, "it is my will that you should not go empty-handed. Go back," continued he, "to the chamber in which you slept, where you will find an empty chest: fill it with whatever you like best, and I will get it conveyed to your house."

The Beast then went away, and the good merchant said to himself:

"If I must die, yet I shall have the consolation of leaving my children some provision."

He returned to the chamber in which he had slept; and having found a great quantity of pieces of gold, filled the chest with them to the very brim, locked it, and, mounting his horse, left the palace. The horse of itself took a path across the forest, and in a few hours they reached the merchant's house. His children gathered round him as he dismounted, but the merchant, instead of embracing them with joy, could not, as he looked at them, refrain from weeping. He held in his hand the bunch of roses, which he gave to Beauty, saying:

"Take these roses, Beauty; little do you think how dear they have cost your unhappy father," and then he gave an account of all that had happened in the palace of the Beast. The two eldest sisters immediately began to shed tears, and to reproach Beauty, who they said would be the cause of her father's death.

"See," said they, "the consequence of the pride of the little wretch; why did she not ask for fine things as we did? But, forsooth, she must distinguish herself; and though she will be the cause of her father's death she does not shed a tear."

"It would be useless," replied Beauty, "to weep for the death of my father, since he will not die. As the Beast will accept one of his daughters, I will give myself up to his fury; and most happy do I think myself in being able at once to save his life, and prove my tenderness to the best of fathers."

"No, sister," said the three brothers, "you shall not die: we will go in search of this monster, and he or we will perish."

"Do not hope to kill him," said the merchant; "for his power is by far too great for this to be possible. I am charmed with the kindness of Beauty, but I will not suffer her life to be exposed. I am old, and cannot expect to live much longer: I shall therefore have lost but a few years of my life, which I regret only for my children's sake."

"Never, my father," cried Beauty, "shall you go to the palace without me; for you cannot prevent my following you: though young, I am not overfond of life, and I had much rather be devoured by the monster than die of the grief your loss would occasion me."

The merchant tried in vain to reason with Beauty, for she was determined to go. He was, indeed, so afflicted with the idea of losing his child, that he never thought of the chest filled with gold; but, retiring to his chamber at night, to his great surprise, perceived it standing by his bedside. He now determined to say nothing to his eldest daughters of the riches he possessed; for he knew very well they would immediately wish to return to town: but he told Beauty his secret, who informed him that two gentleman had been visiting at their cottage during his absence, who had a great affection for her two sisters. She entreated her father to marry them without delay; for she was so sweet-tempered, that she loved them notwithstanding their unkind behavior, which she forgave with all her heart.

PART II

When the three months had passed, the merchant and Beauty prepared to set out for the palace of the Beast; the two sisters rubbed their eyes with an onion, to make believe they shed a great many tears: but both the merchant and his sons shed them in reality. Beauty did not weep, for she thought this would only increase their affliction. They reached the palace in a few hours: the horse, without bidding, entered the stable, and the merchant with his daughter proceeded to the large hall, where they found a table provided with every delicacy, and with it two covers laid on it. The merchant had little appetite; but Beauty, the better to conceal her sorrow, placed herself at table, and, having helped her father, began to eat, thinking all the time that the Beast had surely a mind to fatten her before he ate her up, since he had provided such good cheer. When they had finished their supper they heard a great noise; and the good old man began to bid his poor child farewell, for he knew it was the Beast coming to them. Beauty, on seeing his form, could not help being terrified, but tried as much as possible to conceal her fear. The monster asked her if she had come willingly; she replied, trembling still more:

"Y-e-s."

"You are a good girl," replied he, "and I think myself much obliged to you. Good man," continued he, "you may leave the palace tomorrow morning, and take care to return to it no more. Good-night, Beauty!"

"Good-night, Beast!" answered she; and the monster withdrew.

"Ah! dear child," said the merchant, embracing her, "I am half dead at the thought of your being sacrificed to this frightful monster: believe me, you had better go back, and let me stay."

"No," answered Beauty firmly, "to this I will never consent; you must go home tomorrow morning."

They now wished each other a sorrowful good-night, and went to bed, thinking it would be impossible for them to close their eyes; but no sooner had they lain down, than they fell into a profound sleep, from which they did not awake till morning. Beauty dreamed that a lady approached her, who said:

"I am much pleased, Beauty, with the generous affection you have shown, in being willing to give your life to save that of your father; it shall not go unrewarded."

Beauty related this dream to her father; but though it afforded him some comfort, he could not take leave of his darling child without shedding bitter tears. When the merchant was out of sight, Beauty sat down in the large hall and began to cry also; but as she had a great deal of courage, she soon resolved not to make her unhappy condition still worse by useless sorrow. She determined on taking a view of different parts of the palace, with which she was much delighted. What was her surprise, at coming to a door on which was written, "Beauty's apartment"! She opened it hastily, and her eyes were dazzled by the splendor of everything it contained; but the things that more than all the rest excited her wonder were a large library of books, a harpsichord, and music.

"The Beast is determined I shall not want amusement," said she. The thought then struck her, that it was not likely such provision should have been made for her if she had but one day to live. She opened the library, and perceived a book, on which was written, in letters of gold:

> *"Beauteous lady, dry your tears,*
> *Here's no cause for sighs or fears;*
> *Command as freely as you may,*
> *Compliance still shall mark your sway."*

"Alas!" thought she, "there is nothing I so much desire as to see my poor father, and to know what he is this moment doing."

Great was her amazement, when, casting her eyes on a looking glass that stood near, she saw her home, and her father riding up to the cottage in the deepest affliction. Her sisters had come out to meet him, who, notwithstanding all their endeavors to look sorry, could not help betraying their joy. In a short time this disappeared; but Beauty began to think the Beast was very kind to her; and that she had nothing to fear. About noon she found a table pre-prepared, and delightful concert music played all the time she was eating her dinner, without her seeing a single creature. At supper, when she was going to place herself at table, she heard the noise of the Beast, and could not help trembling in terror.

"Will you allow me, Beauty," said he, "the pleasure of seeing you at sup?"

"That is as you please," answered she.

"Not in the least," said the Beast, "and the Beast you alone command in this place. If you dislike my company, you have only to say so, and I shall leave you. But tell me, Beauty, do you not think me very ugly?"

"Truly, yes," replied she, "for I cannot tell a falsehood; but I think you are very good."

"You are right," continued the Beast; "and, besides my ugliness, I am also ignorant; I know well enough that I am but a beast.

"Pray do not let me interrupt you eating," pursued he: "and be sure you do not want for anything, for all you see is yours, and I shall be grieved if you are not happy."

"You are very good," replied Beauty, "I must confess I think very highly of your disposition; and that makes me almost forget your ugliness."

"Yes, I trust I am good-tempered," said he, "but still I am a monster."

"Many men are more monsters than you," replied Beauty; "and I am better pleased with you in that form, ugly as it is, than with those who, under the form of men, conceal wicked hearts."

"If I had any understanding," resumed the Beast, "I would thank you for what you have said; but I am too stupid to say anything that could give you pleasure."

Beauty supped with an excellent appetite, and had nearly got the better of her dread of the monster; but was ready to sink with horror, when he said:

"Beauty, will you be my wife?"

She was afraid of putting him in a passion by refusing and remained silent for a few moments before saying:

"No, Beast."

The Beast sighed deeply, and said, in a melancholy tone:

"Adieu, Beauty!" and left her, turning his head two or three times as he went, to look at her once more. Beauty, finding herself alone, began to feel the greatest compassion for the poor Beast.

"Alas!" said she, "what a pity it is he should be so very frightful, since he is good-tempered!"

Beauty lived three months in this palace, very contentedly: the Beast visited her every evening, and entertained her with his conversation while she supped, and though what he said was not very clever, yet, perceiving in him every day new virtues, instead of dreading the time of his coming, she continually looked at her watch, to see if it was almost nine o'clock; at which time he never failed to visit her. There was but one thing that made her uneasy; which was that the Beast, before he retired, constantly asked her if she would be his wife, and appeared extremely sorrowful at her refusals. Beauty one day said to him:

"You distress me exceedingly, Beast, in obliging me to refuse you so often: I wish I could prevail on myself to marry you, but I am too sincere to flatter you that this will ever happen."

"I love you exceedingly," replied the Beast; "however, I think myself fortunate in your being pleased to stay with me; promise me, Beauty, that you will never leave me."

Beauty was quite confused when he said this, for she had seen in her glass that her father had fallen sick of grief in her absence, and pined to see her.

"I would willingly promise," said she, "never to leave you entirely; but I have such a longing desire to see my father, that if you refuse me this pleasure I shall die of grief."

"Rather would I die myself, Beauty," replied he, "than cause you affliction. I will send you to your father's cottage; you shall stay there, and your poor Beast shall die of grief."

"No," said Beauty, weeping, "I love you too well to be the cause of your death: I promise to return in a week; you have shown me that my sisters are married, and my brothers gone to the army; my father is therefore all alone. Allow me to pass one week with him."

"You shall find yourself with him tomorrow morning," answered the Beast, "but remember your promise. When you wish to return you have only to put your ring on a table when you go to bed. Adieu, Beauty!"

The Beast sighed, and Beauty went to bed extremely affected to see him so distressed. When she awoke in the morning, she found herself in her father's cottage. Ringing a bell that was at her bedside, a servant entered, and on seeing her, gave a loud shriek; upon which the merchant ran upstairs, and, on beholding his daughter, was ready to die of joy. They embraced again and again; at length, Beauty began to recollect that she had no clothes to put on; but the servant told her she had just found a large chest filled with apparel, embroidered all over with gold and ornamented with pearls and diamonds. Beauty thanked the kind Beast in her thoughts for his attention, and dressed herself in the plainest of gowns, telling the servant to put away the others carefully, for she intended to present them to her sisters: but scarcely had she pronounced these words than the chest disappeared. Her father then observed that no doubt the Beast intended she should keep the whole for herself; and immediately the chest returned to the same place.

While Beauty was dressing herself, notice was sent to her sisters of her arrival, and they lost no time in coming with their husbands to pay her a visit. The husband of the eldest was extremely handsome; but so vain of his person, that he thought of nothing else from morning till night, and wholly disregarded the beauty of his wife. The second had married a man of excellent understanding; but he made no other use of it than to torment and affront all his aquaintances and his wife. The two sisters were ready to burst with envy when they saw Beauty dressed like a princess, and looking so very beautiful; not all the kindness she showed them produced the least effect; their jealousy was still increased when she told them how happily she lived at the palace of the Beast. The envious creatures went secretly into the garden, where they cried with spite, to think of her good fortune.

"Sister," said the eldest, "let us try to keep her here beyond the week allowed by the Beast; he will then be so enraged, that ten to one but he eats her up in a moment."

Having determined on this, they joined her in the cottage, and showed her so much affection, that Beauty could not help crying for joy. When the week was ended, the two sisters began to tear their hair, and counterfeited so much affliction at the thought of her leaving them, that she consented to stay another week; during which Beauty could not help constantly reproaching herself for the unhappiness she knew she must occasion the poor Beast, whom she tenderly loved, and for whose company she much wished. The tenth night of her being at the cottage, she dreamed she was in the garden of the palace, and that the Beast lay expiring, and in a dying voice reproached her with ingratitude. Beauty awaked and burst into tears.

"Am I not very wicked," said she, "to act so unkindly to a Beast who has treated me with such kindness? It is not his fault that he is ugly and stupid; and then he is so good! Which is far better than all the rest. Why do I refuse to marry him? I should certainly be happier with him than my sisters with their husbands, for neither the person nor the understanding of a husband makes his wife happy, but kindness, virtue, and obliging temper; and all these the Beast possesses in perfection. I do not love him, but I feel for him the sincerest friendship, esteem and gratitude."

She put her ring on the table, and soon fell asleep again. In the morning she found herself in the palace of the Beast; she dressed herself with great magnificence, that she might please him the better, and thought she had never passed so long a day. At length the clock struck nine, but no Beast appeared. Beauty imagined she had been the cause of his death; she ran from room to room all over the palace, calling in despair upon his name; but still no Beast came. After seeking for a long time, she recollected her dream, and instantly ran towards the grass plot on which she had seen him; and there she found the poor Beast extended senseless, and to all appearence dead. She threw herself upon his body, thinking nothing at all of his ugliness, and finding his heart still beat, she ran hastily and fetched some water, and threw it on his face. The Beast opened his eyes and said:

"You forgot your promise, Beauty. My grief for the loss of you made me resolve to starve myself to death; at least I shall die content, since I have had the pleasure of seeing you once more."

"No, dear Beast," replied Beauty, "you shall not die; you shall live to become my husband; from this moment I offer you my hand, and swear to be only yours. Alas! I thought I felt only friendship for you; but the pain I feel convinces me that I could not live without seeing you."

Scarcely had Beauty pronounced these words, before the palace was suddenly illuminated, and music, fireworks, and all kinds of amusements announced the most splendid rejoicings. This, however, had no effect on Beauty who watched over her Beast with the most tender anxiety. But what was her amazement, to see all at once at her feet the handsomest prince that was ever seen, who thanked her with utmost tenderness for having broken his enchantment! Though this prince was deserving her whole attention, she could not refrain from asking him what was become of the Beast.

"You see him, Beauty, at your feet," answered the prince. "A wicked fairy had condemned me to keep the form of a beast till a beautiful young lady should consent to marry me, and had forbidden me on pain of death to show any understanding. You alone, dearest Beauty, have had the generosity to judge of me by the goodness of my heart; and, in offering you my crown, the recompense falls infinitely short of what I owe you."

Beauty, in the most pleasing surprise, assisted the handsome prince to rise, and they proceeded together to the palace; when her astonishment was very great to find there her father and all her family, who had been conveyed thither by the beautiful lady she saw in her dream.

"Beauty," said the lady (for she was a great fairy), "receive the reward of the virtuous choice you have made. You have preferred goodness of heart to sense and beauty; you therefore deserve to find these qualities united in the same person. You are going to be a great queen: I hope a crown will not destroy your virtue. As for you, ladies," said the fairy to the eldest sisters, "I have long been witness to the malice of your hearts, and the injustice you have committed. You shall become two statues; but under that form you shall preserve your reason as before, and shall be fixed at the gates of your sister's palace; nor will I inflict on you any greater punishment than that of witnessing her happiness. You will never recover your natural forms till you are fully sensible of your faults; and, to say the truth, I much fear you will ever remain statues. I have sometimes seen that pride, anger and idleness may be conquered; but to amend a malignant and envious temper would be absolutely a miracle."

At the same instant the fairy, with a stroke of her wand, transported all who were present to the young prince's dominions, where he was received with transports of joy by his subjects. He married Beauty, and passed with her a long and happy life, because their actions were founded on virtue.

Jerold, Walter, ed. *The Big Book of Fairy Tales*. London: Blackie and Son Ltd., 1911.

LITTLE CHICKEN KLUCK

ANONYMOUS

This short tale sends a big message to be careful about who you listen to, who you believe, and who you follow.

There once was a little chicken called Kluck. A nut fell on his back, and gave him such a blow that he rolled on the ground. So he ran to the hen, and said: "Henny Penny, run, I think all the world is falling!"

"Who has told thee that, little chicken Kluck?"

"Oh, a nut fell on my back, and struck me so that I rolled on the ground."

"Then let us run," said the hen.

So they ran to the cock, and said: "Cocky Locky, run, I think all the world is falling."

"Who has told thee that, Henny Penny?"

"Little chicken Kluck."

"Who told thee that, little chicken Kluck?"

"Oh, a nut fell on my back, and struck me so that I rolled on the ground."

"Then let us run," said the cock.

So they ran to the duck, and said: "Ducky Lucky, run, I think all the world is falling."

"Who told thee that, Cocky Locky?"

"Henny Penny."

"Who has told thee that, Henny Penny?"

"Little chicken Kluck."

"Who has told thee that, little chicken Kluck?"

"Oh, a nut fell on my back, and struck me so that I rolled on the ground."

"Then let us run," said the duck.

So they ran to the goose, and said: "Goosy Poosy, run, I think all the world is falling."

"Who has told thee that, Ducky Lucky?"

"Cocky Locky."

"Who has told thee that, Cocky Locky?"

"Henny Penny."

"Who has told thee that, Henny Penny?"

"Little chicken Kluck."

"Who has told thee that, little chicken Kluck?"

"Oh, a nut fell on my back, and struck me so I rolled on the ground."

"Then let us run," said the goose.

Then they ran to the fox, and said: "Foxy Coxy, run, I think all the world is falling."

"Who has told thee that, Goosy Poosy?"

"Ducky Lucky."

"Who has told thee that, Ducky Lucky?"

"Cocky Locky."

"Who has told thee that, Cocky Locky?"

"Henny Penny."

"Who has told thee that, Henny Penny?"

"Little chicken Kluck."

"Who has told thee that, little chicken Kluck?"

"Oh, a nut fell on my back, and struck me so I fell on the ground."

"Then let us run," said the fox.

So they all ran into the wood. Then the fox said: "I must now count and see if I have got you all here. I, Foxy Coxy, one; Goosy Poosy, two; Ducky Lucky, three; Cocky Locky, four; Henny Penny, five; and little chicken Kluck, six; Hey! that one I'll snap up." He then said: "Let us run."

So they ran farther into the wood. Then said he: "Now I must count and see if I have got you all here. I, Foxy Coxy, one; Goosy Poosy, two; Ducky Lucky, three; Cocky Locky, four; Henny Penny, five; Hey! that one I'll snap up."

And so he went on till he had eaten them all up.

Jerrold, Walter, ed. *The Big Book of Fairy Tales.* London: Blackie and Sons Ltd., 1911.

Growing Up Around the World

ALL-OF-A-KIND FAMILY

SYDNEY TAYLOR

It's 1912, on New York's Lower East Side, home to immigrant families from all over the world, including many Jewish families from Eastern Europe like the five sisters in the "All of a Kind Family." In this excerpt, Ella, Charlotte, Hennie, Sarah, and Gertie delight in the bustle of the market while their mother shops for the ingredients for their Sabbath dinner.

THE SABBATH

The Sabbath begins Friday evening at dusk and for two days Mama was busy with her preparations. On Fridays she cleaned, cooked and baked. On Thursdays she shopped. Sabbath meals had to be the best of the whole week, so it was most important that she shop carefully. Every Thursday afternoon, Mama went to Rivington Street market where prices were lower than in her neighborhood stores.

Usually she left Gertie in Papa's care and set off alone right after lunch. This Thursday Mama was rather late. The children would soon be home from school so Mama decided that it would be nice if, for once, shopping for the Sabbath could be a family affair.

"Who wants to come to market with me?" she asked the children as soon as they came trooping in.

"I do! I do!" Everybody wanted to go along.

"Gracious, hasn't anybody any other plans for this afternoon?" asked Mama.

"Nothing as exciting as going to market," Ella declared, and her sisters all agreed.

But what about Gertie? It was a long walk for little feet. "Oh, Mama," she pleaded, "me too!"

Mama wasn't going to disappoint her. "All right, but I think it would be a good idea to take the baby carriage along."

"Baby carriage!" Gertie was indignant. "I'm too big for a baby carriage!"

"Of course you are," Mama assured her, "but the carriage will come in handy for all the bundles and if you should happen to get too tired to keep on walking, why, we can have the bundles move over and make room for a very nice little girl. Now hurry, everybody. Into your hats and coats."

Already they could smell the good smells, and in another minute, they were themselves part of the crowd.

"Just look at all the pushcarts!" exclaimed Sarah.

Heaped high with merchandise, they stretched in endless lines up and down the main street and in and out the side streets. They were edged up close to the curb and wedged together so tightly that one could not cross anywhere except at the corners. The pushcart peddlers, usually bearded men in long overcoats or old women in heavy sweaters and shawls, outdid each other in their loud cries to the passersby. All promised bargains—bargains in everything—in fruits and vegetables, crockery, shoelaces, buttons and other notions, in aprons and housedresses, in soap and soap powders, and hundreds of other things.

There were stores in which you could buy fish and stores that carried only dairy products. There were bakeries and meat shops, shoe stores and clothing establishments. In delicatessen shops fat "specials" (frankfurters) hung on hooks driven into the wall and big chunks of "knubble" (garlic) wurst were laid out in neat rows on white trays which bore the sign "A Nickel a Schtickel" (a nickel for a piece). The counters overflowed with heaps of smoked whitefish and carp, and large slabs of smoked red salmon. If one wished, firm, plump salt herrings were fished out of barrels for inspection before buying. Men's red flannel drawers and ladies' petticoats flew in the wind from their show-hooks on dry-goods store fronts.

But it was not enough that the merchandise sold behind closed shop doors could be displayed in showcase windows and store fronts. Their owners had to come out in the open too. They built stands which they either used themselves or rented out to others. Almost anything could be bought at these stands. There were pickle stands where the delicious odor of sour pickles mingled with the smell of sauerkraut and pickled tomatoes and watermelon rind. There were stands where only cereal product were sold—oats, peas, beans, rice and barley—all from open sacks. At other stands, sugar and salt were scooped out of large barrels and weighed to order. Here coffee was bought in the bean, for every household had its own wooden coffee grinder.

And wherever there was a bit of space too small for a regular stand, one could be sure to find the old pretzel woman. Her wrinkled face was almost hidden inside of the woolen kerchief bound round her head. Her old hands trembled as they wrapped up the thick, chewy pretzels.

The sidewalks were choked with people. It was not easy for Mama to push the carriage through the narrow aisles left between pushcarts and stands. The children followed behind in twos and whenever Mama stopped either to buy or look, they stopped too.

"Say, Gertie," Charlotte cried out, "how would you like a necklace like that?" she pointed to the garlic peddler who was coming towards them. No need for a store, a stand, or a pushcart for this peddler. With a basket full of garlic on one arm and a spicy necklace of the same looped around his neck, he was set for business.

The dried mushroom peddlers did business in the same way except that, as Charlotte laughingly said, "They were better dressed." They wore long, heavy, mushroom bracelets about their arms as well as necklaces.

How sharply the shoppers hunted for bargains! And what bargains, if one could believe the peddlers. How carefully every article was examined to make sure it was perfect! It always was, according to the shopkeepers. How the buyers haggled over the price of everything. And how the peddlers swore on their very lives that the price of anything was the lowest at which they could afford to part with it! But above and through all the noise and confusion, ran a feeling of great good nature and cheery contentment.

Only one tongue was spoken here—Yiddish. It was like a foreign land right in the midst of America. In this foreign land, it was Mama's children who were the foreigners since they alone conversed in an alien tongue—English.

At the next corner, Henny bought a fat, juicy sour pickle with her after-lunch penny. She ate it greedily, with noise and gusto, while her sisters watched, their mouths watering. "Selfish! How about giving us a taste, huh?"

Henny pretended that she didn't hear them, but before the pickle was half gone, she stopped teasing and gave each a bite.

Inside Mama's favorite fish store the smell was not so pleasing. "Gertie," suggested Charlotte, "let's squeeze our noses tight and talk to each other while we're squeezing."

And that's just what they did, talking about anything at all just so they could hear the funny sounds which came through their squeezed noses. "Look at the big fish with goggley eyes," said Gertie.

"I hope Mama is not getting any live fish this week," Charlotte said. "I like to see them swimming around in the bathtub, but I don't like it when Papa cleans them afterward."

But Mama was not getting any live fish this time, only pieces of several different kinds of fish, whitefish, yellow pike and winter carp—that meant gefullte fish (stuffed fish) for the Sabbath, yum, yum!

"I wish Mama would hurry up," said Gertie. "I can smell the fish right through my squeezed nose. And I do want to buy something for my penny, don't you?"

"Yes, and not fish!"

Out on the street again, the air seemed sharper and colder. Some of the peddlers had been standing in their places since early morning. They stamped their feet and slapped their arms across their chests trying to warm their chilled bones. But the sweet potato man did not mind the cold. Why should he when he had his nice hot street oven to push before him? When Ella caught sight of him, she said at once, "Just the thing for a cold day." The sweet potato man stopped before them and pulled open one of the drawers of his oven. There rose on the air such a delicious smell that Ella smacked her lips expectantly. Inside she saw the plump sweet potatoes in the gray jackets.

Some were cut open in halves and their rich golden color gave promise of great sweetness. For her penny, Ella got a large half and as she bit into it, she wondered why sweet potatoes baked at home never tasted half so good. When she rejoined the family, four other mouths helped to make short work of that potato.

The chicken market was the next stopping place. It was smelly and noisy with the squawking of fowl. The children gathered about the crates and watched the roosters sticking their long necks through the slats. Mama donned an apron she had brought with her and began to pluck the fowl she selected.

After Mama finished her plucking, the chicken was wrapped up and added to the other bundles in the shopping bag. The family continued on its way.

Gertie turned to Charlotte. "What'll we buy with our pennies?" The answer to that question was just then coming along the street. Candied slices of tangerine and candied grapes mounted on sticks in rows on white trays. The peddler stopped when he heard Gerties's delighted cry. "Penny a stick, little darlings," he said. Charlotte chose grape and Gertie took tangerine. Thus two more pennies were spent.

"I'm almost through," Mama told them, but still Sarah's penny lay warm and snug in her coat pocket. "Aren't you going to spend your penny?" the children asked her. They couldn't be sure because Sarah was saving all her pennies these days—six for the dolly and one penny for the library lady. But today was something special. She had shared in the goodies her sisters had bought. It would only be fair for her to return their generosity. But what could she get?

"Arbis! Shaynicke, guttinke arbishlach! Keuf meine heise arbis!" (Chick peas. Fine, nice chick peas. Buy my hot chick peas!)

The hot-chick-pea peddler was singing the words over and over in a funny Yiddish chant as he rolled a small white oven along the streets. Before Mama could stop her, mischievous Henny gave the carriage a big push so that it rolled away from under Mama's hands. She stooped over it as if she were pushing a great weight and began to chant in imitation:

"Arbis! Shaynicke, guttinke arbislac!"

The children roared with laughter. Even Mama could not hide a smile while she ordered Henny to stop. "Leave her alone, lady," the peddler told Mama. "She's helping me in mine business."

Because he was so good-natured, Sarah decided to give up her penny to him. Everyone watched as he fished out the peas. First he took a small square of white paper from a little compartment on one side of the oven. He twirled the paper about his fingers to form the shape of a cone and then skillfully twisted the pointed end so that the container would not fall apart. He lifted the wagon cover on one side revealing a large white enamel pot. The steam from the pot blew its hot breath in the little girls' faces so they stepped back a bit while the peas were ladled out with a big soup spoon. The wagon cover was dropped back into place and the paper cup handed over to Sarah. The peas were spicy with pepper and salt, and how good they were! They warmed up the children's tummies and made them very thirsty.

With the purchase of a pound of pumpernickel bread, the shopping tour came to an end. They left behind the life and activity of the market and started the weary walk home. By now the children were tired. Gertie uttered not a single word of protest when Mama lifted her up and put her into the carriage together with the bundles. The others wished they were young enough to join her.

Taylor, Sydney. *All-of-a-Kind Family.* New York: Follett Publishing Company, 1951.

. . . AND NOW MIGUEL

JOSEPH KRUMGOLD

Every year the men of the Chavez family drive their flock of sheep to pasture in the Sangre de Cristo Mountains. Twelve-year-old Miguel dreams of nothing but taking this trip into his beloved mountains—but first he must prove to his family that he is ready.

CHAPTER 3

I AM here! Here. The time has come and I am here! I am here!"

The last thing I heard was the clock in the kitchen going nine, ten, eleven times. So now it must be midnight or maybe even after. That's when I heard it. The cry of the first lamb of the New Year.

"Look what's happened," the lamb cried. "Me."

It didn't speak the words, of course. It didn't even sound like the words. But it stands to reason. What else could a new lamb, especially the first lamb born in the whole flock, once he got to his feet and opened his mouth to baa—what else would he say?

"Me! I'm here."

Without taking my head from the pillow, I listened until I was sure. Then I folded back the comforter, and slipped my feet out from Pedro's legs, and took away his arm from around my neck. One would think that Pedro, who sleeps with me in the same bed, was training to be a wrestling champion, the way he sleeps.

Faustina, who sleeps on the other side of our bedroom, she heard me too.

"Miguel?"

"Yes."

"I'm thirsty."

"Down here there is no water." I was underneath the bed looking for my shoes.

"Where d'you think you're going?" Pedro looked down at me from over the side of the bed. He was actually awake.

"It's started. The lambing. I just heard it—the first lamb. I'm going to go and have a look."

"Yah!" Faustina hiccuped and giggled. "He's gonna go look."

"That's what you think," said Pedro.

"Now's bedtime." The way Faustina laughed 'way high up, you'd think this was one big joke.

"In order to grow, we gotta stay in bed," said Pedro. "You know that."

"For you, yes." I didn't even wait to get dressed. I started out with my arms filled with clothes. "I've had enough growing."

I was the first one out of the house, where only my mother and big sisters slept these nights. The men stayed with the flock out in the fields and in the corrals, sleeping in the sheep wagon and around campfires, waiting for many nights now for the lambs to start. And now, surely, it had begun. Out on the veranda where I finished to dress myself, I heard it even more clearly.

"Baa. Aah. It's me. I'm here."

"Mickey. What are you doing?" It was my sister Tomasita.

She was all wrapped around with a bathrobe. "It's not allowed. Go back"

"I know." I was trying to put one leg in my pants, while balancing, and without looking. "I know—but that was last year. Now could be different."

"No, Miquito. Go back!" Tomasita hurried down the path, through the wooden gate to the corrals. And the screen door behind me banged again. I couldn't see who it was because my head was all caught in my jersey, because I was trying to get dressed so fast.

I was putting on the second shoe when my mother came out.

"Miguelito!" My mother was surprised to see me, yet she spoke softly for no one to hear, even though there was no one around who could listen. Only Cyclone, the dog, who was tied to the fence. He started to bark.

"If you will let me tell you something, there is something I have to tell you," I told her. "Like the way I worked hard all the winter. And at school. There was no day in which there was not a new star in my book. You yourself said no one worked harder at the ditching."

This had happened only the week before, the ditching. That is the time at the end of the winter when all the families who live along the same irrigation ditch come together to clean up the ditch. This is in order to make everything ready for when the fields are plowed and the seed is planted. . . .

At ditching time each family is supposed to bring so many men to work for so many days. And my father let me stay home from school in order that I, too, could go along to help. Mr. Martinez said I could count for a half a man, which is not too great a thing, and I asked my father to speak with Mr. Martinez in order that I should be counted three quarters of a man at least. But when he did so, everyone laughed, including my father, because at ditching time everyone does laugh most of the time, and there is a lot of singing as well as wine and other things to drink.

The question though was settled fine. It was agreed that even though I would remain one half a man, since the next day was Saturday and I didn't have to go to school, I would be allowed to work two full days. So that I did end up being counted as one whole man. This was perfect for me, and better for everyone since fractions are hard to keep straight anyway.

To prove it was no mistake I worked as good as I could, using only the biggest shovels and the biggest pickaxes. So that my mother that night made me eat a third mutton chop, just like the older men, because I had worked so hard. And I ate it, too, easily.

And now, when I reminded her, she remembered it all.

"I know," she said. "You already have become one whole man, Miguel. But even a whole man must learn to wait until his time comes. He can work, and he can prepare, but he must know how to wait, too."

"I've learned how to wait. In twelve years, I've learned."

"Is it so hard, then, to wait until morning?"

"Another year. That's how long it will be. This time comes just once every year."

"Miguel!" My mother stopped me. She held me by the chin, tight. She wiped her apron at my eyes. "I have watched you using all your strength to open the gate to the barnyard, the one from which the big stone hangs. But this is not like a gate. To become something different from what you are, it takes more than being strong. Even a little time is needed as well. Go back with the others, with Faustina and Pedro."

"They will be glad to see me!" I kicked off one of my shoes. Not hard. Just enough to hit the door a good bang.

"Back to bed or we'll see about this!" When my mother says, "We'll see about this," sometimes it can hurt. I picked up my shoe and started into the house. When I looked back she was untying Cyclone, who was barking, so even he could go.

Everybody, even the dog, got out that night to see the first lamb.

"And you," said Pedro. He was waiting for me with a smile on his face. "Did you get a good look?"

I didn't answer. With my shoe, I took aim at the floor and let it go. First one, then the other. What difference how much noise I made?

"Okay!" yelled Faustina. "Okay. Okeydokee!" Every few days Faustina learns a new word, and then that's the only word she uses. It doesn't mean anything.

"It's sure nice when someone grows enough." Pedro kept talking behind my back. I sat on the edge of the bed, pulling off my clothes, and he kept talking and laughing. "Everything's sure nice. They get up in the middle of the night. Just like that. Go where they want. Whoopee!" He lay on his back and kicked his feet in the air.

"Okeydokee!" Faustina squealed till she had no more breath.

"Shut up!" I gave a great shout, louder than both of them. When they quieted down, I pointed out the window. "You see out there, far, far away out there." They both crawled across their beds and looked out in the night.

"What is?" asked Faustina.

"You mean the mountains?" said Pedro looking where I was pointing.

"Yes. The Mountains. The Sangre de Cristo. You know what's in those mountains?"

"Clouds," said Faustina.

"Don't be crazy," Pedro told her. "Clouds in the mountains! Clouds are in the sky."

"They come from the mountains. I see them every day, every day, every day."

"You're crazy every day." Pedro tried to stop her.

I stopped Pedro. "I'll tell you what's in those mountains. The biggest fish anywhere, and when they're cooked they taste like the best salted peanuts together with roasted marshmallows. And the best hunting, wild turkeys and bears to shoot at. And camping out every day. And every night getting up whenever you feel like it. And cooking whatever you want to eat."

"Sopapillas with jelly?" These were sort of a puffed-up kind of biscuits, and they were what Faustina liked best.

"Yes," I told her.

"What else?" she asked.

"Up there are pools to swim in, with waterfalls coming down that you can slide in like a sled going down hill in the winter. Only to slide down in the water into a big pool is forty times better. Up there is never hot in the summer. On the very top of each mountain there is snow, like it was a big bunch of ice cream piled up."

"What flavor?" asked Faustina. "Chocolate?"

"No flavor."

"How does it taste then?"

"It tasted cool."

"That's all?"

"That's all."

"Okay," said Faustina.

"What else?" said Pedro.

"And up there are no mountains higher than where you are. When you look up, all you see is the sky. And the air is so clear every breath makes you fill up like a balloon. And when you look down you see everything. The whole Rio Grande Valley, almost the whole of all of New Mexico. No one can see more, or feel better than up there."

Faustina and Pedro kept looking at me even though I stopped talking and the only noise was Cyclone barking, out there where the family was with the new lamb.

"What else?" said Pedro

"What else can there be? That's everything."

"So?" Pedro looked at me. "What's about it?"

Now was the time. For many years it had been a secret that I kept only to myself. A secret of only one person after a while gets too hard to keep. To make it real you have to tell someone else, even though they laugh at you, you've got to tell. Otherwise, all you got left is just one small, dried-up secret that's not worth anything.

"I'm going up there."

"To the Sangre de Cristo?"

"Yes."

"Okay," said Faustina. And she started to crawl back to her pillow.

"Sure," said Pedro. "Someday. We all go."

"Not someday. I go with the others this year. This here year!"

They both stopped from getting under the covers and looked at me. They didn't laugh.

"How do you know?" asked Faustina.

"I will arrange it myself."

"Arrange. That's not the way." Pedro shook his head.

"First you got to know how to do everything. Then when you get into high school, or sometime like that, then it happens."

"Sure," said Faustina as if she knew what was all about.

"It never happens when anyone is so little like us," Pedro said.

"Like who?"

"Us."

"That's you," I told him. "Us—that's not me. You and Faustina are us. But me—I'm Miguel. And what I say is this. I'm going."

"How?"

What could I say? I said, "I have made a plan."

This was a big surprise to them both. They looked at me like I just grew wings.

"Your own plan?" Pedro crawled back to the side of the bed. I nodded my head, yes. "Like what?"

What could I say? I said, "A first-class plan. But I can't tell you about it. You'll see how it works."

"When?" yelled Faustina. "How soon? When can we see?"

"It starts tomorrow."

145

"Tomorrow!" Pedro yelled, too. With no one in the house, there was no reason not to make noise. "Tomorrow begins the plan? And you know how it all works, everything?"

"Everything."

"Wango!" Pedro made like he was throwing rocks all over the bedroom, he was so excited. "This is better than anything. This is as good like when we got the new tractor!"

"Okay," Faustina squealed. "Okeydokee!"

I laughed and yelled, too. It got so I thought I did have a plan, a real, good one. And everything was fixed so it would be all right now. We had a good time making a lot of noise. Pedro climbed up the back of the bed, the iron part where there are bumps and flowers.

"Look at me! I'm, Miguel. I'm way up high. Miguel standing right on top of the mountains."

"I just remembered," yelled Faustina.

"What?"

"I'm, thirsty."

I went and got her a glass of water from the kitchen. Then I put out the lights and undressed and got into bed.

In the quiet, I remembered. I didn't have any plan. In the quiet I heard them beyond the corral, Cyclone barking and the lamb making its kind of noise and the ewe making her kind of noise. All I could do was listen.

But even so, it was good. I had explained the secret. I had come out, like from behind the bushes when we play The Bandits Robbing Schaeffer's Drugstore, which is a drug store in Taos and a game we play at school. I had come out from behind the bushes and that meant, at least, that something had begun. And now that it had begun, I took one good look at the mountains through the window and then I went to sleep.

Krumgold, Joseph. . . .*and now Miguel.* New York: HarperCollins, HarperCollins Children's Books, 1953.

THE BLACK PEARL

SCOTT O'DELL

Everyone in the town of La Paz knows about Manta Diablo, the giant devilfish who guards the Pearl of Heaven, the biggest black pearl in the sea. But sixteen-year-old Ramón, the fearless son of a pearl dealer, decides to look for the pearl in a remote lagoon despite the warnings of the old man who teaches him to dive.

A red haze hung over the water as I floated the canoe on the morning of the fourth day and began to paddle toward the cave where the old man said the Manta Diablo lived.

The sun was up, but the haze hung so thick that I had trouble locating the channel. After I found it, I searched for almost an hour before I sighted the cave. It was hidden behind a rocky pinnacle and faced the rising sun, and the opening was about thirty feet wide and the height of a tall man and curved downward like the upper lip of a mouth. I could not see into the cave because of the red mist, so I drifted back and forth and waited until the sun rose higher and the mist burned away.

I had talked to the old man the night before about the cave. We had eaten supper, and the women and children had gone to bed, and the two of us were sitting around the fire.

"You have fished everywhere in the lagoon," I said, "but not in the cave."

"No," he said. "Nor did my father nor his father."

"Big pearls may grow there."

The old man did not answer. He got up and put wood on the fire and sat down again.

"The great one itself, the Pearl of Heaven, may lie there," I said.

Still he did not answer, but suddenly he looked across the fire. It was a fleeting look that he gave me, and yet, its meaning was as clear as if he had spoken to me and said, "I cannot go to the cave to search for pearls. I cannot go because I fear the Manta Diablo. If you go there, then it is alone. El Diablo cannot blame me."

And that morning when I went down to the beach he did not go with me. And the look he gave me was the same I had seen the night before.

At last, about midmorning, the sun burned away the mist and I could see for a short distance into the cave. I paddled through the mouth and soon found myself in a vast vault-like room. The walls of the room were black and smooth and shone from the light that came in through the opening.

Near the mouth of the cave the water was very clear. I picked up my basket and sink stone, took a deep breath, and slipped over the side of the canoe, remembering all that the old man had taught me.

I reached the bottom after about a fathom and a half. I looped my foot in the rope tied to the sink stone and waited until the bubbles that had risen behind me disappeared and I could find the bed of shells I had noticed from above. The bed was five steps away toward the mouth of the cave. I walked carefully in the sand as I had learned to do.

The shells were the largest I had ever seen. They were half the length of my arm and thick through as my body and covered with weed that looked like a woman's hair. I chose the nearest one, which seemed to be easier to get at than the others. I took out my knife and worked quietly, but a school of small fish kept swimming in front of my eyes, so I failed to pry the shell loose before my lungs began to hurt and I had to go up.

On my second dive I had no sooner reached the bottom than a shadow fell across the bed where I was working. It was the shadow of a gray shark, one of the friendly ones, but by the time he had drifted away my breath was gone.

I dived six times more and worked quickly each time I went down, hacking away with my sharp knife at the base of the big shell where it was anchored to the rock. But it had been growing there for many years, since long before I was born, I supposed, and it would not come free from its home.

By this time it was late in the afternoon, and the light was poor. Also, my hands were bleeding, and my eyes were half-blind with salt from the sea. But I sat in the canoe and thought of all the hours I had spent for nothing.

I filled my lung, and took the sink stone, and went down again. With the first stroke of my knife, the shell came free. It toppled over on one side, and I quickly untied the rope from the sink stone and looped it twice around the shell and swam back to the surface. I pulled up the shell, but it was too heavy for me to lift into the canoe, so I tied it to the stern and paddled out of the cave.

Across the lagoon I could see the old man standing among the trees. From time to time during the day I had caught glimpses of him standing there with his eyes fixed on the cave. I knew that I could drown and he would not try to save me, and he was telling El Diablo all the while that he had not wanted me to go to the cave and that he therefore was not to blame.

"A big one," he said when I dragged the shell ashore. "In my life, I have never seen such a monster. It is the grandfather of all oysters that live in the sea."

"There are many in the cave bigger than this one," I said.

"If there are so many," he answered, "then the Manta Diablo cannot be mad that you have taken only one of them."

"Perhaps a little mad," I said and laughed, "but not much."

The mouth of the oyster was closed, and it was hard to put my blade between the tight edges of the shell.

I wrestled a long time with the oyster. At last, the hard lips began to give a little. Then I could feel the knife sink through the heavy muscles that held them together, and suddenly the lips fell apart.

I put my finger under the frilled edge of the flesh as I had seen my father do. A pearl slid along my finger, and I picked it out. It was about the size of a pea. When I felt again, another of the same size rolled out and then a third. I put them on the other half of the shell so they would not be scratched.

The old man came and leaned over me, as I knelt there in the sand, and held his breath.

Slowly I slid my hand under the heavy tongue of the oyster. I felt a hard lump, so monstrous in size that it could not be a pearl. I took hold of it and pulled it from the flesh, and got to my feet, and held it to the sun, thinking that I must be holding a rock that the oyster had swallowed somehow.

It was round and smooth and the color of smoke. It filled my cupped hand. Then the sun's light struck deep into the thing and moved in silver swirls, and I knew that is was not a rock that I held, but a pearl, the great Pearl of Heaven.

O'Dell, Scott. *The Black Pearl*. New York: Bantam Doubleday Dell for Young Readers, a division of Bantam Doubleday Dell, 1967.

THE ENDLESS STEPPE

ESTHER HAUTZIG

In 1941, the Rudomin family was forced to leave their comfortable home in the Polish village of Vilna for political reasons. After a long journey in a cattle car with many other families they found themselves on the endless steppe of Siberia, where they would have to live and work at a gypsum mine. You may notice that the main character in this story, ten-year-old Esther, has the same first name as the author—that's because this story is an autobiography; the author's own true story.

In the following excerpt Esther and her grandmother have been given permission to walk to a neighboring village and trade some of their things at an outdoor market. Here, Esther sees Siberian people for the first time and gets a rare and wonderful taste of freedom.

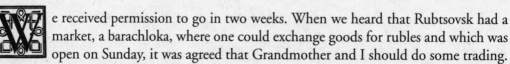e received permission to go in two weeks. When we heard that Rubtsovsk had a market, a barachloka, where one could exchange goods for rubles and which was open on Sunday, it was agreed that Grandmother and I should do some trading. Rubles meant food—potatoes perhaps; anything but bread and brinza. We spent every night deciding which of our few belongings we were ready to sell. One of Mother's lace-trimmed French silk slips went in and out of a bag a dozen times. "I really don't need this for dynamiting gypsum," she said.

"Nor do I need this," Father said, holding up a custom-made silk shirt, "for driving a wagon."

Grandmother wasn't so sure they wouldn't need them, and she herself was most reluctant to part with a black silk umbrella with a slender silver handle.

I thought that Sunday would never come. When it did, Grandmother and I set off down the dust road before anyone else. Along with our wares—the slip, the shirt, and the umbrella, after all—we had wrapped some bread in one of my father's handkerchiefs; the bread was to be our lunch.

It was shortly after six o'clock, the air was still cool and fresh, a hawk was soaring overhead, and, feeling oddly disloyal, I thought that the steppe was just a tiny bit beautiful that morning.

I glanced back over my shoulder. No one was coming after us to order us to return to the mine, but I quickened my pace and urged Grandmother to hurry.

When the mine was out of sight, when there was nothing but Grandmother and me and the steppe, nothing else, not even a hawk in the sky, I didn't shout—I wouldn't dare because of the way sound carried—I didn't sing very loud, but I sang, and my funny little voice sounded strange to me. And I felt light, as if I could do a giant leap over the steppe.

"Grandmother, do you know what?"

"What?"

"We are doing something we want to do. All by ourselves. We are fr-r-r-eeeee. . . ."

"Shh!" Grandmother looked around. "Not so loud."

She was dressed in her best dress, a rumpled blue silk that was also beginning to fade, and her little Garbo hat. In spite of her tininess, Grandmother had always been the grande dame; walking down the dusty road that day, she still was.

We walked for about three hours across the uninhabited steppe without meeting one other person. Before long, I had tied my sweater around my waist—my pleated school skirt and blouse had become my uniform—and Grandmother had opened her umbrella.

We saw a bump in the distance. This turned out to be the first of the widely scattered huts, which meant that before too long we would be in Rubtsovsk.

The village had appeared on the horizon like a mirage always receding from us, but we finally did reach it and it was real. Wonderfully real to my starved eyes.

Rubtsovsk, at that time, had an unused church with its onion top, a bank, a library, a pharmacy, a school—even a movie house and a park with a bandstand. But all I saw that day was a square alive with people and, only vaguely, a rather mean cluster of wooden buildings and huts.

We squeezed our way through the crowd—the men in peaked caps, here and there an old military cap, women in babushkas, friendly faces sometimes scarred from frostbite, friendly voices. And some Kazakhs; Asia at last! Colorful costumes, the women with their long pigtails encased in cloth and leather pouches, and sad to see, men, women, and children, all with rotting teeth. But Kazakhs!

Trading was going on all around us. There were the stalls around the square with produce from the collective farms—and the small farmers too—and there were the buildings with signs proclaiming them to be state-operated stores where one made purchases only if one had been issued ration books, which we had not been. In one corner, sunflower seeds were being roasted over an open fire. The smell was ravishing. "Come on, grandmother." I nudged her. "Let's begin to trade."

We made our way to the baracholka, where wooden horses were set up all over the interior of the square and where piles of stuff were heaped onto blankets or onto the bare stones: old boots, jackets, babushkas, books, pots, pans—anything and everything.

We found a place to stand and, to my surprise, without feeling the least bit self-conscious, I immediately held up my mother's slip, the lacy pink silk blowing in the breeze. In a second, we were surrounded: Where were we from? Where did we live? What did Grandmother do? How old was I? They were exceedingly friendly and frankly inquis-itive, these native Siberians. We answered the questions as fast as we could, with Grandmother doing most of the talking, since she knew Russian well and I hardly spoke it. We coaxed our potential customers to note the beauty of the lace, the fact that there were sixteen ribs in the umbrella. How much? Forty rubles. Forty rubles? There was a roar of laughter. All right, thirty-eight rubles. . . . I caught Grandmother's eye; we smiled at each other; we were born traders and we were having a marvelous time. It was, in fact, the happiest time I had had in a long, long time. The guns, the bombs of World War II were thousands of miles away and at the market place so was the labor camp close by. All around me children were giggling over nothing, girls were showing off their dolls—what if they were made of rags?—and boys were wrestling. These children were just like the children in Vilna. Hunger, fatigue, sorrow, and fright were forgotten: haggling was a wonderfully engrossing game. Rough hands that had scrounged in the earth for potatoes and been frostbitten more that once, fingered the silk, sometimes as if it were a rosary, sometimes as if it were sinful for anything to be that silky, more often to test it for dura-bility. If an egg was around fifteen rubles, how much should a slip with hand-drawn lace be? Hand-drawn, mule-drawn, what difference if you couldn't eat it? We all joined in the laughter. I don't remember who bought Father's shirt and Grandmother's umbrella, but the slip was finally bought by a young woman with lots of orange rouge on her cheeks. She was so plump I wondered how she was going to squeeze into it, but that, I decided, was her worry, not mine.

Feeling very proud of ourselves with our newly acquired rubles, we now became the customers. What to buy? We went to the stalls where the produce was—watermelons, cucumbers, potatoes, milk, flour, white bread—a great luxury—and meat. Everything was incredibly expensive and we walked back and forth from stall to stall, unable to make a decision. I stood perfectly still in front of the roasting sunflower seeds, ostentatiously breathing in and out. Grandmother counted the rubles we had. "Come," she said, "what are grandmothers for?" The first purchase was a small glassful of sunflower seeds. I slit the shell between my teeth and extracted the tiny nut. I nursed it as if it were a piece of precious candy and it could not have tasted better. Siberians love sunflower seeds, and I think ninety percent of them bore a little notch in a front tooth to prove it.

After much deliberation and more bargaining, we bought a piece of meat and a bag of flour. There was a communal outdoor stove at the schoolhouse, and we could boil the meat on it and, after mixing the flour with water, we could bake little cakes, the Siberian cakes of our Diaspora.

By that time, the sun had begun to set, and Grandmother said we must start our long hike home. But I could tell that she was as reluctant to leave this carnival as I was. So, it seemed, was everyone else. The stalls were empty of their produce; like some kind of game, everyone had everyone else's belongings, wrapped in blankets, coats, babushkas, old flour sacks. But having come together in this vast, lonely steppe, having joked and gossiped and even sung songs, no one wanted to leave.

However, as we began our long trudge back we were very gay, thinking only of the baracholka, not of the mine. Grandmother and I had this in common, we were "very" people —either very sad or very gay, with nothing in between. Oh, if we could only live in the village and go to the baracholka every Sunday, Siberia would be bearable. I started to tick off the things I had to sell—three dresses, one blouse, a coat . . . Grandmother laughed. "Stop before you go naked in exchange for a glassful of sunflower seeds."

No matter, I thought, whether I had something to sell or not, I would pray that one day we would be allowed to live in the village within sight and sound of the Sunday baracholka.

Hautzig, Esther. *The Endless Steppe*. New York: HarperCollins, HarperTrophy, 1968.

THE GOLD CADILLAC

MILDRED D. TAYLOR

'lois and her sister, Wilma, live in Ohio in the 1950's. Their father is proud of their brand new gold Cadillac, but when the whole family decides to drive to 'lois's grandparents' farm in Mississippi, 'lois's eyes are opened to an awful fact: racism.

We left the city of Toledo behind, drove through Bowling Green and down through the Ohio countryside of farms and small towns, through Dayton and Cincinnati, and across the Ohio River into Kentucky. On the other side of the river my father stopped the car and looked back at Wilma and me and said, "Now from here on, whenever we stop and there're white people around, I don't want either one of you to say a word. Not one word! Your mother and I'll do all the talking. That understood?"

"Yes, sir," Wilma and I both said, though we didn't truly understand why.

My father nodded, looked at my mother and started the car again. We rolled on, down Highway 25 and through the bluegrass hills of Kentucky. Soon we began to see signs. Signs that read: WHITE ONLY, COLORED NOT ALLOWED. We saw the signs above water fountains and in restaurant windows. We saw them in ice cream parlors and at hamburger stands. We saw them in front of hotels and motels, and on the restroom doors of filling stations. I didn't like the signs. I felt as if I were in a foreign land.

I couldn't understand why the signs were there, and I asked my father what the signs meant. He said they meant we couldn't drink from the water fountains. He said they meant we couldn't stop to sleep in the motels. He said they meant we couldn't stop to eat in the restaurants. I looked at the grand picnic basket I had been enjoying so much. Now I understood why my mother had packed it. Suddenly the picnic did not seem so grand.

Finally we reached Memphis. We got there at a bad time. Traffic was heavy and we got separated from the rest of the family. We tried to find them but it was no use. We had to go on alone. We reached the Mississippi state line and soon after we heard a police siren. A police car came up behind us. My father slowed the Cadillac, then stopped. Two white policemen got out of their car. They eyeballed the Cadillac and told my father to get out.

"Whose car is this, boy?" they asked.

I saw anger in my father's eyes. "It's mine," he said.

"You're a liar," said one of the policemen. "You stole this car."

"Turn around, put your hands on top of that car and spread eagle," said the other policeman.

My father did as he was told. They searched him and I didn't understand why. I didn't understand either why they had called my father a liar and didn't believe that the Cadillac was his. I wanted to ask, but I remembered my father's warning not to say a word, and I obeyed that warning.

The policemen told my father to get in the back of the police car. My father did. One policeman got back into the police car. The other policeman slid behind the wheel of our Cadillac. The police car started off. The Cadillac followed. Wilma and I looked at each other and at our mother. We didn't know what to think. We were scared.

The Cadillac followed the police car into a small town and stopped in front of the police station. The policeman stepped out of our Cadillac and took the keys. The other policeman took my father into the police station.

"Mother-Dear!" Wilma and I cried. "What're they going to do to our daddy? They going to hurt him?"

"He'll be all right," said my mother. "He'll be all right." But she didn't sound so sure of that. She seemed worried.

We waited. More than three hours we waited. Finally my father came out of the police station. We had lots of questions to ask him. He said the police had given him a ticket for speeding and locked him up. But then the judge had come. My father had paid the ticket, and they had let him go.

He started the Cadillac and drove slowly out of the town, below the speed limit. The police car followed us. People standing on steps and sitting on porches and in front of stores stared at us as we passed. Finally we were out of the town. The police car still followed. Dusk was falling. The night grew black and finally the police car turned around and left us.

We drove and drove. But my father was tired now, and my grandparents' farm was still far away. My father said he had to get some sleep, and since my mother didn't drive, he pulled into a grove of trees at the side of the road and stopped.

"I'll keep watch," said my mother.

"Wake me if you see anybody," said my father.

"Just rest," said my mother.

So my father slept. But that bothered me. I needed him awake. I was afraid of the dark, and of the woods, and of whatever lurked there. My father was the one who kept us safe, he and my uncles. But already the police had taken my father away from us once today, and my uncles were lost.

155

"Go to sleep, baby," said my mother. "Go to sleep."

But I was afraid to sleep until my father woke. I had to help my mother keep watch. I figured I had to help protect us too, in case the police came back and tried to take my father away again. There was a long, sharp knife in the picnic basket, and I took hold of it, clutching it tightly in my hand. Ready to strike, I sat there in the back of the car, eyes wide, searching the blackness outside the Cadillac. Wilma, for a while, searched the night too, then she fell asleep. I didn't want to sleep, but soon I found I couldn't help myself as an unwelcome drowsiness came over me. I had an uneasy sleep, and when I woke it was dawn and my father was gently shaking me. I woke with a start, and my hand went up, but the knife wasn't there. My mother had it.

My father took my hand. "Why were you holding the knife 'lois?" he asked.

I looked at him and at my mother. "I — I was scared," I said.

My father was thoughtful. "No need to be scared now, sugar," he said. "Daddy's here and so is Mother-Dear."

Then after a glance at my mother, he got out of the car, walked to the road, looked down it one way, then the other. When he came back and started the motor, he turned the Cadillac north, not south.

"What're you doing?" asked my mother.

"Heading back to Memphis," said my fahter. "Cousin Halton's there. We'll leave the Cadillac and get his car. Driving this car any farther south with you and the girls in the car, it's just not worth the risk."

And so that's what we did. Instead of driving through Mississippi in golden splendor, we traveled its streets and roads and highways in Cousin Halton's solid, yet not so spendid, four-year-old Chevy. When we reached my grandparents' farm, my uncles and aunts were already there. Everybody was glad to see us. They had been worried. They asked about the Cadillac. My father told them what had happened, and they nodded and said he had done the best thing.

We stayed one week in Mississippi. During that week I often saw my father, looking deep in thought, walk off alone across the family land. I saw my mother watching him. One day I ran after my father, took his hand, and walked the land with him. I asked him all the questions that were on my mind. I asked him why the policemen had treated him the way they had and why people didn't want us to eat in the restaurants, or drink from the water fountains, or sleep in the hotels. I told him I just didn't understand all that.

My father looked at me and said that it all was a difficult thing to understand and he didn't really understand it himself. He said it all had to do with the fact that black people had once been forced to be slaves. He said it had to do with our skins being colored. He said it had to do with stupidity and ignorance. He said it had to do with the law, the law that said we could be treated like this here in the South. And for that matter, he added, any other place in these United States where folks thought the same as so many folks did here in the South. But he also said, "I'm hoping one day though we can drive that long road down here and there won't be any signs. I'm hoping one day the police won't stop us just because of the color of our skins and we're riding in a gold Cadillac with northern plates."

Taylor, Mildred D. *The Gold Cadillac*. New York: Dial Books for Young Readers, 1989.

HARRIET THE SPY

Louise Fitzhugh

Harriet M. Welsch, who is in the sixth grade, is determined to become a great author when she grows up. She devises a spy route and carries around a secret notebook in which she writes down observations about the people she spies on. The one person who really understood her, Ole Golly, has just moved away. Harriet's mother tries to be attentive and understanding but doesn't always think the same way Harriet does.

CHAPTER 9

arriet felt so grumpy she knocked off work for the day. That night after supper she tried to practice being an onion. She started by falling down several times, making a great bumping noise each time. The idea was to fall in a rolling way the way an onion would and then roll around in a complete circle several times, then roll slowly to a stop the way an onion would if you put it down on a table. Harriet rolled around and bumped into a chair, knocking it over.

Her mother came to the door. She looked down at Harriet lying there with the chair on top of her. "What are you doing?" she asked mildly.

"Being an onion."

Her mother picked the chair up off Harriet's chest. Harriet didn't move. She was tired.

"What in the world is all that noise I hear in here?"

"I told you. I'm being an onion."

"It's a pretty noisy onion."

"I can't help it. I can't do it right yet. Miss Berry says when I do it right, I won't make a sound."

"Oh, it's for the Christmas pageant . . . is that it?"

"Well, you don't think I'd just be an onion all on my own, do you?"

"None of your lip there, girl. Get up and let me see what you have to do."

Harriet got up and fell over, then rolled and rolled around until suddenly she rolled right under the bed. She came out full of dust mice.

Mrs. Welsch looked horrified. "That terrible maid. I'm going to fire her tomorrow." She looked at Harriet, who stood ready to fall again. "That's the clumsiest dance I ever saw. Miss Berry assigned this?"

"Miss Berry assigned the onion part. I'M making up the DANCE," Harriet said pointedly.

"Oh," said Mrs. Welsch discreetly.

Harriet fell over again, this time rolling away almost into the bathroom.

Mr. Welsch came into the room. "What's going on in here? It sounds like someone hitting a punching bag."

"She's being an onion."

They stood watching Harriet fall over and over again.

Mr. Welsch put his pipe in his mouth and crossed his arms. "According to Stanislavsky, you have to feel like an onion. Do you feel like an onion?"

"Not in the least," said Harriet.

"Oh, come on. What are they teaching you in school these days?" Mrs. Welsch started to laugh.

"No, I'm serious. There's a whole school downtown that's probably rolling all over the floor right this minute."

"I never WANTED to be an onion," Harriet said from the floor.

"And it's a good thing. How many parts do you think are written for onions these days?" Mr. Welsch laughed. "I don't imagine you did want to be an onion. For that matter, who knows if an onion does either."

Mrs. Welsch laughed up at him. "You're so smart. Let's see you fall like an onion."

"Don't mind if I do," said Mr. Welsch, and putting down his pipe, he fell solidly to the floor. The floor shook.

"Honey! Did you hurt yourself?"

Mr. Welsch just lay there flat. "No," he said quietly, "but it's not as easy as it looks." He lay there breathing. Harriet took another fall just to keep him company.

"Why don't you get up, honey?" Mrs. Welsch stood over him with a worried look on her face.

"I'm trying to feel like an onion. The closest I can get is a scallion."

159

Harriet tried to feel like an onion. She found herself screwing her eyes up tight, wrapping her arms around her body, then buckling her knees and rolling to the ground.

"My God, Harriet, are you sick?" Mrs. Welsch rushed over to her.

Harriet rolled round and round the room. It wasn't bad at all, this being an onion. She bumped into her father, who started to laugh. She couldn't keep her face screwed up and laughed at him.

Her father started being an onion in earnest, rolling and rolling. Harriet suddenly jumped up and started to write in her notebook:

I wonder what it would be like to be a table or a chair or a bathtub or another person. I wonder what Ole Golly would say to that. Ole Golly looked like a bird with teeth, but I think I really look like an onion. I wish she would come back.

Harriet was so absorbed in her writing that she had forgotten her parents were in the room. When she finally slammed her book and looked up, they were staring at her in the strangest way.

"What were you doing, dear?" asked Mrs. Welsch in an ever so casual way.

"Writing in my notebook." Harriet began to feel nervous. They were looking at her in such a strange way.

"Oh. Can we see?"

"No!" Harriet almost screamed, then said more quietly, "Of course not, it's secrets."

"Oh," said her father and looked rather hurt.

What is the matter with them? Harriet thought. They both just kept looking at her.

"Is it something for school, dear?" asked Mrs. Welsch.

"No," said Harriet and felt even more nervous. Why didn't they stop looking at her?

"I'm sort of tired, honey. I think I'll go to bed," Mrs. Welsch said to her husband.

"Yeah. Me too," he said, taking up his pipe.

Why are they acting like that? thought Harriet. You'd think I was doing something very funny. Ole Golly never acted like that.

Her parents kissed her good night in a rather melancholy way and went out. She reached for her notebook and was starting to write when she heard her father say, sotto voce, on the steps, "Yes, it makes me feel I don't even know my own child." And Mrs. Welsch answered, "We must try to know her better now that Miss Golly is gone."

Harriet felt puzzled. She wrote:

Why don't they say what they feel? Ole Golly said "Always say exactly what you feel. People are hurt more by misunderstanding than anything else." Am I hurt? I don't feel hurt. I just feel funny all over.

And by the time she went to sleep she felt even funnier.

The next day she felt grumpy again on the way to school. Sport and Janie came running up to her as she was going in and told her that they planned to practice their dances that afternoon and did she want to practice with them at Janie's house. She said "yes" in such a grumpy way, they stared at her. Then, when she breathed in a very labored way and said, "Don't mind me," they really stared. She went on into school, calling back over her shoulder, "I'll be there after my spy route." They just looked at her.

That afternoon she decided to try Mrs. Plumber again even though she knew it was terribly risky. She waited for the maid to leave the kitchen, then darted into the dumbwaiter, her heart pounding so hard she was sure it could be heard. She pulled the ropes gingerly. They worked smoothly at first, but just as she reached the parlor floor there was a terribly loud creak. She sat horrified, not daring to breathe. Then she heard voices.

"Impossible . . . impossible." Mrs. Plumber's voice came out of a pile of pillows, in a whisper filled with horror.

"Nadine!" Mrs. Plumber screamed to the maid. "Nadine!"—a chilling scream fading at the end.

"Yes, ma'am." Harriet could see the maid standing primly to one side of the bed. Mrs. Plumber raised up, looking like a bloated eagle—"Nadine . . . it can't be, it can't beeeee"—and flopped back down, disappearing into pink pillows.

"Doctor's orders, ma'am."

From the pillows: "Confined . . . to . . . bed . . ." —and the tiny voice was lost for a minute— "for . . ."

Well, thought Harriet, feeling agitated and strangely in sympathy with Mrs. Plumber. She did want to be there.

She moved a little to write in her book:

Is Ole Golly right? Is it terrible to get what you want? I want to be a writer, and I'll be finked if I'll be unhappy when I am. Some people just don't think things out.

At that moment there was a querulous shout from Mrs. Plumber.

"What? What was that?"

Harriet looked through her peephole and saw both faces staring right at her. Her mouth opened in speechless terror. They had seen her!! she felt everything stop as in a photograph.

"There's nothing, ma'am."

But of course they couldn't have seen her. They couldn't see through walls.

"There's something in there! I heard it scratching, like a mouse— a rat . . ."

"Oh, I don't think so." Nadine marched firmly to the dumbwaiter and pulled up the door. She jumped and yelled wildly when she saw Harriet.

Harriet started pulling on the ropes. But Nadine recovered herself and stopped the dumbwaiter as it started to move.

"Come out of there, you," she said harshly and pulled Harriet out. Harriet flew through the air on Nadine's arm and landed in a pile at her feet.

"What is that?" Mrs. Plumber shrieked.

"A child, ma'am," said Nadine, holding Harriet by the hood of her sweatshirt.

"Out . . . out . . . get it out of here. . . . That's all I need—all I need today—a child!" And she fell back into the pillows.

Nadine hoisted Harriet into the air and swung her out the door and down the steps. Even though her feet were dangling helplessly and her mind was racing with fear, Harriet took a few mental notes of the interiors as they descended. "There," said Nadine, pushing her out the door, "good riddance. And don't get caught again in there."

Harriet looked back. Nadine winked at her. Feeling ridiculous, she started to run. She didn't stop running until she was at her front door. She sat down on the stoop and panted for a long time. That's the first time in three years of spying that I've been caught, she thought. After she got her breath back she opened up her notebook.

Spies—should not get caught. That is the one essential thing about spies. I am a rotten spy. Of course, how was I to know she was going to do that? But that's no excuse. I knew, I just knew it was too dangerous to go there.

She sat, looking dejectedly at the park. As she stared at the black trees one tear rolled down her cheek. She wrote:

Ole Golly would have had something to say about this. And also about that onion business last night.

Fitzhugh, Louise. *Harriet the Spy.* New York: HarperTrophy, a division of HarperCollins Publishers, 1964.

OTHERWISE KNOWN AS SHEILA THE GREAT

JUDY BLUME

Sheila Tubman lives in an apartment building in the city with her parents and her older sister, Libby. For the summer, Sheila's parents have rented a house in Tarrytown. The house comes with a dog named Jennifer (Sheila is afraid of dogs) and is close to the neighborhood swimming pool (Sheila is also afraid of swimming). But then Sheila meets Mouse Ellis.

PART I

CHAPTER FOUR

The next day I met Mouse Ellis. She is also ten and going into fifth grade. I was sitting on the front steps wondering what to do until it was time to go and register for day camp. Then I saw this girl walking up the road. I watched until she got to the front of my house. She looked at me and waved. I waved back.

She came up our driveway and over to where I was sitting. She held up a purple yo-yo. "I'm Mouse Ellis, Junior Champion of Tarrytown," she said. "I can do eleven different tricks without stopping. How many can you do?"

"I never stopped to count," I told her.

She opened her eyes very wide and offered me her yo-yo. "Go ahead and show me," she said.

"I don't feel like it."

"I'll bet you can't do Shotgun six times in a row."

"I'll bet I can," I told her.

"Okay, let's see you do it then."

"After you," I said.

"Okay." Mouse wound up her yo-yo, held it close to her hip, and next thing I knew, out it flew, right at me, six times in a row.

"Very good," I said.

She handed me her yo-yo. I examined it all over.

"It's a Duncan Imperial," she told me. "The very best yo-yo made."

"It's not bad," I said.

"I'm ready any time you are," Mouse said.

I stood up, held the yo-yo to my hip, threw it out, and whacked myself in the head on my first try.

"Hey, are you okay?" Mouse asked.

"Oh sure," I told her. "But I guess I'll have to tell you the truth now. I didn't want to hurt your feelings before. But where I come from, yo-yo's are for babies. I haven't done Shotgun for about eight years now. That's why I missed."

Mouse looked at me for a while, and I gave her one of my best stares right back. Then she sat down next to me and said, "You'll never know how glad I am that you moved in for the summer. I'm sick of those Egran boys!"

I couldn't help smiling. She wouldn't have stayed if she didn't believe I really was a yo-yoer when I was a little kid. "I'm sleeping in one of the Egran boys' bedrooms," I said. "And guess what I found in the desk?"

"What?" Mouse asked.

"Six tubes of Testor's glue and twenty-seven jars of model paint!"

Mouse laughed. "You must have Bobby's room. He's a model maniac."

"He left a note for me," I said. "He signed it B.E."

"That's Bobby!"

"He wrote that if I touch any of his models, he'll get me someday."

"Ha-ha!" Mouse said. "He's all talk."

"That's what I figured. Anyway, who'd want to fool around with his dumb old models?"

"Not me," Mouse said. "I've got better things to do."

"Me too. Say, is your real name Mouse?"

"No, it's Merle, but everybody calls me Mouse."

"You better watch out," I said. "My father's name is really Bertram, and everybody still calls him Buzz."

"Well, I don't care if people call me Mouse forever. I like it a whole lot better than Merle. And if you ask me, Buzz is a much better name than Bertram. Bertram sounds awful. Nothing against your father, of course."

"I didn't mean that I don't like your nickname," I said. "As long as you like to be called Mouse. Personally, I think it's a very nice name. It's much better than Sheila."

"If you don't like Sheila, you should call yourself something else," Mouse said.

"Like what?" I asked.

"Oh . . . maybe Sugar or Sunny or something like that."

"I don't like Sugar," I said. "But Sunny sounds pretty good. Sunny Tubman . . . yeah, I kind of like that."

"Okay, then that's what I'll call you from now on," Mouse said.

I told Mouse about Libby then, and how she says Mother and Father and pretends to be very grown-up. And Mouse told me about her little sister, Betsy, who still wets the bed every night. We found out we are both going to the same day camp and the same pool.

In a little while Mouse stood up and started to yo-yo again, and I could see why she is Junior Champion of Tarrytown. While she was showing me her tricks I noticed that her legs were a mess of scabs. I hoped they weren't catching.

She must have seen me looking because she said, "They're leftover mosquito bites. I scratch them until they bleed and then I get scabs. Aren't they ugly?"

I didn't tell her the truth. I said, "They're not so bad."

When Mouse was done with her yo-yo tricks she said, "Let's take Jennifer for a walk."

"Jennifer, the dog, you mean?"

"Yes. The Egrans always let me walk her. I love dogs."

I never make friends with dog-lovers. "Do you have one at your house?" I asked, thinking I might as well find out the truth right away. There was no point in getting to like her if it was all for nothing.

"No," Mouse said. "Betsy is allergic to them. She gets hives from dogs."

What a great idea. Why didn't I think of saying that? "Me too," I told Mouse. "I get awful hives from them. You wouldn't believe how big my hives are. They'd make your scabs look practically invisible, they're so huge!"

"Oh, rats!" Mouse said. "I was hoping you and me could take care of Jennifer all summer."

"I'm really sorry," I said.

"Oh, that's okay. I guess I'd rather have a girlfriend than a dog."

I was very happy to hear that.

PART II

e walked down the road to her house then. Mouse yo-yoed all the way. She lives at the bottom of the hill, right around the corner from the swimming pool. Her little sister was out front dragging a candy box by a string.

"That's Betsy," Mouse said. "She's four."

"Why does she have a string around that box?"

"She's walking her dog."

"That box is her dog?" I asked.

"Yes. I told you how she gets hives from real ones. So that box is her pretend dog. She calls it Ootch."

Betsy dragged Ootch over to us. "Who are you?" she asked me.

"I'm Sunny Tubman," I told her, trying out my new name.

"Oh. You don't look like a boy," Betsy said.

"She's not a boy!" Mouse told her.

"Then how come her name is Sonny?"

"It's not that kind of Sonny," Mouse explained. "It's Sunny, like the sun in the sky."

"Ohhh," Betsy said. "Sunny like a sunny day?"

"That's it," Mouse said.

"My real name is Sheila," I said to Betsy. "Maybe you should call me that." I didn't think about Sunny sounding like Sonny. Maybe it wasn't such a good name after all.

Betsy said, "This is my dog. Ootch. Want to pet him?"

"Oh sure." I reached over and tapped the candy box. "Nice doggie," I said. "Nice Ootch."

Betsy picked up her box and held it to her ear. Then she put it back down and said, "Ootch says he likes you. Sunny Sheila. He can always tell a person who really and truly loves dogs."

I didn't say anything. I just smiled.

Mrs. Ellis invited me to stay for lunch. I called home and Mom said I could. Me and Mouse ate peanut butter sandwiches with the crust cut off, and Betsy had four slices of plain salami—no bread or anything. She kept Ootch on the table next to her, and every few minutes she made believe she was feeding some of her salami to that box.

"Ootch loves salami," she told me. "It's his favorite lunch."

That afternoon our mothers took us to the Cultural Arts Center to register for day camp. It is really a private school, but it doesn't look anything like one. It looks like an old house surrounded by lots and lots of big trees. I have never seen a school like that. Mouse told me that she doesn't go there. She goes to regular public school. But Bobby Egran has been going there for years. That's because Bobby refused to do any of his work in public school. All he wanted to do was build models. And since the teachers wouldn't let him, he used to get mad and make a lot of noise. So he was spending most of his time sitting on the bench outside the principal's office. At this school he is allowed to build all kinds of things. Mouse says her mother told her Bobby is some kind of genius, but she doesn't believe it.

Mouse and I explored our day camp together. This is her first year too because she was just ten, which means me and Mouse will be two of the youngest kids there. This makes Libby feel like a double big shot! I told Mouse that Libby thinks she is a great ballerina, but when she dances she really looks like an elephant. Well, not exactly an elephant, but only because she is too skinny to be one.

There are a lot of interesting activities at this day camp. But the one that looks best to me is pottery. You get to use a lot of mushy clay, and you try to shape it into some kind of bowl on a pottery wheel. Me and Mouse signed up for that, first thing. The pottery counselor's name is Denise. She was barefoot. I like to go barefoot too, but I'm afraid I might step on a bee and get stung. That happened to Peter Hatcher's little brother once. I think getting stung on the bottom of your foot would be worse than getting stung someplace ordinary, like your arm. I wonder if Denise has ever stepped on a bee.

When we got home Mouse asked me to go swimming with her. She said, "What's your best stroke? Mine's the crawl."

"I'm the same at every stroke," I said.

"Then maybe you'll join the swimming team. We have races every Sunday."

She didn't understand what I meant, I guess. So I said, "No. I really don't like swimming teams. They take all the fun out of it."

"Well, grab your suit and let's go over anyway. It's steaming out."

"I can't go in today," I said. I wasn't about to tell her I can't swim.

"Why can't you go in?" she asked.

"I'm just getting over a cold."

"Oh, rats! You don't sound sick. Ask your mother."

"I can't," I said. "I promised I wouldn't go in today."

"Can't you even dunk your feet?" Mouse asked.

That didn't sound bad. And it was hot out. "Okay," I said. "I guess dunking my feet can't hurt me. I'll go in and get my suit."

But just then my mother came out and said, "Sheila, we have to go over to the pool now. I want to sign you up for some lessons. It's time you learned how to swim!"

Mouse opened her mouth, but nothing came out.

Blume, Judy. *Otherwise Known as Sheila the Great.* New York: Dell Publishing, 1972.

OVER SEA, UNDER STONE

SUSAN COOPER

Simon, Jane, and Barney Drew visit their eccentric great uncle in Cornwall, England. Exploring the attic one day, they discover an ancient map which shows the location of a sacred grail which is inscribed with the true story of King Arthur. In the following excerpt, they have finally arrived at the spot, a narrow cave on the rocky coast, where they believe the grail may lie.

imon found the loose end of the roll of fishing line and tied it securely round Barney's waist. "If you're going to go first, I can hold on to the line behind you."
"D'you think he ought to?" Jane said.

"Well, I'm not awfully keen on the idea," said Simon, "but he's right about its being narrow, and he may be the only one who can get properly inside. It's all right, I won't lose him. Here—" He handed Jane the roll of line. "Don't let it go slack."

Jane looked at her watch. "It's nearly five o'clock. When you've been in there ten minutes I'll pull on the line twice to tell you."

"That's a good idea," Simon said quickly, glancing at her face. "You pull twice, and if I pull back twice, it means we're all right, but we're staying in there. If I pull three times, it means we're coming out."

"And if I pull three times, it means you've got to come out because the tide's turned."

"Fine. And four pulls from either end means a distress signal—not," Simon added hastily, "that there's going to be any need for it."

"All right," Jane said. "Oh dear. Don't be long."

"Well, we shall have to go slowly. But don't get in a flap, nothing's going to go wrong." Simon patted her on the back, and followed as Barney, straining eagerly at the line round his waist like a dog on a leash, waved one hand briefly and disappeared into the mouth of the cave.

Barney blinked at the darkness. As his eyes grew accustomed to being out of the sunlight, vague objects took shape in the dark. He realized that the light from the entrance penetrated further inside than they had realized; and for the first few yards at least, he could see the faint shine of the slimy green weed covering the walls and roof of the cave, and the glint of water lying along the bottom in a shallow, unmoving stream.

He moved warily forward, one hand up touching the roof and the other stretched out to one side. He could feel a slight steady pull on the line round his waist from Simon holding it behind him.

He moved hesitantly forward, and then some instinct told him to stop. He put out his hand in the silent darkness. It met solid rock a few inches from his face. "Simon! It's a dead end."

"What?" Incredulity and disappointment rose in Simon's voice. He struggled with the matches; he could feel the bottom of the box through them now, and realized that there could not be many left.

In the flickering light, it was difficult to tell shadow from darkness, but they saw that the cave had not actually come to an end. Instead, it changed, just in front of them, to a far narrower passage: tall and thin, with a great boulder wedged between its sides about three feet from the ground. Above their heads, out of reach, the cleft was open to the roof: but there was no way of climbing up to it. The boulder blocked their path.

"We'll never get through that," Simon said in despair.

Barney looked down at the forbidding dark gap that remained at the bottom of the cleft, jagged and sinister through the dancing shadows, and swallowed. He was beginning to wish very much that they were back in the sunlight again.

Then he thought of the grail, "I can get through underneath, if I crawl."

"No" Simon said at once. "It's dangerous."

"But we can't go back now." Barney gained confidence as he began to argue. "We've got this far we may be just a few feet away from it. I'll come out again if it's too narrow. Oh come on, Simon, let me try."

Barney went down on his hands and knees and crawled into the dark opening beneath the wedged rock, holding the dangerously flickering candle in front of him. The draft seemed to be stronger now. The rock brushed his body on all sides, so that he had to keep his head down and his elbows in, and for a moment, he almost panicked with the sense of being shut in.

He crawled a little farther, the floor rough and gritty under his knees, and found, not only that he could stand upright, but that the cave was much wider. The pool of light cast by his carefully guarded flame did not even show the walls on either side.

"Are you all right?" Simon's anxious voice came muffled through the opening behind him.

Barney bent down. "It's okay, it widens out again here, that must be an entrance. . . . I'm going on."

He felt the line at his waist tighten as Simon jerked an answer, and he set off slowly across the cave. The darkness opened before him in the small light from his inch of candle, already burning down and dripping hot wax over his fingernails. When he glanced back over his shoulder he could no longer see the entrance from which he had come.

He went on, sheltering his small dying light, into the dark that gave back, in whispering echoes, the sound of his own steps. And then, above his head, he became aware of a noise stranger than anything he had ever heard.

It seemed to come from nowhere, out of the air; a husky, unearthly humming, very faint and faraway, yet filling the whole cave. It wavered up and down, high and then low like the wind that sings in the trees and telegraphwires. As the thought flickered through Barney's mind, he held the candle up and saw that over his head the roof opened into a kind of chimney, rising up and up and out of sight. He thought for an instant that he saw a point of light shining down, but his own light dazzled his eyes, and he could never be sure. And he realized that the noise he could hear was the wind, far above, blowing over the hole in the rocks, that was the singing of the wind over Kemare Head.

It was almost by accident, as he was looking up, that he saw the ledge. It jutted out from the rocky side of the chimney at the end of the cave, a bump of rock beneath a hollow like a kind of natural cupboard just within his back, from a shape that was not part of the rock.

Hardly daring to breathe, he reached up and found his hand touching the side of something smooth and curved. It rang beneath his finger-nail with the sound of metal. He grasped it and took it down, blinking at the dust which rose from the ledge as he did so. It was a cup, heavy and strangely shaped; swelling out from a thick stem into tall bell shape like the goblets he had seen pictured in his books about King Arthur. He could hardly believe that this, at last, must be the grail.

Cooper, Susan. *Over Sea, Under Stone*. New York: Aladdin Paperbacks, An imprint of Simon & Schuster, 1965.

PHILIP HALL LIKES ME. I RECKON MAYBE.

BETTE GREENE

Beth Lambert has a big crush on Philip Hall, who usually doesn't notice her. But today, as Beth jumps off the schoolbus and runs toward home, he calls out her name. She is in a real hurry because her father has promised to bring a puppy for her. And the new puppy seems even more important than Philip Hall!

I never asked for no allergy. February.

Mr. Barnes stopped the school bus along the side of the highway just at that spot where the dirt road leading to our farm meets the blacktop. First Philip Hall got off. Then I jumped off in front of the faded black-and-white sign at the intersection which read:

> 1 mile
> Lambert Farm
> good turkeys
> good pigs

As I took a flying leap across the frozen drainage ditch that separated the road from the field, I heard Philip calling me.

"Hey, Beth!" He was still standing on the blacktop, just where the bus left him. "You oughtna be going through the field. You might step into an ice puddle."

Of all the days to have to stop and start explaining things to Philip Hall. But at any other time I'd be thinking that he wouldn't be fretting about my feet if he didn't really like me. Now would he? "Frosty feet ain't nothing," I told him. "When you have a spanking new puppy waiting to meet you."

"What if Mr. Grant wouldn't swap a collie dog for one of your pa's turkeys?" asked Philip, grinning as though he hoped it was so.

"That's all you know! When I left the house this morning, my pa was picking out six of our fattest turkeys for swapping." I turned and began running across the field.

"Well, one collie dog is worth more than six of your old turkey," called Philip.

171

I kept on running, pretending not to hear. And anyway, everybody loves to eat turkey. Don't they?

When I reached the rise in the field, I could see our house, a nice pale green. It always surprised me a little to see the house painted because until last year the weathered boards had never ever seen a lick of paint.

That was the year Pa sold mite near three hundred turkeys, not even speaking about the forty-two pigs. And that was when Pa asked Ma what it was she wanted most. And she said that all her life she had wanted to live in a painted house. Especially in a house that was painted green.

As I came closer, I could see the chocolate browness of my mama against the palenesss of the porch. She was hanging work-worn overalls across the porch clothesline. Ma used to always be finished with the laundry by this time of day, but she says that carrying a baby inside tends to slow a person down a mite.

I tiptoed up behind her and threw my arms as far as they would go, which was about half the distance around her ever-widening waist.

"Ohhh!" She jumped. "What you mean scaring me clear out of my wits, girl?"

"Where is he?" I asked. "Where's the collie?"

She put on her I'm-not-fixing-to-any-nonsense face and said, "I don't know nothing about no collie."

"Did Pa make the swap? Did he?"

"Get out of here, girl. Go on into the kitchen."

"Tell me if Pa got the collie," I pleaded. "Now did he?"

Her mouth was still set into that no-nonsense way of hers, but it was different with her eyes. Her eyes were filled up with pure pleasure. "And I told you," she said, "to get on into the kitchen, didn't I?"

Suddenly I understood. I threw open the screen door and, without waiting to close it gently behind me, ran in a straight line through the living room and into the kitchen.

And then I saw him. There in a cardboard carton next to the cookstove was a reddish-brown puppy with a circle of white fluffy hair ringing his neck and spilling down to his chest. I dropped to my knees and showed my open palms. "Hi, puppy. Beautiful little collie puppy."

"He's beautiful, sure enought," said Ma from behind.

The collie just looked at me for a few moments. Then he got to his feet and trotted over.

"And you're friendly too," I said, patting his back. "Hey, that would be a good name for you."

"Friendly," said Ma, smacking her lips like she was word tasting. "That's a right good name."

I gave Friendly a hug and a kiss. "I will now name you—ah-choo!" I tried again. "I will now name—AHHHH-hhhh-choo!!"

Ma shook her head the way she does when she catches me at mischief. "You done gone and got yourself a cold, now, didn't you?"

"AHHHHhhhhhh-ha-ha-ha-choo! I now name you Friendly," I said at last.

By bedtime I was sneezing constantly, and water kept pouring from my sore, itchy eyes. But, thank goodness, all my sneezing didn't seem to bother Friendly, who slept peacefully in his cardboard carton at the foot of my bed.

I could hear my folks in the kitchen talking about what they were always talking about these days—names for our soon-to-be-born baby. When they finally tired of that topic, Ma said, "Beth got me worried. All them wheezing sounds coming from her chest."

"I seen Doc Brenner in town this afternoon," said Pa. "He asked me to kill and clean one of our twenty-pound birds. Said he'd stop by this evening to pick it up."

"When he comes by," said Ma, "ask him to kindly take a look at our Beth."

I climbed out of bed to take off my raggedy tail of a nightgown and put on one that Grandma had given me last Christmas. She had made it out of a sack of Fairy Flake flour, but she dyed it a bright, brilliant orange. It was nice.

Friendly started to bark.

"Don't you be frightened, little Friendly, it's only me, only Beth."

While I patted my new pet, I told him how glad I was that he had come to live with us. "You're going to like it here, you'll see. I'm going to bring all my friends to meet you. Philip Hall, Susan, Bon—ahh-choo-whoo! Ahh choo! Bonnie, Ginny, Esther. You're going to like all my friends, Friendly, but you're going to like me best of all . . . I reckon maybe."

Ma called out, "Is you out of bed, Beth?"

I jumped back into bed before answering. "No m'am, I'm right here. Right here in bed."

I kept my eyes open, waiting for the doctor to come, but after a while my eyelids came together. Sleep stood by waiting for me to fall . . . fall asleep . . . sleep . . . sleep.

"Let me take a look at my old friend, Beth," said a big voice.

My cheeks were being patted. "Doctor's here, Beth honey," Ma was saying.

I pulled myself up to sitting and looked into the face of Dr. Brenner, who said, "This won't hurt," as he placed a freezing stethoscope to my chest.

I jumped. "It's cold."

He rubbed the stethoscope warm with his hands. "That doesn't sound much like the Beth Lambert who caught those turkey-thieving Cooks with only a"— Doc Brenner commenced laughing—"with only a . . ." But again his laughing interfered with his talking, so I just said, "With only a BB gun," while the doctor laughed all the harder.

Greene, Bette. *Philip Hall likes me. I reckon maybe.* New York: Dell Publishing, 1974.

RAMONA AND HER MOTHER

BEVERLY CLEARY

Things are not going so well for Ramona. Beezus, her older sister, is acting like a big shot and gets their mother's attention. Ramona has to go to bed at eight-thirty every night and misses the end of the eight o'clock TV movie. Ramona is feeling really sorry for herself. In these two excerpts you will see how things just get worse.

Chapter 3 NOBODY LIKES RAMONA

In February there came a day for Ramona when everything went wrong, one thing after another, like a row of dominoes falling over. Ramona's mother set it off. "By the way, Ramona," said Mrs. Quimby after breakfast as she hastily tossed potatoes, carrots, and stew meat into the Crock-Pot to simmer while the family was away all day. "Please don't run in the hall in your socks. You might slip and fall."

Ramona's father was next. "And Ramona," he said, pulling strings off celery before slicing it and adding it to the stew, "when you wash your hands, don't leave the dirt on the cake of soap."

Then Beezus, "or wipe it on the towel."

"I haven't had time to get it dirty," said Ramona, who had finished her breakfast. "And I have my shoes on."

"We are talking about yesterday," said her father.

Ramona thought yesterday was a long time ago, hardly worth mentioning. "Everybody picks on me," she said.

"Poor kid." Mr. Quimby kissed his wife on the cheek and each daughter on the top of her head. Then he said, singing the first few words, "Hi-ho, hi-ho, it's off to work I go and at least forty-six changes in produce prices to remember."

Ramona knew her father dreaded Wednesdays, the day prices were changed on fruits and vegetables.

"Maybe things will be easier when you are more used to the job," said Mrs. Quimby. After her husband left to catch the bus, she kissed the girls as if she were thinking about something else and handed Ramona her lunch box and Beezus the brown paper bag that held her sandwich. Seventh-graders thought lunch boxes were babyish. "Scoot along,"

Mrs. Quimby said. "I have to leave early to take the car for brake adjustment, and then I have to take the bus to work."

"I wish Daddy would get used to his job," remarked Beezus as the sisters plodded toward Glenwood School. Clouds hung low, and the wind was cold. For days, the sidewalks had been too wet for roller skating.

"Me, too," said Ramona, who wanted her parents to be happy so their children could be happy, too. "Why doesn't he find another job?"

"Jobs aren't that easy to get," Beezus explained. "Remember how long he was out of work before he found a job at the market."

Ramona did remember. She remembered how discouraged her father had been after a day of job-hunting and how he had disliked standing in line to collect unemployment insurance.

"It might be easier if he had finished college," said Beezus.

"Why didn't he?" asked Ramona.

"Because he and Mother got married," Beezus explained. "And then they had me." Beezus sounded smug, as if being the firstborn made her more important to her parents than Ramona.

But, I'm the baby, thought Ramona. She was glad when school started; maybe her day would improve in school. Ramona liked Mrs. Rudge, her new teacher, who had taken over the second grade when the former teacher left after Christmas to have a baby. She thought Mrs. Rudge liked her, as she liked all the children, but she was not sure exactly where she stood with her. The classroom buzzed softly and busily with the sound of children learning about Indians and cursive writing.

When the morning was half over, Ramona finished her work sheet and was busy filling all the double oo's she could find with crossed eyes and frowns:

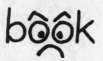

Mrs. Rudge paused beside her desk. Ramona did not have time to hide the frowning oo's.

Mrs. Rudge glanced over Ramona's work sheet. "Why don't you look again?" she suggested. "Is like spelled l-i-c-k?"

"I can't spell," said Ramona. "I'm terrible at spelling." That's what her family said whenever Ramona wrote a note. They always laughed and said, "Ramona is no speller. See how she spells much m-u-c-k." They behaved as if she had done something clever.

Ramona learned right there that Mrs. Rudge was a teacher who did not accept excuses. "There is no such a word as can't," she said, and went on to inspect Becky's work sheet.

How can there be no such word as can't? Ramona wondered. Mrs. Rudge had just said can't. If there was no such word as can't, Mrs. Rudge could not have said there was no such word as can't. Therefore, what Mrs. Rudge had said could not be true. Ramona was left with a vague feeling that Mrs. Rudge did not like her because she did not offer to give Ramona extra help in spelling.

At lunchtime, when Ramona went into the multipurpose room with her lunch box, she found that she had a leftover-pot-roast sandwich in her lunch. She did not like a leftover-pot-roast sandwich because the meat slid out in big pieces when she bit into it. After chewing a while she thought, I won't eat it, and she stuffed the rest of her sandwich into the hole in her milk carton and threw it into the trash can. She sat there arguing with herself about how there had to be a word can't because she just thought it. This was not a good day.

After school at the Kemp's house, Ramona and Howie drank the same old apple juice and ate the same old graham crackers that Mrs. Kemp always set out for them. Sticky Willa Jean, holding Woger by one paw, stood and watched. She was wearing a T-shirt with

Grandma Loves Me printed on the front. The shirt had shrunk so much it showed her navel—tummy button, Mrs. Kemp called it.

Then Howie got out the checkerboard, which he placed on the carpet. Kneeling, he and Ramona began to divide the red and black checkers.

"I want to play." Willa Jean plunked herself down on the carpet, sitting on Woger as if he were a cushion, which was no way to treat a bear, especially a bear like Woger.

"Aw, Willa Jean—" protested Howie, who had his problems with his little sister.

"Now Howie," said Mrs. Kemp, busy with her endless knitting, "play nicely with your sister. She's little, you know."

Howie knew all right.

Willa Jean, pleased to have her grandmother on her side, set a red checker on top of a black checker. "Your turn," she said to Ramona as if she were being generous.

Ramona and Howie shared one hopeless look. They were familiar with Willa Jean's original rules for checkers. Ramona set a black checker on top of Willa Jean's red checker. Howie added red and so on in turn until the tower of checkers grew high and crooked. At last, when Willa Jean set a checker on top, the tower tumbled.

"I won!" crowed Willa Jean as Howie tried to prevent scattered checkers from rolling under the couch. "Grandma, I beat Howie and Wamona!"

"Smart girl!" Mrs. Kemp paused in her knitting to smile down upon her grand-daughter.

The situation was hopeless. "Let's go down in the basement and see if we can think of something to build," said Howie, and Ramona agreed. They would be undisturbed in the basement. Willa Jean was afraid of the furnace.

Safe from interruption, Howie and Ramona decided to build a boat of the scrap lumber Mr. Kemp collected for Howie to work with. They had already built a dog, a cat, and a duck decoy that Mr. Kemp said would never fool a real live duck. Now they sawed and pounded until they had a boat with two decks. They were so good at nailing by now they did not even pound their fingers. Next they found a dowel and sawed off two peices for smokestacks, which Howie studied. "It's going to be hard to nail them to our boat," he said.

"We could use scotch tape," said Ramona, who felt that almost anything could be accomplished with scotch tape.

"I don't think it's strong enough for wood," was Howie's objection. "Glue might be better."

"Scotch tape would work if we use lots of it." Ramona was an experienced user of scotch tape.

In the end, glue won out because Howie thought a boat should look neat. Very, very carefully they spread glue on the ends of the dowels and pressed them in place. They put the top back on the tube of glue, and each held a dowel in place, waiting for the glue to dry. They had not spilled a drop. Fortunately, the glue was quick drying.

"Let's see if our boat will float," said Howie. He pressed the plug of the laundry tub in place and turned on the faucet.

"Howie, what are you two doing down there?" Mrs. Kemp called from the top of the stairs.

"Just seeing if our boat will float," he answered.

"All right," said Mrs. Kemp. "Just don't let the tub overflow."

"We won't," promised Howie.

The boat floated. Howie and Ramona stirred up a storm at sea to make things interesting and watched their boat ride the waves. As it bobbed up and down, Ramona happened to glance up at a shelf above the laundry tub. There she spotted a blue plastic bottle with the picture of a nice old-fashioned lady's face on the label. Bluing!

Ramona knew all about bluing because her mother had used it to make white washing look whiter back in the days before she had gone to work. "If we could get that bottle, we could turn the water blue like a real ocean," she suggested. "It only takes a little bit."

Howie was enthusiastic, but how were they to reach a bottle on such a high shelf? For some reason, Mrs. Rudge's words, there's no such word as can't, ran through Ramona's mind. Of course they could get that bottle of bluing.

Ramona managed to balance on her stomach on the edge of the tub. Then she got one knee up and with a boost from Howie was able to climb up onto the edge of the tub. She stood teetering on the narrow edge, clinging to the front of the shelf with one hand, while she managed to grasp the bottle with the other and hand it down to Howie. As she did so, the top flew off. Bluing splashed over Howie, who tried to catch the top only to have the bottle slip from his fingers into the tub of water, where it poured forth swirls of beautiful deep blue. Ramona was so startled she lost her balance and landed standing up to her knees in blue water.

"Boy, Ramona, see what you've done." Howie looked down at his shirt and jeans, now streaked with blue.

Ramona felt Howie was being most unfair. She did not spill the bluing on purpose. Besides, why wasn't the top of the bottle screwed on tight? Because some grown-up had not screwed it on, that's why. Children weren't the only people who did things wrong. She fumbled through the blue water, now much bluer than any ocean, and pulled the plug. As the water drained out, she and Howie looked at one another. Now what should they do?

Cleary, Beverly. *Ramona and Her Mother.* New York: Avon books, 1979.

ROLL OF THUNDER, HEAR MY CRY

MILDRED D. TAYLOR

Things just aren't fair for Cassie and her family. When Cassie and her brothers walk to school, the schoolbus splashes mud all over their crisply washed and ironed clothes. All the white children on the bus hoot and laugh. In these two excerpts, see how Cassie and her brothers decide to get even. They dig a very large ditch in the road, which they fill with water and when the schoolbus comes down the road, it gets stuck. Then, in the middle of the night Cassie wakes up and sees a gang of men ride into her driveway. Now she's really scared.

CHAPTER 4

assie, what's the matter with you, girl?" Big Ma asked as she thrust three sticks of dried pine into the stove to rekindle the dying morning fire. "You sure are takin' a sorrowful long time to churn that butter."

"Nothin'," I muttered.

"Nothin'?" Big Ma turned and looked directly at me. "You been mopin' 'round here for the past week like you got the whoopin' cough, flu, and measles all put together."

I sighed deeply and continued to churn.

Big Ma reached out and felt my forehead, then my cheeks. Frowning; she pulled her hand away as Mama entered the kitchen. "Mary, feel this child's face," she said. "She seem warm to you?"

Mama cupped my face in her thin hands. "You feel sick, Cassie?"

"No'm."

"How do you feel?"

"All right," I said, still churning.

Mama studied me with the same disturbed look Big Ma wore and a tiny frown line appeared on her brow. "Cassie," she said softly, fixing her dark eyes upon me, "is there something you want to tell me?"

I was on the verge of blurting out the awful truth about the bus and the men in the night, but then I remembered the pact Stacey had made us all swear to when I had told him, Christopher-John, and Little Man about the caravan and I said instead, "No, ma'am," and began to churn again. Abruptly Mama took hold of the churning stick, her eyes searching mine. As she studied me, she seemed about to ask something, then the question faded, and she pulled away, lifting the lid of the churn. "It looks ready now," she said with a sigh. "Dip out the butter like I showed you, and wash it down. I'll take care of the milk."

I scooped the butter from the churning lid onto a plate and went through the curtain to the small pantry off the kitchen to get the molding dish. It had been placed on a high shelf under several other dishes, and I had to stand on a stool to get it. As I eased it out, Mama and Big Ma spoke softly in worried tones on the other side of the curtain.

"Somethin' the matter with that child, Mary."

"She's not sick, Mama."

"There's all sorts of sickness. She ain't ate right for goin' on over a week. She ain't sleepin' right neither. Restless and murmurin' in her sleep all night long. And she won't hardly even go out and play, rather be in here helpin' us. Now, you know that ain't like that child."

There was a moment's pause, then Mama whispered so I could hardly hear her. "You think . . . Mama, you think she could've seen—"

"Oh, Lord, no, child," Big Ma exclaimed hastily. "I checked in there right after they passed, and she was sound asleep. She couldn't've seen them ole devils. The boys neither."

Mama sighed. "The boys, they're not themselves either. All of them, too quiet. Here it is Saturday morning, and they're quiet as church mice. I don't like it, and I can't shake the feeling that it's got something to do with—Cassie!"

Without warning, I had lost my balance and with an absurd topple from the knee-high stool crashed upon the floor with the molding dish. "Cassie, you hurt?" Mama asked, stooping beside me.

"No'm," I mumbled, feeling very clumsy and close to tears. I knew that if I let the tears fall, Mama's suspicion that something was wrong would be confirmed for I never cried about such a silly thing as a fall; in fact, I seldom ever cried. So instead of crying, I jumped up quickly and began to pick up the broken pieces of the dish.

"I'm sorry, Mama," I said.

"That's all right," she said, helping me. When we had swept the chips away with the long field-straw broom, she told me, "Leave the butter, Cassie, and go on in with the boys."

"But, Mama—"

"I'll do the butter. Now go on, do like I say."

I stared up at Mama, wondering if she would ever know what we had done, then joined the boys who were sitting listlessly around the fire absently listening to T.J.

"See, fellows, there's a system to getting out of work," T.J. was expounding as I sat down. "Jus' don't be 'round when it's got to be done. Only thing is, you can't let your folks know that's what you're doin'. See, you should do like me. Like this mornin' when mama wanted to bring back them scissors she borrowed from Miz Logan, I ups and volunteers so she don't have

to make this long trip down here, she bein' so busy and all. And naturally when I got here, y'all wanted me to stay awhile and talk to y'all, so what could I do? I couldn't be impolite, could I? And by the time I finally convince y'all I gotta go, all the work'll be done at home." T.J. chuckled with satisfaction. "Yeah, you just have to use the old brain, that's all."

He was quiet a moment, expecting some comment on his discourse, but no one said a word.

T.J.'s eyes roamed the length of the room, then he admonished, "See, if you was smart like me, Stacey, you'd use the old brain to get the questions on that big test comin' up. Just think, they probably jus' sittin' right here in this very room waitin' to be discovered."

Stacey cast T.J. an annoyed look, but did not speak.

"Ya'll sure are a sorry lot this mornin'," T.J. observed. "A fellow's just wastin' his know-how talkin' to y'all."

"Ain't nobody asked you to give it," said Stacey.

"Well, you don't have to get snippety about it," replied T.J. haughtily. Again, silence prevailed; but that would not do for T.J. "Say, how 'bout we sneak down to that ole Wallace store and learn how to do them new dances?"

"Mama told us not to go down there," Stacey said.

"You some mama's boy or somethin' you gotta do everything your mama tells—"

"You go on if you wanna," said Stacey quietly, not rising to T.J.'s bait, "but we staying here."

Again, silence.

Then T.J. said: "Say, y'all hear the latest 'bout them night men?" Suddenly all eyes turned from the fire and riveted themselves upon him. Our faces were eager question marks; we were totally in T.J.'s power.

What 'bout them?" Stacey asked, almost evenly.

T.J., of course, intended to nurse the moment for as long as he could. "You see when a fellow's as smart as me, he gets to know things that other folks don't. Now, this kind of information ain't for the ears of little kids, so I really shouldn't even tell y'all—"

"Then don't!" said Stacey with smooth finality, turning his back toward the fire as if he cared not at all about the night men. Taking his cue, I nudged Christopher-John and Christopher-John nudged Little Man, and the three of us forced ourselves to stare into the fire in feigned disinterest.

Without a captive audience, T.J. had to reinterest us by getting to the point. "Well, 'bout a week ago, they rode down to Mr. Sam Tatum's place—you know, down the Jackson Road toward Strawberry—and you know what they done?"

Stacey, Little Man, and I kept our eyes upon the fire, but Christopher-John piped eagerly, "What?"

I poked Christopher-John and he turned guiltily around, but T.J., truimphant with an assured audience of one, settled back in his chair ready to prolong the suspense. "You know Mama'd kill me if she knowed I was tellin' this. I heard her and Miz Claire Thompson talkin' 'bout it. They was real scared. Don't know why though. Them ole night men sure wouldn't scare me none. Like I told Claude—"

"Hey, y'all," Stacey said, standing and motioning us up. "Mama said she wanted us to take some milk and butter down to Miz Jackson before noon. We'd better get started."

I nodded, and Christopher-John, Little Man, and I got up.

"Tarred and feathered him!" T.J. announced hastily. "Poured the blackest tar they could find all over him, then plastered him with chicken feathers." T.J. laughed. "Can you imagine that?"

"But why?" asked Little Man, forgetting our ploy.

This time T.J. did not slow down. "I dunno if y'all's little ears should hear this, but it seems he called Mr. Jim Lee Barrett a liar— he's the man who runs the Mercantile down in Strawberry. Mr. Tatum's s'pose to done told him that he ain't ordered up all them things Mr. Barnett done charged him for. Mr. Barnett said he had all them things Mr. Tatum ordered writ down, and when Mr. Tatum asked to see that list of his, Mr. Barnett say'd, 'You callin' me a liar, boy?' And Mr. Tatum says, 'Yessuh, I guess I is!' That done it!"

"Then it wasn't 'cause of the bus?" Christopher-John blurted out.

"Bus? What's a bus got to do with it?"

"Nothin'," said Stacey quickly. "Nothin' at all."

"Well, if anybody said them night men was down in here 'cause of some stupid bus, they crazy," said T.J. authoritatively. " 'Cause my information come direct from Miz Claire Thompson who seen Mr. Tatum herself."

"You sure?" Stacey asked.

"Sure? Sure, I'm sure. When do I ever say anythin' when I ain't sure?"

Stacey smiled with relief. "Come on, let's get the milk."

All of us went into the kitchen, then to the bedrooms to get our coats. When we got outside T.J. remembered that he had left his cap by the fire and ran back to retrieve it. As soon as we were alone, Little Man asked, "Stacey, you really think them night men put tar and feathers all over Mr. Tatum?"

"I s'pose so," said Stacey.

Little Man frowned, but it was Christopher-John who spoke, whispering shrilly as if a stray morning ghost might overhear. "If they ever find out 'bout the bus, you think they gonna put tar and feathers all over us?"

Little Man's frown deepened and he observed gravely, "If they did, we'd never get clean again."

"Cassie," said Christopher-John, his eyes wide, "w-was you real s-scared when you seen 'em?"

Little Man shivered with excitement. "I wish I could've seen 'em."

"Well, I don't," declared Christopher-John. "In fact, I wish I'd never heard of no night men or buses or secrets or holes in the road!" And with that outburst, he stuffed his pudgy hands into his thin jacket, pressed his lips firmly together, and refused to say another word.

Taylor, Mildred D. *Roll of Thunder, Hear My Cry.* New York: Puffin Books, Penguin Books USA Inc., 1976.

THE FIRST SHLEMIEL

Isaac Bashevis Singer

A shlemiel in yiddish means an unlucky person, a chump. The original shlemiel lived with his wife and baby son in a village called Chelm. He was unlucky as well as lazy, unhandy, and foolish. Mr. Shlemiel also had a terrible sweet tooth. Part I and Part II tell the tale of what happens to such a man.

PART I

There are many shlemiels in the world, but the very first one came from the village of Chelm. He had a wife, Mrs. Shlemiel, and a child, Little Shlemiel, but he could not provide for them. His wife used to get up early in the morning to sell vegetables in the marketplace. Mr. Shemiel stayed at home and rocked the baby to sleep. He also took care of the rooster which lived in the room with them, feeding it corn and water.

Mrs. Shlemiel knew that her husband was unhandy and lazy. He also loved to sleep and had a sweet tooth. It so happened that one night she prepared a potful of delicious jam. The next day she worried that while she was away at the market, her husband would eat it all up. So before she left, she said to him, "Shlemiel, I'm going to the market, and I will be back in the evening. There are three things that I want to tell you. Each one is very important."

"What are they?" asked Shlemiel.

"First, make sure the baby does not fall out of his cradle."

"Good. I will take care of the baby."

"Secondly, don't let the rooster get out of the house."

"Good. The rooster won't get out of the house."

"Thirdly, there is a potful of poison on the shelf. Be careful not to eat it, or you will die," said Mrs. Shlemiel, pointing to the pot of jam she had placed high up in the cupboard.

She had decided to fool him, because she knew that once he tasted the delicious jam, he would not stop eating until the pot was empty. It was just before Hanukkah, and she needed the jam to serve with the holiday pancakes.

As soon as his wife left, Shlemiel began to rock the baby and to sing him a lullaby:

I am a big Shlemiel
You are a little Shlemiel

When you grow up,
You will be a big Shlemiel
And I will be an old Shlemiel.
When you have children,
You will be a papa Shlemiel
And I will be a grandpa Shlemiel.

The baby soon fell asleep and Shlemiel dozed too, still rocking the cradle with his foot.

Shlemiel dreamed that he had become the richest man in Chelm. He was so rich that he could eat pancakes with jam not only on Hanukkah, but every day of the year. He spent all day with the other wealthy men of Chelm playing games with a golden dreidel. Shlemiel knew a trick, and whenever it was his turn to spin the dreidel, it fell on the winning "G." He grew so famous that nobles from distant countries came to him and said, "Shlemiel, we want you to be our King."

Shlemiel told them he did not want to be a king. But the nobles fell on their knees before him and insisted until he had to agree. They placed a crown on his head and led him to a golden throne. Mrs. Shlemiel, now a queen, no longer needed to sell vegetables in the market. She sat next to him, and between them they shared a huge pancake spread with jam. He ate from one side and she from the other until their mouths met.

As Shlemiel sat and dreamed his sweet dream the rooster suddenly started crowing. It had a very strong voice. When it came out with a cock-a-doodle-doo, it rang like a bell. Now when a bell rang in Chelm, it usually meant there was a fire. Shlemiel awakened from his dream and jumped up in fright, overturning the cradle. The baby fell out and hurt his head. In his confusion Shlemiel ran to the window and opened it to see where the fire was. The moment he opened the window, the excited rooster flew out and hopped away.

Shlemiel called after it, "Rooster, you come back. If Mrs. Shlemiel finds you gone, she will rave and rant and I will never hear the end of it."

But the rooster paid no attention to Shlemiel. It didn't even look back, and soon it had disappeared from sight.

When Shlemiel realized that there was no fire, he closed the window and went back to the crying baby, who by this time had a big bump on his forehead from the fall. With great effort Shlemiel comforted the baby, righted the cradle, and put him back into it.

Again he began to rock the cradle and sing a song:

In my dream I was a rich Shlemiel
But awake I am a poor Shlemiel.
In my dream I ate pancakes with jam;

Awake I chew bread and onion.
In my dream I was Shlemiel the King
But awake I'm just Shlemiel.

Having finally sung the baby to sleep, Shlemiel began to worry about his troubles. He knew that when his wife returned and found the rooster gone and the baby with a bump on his head, she would be beside herself with anger. Mrs. Shlemiel had a very loud voice, and when she scolded and screamed, poor Shlemiel trembled with fear. Shlemiel could foresee that tonight, when she got home, his wife would be angrier than ever before and would berate him and call him names.

Suddenly Shlemiel said to himself, "What is the sense of such a life? I'd rather be dead." And he decided to end his life. But how to do it? He then remembered what his wife had told him in the morning about the pot of poison that stood on the shelf. "That's what I will do. I will poison myself. When I'm dead she can revile me as much as she likes. A dead Shlemiel does not hear when he is screamed at."

PART II

Shlemiel was a short man and he could not reach the shelf. He got a stool, climbed up on it, took down the pot, and began to eat. "Oh, the poison tastes sweet," he said to himself. He had heard that some poisons have a bitter taste and others are sweet. "But," he reasoned, "sweet poison is better than bitter," and proceeded to finish up the jam. It tasted so good, he licked the pot clean.

After Shlemiel had finished the pot of poison, he lay down on the bed. He was sure that the poison would soon begin to burn his insides and that he would die. But half an hour passed and then an hour, and Shlemiel lay without a single pain in his belly.

"This poison works very slowly," Shlemiel decided. He was thirsty and wanted a drink of water, but there was no water in the house. In Chelm water had to be fetched from an outside well, and Shlemiel was too lazy to go and get it.

Shlemiel remembered that his wife was saving a bottle of apple cider for the holidays. Apple cider was expensive, but when a man is about to die, what is the point of saving money? Shlemiel got out the bottle of cider and drank it down to the last drop.

Now Shlemiel began to have an ache in his stomach, and he was sure that the poison had begun to work. Convinced that he was about to die, he said to himself, "It's not really so bad to die. With such poison I wouldn't mind dying every day." And he dozed off.

He dreamed again that he was a king. He wore three crowns on his head, one on top of the other. Before him stood three golden pots: one filled with pancakes, one with jam, and one with apple cider. Whenever he soiled his beard with eating, a servant wiped it for him with a napkin.

Mrs. Shlemiel, the queen, sat next to him on her separate throne and said, "Of all the kings who ever ruled in Chelm, you are the greatest. The whole of Chelm pays homage to your wisdom. Fortunate is the queen of such a king. Happy is the prince who has you as a father."

Shlemiel was awakened by the sound of the door creaking open. The room was dark and he heard his wife's screechy voice. "Shlemiel, why didn't you light the lamp?"

"It sounds like my wife, Mrs. Shlemiel," Shlemiel said to himself. "But how is it possible that I hear her voice? I happen to be dead. Or can it be that the poison hasn't worked yet and I am still alive?" He got up, his legs shaking, and saw his wife lighting the lamp.

Suddenly she began to scream at the top of her lungs. "Just look at the baby! He has a bump on his head. Shlemiel, where is the rooster, and who drank up the cider! He lost the rooster and let the baby get a bump on his head. Shlemiel, what have you done?"

"Don't scream, dear wife. I'm about to die. You will soon be a widow."

"Die? Widow? What are you talking about? You look healthy as a horse."

"I've poisoned myself," Shlemiel replied.

"Poisoned? What do you mean?" asked Mrs. Shlemiel.

"I've eaten your potful of poison."

And Shlemiel pointed to the empty pot of jam.

"Poison?" said Mrs. Shlemiel. "That's my pot of jam for Hanukkah."

"But you told me it was poison," Shlemiel insisted.

"You fool," she said. "I did that to keep you from eating it before the holiday. Now you've swallowed the whole potful." And Mrs. Shlemiel burst out crying.

Shlemiel too began to cry, but not from sorrow. He wept tears of joy that he would remain alive. The wailing of the parents woke the baby, and he too began to yowl. When the neighbors heard all the crying, they came running, and soon, all of Chelm knew the story. The good neighbors took pity on the Shlemiels and brought them a fresh pot of jam and another bottle of apple cider. The rooster, which had gotten cold and hungry from wandering around outside, returned by itself, and the Shlemiels had a happy holiday after all.

As always in Chelm when an unusual event occurred, the Elders came together to ponder over what had happened. For seven days and seven nights they sat wrinkling their foreheads and tugging at their beards, searching for the true meaning of the incident. At the end the sages all came to the same conclusion: A wife who has a child in the cradle and a rooster to take care of should never lie to her husband and tell him that a pot of jam is a pot of poison, or that a pot of poison is a pot of jam, even if he is lazy, has a sweet tooth, and is a shlemiel besides.

Singer, Isaac Bashevis. *Zlateh the Goat and Other Stories*. New York: HarperCollins Publishers, 1966.

THE MOFFATS

ELEANOR ESTES

It is the very first day of school for Rufus, Janey's little brother. He is terribly excited. Janey and Rufus walk to school together, hand in hand and, on the way, come across Chet and his little brother, Hughie Pudge. Hughie Pudge's reaction to the prospect of school is very different than Rufus's.

Chapter 3 THE FIRST DAY OF SCHOOL

This morning, what a hustle-bustle in the yellow house! And no wonder! It was the first day of school. Not only was it the first day of school for Sylvie, Jane, and Joey, it was also the very first day of school for Rufus. Rufus had never been to school before except for one day last year when Jane brought him to her class for Visiting Day. That day had been more like a party than school, with cookies and oranges, singing games and a spelling bee, instead of lessons. Aside from that day, Rufus had never been to school before. Why should he have been? He was only five and a half. In spite of this, though, he could already print his name RUFUS MOFFAT and count very rapidly up to twenty.

Rufus was so happy he was going to start school, his face was shining. Jane was going to take him this first day. She was going to show him where Room One was and introduce him to the first grade teacher, Miss Andrews. Rufus was radiant as Mama gave him a final going-over, jerking his red tie in place, pulling his stockings up tight, and tying his shoe laces in a double bow.

"There," she said. "Be a good boy. Do as the teacher says, and wait for Jane when school is over."

Then she kissed them both good-by and watched them from the window in the Grape Room all the way down the street. She waved her blue-checked apron after Jane and Rufus, the smallest and last of her children to be starting off to school.

"My, my, it'll be lonesome here without any baby around the house," she said as she started to wind the bobbin on the sewing machine.

Rufus and Jane walked hand in hand. They each had a shiny red apple to eat during recess. When they reached Mr. Brooney's delicatessen store at the end of New Dollar Street, a lively sight greeted them. There was Hughie Pudge, kicking his feet against the big bread box in front of the store, screaming and yelling, "Won't go, won't go!"

His older brother, Chester, was doing his best to quiet him and to pull him away.

"Come on," said Chet. "School's not bad. You know what Mother said. You don't want to grow up to be a dunce, do you? Oh, well, if you do, all right." And with this, Chet shrugged his shoulders and pretended he was going to go off and leave Hughie, hoping his little brother would follow him. But no. Hughie merely howled the louder. So Chet came back and stood beside him helplessly.

"What's the matter?" asked Jane, while Rufus tugged at her arm, impatient to be on his way.

"Aw—Hughie doesn't want to go to school. It's his first day. He did the same thing last year, howled like this, and it ended by his staying home the whole year. Now he's got to go, Mother says, or else he'll grow up a dunce."

Rufus examined Hughie in amazement. Not want to go to school! Imagine! Why, he had looked forward to this day for years, it seemed to him.

Jane tried to take Hughie's hand. "Look," she urged, "Rufus is going to school. You could go with him. You'll be in the same room. Maybe you can sit together. The teacher's nice. Sometimes she has cookies," said Jane.

"Sure," said Rufus, holding out his chubby hand. "Everybody has to go to school. Even God had to go to school."

For a moment Hughie surveyed Rufus with a trace of interest. Hopefully the three others grabbed him by the arm, thinking victory was certain. But Hughie shook them free and started running back towards home. Way down the street they could see Mrs. Pudge shooing with her apron and making gestures with her arms that meant "Go on, go on!" Jane, Chester, and Rufus soon caught up with Hughie. Jane grabbed one arm firmly and Chet the other, and they started to drag him ignominiously in the right direction.

"School is nice," pleaded Jane.

"No, no," screamed Hughie.

"Well," said Jane, dropping his arm in disgust, "if he doesn't want to, he doesn't want to. We might as well leave him, Rufe, or else we'll be late for school."

"What's this, what's this?" a voice boomed behind them. They turned around. Mr. Pennypepper, the new Superintendent of Schools!

"What seems to be the trouble?" asked Mr. Pennypepper, rocking from heel to toe and clinking the keys in his pocket.

"Hughie doesn't want to go to school, sir," answered Chester, red as a beet.

Mr. Pennypepper put on his glasses and examined Hughie critically. Hughie stopped his blubbering and hung his head.

"Nonsense," said Mr. Pennypepper with an air of finality. "We're all going to school."

He took Hughie by one arm and Rufus by the other. Jane took Rufus's other arm and Chester took Hughie's. In this manner, they all proceeded until they reached the boys' school yard.

Here Mr. Pennypepper left them. His last words were, "Now then, Hughie, I see you have changed your mind. That's fine. But," he said, leaning down and whispering in Rufus's ear, "in case he changes his mind again and runs away from school, I want you to bring him back. Yes, I want you to watch out for him today; your responsibility until twelve o'clock."

With that he tipped his hat to the four children and marched up the front steps of the school.

Jane, Rufus, and Hughie stood together for a while watching boys and girls arriving in ones, twos, and threes. Rufus felt rather confused and was glad Jane was right there. But now someone appeared in one of the school windows and rang a bell vigorously.

"First bell," said Jane, speaking from experience. "Now I'll have to go into the girl's school yard until it's time to go in. But, Rufus, when we go in, I'll show you and Hughie where Room One is."

And so she left.

For a moment Rufus had a rather queer feeling. All alone. None of the other Moffats. Not Mama, Sylvie, not Joey or Jane. Yes, even Rufus felt a slight impulse to run home and play as he used to. Play what? he asked himself. Mud pies? he asked himself sarcastically. Pooh! He was too old for all that business now. He was going to school. Soon he would be going home for lunch with all those throngs he'd always envied. With something to show Mama too, maybe. Moreover, he had to mind Hughie.

Estes, Eleanor. *The Moffats.* New York: Harcourt Brace Jovanovich, 1941.

FANTASTIC ANIMALS

THE CRICKET IN TIMES SQUARE

GEORGE SELDEN

Chester Cricket hops into a picnic basket in Connecticut, and ends up being carried all the way to New York City. Alone and far from home, he finds himself in the Times Square subway station. Thankfully, the boy who runs the newsstand hears his pretty chirping and adopts him as a pet. He makes him a cozy bed in a matchbox and goes home for the evening. That's when Chester meets some new friends, Tucker and Harry, and gets to see New York for the first time.

Chapter Four HARRY CAT

Chester buried his head in the Kleenex. He didn't want to see his new friend, Tucker Mouse, get killed. Back in Connecticut he had sometimes watched the one-sided fights of cats and mice in the meadow, and unless the mice were near their holes, the fights always ended in the same way. But this cat had been upon them too quickly: Tucker couldn't have escaped.

There wasn't a sound. Chester lifted his head and very cautiously looked behind him. The cat—a huge tiger cat with gray-green and black stripes along his body—was sitting on his hind legs, switching his tail around his forepaws. And directly between those forepaws, in the very jaws of his enemy, sat Tucker Mouse. He was watching Chester curiously. The cricket began to make frantic signs that the mouse should look up and see what was looming over him.

Very casually Tucker raised his head. The cat looked straight down on him. "Oh him," said Tucker, chucking the cat under the chin with his right front paw, "he's my best friend. Come out from the matchbox."

Chester crept out, looking first at one, then the other.

"Chester, meet Harry Cat," said Tucker. "Harry, this is Chester. He's a cricket."

"I'm very pleased to make your acquaintance," said Harry Cat in a silky voice.

"Hello," said Chester. He was sort of ashamed because of all the fuss he'd made. "I wasn't scared for myself. But I thought cats and mice were enemies."

"In the country, maybe," said Tucker. "But in New York, we gave up those old habits long ago. Harry is my oldest friend. He lives with me over in the drain pipe. So how was scrounging tonight, Harry?"

"Not so good," said Harry Cat. "I was over in the ash cans on the East Side, but those rich people don't throw out as much garbage as they should."

"Chester, make that noise again for Harry," said Tucker Mouse.

Chester lifted the black wings that were carefully folded across his back and with a quick, expert stroke drew the top one over the bottom. A "thrumm" echoed throughout the station.

"Lovely—very lovely," said the cat. "This cricket has talent."

"I thought it was singing," said Tucker. "But you do it like playing a violin, with one wing on the other?"

"Yes," said Chester. "These wings aren't much good for flying, but I prefer music anyhow." He made three rapid chirps.

Tucker Mouse and Harry Cat smiled at each other. "It makes me want to purr to hear it," said Harry.

"Some people say a cricket goes 'chee chee chee,'" explained Chester. "And others say, 'treet treet treet,' but we crickets don't think it sounds like either one of those."

"It sounds to me as if you were going 'crik crik crik,'" said Harry.

"Maybe that's why they call him a 'cricket,'" said Tucker.

They all laughed. Tucker had a squeaky laugh that sounded as if he were hiccuping. Chester was feeling much happier now. The future did not seem nearly as gloomy as it had over in the pile of dirt in the corner.

"Are you going to stay a while in New York?" asked Tucker.

"I guess I'll have to," said Chester. "I don't know how to get home."

"Well, we could always take you to Grand Central Station and put you on a train going back to Connecticut," said Tucker. "But why don't you give the city a try."

Chester shook his head. "I'm afraid I won't get along in New York, he said.

"Oh sure you will!" squeaked Tucker Mouse. "Harry, suppose we take Chester up and show him Times Square. Would you like that, Chester?"

"I guess so," said Chester, although he was really a little leery of venturing out into New York City.

The three of them jumped down to the floor. The crack in the side of the newsstand was just wide enough for Harry to get through. As they crossed the station floor, Tucker pointed out the local sights of interest, such as the Nedick's lunch counter—Tucker spent a lot of time around there—and the Loft's candy store. Then they came to the drain pipe. Chester had to make short, little hops to keep from hitting his head as they went up. There seemed to be hundreds of twistings and turnings, and many other pipes that opened off the main route, but Tucker Mouse knew his way perfectly—even in the dark. At last, Chester saw light above them. One more hop brought him out onto the sidewalk. And there he gasped, holding his breath and crouching against the cement.

They were standing at one corner of the Times building, which is at the south end

of Times Square. Above the cricket, towers that seemed like mountains of light rose up into the night sky. Even this late, the neon signs were still blazing. Reds, blues, greens and yellows flashed down on him. And the air was full of the roar of traffic and the hum of human beings. It was as if Times Square were a kind of shell, with colors and noises breaking in great waves inside it. Chester's heart hurt him, and he closed his eyes. The sight was too terrible and beautiful for a cricket who up to now had measured high things by the height of his willow tree and sounds by the burble of a running brook.

"How do you like it?" asked Tucker Mouse.

"Well—it's—it's quite something," Chester stuttered.

"You should see it New Year's Eve," said Harry Cat.

Gradually Chester's eyes got used to the lights. He looked up. And way far above them above New York, and above the whole world, he made out a star that he knew was a star he used to look at back in Connecticut. When they had gone down to the station and Chester was in the matchbox again, he thought about that star. It made him feel better to think that there was one familiar thing, twinkling above him, amidst so much that was new and strange.

Selden, George. *The Cricket in Times Square*. New York: Farrar, Straus and Giroux, 1960.

THE FAVORITE UNCLE REMUS

JOEL CHANDLER HARRIS

Uncle Remus loves telling stories, especially to his nephew. The dialect he speaks in was used by blacks in Georgia before the end of slavery. If you listen very closely, you'll eventually forget how funny it sounds. And it'll be worth it, because Brer Rabbit, Brer Mink, Brer Tarrypin, Miss Cow and the other animals have some very funny adventures together.

Brer Rabbit is one smart rabbit. He starts building a house and gets all the other animals to help him out. Pretty soon, they're doing all the work. And once they're finished, Brer Rabbit figures out how to get rid of them so he can have the house all to himself.

BRER RABBIT GETS A HOUSE

ne evening, Miss Sally sent a large tray of food to Uncle Remus. The little boy accompanied the bearer of the tray and remained while the old man ate supper, expecting to hear another story when he had finished. Uncle Remus paused, straightened up, looked at the child over his spectacles, and said:

Now den, honey, all dese done fix. You set over dar, and I'll set over yer, en I'll sorter rustle roun' wid my 'membunce en see ef I kin call ter mine de tale 'bout how ole Brer Rabbit got 'im a two-story house widout layin' out much cash.

Uncle Remus stopped talking a little while and pretended to be trying to remember something. Finally he brightened up and began:

Hit tu'n out one time dat a whole lot er de creeturs tuck a notion dat dey'd go in cahoots wid buil'n' un um a house. Ole Brer B'ar, he was 'mongst um, en Brer Fox, en Brer Wolf, en Brer Coon, en Brer Possum. I won't make sho', but it seems like ter me dat plumb down ter ole Brer Mink wuz 'mongst um. Leas'ways, dey wuz a whole passel un um, en dey whirl in, dey did, en dey buil' de house in less'n no time. Brer Rabbit, he make like it make he head swim fer ter climb up on de scaffle, en likewise, he say it make 'im ketch de palsy fer ter wuk in de sun, but he got 'im a squar', en he stuck a pencil behime he year, en he went roun' medjun en markin'—medjun en markin'—en he wuz dat busy dat de udder creeturs say ter deyse'f he doin' most'us sight er wuk, en folks gwine 'long de big road say Brer Rabbit doin' mo' hard wuk dan de whole kit en bilin' un um. Yit all de time Brer Rabbit aint doin' nothin', en he des well bin layin' off in de shade scratchin' de fleas off'n 'im. De udder creeturs, dey buil' de house en, gentermens!, she wuz a fine un, too, mon. She'd 'a' bin a fine un dese days, let 'lone dem days. She had 'er upsta'rs, en down-sta'rs, en chimbleys all roun', en she had rooms fer all de creeturs w'at went inter cahoots en holp make it.

Brer Rabbit, he pick out one er de upsta'rs rooms, en he tuck'n got 'im a gun, en one er dese yer brass cannons, en he tuck'n put um in dar w'en de udder creeturs aint lookin', en den he tuck'n got 'im a tub er nasty slop-water, w'ich likewise he put in dar w'en dey aint lookin'. So den, w'en dey git de house all fix, en w'iles dey wuz all a-settin' in de parlor atter supper, Brer Rabbit, he sorter gap en stretch hisse'f, en make he skuses en say he b'lieve he'll go ter he room. W'en he git dar, en w'iles all de udder creeturs wuz a-laffin' en a-chattin' des ez sociable ez you please, Brer Rabbit, he stick he head out er de do'er he room en sing out:

"W'en a big man like me wanter set down, wharbouts he gwine ter set?" sezee.

Den de udder creeturs dey laff, en holler back:

"Ef big man like you can't set in a cheer, he better set down on de flo'."

"Watch out down dar, den," sez ole Brer Rabbit, sezee, "kaze I'm a gwine ter set down," sezee.

Wid dat, bang! went Brer Rabbit gun. Co'se, dis sorter 'stonish de creeturs, en dey look roun' at wunner nudder much ez ter sy, "W'at in de name er gracious is dat?" Dey listen, en listen, but dey don't year no mo' fuss, en 'twant long 'fo' dey got ter chattin' en jabberin' some mo'. Bimeby, Brer Rabbit stick he head outer he room do', en sing out:

"W'en a big man like me wanter sneeze, wharbouts he gwine ter sneezed at?"

Den de udder creeturs, dey tuck'n holler back:

"Ef big man like you aint a-gone gump, he kin sneeze anywhar he please."

"Watch out down dar, den," sez Brer Rabbit, sezee, "Kaze I'm gwine ter tu'n loose en sneeze right yer," sezee.

Wid dat Brer Rabbit let off his cannon—buldr-um-m-m. De winder glass dey shuck en rattle, en de house shuck like she gwine ter come down, en ole Brer B'ar, he fell out de rockin' cheer—kerblump! W'en de creeturs git sorter settle, Brer Possum en Brer Mink, dey up'n 'low dat Brer Rabbit got sech a monst'us bad cole, dey b'lieve dey'll step out and git some fresh a'r, but dem udder creeturs, dey say dey gwine ter stick it out; en atter w'ile, w'en dey get in a good way, Brer Rabbit, he sing out:

"W'en a big man like me take a chaw terbarker, wharbouts he gwine ter spit?"

Den de udder creeturs, dey holler back, dey did, sorter like deyer mad:

"Big man er little man, spit whar you please."

Den Brer Rabbit, he squall out:

"Dis de way a big man spit!" en wid dat he tilt over de tub er slop-water, en w'en de udder creeturs year it come a-sloshin' down de sta'r-steps, gentermens!, dey des histed deyse'f outer dar. Some un um went out de back do', en some un um went ou de front do', en some un um fell out de winders; some went one way, en some went nudder way; but dey all went sailin' out.

Brer Rabbit, he des tuck'n shot up de house en fassen de winders, en den he go ter bed, he did, en pull de coverled up roun' he years, en he sleep like a man w'at aint owe nobody nothin': en needer do he owe u, kaze ef dem udder creeturs gwine git skeered en run off fum der own house, w'at business is dat er Brer Rabbit? Dat w'at I like ter know

Harris, Joel Chandler. *The Favorite Uncle Remus.* New York: Houghton Miflin, 1948.

CROW AND WEASEL

BARRY LOPEZ

In this fable, inspired by Native American culture, Crow and Weasel go on an expedition to the lands farther north than their people have ever gone before. In the following passage, we join them as they embark on this trip, one that will test the limits of their courage.

Crow and Weasel set out smartly, eager to be off. Over the previous winter they had agreed between themselves that they wanted to travel farther north than anyone had ever gone, farther north than their people's stories went. But their fathers had said no, it was a crazy idea, a boy's idea, and their plans had come to an end. They began talking, instead, about heading south into Aristola country to hunt for horses. Then Mountain Lion had had his dream. In the dream he saw Crow and Weasel standing on the banks of a river, the one called the Floating Ashes, the river farthest to the north in their country. In speaking about it with the other elders, Mountain Lion came to the conclusion that the two young men should revive their plans. So he convinced their fathers.

But Crow and Weasel felt their journey now bore the weight of Mountain Lion's dream. And his words to behave well and to remember their people lay heavily upon them. They forded the creek north of the village and turned to look back. It was hard to tell whether anyone returned their looks.

"We won't see this for a long time," said Crow, musing.

"Yes, but there are good signs for this trip," answered Weasel. "The grass is already good. The horses are young, strong—like us. Our mothers have made spare moccasins and given us dried meat. And I, at least, between the two of us, am a very fine hunter. What more could we ask?"

"We could ask for the blessings of the Above Ones."

The next day they came on the river called Covered with Ashes, or Floating Ashes. It was a broad, fast, dark-water river. When they swam the horses across, Crow especially struggled. They landed far downstream on the other side. From here on, they understood, no one of their people, truly, had ever been. They dried out their things and made prayers to the Ones Above, the way they bad been taught.

That evening they saw the dark line of the forest in the distance.

"From now on," said Crow, as they crawled under their robes, "I think it will get more difficult" He caught his friend's eye. "Also better."

They had never seen anything like the forest. The trees were not at all like alders or cottonwoods, but taller, their leaves like needles, their limbs heavy, their trunks dark. and they were so close together it was hard to ride through them. Crow and Weasel had to get off and lead their horses. They were without a clear view of the sky, and being hemmed in like this made them uneasy and the horses irritable. The silence of the open prairie did not disturb them like this silence, which was oppressive and somehow threatening.

The first night they tried to sleep in the forest Weasel tossed fitfully. He began to wonder what going farther north than anyone had ever gone before really meant. Hadn't they done that, by crossing the Floating Ashes and entering the forest? How far would this forest stretch on?

Crow lay awake most of the night as well. He was disturbed, like his friend, about the way the dampness in the woods and the darkness were crowding them. But he was wondering, too, who the trees might be. They were beings, he knew. If your medicine was strong enough, you might be able to talk with them, ask their advice.

In the morning Weasel wondered how to raise the question of how far they were going to go, but he could sense from Crow's serious mood that he should not say anything.

With extreme care and with a nod of agreement from his companion, Crow took up the medicine pipe Mountain Lion had given them and filled the bowl. He lit the mixture of bearberry leaves and dried willow and offered it with prayers in four directions and to the spirits above and below. Then he turned to a group of trees before him, tall and all of them looking ancient. He held the smoking pipe up to them in his two hands.

"My relatives," Crow began. "My brother and I come from far away in the south. We have never seen any beings like you. We can see that you are old and know that you must be very wise. Please, take pity on us, poor travelers far from home, and tell us who you are and what trail this is that we are on."

Crow held the smoking pipe high over his head. A faint breeze stirred the needles of the trees.

"You young men," began a voice that at first was almost too thin to hear, "are brave to come in here." The horses, which were tied to the trees, stamped and pivoted on their reigns. "You have already traveled far," said the voice, getting stronger now and sounding more like a voice, "but you have farther to go. We are glad to help you. Sit down, and listen."

Crow and Weasel sat together before the trees, and the voice went on. "We knew of your journey from Mountain Lion's dream, which came to us on the wind. And we know of your travels beyond the Floating Ashes River, for it had been passed along by the cotton-woods and the willows. Since our food comes to us from the earth we stand on and our longing for wisdom is satisfied by what comes to us on the wind, we never feel this need that you have to move about, to go off and discover new country. But we respect this way with you.

"The forest is dark. You will have to travel many days before you come again to country that is open. But do not be concerned. You will see a flicker. Follow her. She will show you a path. In one more moon, the Pollen Moon, you will come to our country of lakes. Our people will be very few, until there are none.

"Tell us," said the voice, "do you intend to go farther than that?"

Weasel was about to answer yes, emphatically, but he said nothing.

"Our fathers and mothers," said Crow, "with your help we will travel that far. Beyond that, we do not know. Mountain Lion told us to watch carefully. We will look for signs and try to understand them properly. We're young. We do not know exactly how to do this. Even if we become afraid, or feel lost, we will go on, watching for a sign."

The limbs of the trees before them brushed the air, and they heard the voice again. "Yes," it said. "Be strong. Go now."

Crow and Weasel packed their few things and left. Shortly they saw a yellow-shafted flicker and began to follow her. In the morning they saw her again. It went on like that for several days, following the flashes of golden light from underneath her wings.

Crow whispered his friend's name. "Weasel. Are you awake?"

"Yes. Do you hear something?"

"No. I have been thinking about being in the Floating Ashes River."

"What about it?"

"When we were swimming the horses over, I felt something come up around my legs. It took hold and started to pull me under."

"What! Why didn't you tell me?"

"I am still trying to understand it," said Crow.

"What is there to understand? You just get away from something like that—right away. You don't live in the water. A river, that's not your place."

"You have made this clearer for me," said Crow after a moment.

"What do you mean?"

"I think what it was saying to me was this: with some things in life you don't try to fight. A young man wants to fight everything, it is in him to do that. A grown man knows to leave certain things alone. Some things you don't answer. It doesn't mean you have no courage."

Weasel looked over at Crow in the dark. "My friend, were you afraid to tell me what happened back there because I would say you had no courage?"

"Something like that."

"Well, you may not always get your arrows to fly straight, and sometimes you think too much, but you are courageous, too. Take my word for it."

"It is good to be traveling together," said Crow.

"Yes," said Weasel. "And I will be happy when we are out of these woods."

At the beginning of the Red Berry Moon—and how odd this was, they thought, for the Red Berry Moon would have already come and gone at home—far to the south, they emerged from the trees. The air was immediately warmer, and dryer. The horses, who for so long had walked in a broken gait over the twisting, narrow path, were eager to run, to stretch out.

"Yahoo!" shouted Weasel. "Let's go!"

"Have you no manners?" said Crow, steadying his horse and scowling at his friend. Crow dismounted, gave Weasel his rein and stepped back to the forest.

"Little Sister," he cried out. "Thank you for guiding us here. Thank you for taking care of us all this way. Wherever we go we will remember your kindness. We will hold your people in regard and tell our people always to treat you well. Wah-hey!"

The flicker flew up in the air, flashing the gold beneath her wings one last time, and then flew back into the forest.

Weasel handed Crow his rein.

"It was not good of me to be thinking so much of myself," said Weasel.

"Your exuberance," said Crow, "reminds me not to take life too seriously, although here it was necessary to pay our respects. Now let us go. I'll race you to the top of that ridge!"

Lopez, Barry. *Crow and Weasel.* San Francisco: North Point Press, 1990.

THE VOYAGES OF DOCTOR DOLITTLE

HUGH LOFTING

Young Tommy Stubbins of Puddleby-on-the-Marsh has the honor of accompanying the world-renowned naturalist, Doctor John Dolittle, on an exploratory voyage to South America. Tommy's greatest wish is to one day learn to talk to the animals as Doctor Dolittle can.

During a short stop in the Spanish Capa Blanca Islands, Doctor Dolittle is horrified by the native tradition of weekly bullfights. He challenges their most famous matador to a bullfighting competition, with the condition that if he is the victor, there will no longer be bullfights on the islands. The bulls, anxious to end the fights themselves, are more than happy to help Doctor Dolittle who, of course, speaks their language.

Chapter 8 THE GREAT BULLFIGHT

he next day was a great day in Monteverde. All the streets were hung with flags, and everywhere gaily dressed crowds were to be seen flocking toward the bull-ring, as the big circus was called where the fights took place.

The news of the Doctor's challenge had gone around the town and, it seemed, had caused much amusement to the islanders. The very idea of a mere foreigner daring to match against the great Pepito De Malaga!

The Doctor had borrowed a bullfighter's suit from Don Enrique; and very gay and wonderful he looked in it, though Bumpo and I had hard work getting the waistcoat to close in front and, even then, the buttons kept bursting off it in all directions.

When we set out from the harbor to walk to the bullring, crowds of small boys ran after us making fun of the Doctor's fatness, calling out, "Juan Hagapoco, el grueso matador!" which is Spanish for "John Dolittle, the fat bullfighter."

As soon as we arrived, the Doctor said he would like to take a look at the bulls before the fight began, and we were at once led to the bullpen where, behind a high railing, six enormous black bulls were tramping around wildly.

In a few hurried words and signs, the Doctor told the bulls what he was going to do and gave them careful instructions for their part of the show. The poor creatures were tremendously glad when they heard that there was a chance of bullfighting being stopped, and they promised to do exactly as they were told.

Of course, the man who took us in there didn't understand what we were doing. He merely thought the fat Englishman was crazy when he saw the Doctor making signs and talking in ox tongue.

From there, the Doctor went to the matadors' dressing rooms while Bumpo and I with Polynesia made our way into the bullring and took our seats in the great open-air theater.

It was a very gay sight. Thousands of ladies and gentlemen were there, all dressed in their smartest clothes, and everybody seemed very happy and cheerful.

Right at the beginning, Don Enrique got up and explained to the people that the first item on the program was to be a match between the English Doctor and Pepito de Malaga. He told them what he had promised if the Doctor should win. But the people did not seem to think there was much chance of that. A roar of laughter went up at the very mention of such a thing.

When Pepito came into the ring everybody cheered, the ladies blew kisses, and the men clapped and waved their hats.

Presently, a large door on the other side of the ring was rolled back and in galloped one of the bulls; then the door was closed again. He waved his red cloak, and the bull rushed at him.

Pepito stepped nimbly aside, and the people cheered again.

After about ten minutes of this kind of thing, the small door into the matadors' dressing room opened, and the Doctor strolled into the ring. As soon as his fat figure, dressed in sky-blue velvet, appeared, the crowd rocked in their seats with laughter.

Juan Hagapoco, as they had called him, walked out into the center of the ring and bowed ceremoniously to the ladies in the boxes. Then he bowed to the bull. Then he bowed to Pepito. While he was bowing to Pepito's assistant, the bull started to rush at him from behind.

"Look out! Look out! The bull! You will be killed!" yelled the crowd.

But the Doctor calmly finished his bow. Then turning round he folded his arms, fixed the onrushing bull with his eye, and frowned a terrible frown.

Presently, a curious thing happened: The bull's speed got slower and slower. It almost looked as though he were afraid of that frown. Soon he stopped altogether. The Doctor shook his finger at him. He began to tremble. At last, tucking his tail between his legs, the bull turned around and ran away.

The crowd gasped. This was something new in bullfighting, to have the bull running away from the man instead of the man away from the bull. At last in the tenth lap, with a final burst of speed, Juan Hagapoco, the English matador, caught the poor bull by the tail.

Then leading the now timid creature into the middle of the ring, the Doctor made him do all manner of tricks: standing on the hind legs, standing on the front legs, dancing, hopping, rolling over. He finished by making the bull kneel down; then he got onto his back and did handsprings and other acrobatics on the beast's horns.

Finally, the Doctor turned toward Don Enrique's seat and bowing said in a loud voice, "This bull is no good anymore. He's terrified and out of breath. Take him away, please."

"Does the caballero wish for a fresh bull?" asked Don Enrique.

"No," said the Doctor, "I want five fresh bulls. And I would like them all in the ring at once, please."

At this, a cry of horror burst from the people. They had been used to seeing matadors escaping from one bull at a time. But five! . . . That must mean certain death.

A dreadful silence hung over the great theater as the heavy door into the bull pen was rolled back. Then with a roar, the five big bulls bounded into the ring.

"Look fierce," I heard the Doctor call to them in cattle language. "Don't scatter. Keep close. Get ready for a rush. Take Pepito, the one in purple, first. But for heaven's sake, don't kill him. Just chase him out of the ring. Now then, all together, go for him!"

The bulls put down their heads and, all in line like a squadron of cavalry, charged across the ring straight for poor Pepito.

For one moment, the Spaniard tried his hardest to look brave. But the sight of the five pairs of horns coming at him at full gallop was too much. He turned white to the lips, ran for the fence, vaulted it, and disappeared.

The rest of the show was really well worth seeing. First, all five bulls went raging around the ring, butting at the fence with their horns, pawing up the sand, hunting for something to kill. Then each one in turn would pretend to catch sight of the Doctor for the first time and, giving a bellow of rage, would lower his wicked-looking horns and shoot like an arrow across the ring as though he meant to toss him to the sky.

It was really frightfully exciting. And even I, who knew it was all arranged beforehand, held my breath in terror for the Doctor's life when I saw how near they came to sticking him. But just at the last moment, when the horns' points were two inches from the sky-blue waistcoat, the Doctor would spring nimbly to one side and the great brutes would go thundering harmlessly by, missing him by no more than a hair.

One woman in the crowd got quite hysterical and screamed up to Don Enrique, "Stop the fight! He is too brave a man to be killed. This is the most wonderful matador in the world. Let him live! Stop the fight!"

Then catching each of them by the horns, one after another, he would give their heads a sudden twist and throw them down flat on the sand. The great fellows acted their parts extremely well. They lay there panting on the ground where the Doctor threw them as if they were exhausted and completely beaten.

Then with a final bow to the ladies, John Dolittle took a cigar from his pocket, lit it, and strolled out of the ring.

Lofting, Hugh. *The Voyages of Doctor Dolittle*. New York: Dell Publishing, Bantam Doubleday Dell Publishing Group, Inc., 1988.

FREDDY THE COWBOY

WALTER R. BROOKS

Freddy the Cowboy is only one of the many books by Walter Brooks featuring a remarkable pig named Freddy, and all his friends at Beans' farm, where all of the animals can talk. Freddy has also been a detective, a pilot, and a politician among other professions.

In this story, Freddy rescues a horse named Cyclone (Cy for short) from Mr. Flint, the cruel owner of a dude ranch. The animals then learn that Mr. Flint plans to rob the First Animal Bank, so Freddy puts on his best cowboy accent and challenges him to a shooting contest to dissuade him from his plan. Freddy only uses blanks in his gun—but he manages to win the contest with the help of some crafty mice.

The terms of the shooting match were simple. Four tin cans were put up on posts of the corral. Then when the horses were driven off out of the way into the smaller corral by the house, Mr. Flint would ride down past at a distance of thirty yards and try to shoot the cans off the posts. He was allowed six shots, and would ride at a canter. It was a pretty severe test of marksmanship.

It was a cool, clear night. The moon was high now, and almost bright enough to read by. Certainly, it was bright enough to shoot by. Mr. Flint rode to the end of the corral and then, with his gun swinging in his hand, cantered down once past the posts to get the distance. Then he went back and rode down again, and this time he shot. He fired twice at the first can before he knocked it off the post, but the second and third ones he hit at the first try. With two cartridges left in his gun, he fired more carefully at the fourth can and missed; he fired quickly again and knocked it off the post.

The dudes applauded, and Mr. Flint pulled up besides Freddy. "Let's see you tie that, pig."

"I ain't aimin' to tie it, pardner," said Freddy. "That was right good plain shooting, but what I'm aimin' to show you is something real fancy." He started to pick up four more cans from the pile that had been brought out.

"Jasper'll put up the cans for you," said Mr. Flint.

"I'll put 'em up myself," said Freddy. I've heard of cans bein' fastened down so that they wouldn't fall off if you hit 'em with a cannon." He went over and placed the cans on the posts. And of course, on each post he put a mouse.

209

The mice had been busy, each chewing a wad of gum, and now their job was to stick one end of a piece of string to each can, throw the loose end down, run to the ground, and be ready to pull.

"Now, folks," he said, "this here ain't going to be a real exhibition, because I'm a little out of trainin'. Of course, Flint here has done right well for a feller that ain't never practiced shootin' off anything but his mouth. I wouldn't say nothing about it, except he's seen fit to call me pigs and such-like. And I still wouldn't say anything about it if I hadn't seen him beating a horse—this horse, folks, which I had to buy it off him to keep him from killing it."

Mr. Flint reined in closer to Freddy. "Your keep your mouth shut, you little tramp," he said angrily, "or I'll—Ouch!" he yelled suddenly. For he had forgotten about Cy, who had swung round and nipped him sharply in the leg.

Freddy rode up to the end of the corral. "O.K., Cy," he said, and the pony gathered his legs under him and sprang. They came down past the posts at a dead run. As they passed the first post, Freddy didn't shoot, and Jasper said with a chuckle to Mr. Flint, "The dope ain't even got his gun out."

But opposite the second post Freddy snatched his gun from the holster, and as fast as he could pull the trigger fired four shots—bang, bang, bang, bang!—and at each bang a can jumped or toppled from a post. Indeed, one of them jumped before the bang came—probably because Cousin Augustus was so excited—but nobody noticed.

The dudes had applauded Mr. Flint, but now they shouted and cheered and crowded around Freddy.

"Shucks," said Freddy, "'twasn't anything. I just want to show this Mr. Flint why it ain't healthy for him to talk about fighting me. And also and furthermore, I want to help him to keep out of the way of temptation." He rode up closer to Mr. Flint. "Temptation is a terrible bad thing to get into, Mr. Flint," he said. "Like it might be the temptation to rob a bank. You think how nice it would be to have all that money without working for it—just pulling up a trap door and climbing down and scooping it up. But suppose a bullet—like it might be from this gun of mine—comes climbing down after you, hey? Comes right down and pokes its cold nose into your ribs! Hey? You better think it over carefully, Mr. Flint."

"I don't know what you're talking about," said Mr. Flint sullenly.

"Good," said Freddy. "Then there's no harm done. So good evening, folks. Just hand me my guitar, Jasper." He waved his hand and then rode off, stopping opposite the last post of the corral fence where he pretended to tune his guitar while the mice climbed up Cy's foreleg and into his pockets. Then he went on, singing:

"Yippy-i-dee! Yippy-i-day!
Cowboy Bean is coming this way.

FREDDY THE COWBOY *Walter R. Brooks*

He's sharp as a needle and bright as a dollar,
Wears a No. 3 shoe and a 16 collar.
He's full of vim and he's full of vigor,
Fast on the draw and quick on the trigger.
So all you bandits and thieves take warning,
Or you'll be in a hospital bed by morning,
and the doc'll give you a kind of shake,
And he'll hear the rattle that the bullets make,
And he'll shake his head and he'll say: 'O my!
I can't cure this and I ain't going to try."

Brooks, Walter. *Freddy the Cowboy.* New York: Alfred A. Knopf, 1950.

FROG AND TOAD TOGETHER

Arnold Lobel

Join these two friends–Frog and Toad–on their engrossing adventures. The following excerpt includes the stories of Spring, The Story, *and* Down the Hill.

SPRING

Frog ran up the path to Toad's house. He knocked on the front door. There was no answer.

"Toad, Toad," shouted Frog, "wake up. It is spring!"

"Blah," said a voice from inside the house.

"Toad! Toad!" cried Frog. "The sun is shining! The snow is melting. Wake up!"

"I am not here," said the voice.

Frog walked into the house. It was dark. All the shutters were closed. "Toad, where are you?" called Frog.

"Go away," said the voice from a corner of the room.

Toad was lying in bed. He had pulled all the covers over his head. Frog pushed Toad out of bed. He pushed him out of the house and onto the front porch. Toad blinked in the bright sun.

"Help!" said Toad. "I cannot see anything."

"Don't be silly," said Frog. "What you see is the clear warm light of April. And it means that we can begin a whole new year together, Toad. Think of it," said Frog. "We will skip through the meadows and run through the woods and swim in the river. In the evenings we will sit right here on this front porch and count the stars."

"You can count them, Frog," said Toad. "I will be too tired. I am going back to bed."

Toad went back into the house. He got into the bed and pulled the covers over his head again. "But, Toad," cried Frog, "You will miss all the fun!"

"Listen, Frog," said Toad. "How long have I been asleep?"

"You have been asleep since November," said Frog.

"Well then," said Toad, "a little more sleep will not hurt me. Come back again and wake me up at about half past May. Good night, Frog."

"But, Toad," said Frog, "I will be lonely until then."

Toad did not answer. He had fallen asleep. Frog looked at Toad's calendar. The

212

November page was still on, so Frog tore off the November page. He tore off the December page. And the January page, the February page, and the March page. He came to the April page. Frog tore off the April page too.

Then Frog ran back to Toad's bed. "Toad, Toad, wake up. It is May now."

"What?" said Toad.

"Can it be May so soon?"

"Yes," said Frog.

"Look at your calendar."

Toad looked at the calendar. The May page was on top.

"Why, it is May!" said Toad as he climbed out of bed. Then he and Frog ran outside to see how the world was looking in the spring.

THE STORY

ne day in summer Frog was not feeling well.

Toad said, "Frog, you are looking quite green."

"But I always look green," said Frog. "I am a frog."

"Today you look very green even for a frog," said Toad. "Get into my bed and rest."

Toad made Frog a cup of hot tea. Frog drank the tea, and then he said, "Tell me a story while I am resting."

"All right," said Toad. "Let me think of a story to tell you."

Toad thought and thought. But he could not think of a story to tell Frog.

"I will go out on the front porch and walk up and down," said Toad. "Perhaps that will help me to think of a story."

Toad walked up and down on the porch for a long time. But he could not think of a story to tell Frog. Then toad went into the house and stood on his head.

"Why are you standing on your head?" asked Frog.

"I hope that if I stand on my head, it will help me to think of a story," said Toad. Toad stood on his head for a long time. But he could not think of a story to tell Frog. Then Toad poured a glass of water over his head.

"Why are you pouring water over your head?" asked Frog.

"I hope that if I pour water over my head, it will help me to think of a story," said Toad.

Toad poured many glasses of water over his head.

But he could not think of a story to tell Frog. Then Toad began to bang his head against the wall.

"Why are you banging your head against the wall?" asked Frog.

"I hope that if I bang my head against the wall hard enough, it will help me to think of a story," said Toad.

"I am feeling much better now, Toad," said Frog. "I do not think I need a story anymore."

"Then you get out of bed and let me get into it," said Toad, "because now I feel terrible."

Frog said, "Would you like me to tell you a story, Toad?"

"Yes," said Toad, "if you know one."

"Once upon a time," said Frog, "there were two good friends, a frog and a toad. The frog was not feeling well. He asked his friend the toad to tell him a story. The toad could not think of story. He walked up and down on the porch but he could not think of a story. He stood on his head, but he could not think of a story. He poured water over his head, but he could not think of a story. He banged his head against the wall, but he could not think of a story.

"Then the toad did not feel so well, and the frog was feeling better. So the toad went to bed and the frog got up and told him a story. The end. How was that, Toad?" said Frog.

But Toad did not answer. He had fallen asleep.

DOWN THE HILL

rog knocked at Toad's door.

"Toad, wake up," he cried. "Come out and see how wonderful the winter is!"

"I will not," said Toad. "I am in my warm bed."

"Winter is beautiful," said Frog. "Come out and have fun."

"Blah," said Toad. "I do not have any winter clothes."

Frog came into the house.

"I have brought you some things to wear," he said. Frog pulled snowpants up over the bottom of Toad.

He put a hat and scarf on Toad's head.

"Help!" cried Toad. "My best friend is trying to kill me!"

"I am only getting you ready for winter," said Frog.

Frog and Toad went outside. They tramped through the snow.

"We will ride down this big hill on my sled," said Frog.

"Not me," said Toad.

"Do not be afraid," said Frog. "I will be with you on the sled. It will be a fine, fast ride. Toad, you sit in front. I will sit right behind you."

The sled began to move down the hill.

"Here we go!" said Frog. There was a bump. Frog fell off the sled. Toad rushed past trees and rocks.

"Frog, I am glad that you are here," said Toad.

Toad leaped over a snowbank.

"I could not steer the sled without you, Frog," he said.

"You are right. Winter is fun!"

A crow flew nearby.

"Hello Crow," shouted Toad.

"Look at Frog and me. We can ride a sled better than anybody in the world!"

"But Toad," said the crow, "you are alone on the sled."

Toad looked around. He saw that Frog was not there.

"I AM ALL ALONE!" screamed Toad.

Bang! The sled hit a tree. Thud! The sled hit a rock. Plop! The sled dived into the snow.

Frog came running down the hill. He pulled Toad out of the snow.

"I saw everything," said Frog. "You did very well by yourself."

"I did not," said Toad. "But there is one thing I can do by myself."

"What is that?" asked Frog.

"I can go home," said Toad. "Winter may be beautiful, but bed is much better."

Lobel, Arnold. *Frog and Toad Together.* New York: HarperCollins Publishers, 1970.

OLD MOTHER WEST WIND

Thornton W. Burgess

Old Mother West Wind is a classic collection of tales, first published in 1910, about a group of mischievous woodland creatures.

Chapter 4 WHY JIMMY SKUNK WEARS STRIPES

Jimmy Skunk, as everybody knows, wears a striped suit, a suit of black and white. There was a time, long, long ago, when all the Skunk family wore black. They were very, very proud of them and took the greatest care of them, brushing them carefully ever so many times a day.

There was a Jimmy Skunk then, just as there is now, and he was head of all the Skunk family. Now this Jimmy Skunk was very proud and thought himself very much of a gentleman. He was very independent and cared for no one. Like a great many other independent people, he did not always consider the rights of others. Indeed, it was hinted in the wood and on the Green Meadows that not all of Jimmy Skunk's doings would bear the light of day. It was openly said that he was altogether too fond of prowling about at night. But no one could prove that he was responsible for mischief done in the night, for no one saw him. You see, his coat was so black that in the darkness of the night it was not visible at all.

Now about this time of which I am telling you, Mrs. Ruffed Grouse made a nest at the foot of the Great Pine, and in it she laid fifteen beautiful buff eggs. Mrs. Grouse was very happy, very happy indeed, and all the little meadow folks who knew of her happiness were happy too, for they all loved shy, demure little Mrs. Grouse. Every morning when Peter Rabbit trotted down the Lone Little Path through the wood past the Great Pine he would stop for a few minutes to chat with Mrs. Grouse. Happy Jack Squirrel would bring her the news every afternoon. The Merry Little Breezes of Old Mother West Wind would run up a dozen times a day to see how she was getting along.

One morning Peter Rabbit, coming down the Lone Little Path for his usual morning call, found a terrible state of affairs. Poor little Mrs. Grouse was heartbroken. All about the foot of the Great Pine lay the empty shells of her beautiful eggs. They had been broken and scattered this way and that.

"How did it happen?" asked Peter Rabbit.

"I don't know," sobbed poor little Mrs. Grouse. "In the night when I was fast asleep something pounced upon me. I managed to get away and fly up in the top of the Great Pine. In the morning I found all my eggs broken, just as you see them here."

Peter Rabbit looked the ground over very carefully. He hunted around behind the Great Pine, he looked under the bushes, he studied the ground with a very wise air. Then he hopped off down the Lone Little Path to the Green Meadows. He stopped at the house of Johnny Chuck.

"What makes your eyes so big and round?" asked Johnny Chuck.

Peter Rabbit came very close so as to whisper in Johnny Chuck's ear, and told him all that he had seen. Together they went to Jimmy Skunk's house. Jimmy Skunk was in bed. He was very sleepy and very cross when he came to the door. Peter Rabbit told him what he had seen.

"Too bad! Too bad!" said Jimmy Skunk, and yawned sleepily.

"Won't you join us in trying to find out who did it?" asked Johnny Chuck.

Jimmy Skunk said he would be delighted to come but that he had some other business that morning and he would join them in the afternoon. Peter Rabbit and Johnny Chuck went on. Pretty soon they met the Merry Little Breezes and told them the dreadful story.

"What shall we do?" asked Johnny Chuck.

"We'll hurry over and tell Old Dame Nature," cried the Merry Little Breezes, "and ask her what to do."

So away flew the Merry Little Breezes to Old Dame Nature and told her all the dreadful story. Old Dame Nature listened very attentively. Then she sent the Merry Little Breezes to all the little meadow folks to tell everyone to be at the Great Pine that afternoon. Now whatever Old Dame Nature commanded, all the little meadow folks were obliged to do. They did not dare to disobey her. Promptly at four o'clock that afternoon all the little meadow folks were gathered around the foot of the Great Pine. Brokenhearted Little Mrs. Ruffed Grouse sat beside her empty nest, with all the broken shells about her.

Reddy Fox, Peter Rabbit, Johnny Chuck, Billy Mink, Little Joe Otter, Jerry Muskrat, Hooty the Owl, Bobby Coon, Sammy Jay, Blacky the Crow, Grandfather Frog, Mr. Toad, Spotty the Turtle, the Merry Little Breezes—all were there. Last of all came Jimmy Skunk. Very handsome he looked in his shining black coat, and very sorry he appeared that such a dreadful thing should have happened. He told Mrs. Grouse how badly he felt, and he loudly demanded that the culprit should be found out and severely punished.

Old Dame Nature has the most smiling face in the world, but this time it was very, very grave indeed. First she asked little Mrs. Grouse to tell her story all over again that all might hear. Then each in turn was asked to tell where he had been the night before.

Johnny Chuck, Happy Jack Squirrel, Striped Chipmunk, Sammy Jay and Blacky the Crow had gone to bed when Mr. Sun went down behind the Purple Hills. Jerry Muskrat, Billy Mink, Little Joe Otter, Grandfather Frog and Spotty the Turtle had not left the Smiling Pool. Bobby Coon had been down in Farmer Brown's cornfield. Hooty the Owl had been hunting in the lower end of the Green Meadows. Peter Rabbit had been down in the berry patch. Mr. Toad had been under the big piece of bark which he called a house.

Old Dame Nature called on Jimmy Skunk last of all. Jimmy protested that he had been very, very tired and had gone to bed very early indeed and had slept the whole night through.

Then Old Dame Nature asked Peter Rabbit what he had found among the egg shells that morning.

Peter Rabbit hopped out and laid three long black hairs before Old Dame Nature "These," said Peter Rabbit, "are what I found among the egg shells."

Then Old Dame Nature called Johnny Chuck. "Tell us, Johnny Chuck," said she, "what you saw when you called at Jimmy Skunk's house this morning."

"I saw Jimmy Skunk," said Johnny Chuck, "and Jimmy seemed very, very sleepy. It seemed to me that his whiskers were yellow."

"That will do," said Old Dame Nature, and then she called Old Mother West Wind.

"What time did you come down on the Green Meadows this morning?" asked Old Dame Nature.

"Just at the break of day," said Old Mother West Wind, "as Mr. Sun was coming up from behind the Purple Hills."

"And whom did you see so early in the morning?" asked Old Dame Nature.

"I saw Bobby Coon coming home from old Farmer Brown's cornfield," said Old Mother West Wind. "I saw Hooty the Owl coming back from the other end of the Green Meadows. I saw Peter Rabbit down in the berry patch. Last of all, I saw something like a black shadow coming down the Lone Little Path toward the house of Jimmy Skunk."

Everyone was looking very hard at Jimmy Skunk. Jimmy began to look very unhappy and very uneasy.

"Who wears a black coat?" asked Dame Nature.

"Jimmy Skunk!" shouted all the little meadow folks.

"What might make whiskers yellow?" asked Old Dame Nature.

No one seemed to know at first then Peter Rabbit spoke up. "It might be the yolk of an egg," said Peter Rabbit.

"Who are likely to be sleepy on a bright sunny morning?" asked Old Dame Nature.

"People who have been out all night," said Johnny Chuck, who always goes to bed with the sun.

"Jimmy Skunk," said Old Dame Nature, and her voice was very stern, very stern indeed, and her face was very grave, "Jimmy Skunk, I accuse you of having broken and eaten the eggs of Mrs. Grouse. What have you to say for yourself?"

Jimmy Skunk hung his head. He hadn't a word to say. He just wanted to sneak away by himself.

"Jimmy Skunk," said Old Dame Nature, "because your handsome black coat of which you are so proud had made it possible for you to move about in the night without being seen, and because we can no longer trust you upon your honor, henceforth you and your descendants shall wear a striped coat, which is the sign that you cannot be trusted. Your coat hereafter shall be black and white, so that when you move about in the night you will always be visible."

And that is why to this day Jimmy Skunk wears a striped suit of black and white.

Burgess, Thornton W. *Old Mother West Wind*. New York: Henry Holt and Company, 1990.

REDWALL

BRIAN JACQUES

*In Mossflower country lies Redwall Abbey, where a holy order of peaceful mice has lived for gener-
ations, among them, the eager young novice, Matthias. A sacred tapestry hangs in the Great Hall
of Redwall depicting Martin the Warrior, hero and savior of Redwall, from back in the days when
Cluny the Scourge, an immense and diabolical bilge rat, threatened to take over the Abbey.*

*And now Cluny is back—with an army of hundreds of savage rats; they've stolen the tapestry and
are soon coming back to take it all. In the following two excerpts you will see brave young Matthias
retrieve the precious tapestry from Saint Ninian's church where the rat army is encamped. He winds
up making a loyal new friend, and a heroic rescue of some hostages as well.*

PART I

The rain stopped. Within minutes the hot June sun burst down on Mossflower, as
if in apology for its absence. Clouds of steaming mist arose from the woodland
floor, mingling with the golden shafts slanting down through the trees. The birds
began singing. Each flower and blade of grass was decked out in jeweled pendantry with
necklaces of sparkling raindrops.

The sudden warmth flooded over Matthias, cheering him onwards. Humming a tune
beneath his breath, he strode out with a will, almost breaking from the cover of the trees
straight out into the meadowland. He checked himself just in time. Directly ahead lay a
vast overgrown area which was neither pasture nor meadow. It was the common land that
had once belonged within the curtilage of St. Ninian's.

Matthias crouched at the edge of the woods. He could see the back of the church.
There were ten or twelve rats patrolling it, some distance away. Before he dealt with that
problem there was still the common land to be crossed. Clumps of thistle and slight
ground hummocks would be his only cover. The young mouse spoke his thoughts aloud.
"Hmm, this could present a little problem."

A strange voice answered him. "Problem, a little problem? Well, at least it's not a
fully-grown adult problem."

Matthias squeaked aloud with fright. Whirling about, he looked for the source of the
mystery voice. There was no one about. Taking a grip of himself he squared his shoulders
and called out boldly: "Come out here this instant and show yourself!"

The voice answered. It seemed to come from directly in front of him "Show m'self indeed! How many pairs of eyes d'you want, young feller, eh, eh? Fine state of affairs, bless m'soul! What, what!"

Matthias narrowed his eyes and looked hard. . . still nothing.

"I warn you, come out and show yourself," he shouted irritably. "I'm in no mood for playing games."

As if by magic a lanky hare popped up right beside Matthias. An odd, patchworked creature, his fur was an ashen hue with blots of grey and light-brown-flecked white on the underbelly. He was very tall, with formidable hefty hind legs and a comical, pouched face topped off by two immense ears which flopped about of their own accord. With a court-ly old-fashioned manner the hare made a leg, bowing gracefully. His voice carried a slight-ly affected quaver.

"Basil Stag Hare at your service, sir! Expert scout, hindleg fighter, wilderness guide, and camouflage specialist, ahem, liberator of tender young crops, carrots, lettuce, and other such strange beasts. Pray tell me whom I have the pleasure of addressing, and please state the nature of your little problem."

Matthias decided the peculiar hare was either slightly mad or tipsy, but his outmod-ed manner was certainly friendly. The young mouse humored him accordingly, bowing low with a paw at his waist.

"Good day to you, Mr. Basil Stag Hare. My name is Matthias. I am a novice in the Order of Redwall mice. My immediate problem is to cross this land to the church over yonder without being discovered by the rats who are guarding it."

Basil Stag Hare tapped one of his huge feet gently on the ground. "Matthias," he laughed. "What an odd name, to be sure!"

The young mouse laughed back as he replied, "Not half as odd as your own name. Whoever heard of a hare being called Basil Stag?"

The hare disappeared momentarily. He reappeared next to Matthias. "Ah well, Hare's the family name, don't y'know. My parents named me Basil, though the old mater want-ed to be called Columbine Agnes. Always longed for a young lass, she did."

"But why Stag?" Matthias inquired.

"Noble creatures, stags," the hare sighed. "Did I ever tell you I wanted to be one; a mag-nificent royal stag with great coat-hanger antlers? So, I went down to the jolly old river one night and christened m'self Stag! Had two toads and a newt as witnesses, y'know. Oh yes."

Matthias was unable to hide his merriment. He sat down and chuckled. Basil start-ed chuckling too. He sat down beside Matthias.

"I think I'm going to like you, m'boy," he cried "Now, what about getting you to that church? Why, there's nothing simpler. but enough time for that later, young rip. How about telling me what brings you here? I love listening to good yarn, y'know. Oh, by the way, I hope you like fennel and oatcakes. Of course you do! You'll share lunch with me—of course you will—young 'un like yourself."

In a flash Basil had lugged a haversack from the undergrowth and was spreading a repast on the grass between them. For the next half hour Matthias related his story between mouthfuls of the hare's tasty luncheon. Basil listened intently, interrupting only when he required clarification on some point.

Matthias finished his tale and sat back awaiting comment. Basil's long ears flopped up and down like railway signals as he digested his food and his friend's information.

"Hmm, rats. I knew they'd come eventually, through intelligence on me grapevine, y'know. Could feel it in the old ears, too. As for Redwall, I know it well. Excellent type, Abbot Mortimer. Splendid chap. I heard the Joseph Bell tolling out the sanctuary message. Huh, even had some cheeky old hedgehog telling me to run for it. Couldn't go, of course. Dear me, no. That'd never do. Chap deserting his post; bit of a bad show, what, what? I prefer me own company, y'know. Present company excepted, of course."

"Oh, of course," Matthias agreed. He had taken enormously to the hare. Basil sprang up in a smart military fashion and saluted.

"Right, first things first! Must get you across to the church, young feller, me mouse. I say, that green thingummyjig you're wearin'—habit, isn't it? Capital camouflage You just try lying down anywhere in the shadows. Believe you me, you'd have trouble finding yourself. Well, come on, young bucko. We can't sit about here all day like two fat rabbits at a celery chew. Up and at 'em! Quick's the word and sharp's the action! Nip about a bit, young un."

Again Basil vanished, only to reappear some three yards out on the common. "Come on, Matthias. Tack to the left and wheel to the right. Bob and weave, duck and wriggle. Look, it's easy."

Matthias hurried to follow, keeping in mind Basil's instructions. Surprisingly, they seemed to work perfectly and before long the two friends had covered nearly three-quarters of the common land. Matthias could even count the whiskers on some of the rats. he covered his mouth with a paw to stifle a giggle.

"It's really very simple, isn't it, Basil? How am I doing?"

The hare bobbed up beside him. "Capital! Bung ho! Like a duck to water, young feller. Flop me ears if you aren't the best pupil I've ever had. By the way, is there anything I can do to help?"

Matthias stopped and looked serious. "Yes, there is, Basil, but I feel reluctant to ask you to involve yourself in my fight."

Basil Stag Hare snorted. "Rubbish. My fight indeed! D'you fondly imagine that I'd sit there munching at the old nosebag while some ugly great rodent and his band of yahoos run about conquering my countryside? Huh, never let it be said in the mess that Basil Stag Hare was backward in coming forward! Ask away, Matthias, you young curmudgeon."

PART II

The hare puffed out his narrow chest and stood with paw on heart, his eyes closed and ears standing straight up. He awaited orders. The young mouse, hiding a smile at Basil's noble pose, said admiringly, "Oh, Mr. Hare, you do look heroic standing like that! Thank you!"

Matthias expressed his wishes to the "Stag," "Would it be possible for you to create some kind of diversion while I'm getting the tapestry? Could you keep the rats occupied, Basil?"

The hare twitched his ears confidently. "Say no more, laddie. You've come to the right stag. Listen carefully. They took a piece of planking out of the fence by the lych-gate. That's where you'll slide through. When you've got what you came for, then make your exit the same way. I'll be somewhere about keeping an eye on you. Right, off you go."

Matthias went swiftly, still remembering to bob and weave as Basil had taught him. He made it with ease to the fence, glancing back to check on his companion.

Basil went into a speedy run. He cleared the fencetop at a bound and tapped the nearest rat on the back.

"I say, old thing, where's this leader feller? Cluny, or Loony, whatever you call him."

Completely staggered, the rat stood slack jawed. Basil left him and popped up beside another rat. "Phew! Dear, dear, don't you chaps ever take a bath? Listen here, you dreadful creature. D'you realize that you smell to high heaven? Er, by the way, did your parents ever call you Pongo, or did they smell as bad as you?"

It took the rat sentries a moment or two to recover from their surprise. Then they let out yells of rage and tried to seize the impudent hare.

It was like trying to catch smoke with their claws, Basil ran rings round them, keeping up a steady stream of insults and adding to the rats' bad temper. They shouted angrily:

"Grab that big skinny rabbit, lads."

"Big skinny rabbit yourself! Catsmeat!"

"Blast, he's as slippery as a greased pig."

"Some of my best friends are grease pigs, bottle nose. Oops! Missed me again, you old butterfingers, you."

Matthias chuckled quietly and shook his head in admiration. He watched twelve rats falling over each other and bumping heads as they chased his friend around the common land. Every now and then Basil would pause and strike his "Noble Stag" attitude, letting the rats get to within a whisker of him. Nimbly he would kick out with his long, powerful legs and send them all sprawling in a heap. Adding insult to injury, he danced around the fallen sentries, sprinkling them with daisies until they arose, cursing him, to continue the case.

Wary that there might be other rats about, Matthias climbed into the church through a broken stained-glass window. He dropped down into the chapel. The young mouse wrinkled his nose in disgust. The beautiful old church was rank with the heavy odor of rats. Furniture was overturned, statuary broken, walls stained; the pages of torn hymn books lay about everywhere.

Where was the fragment of tapestry?

And where was Cluny with the rest of his army?

Instant realization sent a leaden weight thudding into the pit of Matthias's stomach! They had gone to attack Redwall. Cluny must have the tapestry with him.

Hastily he climbed back out of the window. Halfway across to the fence he noticed a small shed. Somebody was pounding upon its locked door and calling his name aloud.

"Matthias, quickly, over here in the hut."

Through a small gap in the door he could see the Vole family. Their paws were tightly bound. Colin Vole huddled piteously on some dirty sacking in a corner, while Mr. Abram Vole and his wife batted away at the door with their paws tied together. Matthias called through he crack to them, "Stop banging! Stay quiet! I'll have you out of there as soon as I can break the lock."

Matthias cast about for something that would force the padlock and hasp. Doubtless some rat had the key, but there was no time for that.

By a stroke of luck he found an iron spike that had been thrown at Basil by one of the rats. Forcing the spike in the hoop of the lock, Matthias levered away.

"It's not budging," he muttered.

In his frustration Matthias swung the spike at the lock. It bounced off, lodging deep between the hasp and the woodwork. he grunted in exasperation, pulling it savagely towards himself to loosen it. Taken off balance, he went head over tail. The hasp had broken; it came away bringing with it some twisted rusty screws. The door swung open.

Drawing his dagger, Matthias hastily cut the bindings from the paws of the Voles, issuing orders as he worked. "Follow me and do as I say. Move as quickly and quietly as you can."

Cautiously, they slid through the broken fence and began making their way across the common. There was no sight of the rat sentries. Matthias guessed that they were off somewhere, still trying to catch the elusive hare.

Jacques, Brian. *Redwall*. New York: Avon Books, 1986.

PETER RABBIT AND HIS FRIENDS

BEATRIX POTTER

The very, very energetic Mrs. Tiggy-winkle is a laundress as well as a hedgehog. Lucie loses her pocket-handkerchiefs and searches high and low for them. She finally comes across Mrs. Tiggy-winkle's farm house and stays for a cup of tea.

THE TALE OF MRS. TIGGY-WINKLE

NCE upon a time there was a little girl called Lucie, who lived at a farm called Little-town. She was a good little girl—only she was always losing her pocket-handkerchiefs!

One day little Lucie came into the farm yard crying—oh, she did cry so! "I've lost my pocket-handkin! Three handkins and a pinny! Have you seen them, Tabby Kitten?"

The kitten went on washing her white paws; so Lucie asked a speckled hen—

"Sally Henny-penny, have you found three pocket-handkins?"

But the speckled hen ran into a barn, clucking–

"I go barefoot, barefoot, barefoot!" And then Lucie asked Cock Robin sitting on a twig. Cock Robin looked sideways at Lucie with his bright black eye, and he flew over a stile and away.

Lucie climbed upon the stile and looked up at the hill behind Little-town—a hill that goes up—up—into the clouds as though it had no top!

And a great way up the hillside she thought she saw some white things spread upon the grass.

Lucie scrambled up the hill as fast as her short legs would carry her; she ran along a steep path way—up and up—until Little-town was right away down below—she could have dropped a pebble down the chimney!

Presently she came to a spring, bubbling out from the hillside.

Someone had stood a tin can upon a stone to catch the water—but the water was already running over, for the can was no bigger than an egg-cup! And where the sand upon the path was wet—there were footmarks of a very small person.

Lucie ran on and on.

The path ended under a big rock. The grass was short and green, and there were clothes-props cut from bracken stems, with lines of plaited rushes, and a heap of tiny clothes pins—but no pocket-handkerchiefs!

But there was something else—a door!—straight into the hill; and inside it someone was singing—

"Lily-white and clean, oh!
With little frills between, oh!
Smooth and hot—red rusty spot
Never here be seen, oh!"

Lucie knocked—once—twice, and interrupted the song. A little frightened voice called out "Who's that?"

Lucie opened the door: and what do you think there was inside the hill?—a nice clean kitchen with a flagged floor and wooden beams—just like any other farm kitchen. Only the ceiling was so low that Lucie's head nearly touched it; and the pots and pans were small, and so was everything there.

There was a nice hot, singey smell; and at the table, with an iron in her hand, stood a very stout short person staring anxiously at Lucie.

Her print gown was tucked up, and she was wearing a large apron over her striped petticoat. Her little black nose went sniffle, sniffle, snuffle, and her eyes went twinkle, twinkle; and underneath her cap—where Lucie had yellow curls—that little person had PRICKLES!

"Who are you?" said Lucie. "Have you seen my pocket-handkins?"

The little person made a bob-curtsey—"Oh yes, if you please'm; my name is Mrs. Tiggy-winkle; oh yes, if you please'm, I'm an excellent clear-starcher!" And she took something out of a clothesbasket, and spread it on the ironing-blanket.

"What's that thing?" said Lucie—"that's not my pocket-handkin?"

"Oh no, if you please'm; that's a damask table cloth belonging to Jenny Wren; look how it's stained with currant wine! It's very bad to wash!" said Mrs. Tiggy-winkle.

Mrs. Tiggy-winkle's nose went sniffle, sniffle, snuffle, and her eyes went twinkle, twinkle; and she fetched another hot iron from the fire.

There's one of my pocket-handkins!" cried Lucie—"And there's my pinny!"

Mrs. Tiggy-winkle ironed it, and goffered it, and shook out the frills.

"Oh, that is lovely!" said Lucie.

"And what are those long yellow things with fingers like gloves?"

"Oh, that's a pair of stockings belonging to Sally Henny-penny—look how she's worn the heels out with scratching in the yard! She'll very soon go barefoot!" said Mrs. Tiggy-winkle.

"Why, there's another handkersniff—but it isn't mine; it's red?"

"Oh no, if you please'm; that one belongs to old Mrs. Rabbit; and it did so smell of onions! I've had to wash it separately, I can't get out that smell."

"There's another one of mine," said Lucie.

"What are those funny little white things?"

"That's a pair of mittens belonging to Tabby Kitten; I only have to iron them; she washes them herself."

"There's my last pocket-handkin!" said Lucie.

"And what are you dipping into the basin of starch?"

"They're little dicky shirt-fronts belonging to Tom Titmouse—most terrible particular!" said Mrs. Tiggy-winkle. "Now I've finished my ironing; I'm going to air some clothes."

"What are these dear soft, fluffy things?" said Lucie.

"Oh those are woolly coats belonging to the little lambs at Skelghyl."

"Will their jackets take off?" asked Lucie.

"Oh yes, if you please'm; look at the sheep-mark on the shoulder. And here's one marked for Gatesgarth, and three that come from Little-town. They're always marked at washing!" said Mrs. Tiggy-winkle.

And she hung up all sorts and sizes of clothes—small brown coats of mice; and one velvety black moleskin waist coat; and a red tail coat with no tail belonging to Squirrel

Nutkin; and a very-much-shrunk blue jacket belonging to Peter Rabbit; and a petticoat, not marked, that had gone lost in the washing—and at last the basket was empty!

Then Mrs. Tiggy-winkle made tea— a cup for herself and a cup for Lucie. They sat before the fire on a bench and looked sideways at one another. Mrs. Tiggy-winkle's hand, holding the tea cup, was very brown, and very, very wrinkly with the soap suds; and all through her gown and her cap, there were hairpins sticking wrong end out; so that Lucie didn't like to sit too near her.

When they had finished tea, they tied up the clothes in bundles; and Lucie's pocket-handkerchiefs were folded up inside her clean pinny, and fastened with a silver safety pin.

And then they made up the fire with turf, and came out and locked the door, and hid the key under the door sill.

Then away down the hill trotted Lucie and Mrs. Tiggy-winkle with the bundles of clothes!

All the way down the path little animals came out of the fern to meet them; the very first that they met were Peter Rabbit and Benjamin Bunny!

And she gave them their nice clean clothes; and all the little animals and birds were so very much obliged to dear Mrs. Tiggy-winkle.

So that at the bottom of the hill when they came to the stile, there was nothing left to carry except Lucie's one little bundle.

Lucie scrambled up the stile with the bundle in her hand; and then she turned to say "good night," and to thank the washer-woman—but what a very odd thing! Mrs. Tiggy-winkle had not waited either for thanks or for the washing bill!

She was running, running, running up the hill—and where was her white frilled cap! And her shawl? And her gown—and her petticoat?

And how small she had grown—and how brown—and covered with PRICKLES!

Why! Mrs. Tiggy-winkle was nothing but a HEDGEHOG!

(Now some people say that little Lucie had been asleep upon the stile—but then how could she have found three clean pocket-handkins and a pinny, pinned with a silver safety pin?

And besides—I have seen that door into the back of the hill called Cat Bells—and besides I am very well acquainted with dear Mrs. Tiggy-winkle!)

THE END.

Potter, Beatrix. *Peter Rabbit and Eleven Other Favorite Tales.* Adapted by Pat Stewart. New York: Dover, 1994.

THE WIND IN THE WILLOWS

KENNETH GRAHAME

Moles, rats, toads, and badgers are usually very disagreeable animals, but in these stories they're lovable. Rat, called "Ratty," is good friends with Toad who is always coming up with fantastic schemes and adventures. Mole, who is also a friend of Rat's, wants to meet Toad.

PART I

Chapter II THE OPEN ROAD

"Ratty," said the Mole suddenly, one bright summer morning, "if you please, I want to ask you a favor."

The Rat was sitting on the river bank, singing a little song. He had just composed it himself, so he was very taken up with it, and would not pay proper attention to Mole or anything else. Since early morning he had been swimming in the river, in company with his friends the ducks. And when the ducks stood on their heads suddenly, as ducks will, he would dive down and tickle their necks, just under where their chins would be if ducks had chins, till they were forced to come to the surface again in a hurry, spluttering and angry and shaking their feathers at him, for it is impossible to say quite all you feel when your head is under water. At last they implored him to go away and attend to his own affairs and leave them to mind theirs. So the Rat went away, and sat on the river bank in the sun, and made up a song about them, which he called

"DUCKS' DITTY"

All along the backwater,
Through the rushes tall,
Ducks are a-dabbling,
Up tails all!

Ducks' tails, drakes' tails,
Yellow feet a-quiver,
Yellow bills all out of sight
Busy in the river!

Slushy green undergrowth
Where the roach swim—
Here we keep our larder,
Cool and full and dim.

Everyone for what he likes!
We like to be
Heads down, tails up,
Dabbling free!

High in the blue above
Swifts whirl and call—
We are down a-dabbling
Up tails all!

"I don't know that I think so very much of that little song, Rat," observed the Mole cautiously. He was no poet himself and didn't care who knew it, and he had a candid nature.

"Nor don't the ducks neither," replied the Rat cheerfully. "They say, 'Why can't fellows be allowed to do what they like when they like and as they like, instead of other fellows sitting on banks and watching them all the time and making remarks and poetry and things about them? What nonsense it all is!' That's what the ducks say."

"So it is, so it is," said the Mole, with great heartiness.

"No, it isn't!" cried the Rat indignantly.

"Well then, it isn't, it isn't," replied the Mole soothingly. "But what I wanted to ask you was, won't you take me to call on Mr. Toad? I've heard so much about him, and I do so want to make his acquaintance."

"Why, certainly," said the good-natured Rat, jumping to his feet and dismissing poetry from his mind for the day. "Get the boat out, and we'll paddle up there at once. Its never the wrong time to call on Toad. Early or late he's always the same fellow. Always good-tempered, always glad to see you, always sorry when you go!"

"He must be a very nice animal," observed the Mole, as he got into the boat and took the sculls, while the Rat settled himself comfortably in the stern.

"He is indeed the best of animals," replied Rat. "So simple, so good-natured, and so affectionate. Perhaps he's not very clever—we can't all be geniuses, and it may be that he is both boastful and conceited. But he has got some qualities, has Toady.

Rounding a bend in the river, they came in sight of a handsome, dignified old house of mellowed red brick, with well-kept lawns reaching down to the water"s edge.

"There's Toad Hall," said the Rat; "and that creek on the left, where the notice-board says, 'Private. No landing allowed,' leads to his boat house, where we'll leave the boat. The stables are over there to the right. That's the banqueting-hall you're looking at now—very old, that is. Toad is rather rich, you know, and this is really one of the nicest houses in these parts, though we never admit as much to Toad."

They glided up the creek, and the Mole shipped his sculls as they passed into the shadow of a large boathouse. Here they saw many handsome boats, slung from the cross-beams or hauled up on a slip, but none in the water, and the place had an unused and a deserted air.

The Rat looked around him. "I understand," said he. "Boating is played out. He's tired of it, and done with it. I wonder what new fad he has taken up now? Come along and let's look him up. We shall hear all about it quite soon enough."

They disembarked and strolled across the gay flower-decked lawns in search of Toad, whom they presently happened upon resting in a wicker garden chair, with a preoccupied expression of face, and a large map spread out on his knees.

"Hooray!" he cried, jumping up on seeing them, "this is splendid!" He shook the paws of both of them warmly, never waiting for an introduction to the Mole. "How kind of you!" he went on, dancing round them. "I was just going to send a boat down the river for you, Ratty, with strict orders that you were to be fetched up here at once, whatever you were doing. I want you badly—both of you. Now what will you take? Come inside and have something! You don't know how lucky it is, your turning up just now!"

"Let's sit quiet a bit, Toady!" said the Rat, throwing himself into an easy chair, while the Mole took another by the side of him and made some civil remark about Toad's 'delightful residence.'

"Finest house on the whole river," cried Toad boisterously. "Or anywhere else, for that matter," he could not help adding.

Here the Rat nudged the Mole. Unfortunately, the Toad saw him do it and turned very red. There was a moment's painful silence. Then Toad burst out laughing. "All right, Ratty," he said. "It's only my way, you know. And it's not such a very bad house, is it? You know you rather like it yourself. Now, look here. Let's be sensible. You are the very animals I wanted. You've got to help me. It's most important!"

"It's about your rowing, I suppose," said the Rat, with an innocent air. "You're getting on fairly well, though you splash a good bit still. With a great deal of patience, and any quantity of coaching, you may—"

"O pooh! boating!" interrupted the Toad, in great disgust. "Silly boyish amusement. I've given that up long ago. Sheer waste of time, that's what it is. It makes me downright sorry to see you fellows, who ought to know better, spending all your energies in that aimless manner. No, I've discovered the real thing, the only genuine occupation for a lifetime. I propose to devote the remainder of mine to it and can only regret the wasted years that lie behind me, squandered in trivialities. Come with me, dear Ratty, and your amiable friend also, if he will be so very good, just as far as the stable yard, and you shall see what you shall see!"

PART II

He led the way to the stable yard accordingly, the Rat following with a most mistrustful expression; and there, drawn out of the coach-house into the open, they saw a gypsy caravan, shining with newness, painted a canary-yellow picked out with green, and red wheels.

"There you are!" cried the Toad, straddling and expanding himself. "There's real life for you, embodied in that little cart. The open road, the dusty highway, the heath, the common, the hedgerows, the rolling downs! Camps, villages, towns, cities! Here today, up and off to somewhere else tomorrow. Travel, change, interest, excitement! The whole world before you, and a horizon that's always changing! And mind! This is the very finest cart of its sort that was ever built, without any exception. Come inside and look at the arrangements. Planned 'em all myself, I did!"

The Mole was tremendously interested and excited, and followed him eagerly up the steps and into the interior of the caravan. The Rat only snorted and thrust his hands deep into his pockets, remaining where he was.

It was indeed very compact and comfortable. Little sleeping bunks— a little table that folded up against the wall—a cooking-stove, lockers, bookshelves, a bird cage with a bird in it; and pots, pans, jugs and kettles of every size and variety.

"All complete!" said the Toad triumphantly, pulling open a locker. "You see—biscuits, potted lobster, sardines—everything you can possibly want. Soda-water here—baccy there—letter-paper, bacon, jam, cards, and dominoes—you'll find that nothing whatever has been forgotten, when we make our start this afternoon."

"I beg your pardon," said the Rat slowly, as he chewed a straw, "but did I overhear you say something about 'we,' and 'start,' and 'this afternoon?'"

"Now, you dear good old Ratty," said Toad imploringly, "don't begin talking in that stiff and sniffy sort of way, because you know you've got to come. I can't possibly manage without you, so please consider it settled and don't argue—it's the only thing I can't stand. You surely don't mean to stick to your dull, fusty old river all your life, and just live in a hole in a bank, and boat? I want to show you the world! I'm going to make an animal of you, my boy!"

"I don't care," said the Rat doggedly. "I'm not coming, and that's flat. And I am going to stick to my old river, and live in a hole, and boat, as I've always done. And what's more, Mole's going to stick to me and do as I do, aren't you, Mole?"

"Of course I am," said the Mole loyally. "I'll always stick to you, Rat, and what you say is to be—has got to be. All the same, it sounds as if it might have been—well, rather fun, you know!" He added, wistfully. Poor Mole! The life Adventurous was so new a thing to him, and so thrilling; and this fresh aspect of it was so tempting; and he had fallen in love at first sight with the canary-colored cart and all its little fitments.

Grahame, Kenneth. *The Wind in the Willows*. New York: Signet Classics, Penguin Books USA, 1969.

THE TRUMPET OF
THE SWAN

E. B. WHITE

Louis is a Trumpeter Swan without a voice. He learned to write on a slate that he carries around his neck, but this doesn't help him communicate with a young swan whom he loves. His proud father, who, as a grown-up male swan, is known as a cob, decides to help his son declare his love by getting him a trumpet.

Chapter 9   THE TRUMPET

As the cob flew toward Billings on his powerful, white wings, all sorts of troublesome thoughts whirled in his head. The cob had never gone looking for a trumpet before. He had no money to pay for a tumpet. He feared he might arrive after the shops had closed for the day. He realized that in the whole continent of North America he was undoubtedly the only Trumpeter Swan who was on his way to a city to get a trumpet.

"This is a queer adventure," he said to himself. "Yet, it is a noble quest. I will do anything to help my son Louis—even if I run into real trouble."

Toward the end of the afternoon, the cob looked ahead and in the distance saw the churches and factories and shops and homes of Billings. He decided to act quickly and boldly. He circled the city once, looking for a music store. Suddenly he spied one. It had a very big, wide window, solid glass. The cob flew lower and circled so he could get a better look. He gazed into the store. He saw a drum painted gold. He saw a fancy guitar with an electric cord. He saw a small piano. He saw banjos, horns, violins, mandolins, cymbals, saxophones, marimbaphones, cellos, and many other instruments. Then he saw what he wanted: he saw a brass trumpet hanging by a red cord.

"Now is my time to act!" he said to himself. "Now is my moment for risking everything on one bold move, however shocking it may be to my sensibilities, however offensive it may be to the laws that govern the lives of men. Here I go! May good luck go with me!"

With that, the old cob set his wings for a dive. He aimed straight at the big window. He held his neck straight and stiff, waiting for the crash. He dove swiftly and hit the window going full speed. The glass broke. The noise was terrific. The whole store shook. Musical instruments fell to the floor. Glass flew everywhere. A salesgirl fainted. The cob felt a twinge of pain as a jagged piece of broken glass cut into his shoulder, but he grabbed the trumpet in his beak, turned sharply in the air, flew back through the hole in the window, and began climbing fast over the roofs of Billings. A few drops of blood fell to the ground below. His shoulder hurt. But he had succeeded in getting what he had come for. Held firmly in his bill, its red cord dangling, was a beautiful brass trumpet.

You can imagine the noise in the music store when the cob crashed through the window. At the moment the glass broke, one of the clerks was showing a bass drum to a customer, and the clerk was so started at seeing a big white bird come flying through the window, he hit the drum a tremendous wallop.

"Bom!" went the drum.

"Crash!" went the splinters of flying glass.

When the salesgirl fainted, she fell against the keys of the piano.

"Rrrongee-rrrongee-rrrongee!" went the piano.

The owner of the store grabbed his shotgun, which went off by mistake, blasting a hole in the ceiling and sending down a shower of plaster. Everything was flying around and falling and making a noise.

"Bom!" went the drum.

"Plunk!" went the banjo.

"Rrrongee-rrrongee-rrrongee!" went the piano.

"Ump!" went the bull fiddle.

"Help!" screamed a clerk. "We've been robbed."

"Make way!" shouted the owner. He ran for the door, stepped outside, and fired another shot—bang!—at the disappearing bird. His shot was too late. The cob was safe in the sky, beyond the range of gunfire. He was headed home, toward the southwest, high above the roofs and spires of Billings. In his beak was the trumpet. In his heart was the pain of having committed a crime.

"I have robbed a store," he said to himself. "I have become a thief. What a miserable fate for a bird of my excellent character and high ideals! Why did I do this? What led me to commit this awful crime? My past life has been blameless—a model of good behavior and correct conduct. I am by nature law-abiding. Why, oh, why did I do this?"

Then the answer came to him, as he flew steadily on through the evening sky. "I did it to help my son. I did it for love of my son Louis."

Back in Billings, the news spread rapidly. This was the first time a swan had broken into a music store and made off with a trumpet. A lot of people refused to believe it had happened. The editor of the newspaper sent a reporter to the store to look around. The reporter interviewed the owner and wrote an article about the event for the paper. The article was headed:

LARGE BIRD BREAKS INTO MUSIC STORE
White Swan Crashes Through Window and
Makes Off With Valuable Trumpet

Everybody in Billings bought a copy of the paper and read all about the extraordinary event. It was talked about all over town. Some people believed it; others said it never could have happened. They said the store owner had just invented it to get some publicity for his store. But the clerks in the store agreed that it had really happened. They pointed to the drops of blood on the floor.

The police came to look over the damage, which was estimated at nine hundred dollars. The police promised they would try to find the thief and arrest him, but the police were sorry to hear that the thief was a bird. "Birds are a special problem," they said, "Birds are hard to deal with."

Back at the Red Rock Lakes, Louis's mother waited anxiously for her husband to return. When he showed up in the night sky, she saw that he had a trumpet with him. It was slung around his neck by its cord.

"Well," she said, as he glided to a stop in the water, "I see you made it."

"I did, my dear," said the cob. "I traveled fast and far, sacrificed my honor, and I have returned. Where is Louis? I want to give him his trumpet right away."

"He's over there sitting on a muskrat house, dreaming about that empty-headed young female he's so crazy about."

The cob swam over to his son and made a presentation speech.

"Louis," he said, "I have been on a journey to the haunts of men. I visited a great city teeming with life and commerce. Whilst there, I picked up a gift for you, which I now bestow upon you with my love and my blessing. Here, Louis, is a trumpet. It will be your voice—a subsitute for the voice God failed to give you. Learn to blow it, Louis, and life will be smoother and richer and gayer for you! With the help of this horn, you will be able at last to say ko-hoh, like every other swan. The sound of music will be in our ears. You will be able to attract the attention of desirable young females. Master this trumpet, and you will be able to play love songs for them, filling them with ardor and surprise and longing. I hope it will bring you happiness, Louis, and a new and better life. I procured it at some personal sacrifice to myself and my pride, but won't go into that now. The long and short of it is, I had no money; I took the trumpet without paying for it. This was deplorable. But the important thing is that you learn to play the insrument."

So saying, the cob removed the trumpet from around his neck and hung it on Louis, alongside the slate and the white chalk pencil.

"Wear it in health!" he said. "Blow it in happiness! Make the woods and the hills and the marshes echo with the sounds of your youthful desire!"

Louis wanted to thank his father, but he was unable to say a word. And he knew it would do no good to write "Thank you" on the slate beause his father wouldn't be able to read it, never having had an education. So Louis just bobbed his head and waggled his tail and fluttered his wings. The cob knew by these signs that he had found favor in the sight of his son and that the gift of a trumpet was acceptable.

White, E.B. *The Trumpet of the Swan.* New York: Harper Collins Publishers, 1970.

ZLATEH THE GOAT

Isaac Bashevis Singer

It's a mild winter and Aaron's father, who is a furrier, is having a tough time making ends meet. He asks his son to sell Zlateh, their goat, to the butcher in town. This tale follows Aaron and Zlateh on a scary trip to the butcher's and then recounts how Zlateh becomes the family hero.

At Hanukkah time the road from the village to the town is usually covered with snow, but this year the winter had been a mild one. Hanukkah had almost come, yet little snow had fallen. The sun shone most of the time. The peasants complained that because of the dry weather there would be a poor harvest of winter grain. New grass sprouted, and the peasants sent their cattle out to pasture.

For Reuven the furrier it was a bad year, and after long hesitation he decided to sell Zlateh the goat. She was old and gave little milk. Feyvel the town butcher had offered eight gulden for her. Such a sum would buy Hanukkah candles, potatoes and oil for pancakes, gifts for the children, and other holiday necessaries for the house. Reuven told his oldest boy Aaron to take the goat to town.

Aaron understood what taking the goat to Feyvel meant, but he had to obey his father. Leah, his mother, wiped the tears from her eyes when she heard the news. Aaron's younger sisters, Anna and Miriam, cried loudly. Aaron put on his quilted jacket and a cap with earmuffs, bound a rope around Zlateh's neck, and took along two slices of bread with cheese to eat on the road. Aaron was supposed to deliver the goat by evening, spend the night at the butcher's, and return the next day with the money.

While the family said good-bye to the goat, and Aaron placed the rope around her neck, Zlateh stood as patiently and good-naturedly as ever. She licked Reuven's hand. She shook her small white beard. Zlateh trusted human beings. She knew that they always fed her and never did her any harm.

When Aaron brought her out on the road to town, she seemed somewhat astonished. She'd never been led in that direction before. She looked back at him questioningly, as if to say, "Where are you taking me?" But after a while she seemed to come to the conclusion that a goat shouldn't ask questions. Still, the road was different. They passed new fields, pastures, and huts with thatched roofs. Here and there a dog barked and came running after them, but Aaron chased it away with his stick.

The sun was shining when Aaron left the village. Suddenly the weather changed. A large black cloud with a bluish center appeared in the east and spread itself rapidly over the sky. A cold wind blew in with it. The crows flew low, croaking. At first it looked as if it would rain, but instead it began to hail as in summer. It was early in the day, but it became dark as dusk. After a while the hail turned to snow.

In his twelve years Aaron had seen all kinds of weather, but he had never experienced a snow like this one. It was so dense it shut out the light of the day. In a short time their path was completely covered. The wind became as cold as ice. The road to town was narrow and winding. Aaron no longer knew where he was. He could not see through the snow. The cold soon penetrated his quilted jacket.

At first Zlateh didn't seem to mind the change in weather. She too was twelve years old and knew what winter meant. But when her legs sank deeper and deeper into the snow she began to turn her head and look at Aaron in wonderment. Her mild eyes seemed to ask, "Why are we out in such a storm?" Aaron hoped that a peasant would come along with his cart, but no one passed by.

The snow grew thicker, falling to the ground in large, whirling flakes. Beneath it Aaron's boots touched the softness of a plowed field. He realized that he was no longer on the road. He had gone astray. He could no longer figure out which was east or west, which way was the village, the town. The wind whistled, howled, whirled the snow about in eddies. It looked as if white imps were playing tag on the fields. A white dust rose above the ground. Zlateh stopped. She could walk no longer. Stubbornly she anchored her cleft hooves in the earth and bleated as if pleading to be taken home. Icicles hung from her white beard, and her horns were glazed with frost.

Aaron did not want to admit the danger, but he knew just the same that if they did not find shelter they would freeze to death. This was no ordinary storm. It was a mighty blizzard. The snowfall had reached his knees. His hands were numb, and he could no longer feel his toes. He choked when he breathed. His nose felt like wood, and he rubbed it with snow. Zlateh's bleating began to sound like crying. Those humans in whom she had so much confidence had dragged her into a trap. Aaron began to pray to God for himself and for the innocent animal.

Suddenly he made out the shape of a hill. He wondered what it could be. Who had piled snow into such a huge heap? He moved foward, dragging Zlateh after him. When he came near it, he realized that it was a large haystack which the snow had blanketed.

Aaron realized immediately that they were saved. With great effort he dug his way through the snow. He was a village boy and knew what to do. When he reached the hay, he hollowed out a nest for himself and the goat. No matter how cold it may be outside, in the hay it is always warm. And hay was food for Zlateh. The moment she smelled it she became contented and began to eat. Outside the snow continued to fall. It quickly covered the passageway Aaron had dug. But a boy and an animal need to breathe, and there was hardly any air in their hideout. Aaron bored a kind of a window through the hay and snow and carefully kept the passage clear.

Zlateh, having eaten her fill, sat down on her hind legs and seemed to have regained her confidence in man. Aaron ate his two slices of bread and cheese, but after the difficult journey he was still hungry. He looked at Zlateh and noticed her udders were full. He lay down next to her, placing himself so that when he milked her he could squirt the milk into his mouth. It was rich and sweet. Zlateh was not accustomed to being milked that way, but she did not resist. On the contrary, she seemed eager to reward Aaron for bringing her to a shelter whose very walls, floor, and ceiling were made of food.

Through the window Aaron could catch a glimpse of the chaos outside. The wind carried before it whole drifts of snow. it was completely dark, and he did not know whether night had already come or whether it was the darkness of the storm. Thank god that in the hay it was not cold. The dried hay, grass, and field flowers exuded the warmth of the summer sun. Zlateh ate frequently; she nibbled from above, below, from the left and right. Her body gave forth an animal warmth, and Aaron cuddled up to her. He had always loved Zlateh, but now she was like a sister. He was alone, cut off from his family, and wanted to talk. He began to talk to Zlateh. "Zlateh, what do you think about what has happened to us?" he asked.

"Maaaa," Zlateh answered.

"If we hadn't found this stack of hay, we would both be frozen stiff by now," Aaron said.

"Maaaa," was the goat's reply.

"If the snow keeps on falling like this, we may have to stay here for days," Aaron explained.

"Maaaa," Zlateh bleated.

"What does 'Maaaa' mean?" Aaron asked. "You'd better speak up clearly."

"Maaaa. Maaaa," Zlateh tried.

"Well, let it be 'Maaaa' then," Aaron said patiently. "You can't speak, but I know you understand. I need you and you need me. Isn't that right?"

"Maaaa."

Aaron became sleepy. He made a pillow out of some hay, leaned his head on it, and dozed off. Zlateh too fell asleep.

When Aaron opened his eyes, he didn't know whether it was morning or night. The snow had blocked up his window. He tried to clear it, but when he had bored through to the length of his arm, he still hadn't reached the outside. Luckily he had his stick with him and was able to break through to the open air. It was still dark outside. The snow continued to fall and the wind wailed, first with one voice and then with many. Sometimes it had the sound of devilish laughter. Zlateh too awoke, and when Aaron greeted her, she answered, "Maaaa." Yes, Zlateh's language consisted of only one word, but it meant many things. Now she was saying, "We must accept all that God gives us—heat, cold, hunger, satisfaction, light, and darkness."

Aaron had awakened hungry. He had eaten up his food, but Zlateh had plenty of milk.

For three days Aaron and Zlateh stayed in the haystack. Aaron had always loved Zlateh, but in these three days he loved her more and more. She fed him with her milk and helped him keep warm. She comforted him with her patience. He told her many stories, and she always cocked her ears and listened. When he patted her, she licked his hand and his face. Then she said, "Maaaa," and he knew it meant, I love you too.

The snow fell for three days, though after the first day it was not as thick and the wind quieted down. Sometimes Aaron felt that there could never have been a summer, that the snow had always fallen, ever since he could remember. He, Aaron, never had a father or mother or sisters. He was a snow child, born of the snow, and so was Zlateh. It was so quiet in the hay that his ears rang in the stillness. Aaron and Zlateh slept all night and a good part of the day. As for Aaron's dreams, they were all about warm weather. He dreamed of green fields, trees covered with blossoms, clear broods, and singing birds. By the third night the snow had stopped, but Aaron did not dare to find his way home in the darkness. The sky became clear and the moon shone, casting silvery nets on the snow. Aaron dug his way out and looked at the world. It was all white, quiet, dreaming dreams of heavenly splendor. The stars were large and close. The moon swam in the sky as in a sea.

On the morning of the fourth day Aaron heard the ringing of sleigh bells. The haystack was not far from the road. The peasant who drove the sleigh pointed out the way to him—not to the town and Feyvel the butcher, but home to the village. Aaron had decided in the haystack that he would never part with Zlateh.

Aaron's family and their neighbors had searched for the boy and the goat but had found no trace of them during the storm. They feared they were lost. Aaron's mother and sisters cried for him; his father remained silent and gloomy. Suddenly one of the neighbors came running to their house with the news that Aaron and Zlateh were coming up the road.

There was great joy in the family. Aaron told them how he had found the stack of hay and how Zlateh had fed him with her milk. Aaron's sisters kissed and hugged Zlateh and gave her a special treat of chopped carrots and potato peels, which Zlateh gobbled up hungrily.

Nobody ever again thought of selling Zlateh, and now that the cold weather had finally set in, the villagers needed the services of Reuven the furrier once more. When Hanukkah came, Aaron's mother was able to fry pancakes every evening, and Zlateh got her portion too. Even though Zlateh had her own pen, she often came to the kitchen, knocking on the door with her horns to indicate that she was ready to visit, and she was always admitted. In the evening Aaron, Miriam, and Anna played Dreidel. Zlateh sat near the stove watching the children and the flickering of the Hanukkah candles.

Once in a while Aaron would ask her, "Zlateh, do you remember the three days we spent together?"

And Zlateh would scratch her neck with a horn, shake her white bearded head and come out with the single sound which expressed all her thoughts, and all her love.

Singer, Isaac Bashevis. *Zlateh the Goat and Other Stories.* New York: HarperCollins Publishers, 1966.

KIDS FROM ANOTHER TIME

CENTERBURG TALES

DADDY-LONG-LEGS

EIGHT COUSINS, OR AUNT HILL

ROSE IN BLOOM

HANS BRINKER OR THE SILVER SKATES

LITTLE HOUSE IN THE BIG WOODS

OLIVER TWIST

POLLYANNA

THE SECRET GARDEN

CENTERBURG TALES: MORE ADVENTURES OF HOMER PRICE

ROBERT MCCLOSKEY

Homer Price's grandfather, Grandpa Hercules, has something up his sleeve. And Homer wants to know what it is. So, when Homer's mother asks him to go over and tell his grandfather that there's a large express package waiting for him at the post office, Homer jumps at the chance. Homer's mom tells him not to stay too long, but as usual, Homer gets pulled along into an adventure.

Chapter IV THE GRAVITTY-BITTIES

The following Monday afternoon Homer's mother met him at the door. "Homer, the station agent has just phoned and said that a large express package has arrived for your grandfather Hercules. Would you please run over and tell him about it?"

"Yup," said Homer.

"And don't stay too long," she reminded quickly, because Homer was already down the steps and almost to the road.

"Where're you going, Homer?" called Freddy from his front porch.

"Grandpa Herc has a package at the express office," said Homer, "and I'm on my way over to tell him about it."

"I could come along and help you tell him, Homer," Freddy offered, falling into step beside Homer.

"There he is," said Homer, pointing across the road and up toward the little knoll where Grampa Herc's house and chickencoops stood.

"You've got a package!" panted Freddy, out of breath from running up the hill.

"At the express office," explained Homer. "The station agent just phoned. Perhaps you'd like to have us come along and see what's in it."

"Wu-a-ll now!" said Grampa Hercules. "Wonder who could be sendin' me an express package? Haven't ordered anything, no birthdays or anniversaries this month. Just let me get my hat, and we'll walk down to the station and see what this is all about."

As they crossed the town square the sheriff came out of the barbershop and called, "You've got a package down at the station—came on the afternoon train!"

Grampa Hercules nodded his head and kept right on striding, followed by Homer and Freddy, Ginny Lee and several other girls and boys collected from around the monument and followed, so that by the time Grampa Herc reached the station he had a considerable crowd to help him claim his package. There on the station platform stood a tremendous carton.

"Nothing pasted on it to tell what's inside," Uncle Ulysses stated. "Just says, 'USE NO HOOKS' and 'HANDLE WITH CARE.'"

"Hercules!" called the station agent, pushing through the crowd and handing Grampa Herc a yellow paper. "This telegram just arrived from New York."

Grampa Herc fumbled in his pocket. "Forgot my glasses. Here, Homer, read this for me like a good young un."

Homer read: "'Have sent you four months' supply of sensational new breakfast food. Stop. Please use as instructed by directions on box. Stop. Anxiously await your experiment reaction before selling product to buying public. Gabby and Maxwell.'"

"Four months' supply of breakfast food!" said Uncle Ulysses with a chuckle.

"That's certainly a lot of food!" said the station agent, starting back to his office.

"And a lot of box tops!" said Homer.

"Oh, boy!" shouted Freddy. "Let's open the carton and see what they're giving away."

Grampa Hercules took out his pocketknife and carefully slit the tape that sealed the carton. He picked out one of the boxes and read "GRAVITTY-BITTIES' printed in large letters across the front. Then, after squinting a bit, Grampa Herc handed the box to Homer so he could read the fine print.

"'Gravitty-Bitties,'" read Homer, "'the breakfast food of champion jumpers. The sensational cereal of packaged power with the GRAVITTY BOX BOTTOM.'"

"What's that?" Ginny Lee asked.

"'See directions on reverse side,'" Homer read. Then he turned the box over and continued, "'Eat a box of feather-light Gravitty-Bitties for breakfast every morning for four months and become a champion jumper. All you have to do is this:

"'First—Eat the Gravitty-Bitties.

"'Second—Pin the Gravitty-Bitty box bottom, which is made of pure lead, to the inside of your coat or jacket. Each Gravitty-Bitty box bottom comes complete with attached safety-catch pin.

"'And last—Practice jumping.

"'Be Sure you eat your box of feather-light enriched Gravitty-Bitties every morning for four months and

"'Be sure you pin another pure lead Gravitty-Bitty box bottom inside your jacket every morning for four months. Then, take off your jacket and JUMP! Your friends will be SURPRISED!'"

"I'll be durned," said Uncle Ulysses, scratching his head.

"Don't this setup remind you of a story, Hercules?" asked the sheriff slyly.

"Hercules," called the station agent, "it looks like you're getting to be a popular fellow. Here's another telegram."

"Uh-h? Oh, yes," said Grampa Hercules in a dazed sort of way. He motioned for Homer to read it.

"It says," Homer began, "'Please time four months' test of Gravitty-Bitty breakfasts to end morning of July Fourth. Stop. Arranging with radio, television, and news services to cover jump. Gabby and Maxwell.'"

"Well, Grampa Hercules," said Uncle Ulysses, "it looks like we'll have a chance to find out what's wrong with that story of yours."

"Now look here!" cried Grampa Hercules. "Ther's not a thing wrong with that story in its place. These two crazy fellas 're trying to put my story in a box and make it something to eat! The trouble with these advertising people is that they don't know where words and stories stop and what isn't words and stories begin. They get it all confused and printed on a fancy package and commence to believe it's every word true!"

"Well," said Uncle Ulysses, "in a world full of television and rocket ships, it's sort of hard for anybody not to be confused. I'll admit I'm puzzled," Uncle Ulysses continued. "This theory sounds good, but I don't think that gold or rocks or Gravitty-Bitty box bottoms can help a man jump like that. Still, I can't understand why it wouldn't work."

"Oh, pshaw!" said the sheriff. "It's just like all of Hercules' tales—just like breakin' through the ice, like the clock spull of farrows—I mean birds. There's some catch to it, something that's not quite right."

"Now, Sheriff!" began Grampa Hercules.

Ginny Lee put her small hand in Grampa Hercules' wrinkled brown one and said, "Don't you worry about what he says. We all like your stories!"

250

"And," continued Ginny Lee, turning toward the sheriff and Uncle Ulysses, "Grandpa Herc will show you men on the Fourth of July, so there!"

A loud cheer of approval went up from the crowd of children. Grampa Herc stroked his chin, looking uncomfortable.

Ginny Lee turned to him and inquired anxiously, "Won't you Grampa Herc?"

"U-u-u-uh-h," mumbled Grampa Hercules in a flustered sort of way, while some of the children cheered and whistled their approval.

"Come on, everybody," Ginny Lee commanded the children. "We'll help Grampa Herc carry his Gravitty-Bitties home."

She supervised most efficiently while each of the children filed by and received several boxes of Gravitty-Bitties. Then Ginny Lee, still hand in hand with Grampa Hercules, led the way, and all the girls and boys carrying heavy lead-bottomed boxes of breakfast food followed behind, leaving the sheriff and Uncle Ulysses standing on the platform with the large empty carton.

McCloskey, Robert. *Centerburg Tales*. New York: Puffin Books, a division of Penguin Books USA Inc., 1951.

DADDY-LONG-LEGS

Jean Webster

Jerusha (Judy) Abbott is given the chance of a lifetime when a trustee of the John Grier orphanage offers to send her to college. He believes that Jerusha has originality and should study to become a writer. He will pay all of her bills and in return all she needs to do is write a monthly letter to him about her studies and her daily life. The following excerpt is a collection of letters reporting her observations of her new surroundings and reflections on where she has come from.

Chapter 2 THE LETTERS OF MISS JERUSHA ABBOTT TO MR. DADDY-LONG-LEGS

215 Fergussen Hall,
September 24th

Dear Kind-Trustee-Who-Sends-Orphans-to-College,
Here I am! I traveled yesterday for four hours in a train. It's a funny sensation isn't it? I never rode in one before.

College is the biggest, most bewildering place—I get lost whenever I leave my room. I will write you a description later when I'm feeling less muddled; also I will tell you about my lessons. Classes don't begin until Monday morning, and this is Saturday night. But I wanted to write a letter first just to get acquainted.

It seems queer to be writing letters to somebody you don't know. It seems queer for me to be writing letters at all—I've never written more than three or four in my life, so please overlook it if these are not a model kind.
Before leaving yesterday morning, I had a very serious talk with Mrs. Lippett. She told me how to behave all the rest of my life, and especially how to behave toward the kind gentleman who is doing so much for me. I must take care to be Very Respectful.

But how can one be very respectful to a person who wished to be called John Smith? Why couldn't you have picked out a name with a little personality? I might as well write letters to Dear Hitching-Post or Dear Clothes-Pole.

I have been thinking about you a great deal this summer; having somebody take an interest in me after all these years, makes me feel as though I had found a sort of family. It seems as though I belonged to somebody now, and it's a very comfortable sensation. I must say, however, that when I think about you, my imagination has very little to work upon. There are just three things that I know:

> I. You are tall.
> II. You are rich.
> III. You hate girls.

I suppose I might call you Dear Mr. Girl-Hater, only that's sort of insulting to me. Or Dear Mr. Rich-man, but that's insulting to you, as though money were the only important thing about you. Besides, being rich is such a very external quality. Maybe you won't stay rich all your life; lots of very clever men get smashed up in Wall Street. But at least you will stay tall all your life! so I've decided to call you Dear Daddy-Long-Legs. I hope you won't mind. It's just a private pet name—we won't tell Mrs. Lippett.

The ten o'clock bell is going to ring in two minutes. Our day is divided into sections by bells. We eat and sleep and study by bells. It's very enlivening; I feel like a firehorse all of the time. There it goes! Lights out. Good night. Observe with what precision I obey rules—due to my training in the John Grier Home.

> Yours most respectfully,
> Jerusha Abbott

To Mr. Daddy-Long-Legs Smith
October 1st

Dear Daddy-Long-Legs,
I love college and I love you for sending me—I'm very, very happy, and so excited every moment of the time that I can scarcely sleep. You can't imagine how different it is from the John Grier Home. I never dreamed there was such a place in the world. I'm feeling sorry for everybody who isn't a girl and who can't come here; I am sure the college you attended when you were a boy couldn't have been so nice.

My room is up in a tower that used to be the contagious ward before they built the new infirmary. There are three other girls on the same floor of the tower—a senior, who wears spectacles and is always asking us please to be a little more quiet, and two freshmen named Sallie McBride and Julia Rutledge Pendleton. Sallie has red hair and a turn-up nose and is quite friendly; Julia comes from one of the first families in New York and hasn't noticed me yet. They room together and the senior and I have singles; they are very scarce, but I got one without even asking. I suppose the registrar didn't think it would be right to ask a properly brought-up girl to room with a foundling. You see there are advantages!

My room is on the northwest corner with two windows and a view. After you've lived in a ward for eighteen years with twenty roommates, it is restful to be alone. This is the first chance I've ever had to get acquainted with Jerusha Abbott. I think I'm going to like her.

Do you think you are?

Tuesday

They are organizing the freshman basketball team and there's just a chance that I shall make it. I'm little of course, but terribly quick and wiry and tough. While the others are hopping about in the air, I can dodge under their feet and grab the ball. It's loads of fun practicing—out in the athletic field in the afternoon with the trees all red and yellow and the air full of the smell of burning leaves, and everybody laughing and shouting. These are the happiest girls I ever saw—and I am the happiest of all!

I meant to write a long letter and tell you all the things I'm learning (Mrs. Lippett said you wanted to know) but 7th hour has just rung, and in ten minutes I'm due at the athletic field in gymnasium clothes. Don't you hope I'll make the team?

>Yours always,
>Jerusha Abbott

P.S. (9 o'clock)
Sallie McBride just poked her head in at my door. This is what she said: "I'm so homesick that I simply can't stand it. Do you feel the same way?" I smiled a little and said no, I thought I could pull through. At least home-sickness is one disease that I've escaped! I never heard of anybody being asy-lumsick, did you?

October 10th

Dear Daddy-Long-Legs,
Did you ever hear of Michael Angelo?

He was a famous artist who lived in Italy in the Middle Ages. Everybody in English Literature seemed to know about him and the whole class laughed because I thought He was an archangel. He sounds like an archangel, does-n't he? The trouble with college is that you are expected to know such a lot of things you've never learned. It's very embarrassing at times. But now, when the girls talk about things that I never heard of, I just keep still and look them up in the encyclopedia.

I made an awful mistake the first day. Somebody mentioned Maurice Maeterlinck, and I asked if she was a freshman. That joke has gone all over college. But anyway, I'm just as bright in class as any of the others—and brighter than some of them!

Do you care to know how I've furnished my room? It's a symphony in brown and yellow. The wall was tinted buff, and I've bought yellow denim curtains and cushions and a mahogany desk (secondhand for three dollars) and rattan chair and a brown rug with an ink spot in the middle. I stand the chair over the spot.

The windows are up high; you can't look out from an ordinary seat. But I unscrewed the looking glass from the back of the bureau, upholstered the top, and moved it up against the window seat. It's just the right height for a window seat. You pull out the drawers like steps and walk up. Very comfortable!

Sallie McBride helped me choose the things at the senior auction. She has lived in a house all her life and knows about furnishing. You can't imagine what fun it is to shop and pay with a real five-dollar bill and get some change—when you've never had more than a nickel in your life. I assure you, Daddy dear, I do appreciate that allowance.

Sallie is the most entertaining person in the world—and Julia Rutledge Pendleton the least so. It's queer what a mixture the registrar can make in the matter of roommates. Sallie thinks everything is funny—even flunking—and Julia is bored at everything. She never makes the slightest effort to be amiable. She believes that if you are a Pendleton, that fact alone admits you to heaven without any further examination. Julia and I were born to be enemies.

And now I suppose you've been waiting very impatiently to hear what I am learning?

I. Latin: Second Punic War. Hannibal and his forces pitched camp at Lake Trasimenus last night. They prepared an ambuscade for the Romans, and a battle took place at the fourth watch this morning. Romans in retreat.

II. French: 24 pages of the The Three Musketeers and third conjugation, irregular verbs.

III. Geometry: Finished cylinders; now doing cones.

IV. English: Studying exposition. My style improves daily in clearness and brevity.

V. Physiology: Reached the digestive system. Bile and the pancreas next time. Yours, on the way to being educated,

    Jerusha Abbott

PS. I hope you never touch alcohol, Daddy? It does dreadful things to your liver.

Wednesday

Dear Daddy-Long-Legs,
I've changed my name.

I'm still "Jerusha" in the catalog, but I'm "Judy" everyplace else. It's sort of too bad, isn't it, to have to give yourself the only pet name you ever had? I didn't quite make up the Judy though. That's what Freddie Perkins used to call me before he could talk plain.

I wish Mrs. Lippett would use a little more ingenuity about choosing babies' names. She gets the last names out of the telephone book—you'll find Abbott on the first page—and she picks the Christian names up anywhere; she got Jerusha from a tombstone. I've always hated it; but I rather like Judy. It's such a silly name. It belongs to the kind of girl I'm not—a sweet little blue-eyed thing, petted and spoiled by all the family, who romps her way through life without any cares. Shouldn't it be nice to be like that? Whatever faults I may have, no one can ever accuse me of having been spoiled by my family! But it's sort of fun to pretend I've been. In the future please always address me as Judy.

Do you want to know something? I have three pairs of kid gloves. I've had kid mittens before from the Christmas tree, but never real kid gloves with five fingers. I take them out and try them on every little while. It's all I can do not to wear them to classes.

(Dinner bell. Good-bye.)

Friday

What do you think, Daddy? The English instructor said that my last paper shows an unusual amout of originality. She did, truly. Those were her words. It doesn't seem possible, does it, considering the eighteen years of training that I've had? The aim of the John Grier Home (as you doubtless know and heartily approve of) is to turn the ninety-seven orphans into ninety-seven twins.

The unusual artistic ability which I exhibit was develped at an early age through drawing chalk pictures of Mrs. Lippett on the woodshed door.

I hope that I don't hurt your feelings when I criticize the home of my youth? But you have the upper hand, you know, for if I become too impertinent you can always stop payment on your checks. That isn't a very polite thing to say—but you can't expect me to have any manners; a foundling asylum isn't a young ladies' finishing school.

You know, Daddy, it isn't the work that is going to be hard in college. It's the play. Half the time I don't know what the girls are talking about; their jokes seem to relate to a past that everyone but me has shared. I'm a foreigner in the world and I don't understand the language. It's a miserable feeling. I've had it all my life. At the high school the girls would stand in groups and just look at me. I was queer and different and everybody knew it. I could feel "John Grier Home" written on my face. And then a few charitable ones would make a point of coming up and saying something polite. I hated every one of them—the charitable ones most of all.

Nobody here knows that I was brought up in an asylum. I told Sallie McBride that my mother and father were dead, and that a kind old gentleman was sending me to college—which is entirely true so far as it goes. I don't want you to think I am a coward, but I do want to be like the other girls, and that Dreadful Home looming over my childhood is the one great big difference. If I can turn my back on that and shut out the remembrance, I think I might be just as desirable as any other girl. I don't believe there's any real, underneath difference, do you?

Anyway, Sallie McBride likes me!

      Yours ever,
      Judy Abbott
      (Née Jerusha))

Saturday morning

I've just been reading this letter over and it sounds pretty uncheerful. But can't you guess that I have a special topic due Monday morning and a review in geometry and a very sneezy cold?

Sunday

I forgot to mail this yesterday so I will add an indignant postscript. We had a bishop this morning, and what do you think he said?

"The most beneficent promise made us in the Bible is this, 'The poor ye have always with you.' They were put here in order to keep us charitable."

The poor, please observe, being a sort of useful domestic animal. If I hadn't grown up into such a perfect lady, I should have gone up after service and told him what I thought.

Webster, Jean. *Daddy-Long-Legs*. New York: Penguin Books USA Inc., 1912.

EIGHT COUSINS, OR AUNT HILL

LOUISA MAY ALCOTT

Writing in the late nineteenth century, Louisa May Alcott often concerned herself, as she did in her famous novel Little Women, *with girls coming of age during a period in history when women were beginning to hope for more independence. In* Eight Cousins *and its sequel* Rose in Bloom, *Rose Campbell grows from a shy and sickly orphan to a strong and self-possessed young woman with her own ideas about how her life should be led.*

In Eight Cousins *we meet Rose, recently orphaned and sent to live amid relatives she has never known: six aunts, seven boy cousins, and Uncle Alec, who is her guardian. In this excerpt Uncle Alec, who has resolved to "cure" Rose of her sadness and her delicate nature, shows Rose his splendid new chambers, but Rose soon deduces that the beautiful room, with all its girlish charm, is actually a surprise for her.*

Now take a good look, and tell me what you think of it," said Alec, opening the door and letting her enter before him.

Rose walked to the middle of the room, stood still, and gazed about her with eyes that brightened as they looked, for all was changed.

This chamber had been built out over the library to suit some fancy and had been unused for years, except at Christmastimes, when the old house overflowed. It had three windows—one to the east, that overlooked the bay; one to the south, where the horse chestnuts waved their green fans; and one to the west, toward the hills and the evening sky. A ruddy sunset burned there now, filling the room with an enchanted glow; the soft murmur of the sea was heard, and a robin chirped "Good night!" among the budding trees.

Rose saw and heard these things first, and felt their beauty with a child's quick instinct; then her eye took in the altered aspect of the room, once so shrouded, still, and solitary, now so full of light and warmth and simple luxury.

India matting covered the floor, with a gay rug here and there; the antique andirons shone on the wide hearth, where a cheery blaze dispelled the dampness of the long-closed room. Bamboo lounges and chairs stood about, and quaint little tables in cozy corners; one bearing a pretty basket, one a desk, and on a third lay several familiar-looking books. In a recess stood a narrow white bed, with a lovely Madonna hanging over it. The Japanese screen, half folded back, showed a delicate toilet-service of blue and white set forth on a marble slab, and nearby was the great bath-pan, with Turkish towels and a sponge as big as Rose's head.

Uncle must love cold water like a duck, she thought with a shiver.

Then her eyes went on to the tall cabinet, where a half-open door revealed a tempting array of the drawers, shelves, and "cubbyholes," which so delight the hearts of children.

What a grand place for my new things, she thought, wondering what her uncle kept in that cedar retreat.

Oh, me, what a sweet toilet table! was her next mental exclamation, as she approached this inviting spot.

A round old-fashioned mirror hung over it, with a gilt eagle atop, holding in his beak the knot of blue ribbon that tied up a curtain of muslin falling on either side of the table, where appeared little ivory-handled brushes, two slender silver candle sticks, a porcelain matchbox, several pretty trays for small matters, and most imposing of all, a plump blue silk cushion, coquettishly trimmed with lace, and pink rosebuds at the corners.

That cushion rather astonished Rose; in fact, the whole table did, and she was just thinking with a sly smile, Uncle is a dandy, but I never should have guessed it, when he opened the door of a large closet, saying, with a careless wave of the hand—

"Men like plenty of room for their rattletraps; don't you think that ought to satisfy me?"

Rose peeped in and gave a start, though all she saw was what one usually finds in closets—clothes and boots, boxes and bags. Ah! but you see these clothes were small black and white frocks; the row of little boots that stood below had never been on Dr. Alec's feet; the green bandbox had a gray veil straying out of it, and—yes! the bag hanging on the door was certainly her own piece bag, with a hole in one corner. She gave a quick look round the room and understood now why it had seemed too dainty for a man, why her Testament and prayer book were on the table by the bed, and what those rosebuds meant on the blue cushion. It came upon her in one delicious burst that this little paradise was all for her, and not knowing how else to express her gratitude, she caught Dr. Alec round the neck, saying impetuously, "Oh, Uncle, you are too good to me!"

"You like it, then? But why do you think it is yours, my lass?" asked Dr. Alec as he sat down looking well pleased and drew his excited little niece to his knee.

"I don't think, I know it is for me; I see it in your face, and I feel as if I didn't half deserve it. Aunt Jessie said you would spoil me, and I must not let you. I'm afraid this looks like it, and perhaps—oh, me!—perhaps I ought not to have this beautiful room after all!" And Rose tried to look as if she could be heroic enough to give it up if it was best.

"I owe Mrs. Jessie one for that," said Dr. Alec, trying to frown, though in his secret soul he felt that she was quite right. Then he smiled that cordial smile, which was like sunshine on his brown face, as he said, "This is part of the cure, Rose, and I put you here that you might take my three great remedies in the best and easiest way. Plenty of sun, fresh air, and cold water; also cheerful surroundings and some work; for Phebe is to show you how to take care of this room, and be your little maid as well as friend and teacher. Does that sound hard and disagreeable to you, dear?

"No sir; very, very pleasant, and I'll do my best to be a good patient. But I really don't think anyone could be sick in this delightful room," she said, with a long sigh of happiness as her eye went from one pleasant object to another.

Alcott, Louisa May. *Eight Cousins, or Aunt Hill.* New York: Dell Publishing, a division of Bantam Doubleday Dell Publishing Group, Inc., 1875.

ROSE IN BLOOM

LOUISA MAY ALCOTT

In the sequel to Eight Cousins, Rose in Bloom, Rose Campbell's story continues, though now she is a wealthy and beautiful young woman, having come into her inheritance and traveled the world with her maid and best friend, Phebe, and wise Uncle Alec as her chaperone. In this section she is reunited with her aunts and six cousins. Though they marvel at how lovely she's become, her views on the duties of women manage to ruffle a few feathers.

ear child! how nice it is to see her safely back, so well and happy and like her sweet little self!" said Aunt Plenty, folding her hands as if giving thanks for a great happiness.

"I shouldn't wonder if you found that you'd brought a firebrand into the family, Alec. Two, in fact; for Phebe is a fine girl, and the lads have found it out already, if I'm not mistaken," added Uncle Mac, with a nod toward the other room.

Rose and Phebe, sitting side by side on the sofa, had evidently assumed at once the places which they were destined to fill by right of youth, sex, and beauty; for Phebe had long since ceased to be the maid and become the friend, and Rose meant to have that fact established at once.

Jamie occupied the rug, on which Will and Geordie stood at ease, showing their uniforms to the best advantage; for they were now in a great school, where military drill was the delight of their souls. Steve posed gracefully in an armchair, with Mac lounging over the back of it; while Archie leaned on one corner of the low chimneypiece looking down at Phebe as she listened to his chat with smiling lips, and cheeks almost as rich in color as the carnations in her belt.

Aunt Plenty said warmly,—

"Bless the dears! Anyone might be proud of such a bonny flock of bairns as that."

"I am all ready to play chaperon as soon as you please, Alec; for I suppose the dear girl will come out at once, as she did not before you went away."

"You must settle all those matters with Rose: I am no longer captain, only first mate now, you know," answered Dr. Alec. "I've done my best to fit Rose for what may come, as far as I can foresee it; but now she must stand alone. I can only stand by ready to share the joy and sorrow and watch her shape her life."

"Why, Alec, what is the child going to do, that you need look so solemn?" exclaimed Mrs. Clara.

"Hark! and let her tell you herself," answered Dr. Alec, as Rose's voice was heard saying very earnestly—

"Now you have all told your plans for the future, why don't you ask us ours?"

"Because we know that there is only one thing for a pretty girl to do—break a dozen or so of hearts before she finds one to suit, then marry and settle," answered Charlie, as if no other reply was possible.

"That may be the case with many, but not with us; for Phebe and I believe that it is as much a right and a duty for women to do something with their lives as for men; and we are not going to be satisfied with such frivolous parts as you give us," cried Rose, with kindling eyes. "I mean what I say, and you cannot laugh me down. Would you be contented to be told to enjoy yourself for a little while, then marry and do nothing more till you die?" she added, turning to Archie.

"Of course not: that is only a part of a man's life," he answered decidedly.

"A very precious and lovely part, but not all," continued Rose; "neither should it be for a woman: for we've got minds and souls as well as hearts; ambition and talents, as well as beauty and accomplishments; and we want to live and learn as well as love and be loved. I'm sick of being told that is all a woman is fit for! I won't have anything to do with love till I prove that I am something beside a housekeeper and baby-tender!"

"Heaven preserve us! here's woman's rights with a vengeance!" cried Charlie, starting up with mock horror, while the others regarded Rose with mingled surprise and amusement, evidently fancying it all a girlish outbreak.

"Ah, you needn't pretend to be shocked: you will be in earnest presently; for this is only the beginning of my strong-mindedness," continued Rose, nothing daunted by the smiles of good-natured incredulity or derision on the faces of her cousins. "I have made up my mind not to be cheated out of the real things that make one good and happy; and, just because I'm a rich girl, fold my hands and drift as so many do. I haven't lived with Phebe all these years in vain: I know what courage and self-reliance can do for one; and I sometimes wish I hadn't a penny in the world so that I could go and earn my bread with her and be as brave and independent as she will be pretty soon."

It was evident that Rose was in earnest now; for, as she spoke, she turned to her friend with such respect as well as love in her face that the look told better than any words how heartily the rich girl appreciated the virtues hard experience had given the poor girl and how eagerly she desired to earn what all her fortune could not buy for her.

Something in the glance exchanged between the friends impressed the young men in spite of their prejudices; and it was in a perfectly serious tone that Archie said—

"I fancy you'll find your hands full, cousin, if you want work; for I've heard people say that wealth has its troubles and trials as well as poverty."

"I know it, and I'm going to try and fill my place well. I've got some capital little plans all made and have begun to study my profession already," answered Rose, with an energetic nod.

"Could I ask what it is to be?" inquired Charlie, in a tone of awe.

"Guess!" and Rose looked up at him with an expression half-earnest, half-merry.

"Well, I should say that you were fitted for a beauty and a belle; but, as that is evidently not to your taste, I am afraid you are going to study medicine and be a doctor."

"Now, Charlie, you know how well women have succeeded in this profession, and what a comfort Dr. Mary Kirk was to dear Aunt Peace. I did want to study medicine; but uncle thought it wouldn't do to have so many M.D.'s in one family. Besides, I seem to have other work put into my hands that I am better fitted for."

"You are fitted for anything that is generous and good; and I'll stand by you, no matter what you've chosen," cried Mac heartily; for this was a new style of talk from a girl's lips, and he liked it immensely.

"Philanthropy is a generous, good, and beautiful profession; and I've chosen it for mine because I have much to give. I'm only the steward of the fortune papa left me; and I think, if I use it wisely for the happiness of others, it will be more blest than if I keep it all for myself."

Alcott, Louisa May. *Rose in Bloom*. New York: Little, Brown and Company, 1876, 1927.

HANS BRINKER OR THE SILVER SKATES

Mary Mapes Dodge

A big skating race is soon to take place on the frozen canals of Holland. But how can two poor children compete for the precious prize—ice skates with real silver blades—when their slow, handmade skates have blades of wood?

HANS AND GRETEL FIND A FRIEND

At noon our young friends poured forth from the schoolhouse, intent upon having an hour's practice upon the canal.

They had skated but a few moments when Carl Schummel said mockingly to Hilda, "There's a pretty pair just coming upon the ice! The little ragpickers! Their skates must have been a present from the king direct."

"They are patient creatures," said Hilda gently. "It must have been hard to learn to skate upon such queer affairs. They are very poor peasants, you see. The boy has probably made the skates himself."

Carl was somewhat abashed.

Hilda laughed pleasantly and left him. After joining a small detachment of the racers and sailing past every one of them, she halted beside Gretel, who, with eager eyes, had been watching the sport.

"What is your name, little girl?"

"Gretel, my lady," answered the child, somewhat awed by rank, though they were nearly of the same age, "and my brother is called Hans."

"Hans is a stout fellow," said Hilda cheerily, "and seems to have a warm stove somewhere within him, but you look cold. You should wear more clothing, little one."

Gretel, who had nothing else to wear, tried to laugh as she answered, "I am not so very little. I am past twelve years old."

"Oh, I beg your pardon. You see, I am nearly fourteen and so large for my age that other girls seem small to me, but that is nothing. Perhaps you will shoot up far above me yet, but not unless you dress more warmly, though. Shivering girls never grow."

Hans flushed as he saw tears rising in Gretel's eyes.

"My sister has not complained of the cold, but this is bitter weather, they all say." And he looked sadly upon Gretel.

"It is nothing," said Gretel. "I am often warm—too warm when I am skating. You are good, jufvrouw,* to think of it."

"No, no," answered Hilda, quite angry at herself. "I am careless, cruel, but I meant no harm. I wanted to ask you—I mean, if—" And here Hilda, coming to the point of her errand, faltered before the poorly clad but noble-looking children she wished to serve.

"What is it, young lady?" exclaimed Hans eagerly. "If there is any service I can do, any—"

"Oh, no, no," laughed Hilda, shaking off her embarrassment. "I only wished to speak to you about the grand race. Why do you not join it? You both can skate well, and the ranks are free. Anyone may enter for the prize."

Gretel looked wistfully at Hans, who, tugging at his cap, answered respectfully:

"Ah, jufvrouw, even if we could enter, we could skate only a few strokes with the rest. Our skates are hard wood, you see"—holding up the sole of his foot—"but they soon become damp, and then they stick and trip us."

Looking down with a sigh at the two pairs of feet so very different in size, she asked: "Which of you is the better skater?"

"Gretel," replied Hans promptly.

"Hans," answered Gretel in the same breath.

Hilda smiled.

"I cannot buy you each a pair of skates, or even one good pair, but here are eight kwartjes. Decide between you which stands the best chance of winning the race, and buy the skates accordingly. I wish I had enough to buy better ones. Good-bye!" And, with a nod and a smile, Hilda, after handing the money to the electrified Hans, glided swiftly away to rejoin her companions.

"Jufvrouw! Jufvrouw van Gleck!" called Hans in a loud tone, stumbling after her as well as he could, for one of his skate strings was untied.

"We cannot take this money," panted Hans, "though we know your goodness in giving it."

"Why not, indeed?" asked Hilda, flushing.

"Because," replied Hans, bowing like a clown but looking with the eye of a prince at the queenly girl, "We have not earned it."

Hilda was quick-witted. She had noticed a pretty wooden chain upon Gretel's neck. "Carve me a chain, Hans, like the one your sister wears."

"That I will, lady, with all my heart. We have whitewood in the house, fine as ivory; you shall have one tomorrow." And Hans hastily tried to return the money.

*Miss; young lady (pronounced yuffrow).

"No, no," said Hilda decidely. "That sum will be but a poor prize for the chain." And off she darted, outstripping the fleetest among the skaters.

Hans shook his head. "The young lady would have given us the money to buy skates, but if I earn it, Gretel, it shall be spent for wool. You must have a warm jacket."

"Oh!" cried Gretel in real dismay, "not buy the skates? Why, I am not often cold! Mother says the blood runs up and down in poor children's veins, humming, 'I must keep 'em warm! I must keep 'em warm.'"

"Now mind," cried Gretel, seeing her advantage, "I'll feel awful if you give up the skates. I don't want them. I'm not so stingy as that; but I want you to have them, and then when I get bigger, they'll do for me—oh—count the pieces Hans. Did ever you see so many!"

Hans turned the money thoughtfully in his palm. Never in all his life had he longed so intensely for a pair of skates, for he had known of the race and had fairly ached for a chance to test his powers with the other children. He felt confident that with a good pair of steel runners he could readily outdistance most of the boys on the canal. Then, too, Gretel's argument was so plausible. On the other hand, he knew that she, with her strong but lithe little frame, needed but a week's practice on good runners to make her a better skater than Rychie Korbes or even Katrinka Flack. As soon as this last thought flashed upon him, his resolve was made. If Gretel would not have the jacket, she should have the skates.

"No, Gretel," he answered at last, "I can wait. Someday I may have money enough saved to buy a fine pair. You shall have these."

Gretel's eyes sparkled, but in another instant she insisted rather faintly, "The young lady gave the money to you, Hans. I'd be real bad to take it."

Hans shook his head resolutely as he trudged on, causing his sister to half skip and half walk in her effort to keep beside him. By this time they had taken off their wooden "rockers" and were hastening home to tell their mother the good news.

"Oh! I know!" cried Gretel in a sprightly tone. "You can do this. You can get a pair a little too small for you, and too big for me, and we can take turns and use them. Won't that be fine?" Gretel clapped her hands again.

Poor Hans! This was a strong temptation, but he pushed it away from him, brave-hearted fellow that he was.

"Nonsense, Gretel. You could never get on with a big pair. You stumbled about with these, like a blind chicken, before I curved off the ends. No, you must have a pair to fit exactly, and you must practice every chance you can get until the twentieth comes. My little Gretel shall win the silver skates."

Dodge, Mary Mapes. *Hans Brinker or The Silver Skates*. New York: Scholastic Inc., 1988.

LITTLE HOUSE IN THE BIG WOODS

LAURA INGALLS WILDER

More than one hundred years ago, in a small log house in the woods of Wisconsin, a little girl named Laura lived with her ma, pa, and sisters, Mary and Carrie. In the following excerpt you will see just how they live off the land. At harvest time they help Uncle Henry with his work in the fields and Laura gets to spend the day with her cousins.

HARVEST

Pa and Uncle Henry traded work. When the grain got ripe in the fields, Uncle Henry came to work with Pa, and Aunt Polly and all the cousins came to spend the day. Then Pa went to help Uncle Henry cut his grain, and Ma took Laura and Mary and Carrie to spend the day with Aunt Polly.

Ma and Aunt Polly worked in the house and all the cousins played together in the yard till dinnertime. Aunt Polly's yard was a fine place to play because the stumps were so thick. The cousins played jumping from stump to stump without ever touching the ground.

Even Laura, who was littlest, could do this easily in the places where the smallest trees had grown close together. Cousin Charley was a big boy, going on eleven years old, and he could jump from stump to stump all over the yard. The smaller stumps he could jump two at a time, and he could walk on the top rail of the fence without being afraid.

Pa and Uncle Henry were out in the field, cutting the oats with cradles. A cradle was a sharp steel blade fastened to a framework of wooden slats that caught and held the stalks of grain when the blade cut them. Pa and Uncle Henry carried the cradles by their long, curved handles, and swung the blades into the standing oats. When they had cut enough to make a pile they slid the cut stalks off the slats into neat heaps on the ground.

It was hard work, walking around and around the field in the hot sun, and with both hands swinging the heavy cradles into the grain and cutting it, then sliding it into the piles.

After all the grain was cut, they must go over the field again. This time they would stoop over each pile, and taking up a handful of the stalks in each hand they would knot them together to make a longer strand. Then, gathering up the pile of grain in their arms, they would bind it tightly around with the band they had made, and tie the band, and tuck its ends.

After they made seven such bundles, then the bundles must be shocked. To make a shock, they stood five bundles upright, snugly together with the oat heads up. Then over these they put two more bundles, spreading out the stalks to make a little roof and shelter the five bundles from dew and rain.

Every stalk of the cut grain must always be safely in the shock before dark, for lying on the dewey ground all night would spoil it.

Pa and Uncle Henry were working very hard because the air was so heavy and hot and still that they expected rain. The oats were ripe, and if they were not cut and in the shock before rain came, the crop would be lost. Then Uncle Henry's horses would be hungry all winter.

At noon Pa and Uncle Henry came to the house in a great hurry and swallowed their dinner as quickly as they could. Uncle Henry said that Charley must help them that afternoon.

Laura looked at Pa, when Uncle Henry said that. At home, Pa had said to Ma that Uncle Henry and Aunt Polly spoiled Charley. When Pa was eleven years old, he had done a good day's work every day in the fields, driving a team. But Charley did hardly any work at all.

Now Uncle Henry said that Charley must come to the field. He could save them a great deal of time. He could go to the spring for water, and he could fetch them the water-jug when they needed a drink. He could fetch the whetstone when the blades needed sharpening.

All the children looked at Charley. Charley did not want to go to the field. He wanted to stay in the yard and play. But, of course, he did not say so.

Pa and Uncle Henry did not rest at all. They ate in a hurry and went right back to work, and Charley went with them.

Now Mary was oldest, and she wanted to play a quiet, ladylike play. So in the afternoon the cousins made a playhouse in the yard. The stumps were chairs and tables and stoves, and leaves were dishes, and sticks were the children.

On the way home that night, Laura and Mary heard Pa tell Ma what happened in the field.

Instead of helping Pa and Uncle Henry, Charley was making all the trouble he could. He got in their way so they couldn't swing the cradles. He hid the whetstone, so they had to hunt for it when the blades needed sharpening. He didn't bring the water-jug till Uncle Henry shouted at him three or four times, and then he was sullen.

After that he followed them around, talking and asking questions. They were working too hard to pay attention to him, so they told him to go away and not bother them.

But they dropped their cradles and ran to him across the field when they heard him scream. The woods were all around the field, and there were snakes in the oats.

When they got to Charley there was nothing wrong, and he laughed at them. He said "I fooled you that time!"

Pa said if he had been Uncle Henry, he would have tanned that boy's hide for him right then and there. But Uncle Henry did not do it.

So they took a drink of water and went back to work.

Three times Charley screamed, and they ran to him as fast as they could, and he laughed at them. He thought it was a good joke. And still, Uncle Henry did not tan his hide.

Then a fourth time he screamed, louder than ever. Pa and Uncle Henry looked at him, and he was jumping up and down, screaming. They saw nothing wrong with him, and they had been fooled so many times that they went on with their work.

Charley kept on screaming, louder and shriller. Pa did not say anything, but Uncle Henry said, "Let him scream." So they went on working and let him scream.

He kept on jumping up and down, screaming. He did not stop. At last Uncle Henry said:

"Maybe something really is wrong."

They laid down their cradles and went across the field to him.

And all that time Charley had been jumping up and down on a yellow jackets' nest!

The yellow jackets lived in a nest in the ground, and Charley stepped on it by mistake. Then all the little bees in their bright yellow jackets came swarming out with their red-hot stings, and they hurt Charley so that he couldn't get away.

He was jumping up and down and hundreds of bees were stinging him all over. They were stinging his face and his hands and his neck and his nose; they were crawling up his

pants' legs and stinging and crawling down the back of his neck and stinging. The more he jumped and screamed, the harder they stung.

Pa and Uncle Henry took him by the arms and ran him away from the yellow jackets' nest. They undressed him, and his clothes were full of yellow jackets, and their stings were swelling up all over him. They killed the bees that were stinging him, and they shook the bees out of his clothes, and then they dressed him again and sent him to the house.

Laura and Mary and the cousins were playing quietly in the yard, when they heard a loud, blubbering cry. Charley came bawling into the yard, and his face was so swollen that the tears could hardly squeeze out of his eyes.

His hands were puffed up, and his neck was puffed out, and his cheeks were big, hard puffs. His fingers stood out stiff and swollen. There were little, hard, white dents all over his puffed-out face and neck.

Laura and Mary and the cousins stood and looked at him.

Ma and Aunt Polly came running out of the house and asked him what was the matter. Charley blubbered and bawled. Ma said it was yellow jackets. She ran to the garden and got a big pan of earth, while Aunt Polly took Charley into the house and undressed him.

They made a big panful of mud and plastered him all over with it. They rolled him up in an old sheet and put him to bed. His eyes were swollen shut and his nose was a funny shape. Ma and Aunt Polly covered his whole face with mud and tied the mud on with cloths. Only the end of his nose and his mouth showed.

Aunt Polly steeped some herbs, to give him for his fever. Laura and Mary and the cousins stood around for some time, looking at him. It was dark that night when Pa and Uncle Henry came from the field. All the oats were in the shock, and now the rain could come, and it would not do any harm.

Pa could not stay to supper; he had to get home and do the milking. The cows were already waiting at home, and when cows are not milked on time they do not give up so much milk. He hitched up quickly, and they all got into the wagon.

Pa was very tired and his hands ached so that he could not drive very well, but the horses knew the way home. Ma sat beside him with Baby Carrie, and Laura and Mary sat on the board behind them. Then they heard Pa tell about what Charley had done.

Laura and Mary were horrified. They were often naughty, themselves, but they had never imagined that anyone could be as naughty as Charley had been. He hadn't worked to help save the oats. He hadn't minded his father when his father spoke to him. He had bothered Pa and Uncle Henry when they were hard at work.

Then Pa told about the yellow jackets' nest, and he said:

"It served the little liar right."

After she was in the trundle that night, Laura lay and listened to the rain drumming on the roof and streaming from the eaves, and she thought about what Pa had said.

She thought about what the yellow jackets had done to Charley. She thought it served Charley right, too. It served him right because he had been so monstrously naughty. And the bees had a right to sting him, when he jumped on their home.

But she couldn't understand why Pa had called him a little liar. She didn't understand how Charley could be a liar, when he had not said a word.

Wilder, Laura Ingalls. *Little House in the Big Woods*. New York: HarperTrophy, a division of HarperCollins Publishers, Inc., 1932.

OLIVER TWIST

CHARLES DICKENS

Oliver Twist has lived in a dreary orphanage since he was nine. Then he runs away and sets out for London. When he gets to a small town outside London he meets a young boy about his own age. This strange boy befriends him and later introduces Oliver to a gang of pickpockets.

CHAPTER 7

Oliver reached the stile at which the by path terminated and once more gained the high road. It was eight o'clock now. Though he was nearly five miles away from the town, he ran and hid behind the hedges, by turns, till noon: fearing that he might be pursued and overtaken. Then he sat down to rest by the side of the milestone, and began to think, for the first time, where he had better go and try to live.

The stone by which he was seated bore, in large characters, an intimation that it was just seventy miles from that spot to London. The name awakened a new train of ideas in the boy's mind. London—that great large place!—nobody—not even Mr. Bumble—could ever find him there! He had often heard the old men in the workhouse, too, say that no lad of spirit need want in London and that there were ways of living in that vast city, which those who had been bred up in country parts had no idea of. It was the very place for a homeless boy, who must die in the streets unless someone helped him. As these things passed through his thoughts, he jumped upon his feet and again walked forward.

He had diminished the distance between himself and London by full four miles more before he recollected how much he must undergo ere he could hope to reach his place of destination. As this consideration forced itself upon him, he slackened his pace a little, and meditated upon his means of getting there. He had a crust of bread, a coarse shirt, and two pairs of stockings in his bundle. He had a penny too—a gift of Sowerberry's after some funeral in which he had acquitted himself more than ordinarily well—in his pocket. A clean shirt, thought Oliver, is a very comfortable thing, and so are two pairs of darned stockings, and so is a penny; but they are small helps to a sixty-five miles' walk in winter-time. But Oliver's thoughts, like those of most other people, although they were extremely ready and active to point out his difficulties, were wholly at a loss to suggest any feasible mode of surmounting them; so, after a good deal of thinking to no particular purpose, he changed his little bundle over to the other shoulder and trudged on.

Oliver walked twenty miles that day, and all that time tasted, nothing but the crust of dry bread and a few draughts of water, which he begged at the cottage doors by the roadside. When the night came, he turned into a meadow, and creeping close under a hay rick, determined to lie there till morning. He felt frightened at first, for the wind moaned dismally over the empty fields, and he was cold and hungry, and more alone than he had ever felt before. Being very tired with his walk, however, he soon fell asleep and forgot his troubles.

He felt cold and stiff when he got up next morning and so hungry that he was obliged to exchange the penny for a small loaf in the very first village through which he passed. He had walked no more than twelve miles when night closed in again. His feet were sore and his legs so weak that they trembled beneath him. Another night passed in the bleak damp air made him worse; when he set forward on his journey next morning he could hardly crawl along.

In some villages, large painted boards were fixed up warning all persons who begged within the district that they would be sent to jail. This frightened Oliver very much and made him glad to get out of those villages with all possible expedition. In others, he would stand about the inn yards and look mournfully at everyone who passed, a proceeding which generally terminated in the landlady's ordering one of the post boys who were lounging about, to drive that strange boy out of the place, for she was sure he had come to steal something. If he begged at a farmer's house, ten to one but they threatened to set the dog on him; and when he showed his nose in a shop, they talked about the beadle—which brought Oliver's heart into his mouth—very often the only thing he had there for many hours together.

In fact, if it had not been for a good-hearted turnpike man and a benevolent old lady, Oliver's troubles would have been shortened by the very same process which had put an end to his mother's; in other words, he would most assuredly have fallen dead upon the king's highway. But the turnpike man gave him a meal of bread and cheese; and the old lady, who had a shipwrecked grandson wandering barefoot in some distant part of the earth, took pity upon the poor orphan and gave him what little she could afford—and more—with such kind and gentle words, and such tears of sympathy and compassion, that they sank deeper into Oliver's soul than all the sufferings he had ever undergone.

Early on the seventh morning after he had left his native place, Oliver limped slowly into the little town of Barnet. The window shutters were closed; the street was empty; not a soul had awakened to the business of the day. The sun was rising in all its splendid beauty; but the light only served to show the boy his own lonesomeness and desolation as he sat, with bleeding feet and covered with dust, upon a cold doorstep.

He had been crouching on the step for some time, wondering at the great number of public houses (every other house in Barnet was a tavern, large or small), gazing listlessly at the coaches as they passed through and thinking how strange it seemed that they could do, with ease, in a few hours, what it had taken him a whole week of courage and determination beyond his years to accomplish when he was roused by observing that a boy, who had passed him carelessly some minutes before, had returned and was now surveying him most earnestly from the opposite side of the way. He took little heed of this at first; but the boy remained in the same attitude of close observation so long, that Oliver raised his head and returned his steady look. Upon this, the boy crossed over, and walking close up to Oliver, said,

"Hullo, my covey! What's the row?"

The boy who addressed this inquiry to the young wayfarer was about his own age, but one of the queerest-looking boys that Oliver had ever seen. He was a snub-nosed, flat-browed, common-faced boy enough, and as dirty a juvenile as one would wish to see; but he had about him all the airs and manners of a man.

Dickens, Charles. *Oliver Twist*. New York: Puffin Books, a division of Penguin Books USA Inc., 1837, 1994.

POLLYANNA

Eleanor H. Porter

Pollyanna is orphaned and has to go live with her stern aunt Polly and sleep in a tiny attic room. But she remains an eternal optimist.

In this passage, Nancy, the housekeeper, finds Pollyanna after she ran off to explore and missed dinner. Nancy is ordered to give her only bread and milk for dinner as punishment, but that doesn't dampen Pollyanna's indomitable spirit. Here, she explains her "game" to the disbelieving Nancy.

Chapter 5 THE GAME

or the land's sake Miss Pollyanna, what a scare you did give me," panted Nancy, hurrying up to the big rock, down which Pollyanna had just regretfully slid.

"Scare? Oh, I'm so sorry. But you mustn't, really, ever get scared about me, Nancy. Father and the Ladies' Aid used to do it, too, till they found I always came back all right."

"But I didn't even know you'd went," cried Nancy, tucking the little girl's hand under her arm and hurrying her down the hill. "I didn't see you go, and nobody didn't. I guess you flew right up through the roof."

Pollyanna skipped gleefully.

"I did,—only I flew down instead of up. I came down the tree."

Nancy stopped short.

"You did—what?"

"Came down the tree, outside my window."

"My stars and stockings!" gasped Nancy, hurrying on again. "I'd like ter know what yer aunt would say ter that!"

"Would you? Well, I'll tell her, then, so you can find out," promised the little girl cheerfully.

"Mercy!" gasped Nancy. "No—no!"

"Why, you don't mean she'd care!" cried Pollyanna, plainly disturbed.

"No—er—yes—well, never mind. I—I ain't so very particular about knowin' what she'd say, truly," stammered Nancy, determined to keep one scolding from Pollyanna, if nothing more. "But, say, we better hurry."

For a moment there was silence. The sky was darkening fast and Pollyanna took a firmer hold of her friend's arm.

"I reckon I'm glad, after all, that you did get scared—a little, 'cause then you came after me." She shivered.

"Poor little lamb! And you must be hungry too. I—I'm afraid you'll have ter have bread and milk in the kitchen with me. Yer aunt didn't like it—because you didn't come down ter supper, ye know."

"But I couldn't. I was up here."

"Yes, but—she didn't know that, you see," observed Nancy dryly, stifling a chuckle. "I'm sorry about the bread and milk, I am, I am."

"Oh, I'm not. I'm glad."

"Glad! Why?"

"Why, I like bread and milk, and I'd like to eat with you. I don't see any trouble about being glad about that."

"You don't seem ter see any trouble bein' glad about everythin'" retorted Nancy, choking a little over her remembrance of Pollyanna's brave attempts to like the bare little attic room.

Pollyanna laughed softly.

"Well, that's the game, you know, anyway."

"The—game?"

"Yes, the 'just being glad' game."

"Whatever in the world are you talkin' about?"

"Why, it's a game Father told it to me, and it's lovely," rejoined Pollyanna. "We've played it always, ever since I was a little, little girl. I told the Ladies' Aid, and they played it—some of them."

"What is it? I ain't much on games, though."

Pollyanna laughed again, but she sighed, too, and in the gathering twilight her face looked thin and wistful.

"Why, we began it on some crutches that came in a missionary barrel."

"Crutches!"

"Yes. You see I'd wanted a doll, and Father had written them so. But when the barrel came the lady wrote that there hadn't any dolls come in, but the little crutches had. So she sent 'em along as they might come in handy for some child, sometime. And that's when we began it."

"Well, I must say I can't see any game about that," declared Nancy, almost irritably.

"Oh, yes; the game was to just find something about everything to be glad about—no matter what 'twas," rejoined Pollyanna earnestly. "and we began right then—on the crutches."

"Well, goodness me! I can't see anythin' ter be glad about—gettin' a pair of crutches when you wanted a doll!"

279

Pollyanna clapped her hands.

"There is—there is," she crowed. "but I couldn't see it, either, Nancy, at first," she added with quick honesty. "Father had to tell it to me."

"Well, then, suppose you tell me," almost snapped Nancy.

"Goosey! Why, just be glad because you don't—need—'em!" exulted Pollyanna triumphantly "You see it's just as easy—when you know how!"

"Well, of all the queer doin's!" breathed Nancy, regarding Pollyanna with almost fearful eyes.

"Oh, but it isn't queer—it's lovely," maintained Pollyanna enthusiastically. "And we've played it ever since. And the harder 'tis, the more fun 'tis to get 'em out. Only—only—sometimes it's almost too hard— like when you father goes to heaven, and there isn't anybody but a Ladies Aid left."

"Yes or when you're put in a snippy little room way at the top of the house with nothin' in it," growled Nancy.

Pollyanna sighed.

"That was a hard one, at first," she admitted, "specially when I was so kind of lonesome. I just didn't feel like playing the game anyway, and I had been wanting pretty things so! Then I happened to think how I hated to see my freckles in the looking glass, and I saw that lovely picture out the window too. So then I knew I'd found the things to be glad about. You see, when you're hunting for the glad things, you sort of forget the other kind—like the doll you wanted, you know."

"Most generally it doesn't take so long," sighed Pollyanna, "and lots of times now I just think of them without thinking, you know. I've got so used to playing it. It's a lovely game. F-father and I used to like it so much," she faltered. "I suppose, though, it—it'll be a little harder now, as long as I haven't anybody to play it with. Maybe Aunt Polly will play it, though," she added as an afterthought.

"My stars and stockings—her!" Breathed Nancy behind her teeth. Then, aloud, she said doggedly, "See here, Miss Pollyanna, I ain't sayin' that I'll play it very well, and I ain't sayin' that I know how, anyway. But I'll play it with ye, after a fashion—I just will, I will!"

"Oh, Nancy!" exulted Pollyanna, giving her a rapturous hug. "That'll be splendid! Won't we have fun?"

"Er—maybe," conceded Nancy, in open doubt. "but you musn't count too much on me, ye know. I never was no case fur games, but I'm a-goin' ter have someone ter play it with, anyhow," she finished as they entered the kitchen together.

Pollyanna ate her bread and milk with good appetite. Then, at Nancy's suggestion, she went into the sitting room, where her aunt sat reading.

Miss Polly looked up coldly.

"Have you had your supper, Pollyanna?"

"Yes, Aunt Polly."

POLLYANNA *Eleanor H. Porter*

"I'm very sorry, Pollyanna, to have been obliged so soon to send you into the kitchen to eat bread and milk."

"But I was real glad you did it, aunt Polly. I like bread and milk, and Nancy too. You mustn't feel bad about that one bit."

Aunt Polly sat suddenly a little more erect in her chair.

"Pollyanna, it's quite time you were in bed. Breakfast will be at half past seven. See that you are down to that. Good night."

Quite as a mater of course Pollyanna came straight to her aunt's side and gave her an affectionate hug.

"I've had such a beautiful time so far." She sighed happily. "I know I'm going to just love living with you—but then, I knew I should before I came. Good night," she called cheerfully as she ran from the room.

Porter, Eleanor H. *Pollyanna.* New York: Bantam Doubleday Dell Publishing Group, Inc., 1986.

THE SECRET GARDEN

FRANCES HODGSON BURNETT

Mary Lennox is raised by a nurse (her Ayah) in her parents' grand house in India. When they die in a cholera epidemic, Mary is brought to live with her uncle on the Yorkshire moors. In this excerpt you will learn that other than the servants, she is all alone until she makes friends with Dickon who lives among the animals and birds, a robin who leads her to the secret garden, and Colin, a strange boy who almost never leaves his bed.

Chapter 17   A TANTRUM

She had got up very early in the morning and had worked hard in the garden, and she was tired and sleepy, so as soon as Martha had brought her supper and she had eaten it, she was glad to go to bed. As she laid her head on the pillow she murmured to herself:

"I'll go out before breakfast and work with Dickon and then afterward—I believe—I'll go to see him."

She thought it was the middle of the night when she was awakened by such dreadful sounds that she jumped out of bed in an instant. What was it—what was it? The next minute she felt quite sure she knew. Doors were opened and shut, and there were hurrying feet in the corridors, and someone was crying and screaming at the same time, screaming and crying in a horrible way.

"It's Colin," she said. "He's having one of those tantrums the nurse called hysterics. How awful it sounds."

As she listened to the sobbing screams she did not wonder that people were so frightened that they gave him his own way in everything rather than hear them. She put her hands over her ears and felt sick and shivering.

"I don't know what to do. I don't know what to do," she kept saying. "I can't bear it."

Once she wondered if he would stop if she dared go to him and then she remembered how he had driven her out of the room and thought that perhaps the sight of her might make him worse. Even when she pressed her hands more tightly over her ears she could not keep the awful sounds out. She hated them so and was so terrified by them that suddenly they began to make her angry, and she felt as if she should like to fly into a tantrum herself and frighten him as he was frightening her. She was not used to any one's tempers but her own. She took her hands from her ears and sprang up and stamped her foot.

"He ought to be stopped! Somebody ought to make him stop! Somebody ought to beat him!" she cried out.

Just then she heard feet almost running down the corridor, and her door opened, and the nurse came in. She was not laughing now by any means. She even looked rather pale.

"He's worked himself into hysterics," she said in a great hurry. "He'll do himself harm. No one can do anything with him. You come and try, like a good child. He likes you."

"He turned me out of the room this morning," said Mary, stamping her foot with excitement.

The stamp rather pleased the nurse. The truth was that she had been afraid she might find Mary crying and hiding her head under the bedclothes

"That's right," she said. "You're in the right humor. You go and scold him. Give him something new to think of. Do go, child, as quick as ever you can."

It was not until afterward Mary realized that the thing had been funny as well as dreadful—that it was funny that all the grown-up people were so frightened that they came to a little girl just because they guessed she was almost as bad as Colin himself.

She flew along the corridor, and the nearer she got to the screams, the higher her temper mounted. She felt quite wicked by the time she reached the door. She slapped it open with her hand and ran across the room to the four-posted bed.

"You stop!" she almost shouted. "You stop! I hate you! Everybody hates you! I wish everybody would run out of the house and let you scream yourself to death! You will scream yourself to death in a minute, and I wish you would!"

A nice, sympathetic child could neither have thought nor said such things, but it just happened that the shock of hearing them was the best possible thing for this hysterical boy whom no one had ever dared to restrain or contradict.

He had been lying on his face beating his pillow with his hands, and he actually almost jumped around, he turned so quickly at the sound of the furious little voice. His face looked dreadful, white and red and swollen, and he was gasping and choking; but savage little Mary did not care an atom.

"If you scream another scream," she said, "I'll scream too—and I can scream louder than you can, and I'll frighten you, I'll frighten you!"

He actually had stopped screaming because she had startled him so. The scream which had been coming almost choked him. The tears were streaming down his face, and he shook all over.

"I can't stop!" he gasped and sobbed. "I can't—I can't!"

"You can!" shouted Mary. "Half that ails you is hysterics and temper—just hysterics—hysterics—hysterics!" And she stamped each time she said it.

"I felt the lump—I felt it," choked out Colin. "I knew I should. I shall have a hunch on my back, and then I shall die," and he began to writhe again and turned on his face and sobbed and wailed, but he didn't scream.

"You didn't feel a lump!" contradicted Mary fiercely. "If you did, it was only a hysterical lump. Hysterics makes nothing but hysterics! Turn over and let me look at it!"

She liked the word "hysterics" and felt somehow as if it had an effect on him. He was probably like herself and had never heard it before.

"Nurse," she commanded, "come here and show me his back this minute!"

The nurse, Mrs. Medlock and Martha had been standing huddled together near the door staring at her, their mouths half open. All three had gasped with fright more than once. The nurse came forward as if she were half afraid. Colin was heaving with great breathless sobs.

"Perhaps he—he won't let me," she hesitated in a low voice.

Colin heard her, however, and he gasped out between two sobs:

"Sh-show her! She—She'll see then!"

It was a poor, thin back to look at when it was bared. Every rib could be counted and every joint of the spine, though Mistress Mary did not count them as she bent over and examined them with a solemn, savage little face. She looked so sour and old-fashioned that the nurse turned her head aside to hide the twitching of her mouth. There was just a minute's silence, for even Colin tried to hold his breath while Mary looked up and down his spine, and down and up, as intently as if she had been the great doctor from London.

"There's not a single lump there!" she said at last. "There's not a lump as big as a pin—except backbone lumps, and you can only feel them because you're thin. I've got backbone lumps myself, and they used to stick out as much as yours do, until I began to get fatter, and I am not fat enough yet to hide them. There's not a lump as big as a pin! If you ever say there is again, I shall laugh!"

No one but Colin himself knew what effect those crossly spoken childish words had on him. If he had ever had anyone to talk to about his secret terrors—if he had ever dared to let himself ask questions—if he had had childish companions and had not lain on his back in the huge, closed house, breathing an atmosphere heavy with the fears of people who were, most of them, ignorant and tired of him he would have found out that most of his fright and illness was created by himself. But he had lain and thought of himself and his aches and wearinesss for hours and days and months and years. And now that an angry, unsympathetic little girl insisted obstinately that he was not as ill as he thought he was, he actually felt as if she might be speaking the truth.

"I didn't know," ventured the nurse, "that he thought he had a lump on his spine. His back is weak because he won't try to sit up. I could have told him there was no lump there."

Colin gulped and turned his face a little to look at her.

"C-Could you?" he said pathetically.

"Yes, sir."

"There!" said Mary, and she gulped too.

Colin turned on his face again, and but for his long-drawn broken breaths, which were the dying down of his storm of sobbing, he lay still for a minute, though great tears streamed down his face and wet the pillow. Actually, the tears meant that a curious great relief had come to him. Presently he turned and looked at the nurse again, and strangely enough, he was not like a Rajah at all as he spoke to her.

"Do you think—I could—live to grow up?" he said.

The nurse was neither clever nor soft-hearted, but she could repeat some of the London doctor's words.

"You probably will if you will do what you are told to do and not give way to your temper and stay out a great deal in the fresh air."

Colin's tantrum had passed, and he was weak and worn out with crying, and this per-haps made him feel gentle. He put out his hand a little toward Mary, and I am glad to say that, her own tantrum having passed, she was softened too and met him half-way with her hand, so that it was a sort of making up.

"I'll—I'll go out with you, Mary," he said. "I shan't hate fresh air if we can find—" He remembered just in time to stop himself from saying "if we can find the secret garden" and he ended, "I shall like to go out with you if Dickon will come and push my chair. I do so want to see Dickon and the fox and the crow."

The nurse remade the tumbled bed and shook and straightened the pillows. Then she made Colin a cup of beef tea and gave a cup to Mary, who really was very glad to get it after her excitement. Mrs. Medlock and Martha gladly slipped away, and after everything was neat and calm and in order the nurse looked as if she would very gladly slip away also. She was a healthy young woman who resented being robbed of her sleep, and she yawned quite openly as she looked at Mary, who had pushed her big footstool close to the four-posted bed and was holding Colin's hand.

"You must go back and get your sleep out," she said. "He'll drop off after a while—if he's not too upset. Then I'll lie down myself in the next room."

"Would you like me to sing you that song I learned from my Ayah?" Mary whispered to Colin.

His hand pulled hers gently, and he turned his tired eyes on her appealingly.

"Oh, yes!" he answered. "It's such a soft song. I shall go to sleep in a minute."

"I will put him to sleep," Mary said to the yawning nurse. "You can go if you like."

Burnett, Frances Hodgson. *The Secret Garden*. New York: Harper Trophy, Harper Collins Publishers, 1987.

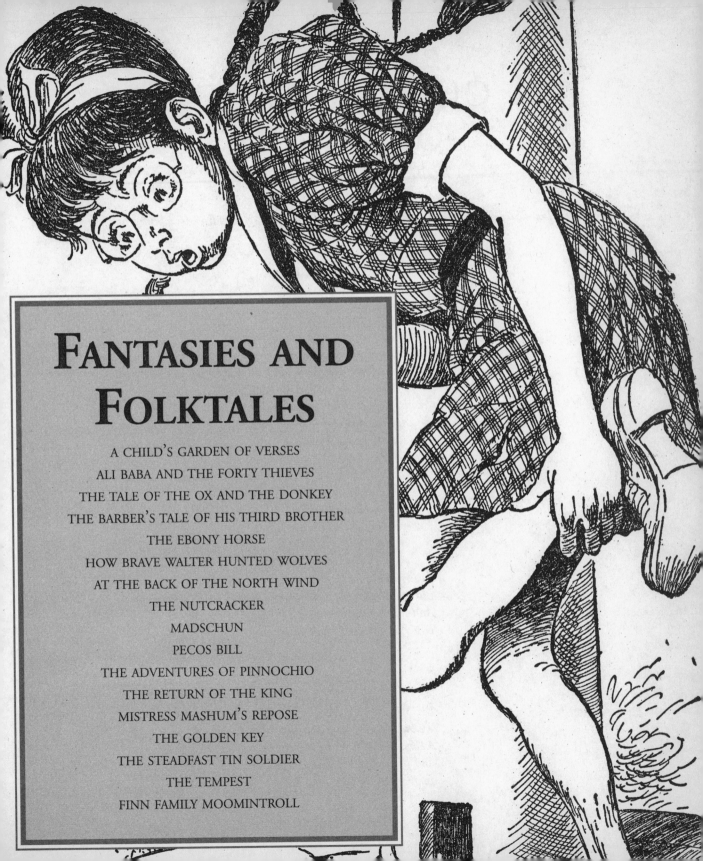

Fantasies and Folktales

A CHILD'S GARDEN
OF VERSES

ROBERT LOUIS STEVENSON

Robert Louis Stevenson's poems for children evoke a world of imaginary friends, whimsy, and play.

YOUNG NIGHT THOUGHT

All night long, and every night,
When my mamma puts out the light,
I see the people marching by,
As plain as day, before my eye.

Armies and emperors and kings,
All carrying different kinds of things,
And marching in so grand a way,
You never saw the like by day.

So fine a show was never seen
At the great circus on the green;
For every kind of beast and man
Is marching in that caravan.

At first they move a little slow,
But still the faster on they go,
And still beside them close I keep
Until we reach the town of Sleep.

A GOOD PLAY

We built a ship upon the stairs
All made of the back-bedroom chairs,
And filled it full of sofa pillows
To go a-sailing on the billows.

We took a saw and several nails,
And water in the nursery pails;
And Tom said, "Let us also take
An apple and a slice of cake";
Which was enough for Tom and me
To go a-sailing on, till tea.

We sailed along for days and days,
And had the very best of plays;
But Tom fell out and hurt his knee,
So there was no one left but me.

THE LAND OF NOD

From breakfast on all through the day
At home among my friends I stay;
But every night I go abroad
Afar into the land of Nod.

All by myself I have to go,
With none to tell me what to do—
All alone beside the streams
And up the mountainsides of dreams.

The strangest things are there for me,
Both things to eat and things to see,
And many frightening sights abroad
Till morning in the land of Nod.

Try as I like to find the way,
I never can get back by day,
Nor can remember plain and clear
The curious music that I hear.

MY SHADOW

I have a little shadow that goes in and out with me,
And what can be the use of him is more than I can see.
He is very, very like me from the heels up to the head;
And I see him jump before me, when I jump into my bed.

The funniest thing about him is the way he likes to grow—
Not at all like proper children, which is always very slow;
For he sometimes shoots up taller like an india-rubber ball,
And sometimes gets so little that there's none of him at all.

He hasn't got a notion of how children ought to play,
And can only make a fool of me in every sort of way.
He stays so close beside me, he's a coward you can see;
I'd think shame to stick to nursie as that shadow sticks to me!

One morning, very early, before the sun was up,
I rose and found the shining dew on every buttercup;
But my lazy little shadow, like an arrant sleepyhead,
Had stayed at home behind me and was fast asleep in bed.

MY BED IS A BOAT

My bed is like a little boat;
    Nurse helps me when I embark;
She girds me in my sailor's coat
    And starts me in the dark.

At night, I go on board and say
    Good night to all my friends on shore;
I shut my eyes and sail away
    And see and hear no more.

And sometimes things to bed I take,
As prudent sailors have to do;

Perhaps a slice of wedding cake,
Perhaps a toy or two.

All night across the dark we steer:
But when the day returns at last,
Safe in my room, beside the pier,
I find my vessel fast.

FAREWELL TO THE FARM

The coach is at the door at last;
The eager children, mounting fast
And kissing hands, in chorus sing:
Good-bye, good-bye, to everything!

To house and garden, field and lawn,
The meadow-gates we swang upon,
To pump and stable, tree and swing,
Good-bye, good-bye, to everything!

And fare you well for evermore,
O ladder at the hayloft door,
O hayloft where the cobwebs cling,
Good-bye, good-bye, to everything!

Crack goes the whip, and off we go;
The trees and houses smaller grow;
Last, round the woody turn we swing:
Good-bye, good-bye, to everything!

NORTH-WEST PASSAGE

1. Good Night
When the bright lamp is carried in,
The sunless hours again begin;
O'er all without, in field and lane,
The haunted night returns again.

Now we behold the embers flee
About the firelit hearth; and see
Our faces painted as we pass,
Like pictures, on the window-glass.

Must we to bed indeed? Well then,
Let us arise and go like men,
And face with an undaunted tread
The long black passage up to bed.

Farewell, O brother, sister, sire!
O pleasant party round the fire!
The songs you sing, the tales you tell,
Till far tomorrow, fare ye well!

2. Shadow March
All round the house is the jet-black night;
It stares through the windowpane;
It crawls in the corners, hiding from the light,
And it moves with the moving flame.

Now my little heart goes a-beating like a drum,
With the breath of the Bogie in my hair;
And all round the candle the crooked shadows come
And go marching along up the stair.

The shadow of the balusters, the shadow of the lamp,
The shadow of the child that goes to bed—

All the wicked shadows coming, tramp, tramp, tramp,
With the black light overhead.

3. In Port
Last, to the chamber where I lie
My fearful footsteps patter nigh,
And come from out the cold and gloom
Into my warm and cheerful room.

There, safe arrived, we turn about
To keep the coming shadows out,
And close the happy door at last
On all the perils that we past.

Then, when mamma goes by to bed,
She shall come in with tiptoed tread,
And see me lying warm and fast
And in the Land of Nod at last.

THE UNSEEN PLAYMATE

When children are playing alone on the green,
In comes the playmate that never was seen.
When children are happy and lonely and good,
The friend of the Children comes out of the wood.

Nobody heard him and nobody saw,
His is a picture you never could draw,
But he's sure to be present, abroad or at home,
When children are happy and playing alone.

He lies in the laurels, he runs on the grass,
He sings when you tinkle the musical glass;
Whene'er you are happy and cannot tell why,
The friend of the Children is sure to be by!

He loves to be little, he hates to be big,
'Tis he that inhabits the caves that you dig;

'Tis he when you play with your soldiers of tin
That sides with the Frenchmen and never can win.

'Tis he, when at night you go off to your bed,
Bids you go to sleep and not trouble your head;
For wherever they're lying, in cupboard or shelf,
'Tis he will take care of your playthings himself!

BLOCK CITY

What are you able to build with your blocks?
Castles and palaces, temples and docks.
Rain may keep raining, and others go roam,
But I can be happy and building at home.

Let the sofa be mountains, the carpet be sea,
There I'll establish a city for me:
A kirk and a mill and a palace beside,
And a harbor as well where my vessels may ride.

Great is the palace with pillar and wall,
A sort of tower on the top of it all,
And steps coming down in an orderly way
To where my toy vessels lie safe in the bay.

This one is sailing and that one is moored:
Hark to the song of the sailors on board!
And see on the steps of my palace, the kings
Coming and going with presents and things!

Now I have done with it, down let it go!
All in a moment the town is laid low.
Block upon block lying scattered and free,
What is there left of my town by the sea?

Yet as I saw it, I see it again,
The kirk and the palace, the ships and the men,
And as long as I live, and where'er I may be,
I'll always remember my town by the sea.

THE LITTLE LAND

When at home alone I sit
And am very tired of it,
I have just to shut my eyes
To go sailing through the skies—
To go sailing far away
To the pleasant Land of Play;
To the fairy land afar
Where the Little People are;
Where the clover-tops are trees,
And the rain-pools are the seas,
And the leaves like little ships
Sail about on tiny trips;
And above the daisy tree
Through the grasses,
High o'erhead the Bumble Bee
Hums and passes.

In that forest to and fro
I can wander, I can go;
See the spider and the fly,
And the ants go marching by
Carrying parcels with their feet
Down the green and grassy street.
I can in the sorrel sit,
Where the ladybird alit.
I can climb the jointed grass,
And on high
See the greater swallows pass
In the sky,
And the round sun rolling by
Heeding no such things as I.

Through that forest I can pass
Till, as in a looking glass,
Humming fly and daisy tree
And my tiny self I see,
Painted very clear and neat

On the rain-pool at my feet.
Should a leaflet come to land
Drifting near to where I stand,
Straight I'll board that tiny boat
Round the rain-pool sea to float.

Little thoughtful creatures sit
On the grassy coast of it.
Little things with lovely eyes
See me sailing with surprise.
Some are clad in armor green—
(These have sure to battle been!)—
Some are pied with every hue,
Black and crimson, gold and blue;
Some have wings and swift are gone;
But they all look kindly on.

When my eyes I once again
Open, and see all things plain:
High bare walls, great bare floor;
Great knobs on drawer and door;
Great big people perched on chairs,
Stitching tucks and mending tears,
Each a hill that I could climb,
And talking nonsense all the time—
O dear me,
That I could be
A sailor on the rain-pool sea,
A climber in the clover tree,
And just come back; a sleepyhead,
Late at night to go to bed.

Stevenson, Robert Louis. *A Child's Garden of Verses*. New York: Penguin Books USA, 1994.

The Tales of the Arabian Nights are a collection of stories that have been passed down from story tellers from the Far and Middle East. They started as oral tales and then were written down so that they would be preserved.

ALI BABA AND THE FORTY THIEVES

Ali Baba learns the magic words that one must utter to enter the cave where a group of robbers keep their stolen bounty.

nce upon a time, there were two brothers named Kasim and Ali Baba, who lived in a certain city of Persia. When their father died, they each received an equal share of his wealth and lost no time in spending and wasting it all. The elder brother, Kasim, however, married the daughter of a rich merchant, so that when his father-in-law passed away, he became the owner of a large shop that contained valuable merchandise and a storehouse of precious goods. Moreover, he inherited a great deal of gold buried in the ground. Thus, he became known throughout the town as a prosperous merchant.

Meanwhile, Ali Baba had married a poor and needy woman and lived with her in a dismal hovel. He eked out a scanty livelihood by gathering wood in a forest and selling it for fuel on his three donkeys in the bazaars around town.

Now, one day it so happened that Ali Baba had cut some dead branches and had placed the load on his donkeys when suddenly he perceived a cloud of dust high in the air and moving rapidly toward him from the right. When he took a closer look, he was able to distinguish a troop of horsemen who would soon reach him, and this sight caused him great alarm, for he was afraid that they might be bandits who would slay him and drive off his donkeys. So, he began to run, but since he could not possibly escape the forest in time to avoid them, he drove his donkeys into some nearby bushes and scampered up a huge tree, where he hid himself behind some leaves. Fortunately, he could observe everything beneath him without fear of being seen by the people below, and the first thing he noticed was an immense rock that towered above the tree. When the horsemen finally arrived, it was right in front of this rock that they dismounted, and he could see that they were all young and strong. Moreover, it was clear from their looks and demeanor that they

were a group of robbers, about forty in all, who had attacked a caravan and had carried off the spoils and booty to this place with the intention of hiding it safely in some cache.

Indeed, the saddlebags which the men took from their horses proved to be full of gold and silver, and the men slung their bags over their shoulders. Then the robber who appeared to be their captain led the way and pushed through thorns and thickets until he came to a certain spot, where he uttered, "Open, Sesame!"

All at once a wide doorway appeared in the face of the rock, allowing the robbers to enter, and then the portal shut by itself. Although they were now inside the cave, Ali Baba remained perched on the tree, for he knew that the robbers could come out of the cave at any moment and slay him if they caught him descending the tree. Nevertheless, after waiting for a long time, he became tired and decided to mount one of their horses, herd his donkeys together, and then head toward the town. Just as he reached his decision, the portal flew open and the chief emerged. Standing at the entrance, he counted his men as they came out, and finally he spoke the magic words "Shut, Sesame!" and the door closed by itself. After he inspected his men, they all slung their saddlebags onto their horses and bridled them. As soon as they were ready, they rode off, and their chief led them in the direction that they had come from.

However, Ali Baba did not budge from the tree until they were clear out of sight, for he was afraid that one of them might return and spot him. When he finally descended, he thought to himself, "Why not try those magic words and see if the door will open and close at my bidding?" So he called aloud, "Open, Sesame!" And no sooner had he said those words than the portal flew open, and he entered a large, vaulted cavern through the portal about the size of a man, and hewn in stone. There was also light that came though air holes and bull's-eyes in the upper surface of the rock that formed the ceiling.

He had expected to find nothing but a dark and gloomy den and therefore was surprised to see the whole cave filled with bales of all kinds of material, heaped from floor to ceiling with camel loads of silks, brocades, embroidered cloths, and mounds of different-colored carpets. In addition, he came across countless gold and silver coins, some piled on the ground and others bound in leather bags and sacks. Upon seeing such an abundance of goods and money, Ali Baba concluded that the thieves must have been storing their loot in this place for many decades and not just the last few years.

Although the door to the cave had closed once he had entered, Ali Baba was not dismayed, because he remembered the magic words, which he used to open the door once again so he could carry out some of the spoils. He paid no attention to the precious materials but rather concentrated on gathering as many sacks of coins as he thought his donkeys could carry. Then he loaded them on the beasts and covered his plunder with sticks and branches so that nobody would detect the bags. Finally, he cried out, "Close, Sesame!" and immediately the door shut, for the spell had been so conceived that if anyone entered the cave, its portal shut automatically behind him, and if he wanted to leave the cave, the door would not open again unless he uttered the words, "Open, Sesame!"

Now that Ali Baba had loaded his donkeys he drove them toward the town as fast as he could, and after reaching home, he led them into the yard and shut the outer door. Then he took off the sticks and branches from the donkeys and carried the bags of gold to his wife, who immediately began feeling what was inside. When she realized that they were full of coins, however, she suspected that Ali Baba had robbed some people and began reproaching him for having done such an evil thing.

And Scheherazade noticed that dawn was approaching and stopped telling her story. When the next night arrived, however, she received the king's permission to continue her tale and said,

Upset by his wife's reaction, Ali Baba told her that he had not robbed anyone, and that instead of berating him she should rejoice with him at their good fortune. Thereupon, he told her about his adventure and began to pour heaps of gold on the floor right before her eyes so that she was dazzled by the sight and delighted in his account of the events in the forest. Then she stooped down and began counting coin after coin until Ali Baba said, "Silly woman, how long are you going to do that? Let me dig a hole to hide this treasure so that nobody will know about it."

THE TALE OF THE OX
AND THE DONKEY

A merchant who is able to understand the language of birds and animals overhears his ox give some important advice to his donkey.

There was once a merchant who owned a great deal of money and men, and who had a large number of cattle and camels. He also had a wife and family and dwelt in the country, since he knew a great deal about farming and agriculture. Now, Allah Almighty had endowed him with the ability to understand the language of birds and beasts of every kind. However, it was decreed that if he were to divulge the gift to anyone, he would be punished by death. So, out of fear, he kept his unusual gift a secret.

In his barn he had an ox and donkey, each tethered in his own stall next to one another. One day, when the merchant was sitting nearby with his servants, and children playing around him, he heard the ox say to the ass, "Greetings, friend. I hope that you continued to enjoy your rest and good care. Everything under you is swept neatly and watered down. Men wait on you and feed you sifted barley, and give you pure spring water to drink. On the other hand, I (unhappy creature!) am led forth in the middle of the night when they set the plow and something called a yoke on my neck. I'm exhausted from cleaving the earth from dawn to dusk. I'm forced to do more than I can and to bear all kinds of mistreatment every night. And at the end of my work they take me back with my sides torn, my neck flayed, my legs aching, and my eyelids sore with tears. Then they shut me up in the barn and throw me beans and hay mixed with dirt and chaff. And I lie in dung and filth, and there is nothing but a foul stench throughout the night. But you are always in a clean place and are always able to relax, except when the master has some business in town, and that's very seldom. Then he just mounts you and rides to the town and returns right away. This is the way things are: I toil and have no rest, while you relax and have leisure time. You sleep while I am sleepless. I starve while you have all you want to eat."

When the ox stopped speaking, the donkey turned toward him and said, "Oh you lost soul! Whoever dubbed you bull head did not lie, for you are denser than the simplest of simpletons! With all your zeal, you foolishly toil for the master, and wear yourself out and kill yourself for the comfort of someone else. At the call of dawn you set out to work and don't return until sundown, and throughout the livelong day you endure all kinds of hardships such as beatings and cursing. Now listen to me, carefully. When you go into the fields and they lay that thing called the yoke on your neck, lie down and don't get up again, even though they hit you with the switch. And if you do have to rise, lie down a second time. And when they bring you home and offer you beans, fall backward and only sniff your food. Don't taste it. Withdraw and content yourself only with the hay and chaff. Pretend you are sick, and continue to do this for two or three days. This way you'll be able to gain some rest from all your hard work."

When the ox heard these words, he knew that the donkey was his friend and thanked him. "This is good advice," he said, and prayed that the ass would be blessed with a fine reward.

The next day, the driver took the ox, set the plow on his neck, and made him work as usual. But the ox took the donkey's advice and shirked the plowing. Consequently, the plowman drubbed him until the ox broke the yoke and made off. But the man caught up to him and tanned him until he thought he would die. Nevertheless, he did nothing but stand still and drop down until evening came. Then the plowman led him home and put him into his stall, but the ox drew back from his manger and neither stamped, nor butted, nor bellowed as he was accustomed to do. Such strange behavior puzzled the plowman. Then he brought the ox beans and husks, but the animal sniffed at them and lay down as far from them as he could and spent the whole night fasting. Next morning the plowman came and saw the manger full of beans, the hay untasted, and the ox lying on his back in a most sorry plight with his legs outstretched and a swollen belly. Of course, he was very worried about him and said to himself, "By Allah, he has certainly become sick, and this is why he wouldn't plow yesterday." Then he went to the merchant and reported, "Master, the ox is sick. He refused his fodder last night, and he hasn't tasted a scrap of it this morning."

Now the merchant understood what all this meant, because he had overheard the talk between the ox and the ass. So he said, "Take that rascal donkey, and set the yoke on his neck. Tie him to the plow and make him do the ox's work."

Accordingly, the plowman took the ass and made him do the ox's work the entire day long. And when the donkey let up out of weakness, the driver made him feel his stick until the animal's ribs were sore and his sides were sunken and his neck flayed by the yoke. When the ass returned home in the evening, he could hardly drag his limbs along. Meanwhile, the ox had spent the day lying at full length and had eaten his fodder with an excellent appetite. He continually heaped blessings on the donkey for his good advice, not knowing how the donkey had suffered and that it was on his account. So, when night set in and the donkey returned to the barn, the ox rose up before him in his honor and said, "May good tidings warm your heart, my friend! Because of you I have rested the entire day, and I have eaten my food in peace and quiet."

But the ass did not reply, because his heart was burning with rage, and he was exhausted from the beating he had gotten. Indeed, he regretted that he had given the ox such good advice and said to himself, "This is the result of your folly in giving good counsel. I was living in joy and happiness until I mixed into somebody else's business. So now I must think of something and trick the ox so that he'll return to this place. Otherwise, I'll die." Then he went wearily to his stall, while the ox continued to thank and bless him.

Burton, Richard, F. trans. *Arabian Nights: The Marvels and Wonders of the Thousand and One Nights*. Adapted by Jack Zipes. New York: Penguin Books USA, 1991.

THE HUNCHBACK'S TALE: THE BARBER'S TALE OF HIS THIRD BROTHER

Al-Fakik is a blind man who asks for alms. One day he goes to a grand house and begs the house's master for something. The master tells Al-Fakik he has nothing to give and then secretly follows him when he leaves.

My third brother's name was Al-Fakik, the Gabbler, who was blind. Now, one day fate and fortune drove him to a fine large house, and he knocked at the door and asked to speak to the owner so that he might beg something from him.

"Who's at the door?" asked the master of house. But my brother did not utter a word, and soon he heard the master repeat, "Who's there?"

Again my brother did not say a word, and all at once he heard the master walk to the door, open it, and say, "What do you want?"

My brother answered, "Something for Allah Almighty's sake."

"Are you blind?" asked the man.

And my brother answered, "Yes."

"Stretch out your hand," the man said.

So my brother stretched out his hand, thinking that he would receive something, but the man took it, drew him into the house, and led him up the stairs until they reached the terrace on top of the house. All the while, my brother kept thinking that he would surely receive some food or money. Finally, the man asked him, "What do you want, blind man?"

And he answered, "Something for the Almighty's sake."

"May Allah open some other door for you," replied the man.

"But why didn't you tell me this when we were downstairs?"

"You cadger, why didn't you answer me when I first called to you?"

"And what do you mean to do now?"

"There's nothing in the house to give you."

"Well, then, take me downstairs."

"The way is right before you."

So my brother rose and made his way downstairs until he came within twenty steps of the door. There his foot slipped, and he rolled to the bottom of the stairs and hurt his head. After leaving, he did not know where to turn and soon encountered two other blind men, companions of his, who asked him what he had earned that day.

So he told them what had happened to him and added, "My brothers, I need to take some of our common money and buy some provisions so I can eat."

Now, the master of the house had followed him and overheard their conversation. Of course, neither my brother nor his comrades were aware of this. So my brother went to their common lodgings and sat down to wait for his companions. The landlord entered after him without being heard, and when the other blind men arrived, my brother said to them, "Bolt the door, and search the house in case some stranger may have followed us."

Upon hearing this, the man grabbed hold of a rope that hung from the ceiling and clung to it, while they went around the house and searched but found no one. So they came back and sat down next to my brother, took out their money, which they counted, and there were twelve thousand dirhams. Each took what he needed, and they buried the rest in the corner of the room. Then they set some food before them and sat down to eat. Soon my brother heard an unfamiliar pair of jaws munching by his side, and he said to his friends, "There's a stranger among us," and he stretched out his hand and seized the house master, whereupon they all fell on top of him and beat him. When they got tired of pounding him, they shouted, "Oh Moslems! There's a thief here! He's trying to take our money!"

All at once a crowd of people gathered in their lodgings, but the intruder pretended to be one of the blind and complained and shut his eyes like them so that nobody would know whether he was blind or not. "Oh Moslems," he cried out "May Allah save me! Take me to the governor, for I have some important information for him!"

Suddenly the watch appeared, and they seized the whole lot of them (my brother included) and dragged them to the governor's house. Once there, the governor asked, "Tell me what's going on here!"

"Look and find out for yourself," said the intruder. "Not a word will be wrung from us unless you torture us. So begin by beating me, and after me, beat our leader." And he pointed to my brother.

So they threw the man down on the ground and gave him four hundred blows on his backside. The beating was so painful that he was forced to open one eye, and as they increased their blows, he opened the other. When the governor saw this, he said, "What do we have here, you scoundrel?"

"Pardon, oh Governor!" he exclaimed. "All four of us have pretended to be blind so that we can enter houses, gaze upon the unveiled faces of the women, and bring about their corruption. By doing this we've gained a great deal of money, and our savings amount to twelve thousand dirhams. Well, when I insisted on having my share, which amounts to three thousand, my companions refused, took my money away, and beat me. So, by Allah, I need your protection. It's better that you have my share than they. And if you really want to find out if I'm speaking the truth, beat every one of my companions as you've beaten me, and they'll surely open their eyes."

The governor gave orders for the interrogation to begin with my brother, and they bound him to the whipping post. "Oh scum of the earth!" the governor exclaimed. "Have you been abusing the gracious gifts of Allah by pretending to be blind?"

"Allah, Allah!" cried my brother. "There's not one of us who can really see."

Then they beat him until he fainted, and the governor cried, "Leave him alone until he comes to. Then beat him again." After this the governor had each of the blind men receive three hundred blows, while the imposter kept saying to them, "Open your eyes, or they'll keep beating you." At last this man said to the governor, "Send someone with me to bring you the money, for these fellows refuse to open their eyes and be disgraced in front of all the people."

So the governor sent some guards with the imposter to fetch the money, and he gave this man his pretended share, or three thousand dirhams. Then he kept the rest for himself and banished the three blind men from the city. But I, oh Commander of the Faithful, went out and overtook my brother. After questioning him about what had happened, he told me the tale that I've told you, and I brought him secretly back to the city, where I gave him an allowance for food and drink.

Burton, Richard F., trans. *Arabian Nights: The Marvels and Wonders of the Thousand and One Nights.* Adapted by Jack Zipes. New York: Penguin Books USA, 1991.

THE EBONY HORSE

Sabur, king of Persia, entertains three wise old men. The sages bring the king fantastic inventions and he promises to grant them whatever they wish if their gifts prove to be as ingenious as they claim them to be.

King Sabur had three daughters as beautiful as flower gardens in full bloom and a son as handsome as the moon. And it was his custom to celebrate two holidiays during the year, the Nau-Roz, or New Year, and Mihgan, or the Autumnal Equinox. On both occasions he threw open his palace, gave alms to the people, made proclamations of safety and security, and promoted his chamberlains and viceroys. The people of his realm came to him, saluted him, and celebrated these holy days with joy, and they also brought him gifts, servants and eunuchs.

Now, King Sabur loved science and geometry, and on one holiday, as he sat on his throne, three wise men entered his palace and approached him. They were cunning inventors and masters of all sorts of crafts. Indeed, they could make things so unusual and rare that it was impossible to discern how they were invented. These men were versed in the knowledge of the occult and knew all about the mysteries of the world. Each one was from a different country and spoke a foreign language. The first was a Hindi, or Indian, the second a Roumi, or Greek, and the third a Farsi, or Persian.

When the Indian stepped forward, he prostrated himself before the king, wished him a joyous holiday, and placed before him a gift befitting his dignity: it was a man of gold set with precious gems and jewels and holding a golden trumpet in his hand.

When Sabur saw this, he said, "Tell me, sage, what can this figure do?"

And the Indian answered, "My lord, if this figure is placed at the gate of your city, he will be a most powerful protector, for whenever an enemy tries to enter, the figure will blow his trumpet against him, and he will be seized with palsy and drop dead."

The king was extremely astonished by this gift and declared, "By Allah, if you are telling the truth, I'll grant you anything you desire."

Then the Greek stepped forward, and after prostrating himself before the king, he gave him a silver basin with a golden peacock and twenty-four golden chicks in the middle of it. Sabur looked at the basin and then inquired, "Tell me, sage, what can this peacock do?"

"My lord," he answered, "whenever an hour of the day or night elapses, it pecks one of its young, cries out and flaps its wings every hour on the hour. Then, when the end of the mouth arrives, it will open its month, and you will see the crescent inside it."

And the king said, "If you're telling the truth, I'll grant anything you wish or desire."

Then the Persian sage stepped forward, and after prostrating himself before the king, he presented him with a horse made of the darkest ebony wood with a gold and jeweled inlay and with saddle, stirrups, and bridle suitable for the majesty of the king. When Sabur saw the horse, he was extremely astonished and admired the beauty of its form and style. So he asked, "What can this wooden horse do? Tell me its virtue and whether it can move."

"My lord," the Persian answered, "if one mounts this horse, it will carry him wherever he wants. It can ride through the air and cover the space of a year in a single day."

The king was amazed by these wonders, especially since they came all on the same day, and he turned to the Persian sage and said, "By Allah, if you are telling the truth, I'll certainly grant you whatever you desire."

Then he entertained the sages for three days so he could try out their gifts. During that time each one demonstrated what his invention could do: the man of gold blew his trumpet; the peacock pecked its chicks; and the Persian sage mounted the ebony horse, which soared with him high in the air and descended again. When King Sabur saw all this, he was amazed and overcome with joy. Then he said to the three sages, "I'm now convinced of the truth of your words, and it behooves me to keep my promise. So, you may now ask for whatever you want, and I shall grant your wishes."

Well, news about the beauty of the king's three daughters had reached these sages, and thus they asked, "If the king is content with us and our gifts and allows us to make a request, we beg that he give us his three daughters in marriage so that we may become his sons-in-law."

"Your wish is granted," the king said and ordered the kazi to come right away so that he could marry his daughters to these sages.

Now it so happened that the princesses were behind a curtain and witnessed the entire scene. The youngest saw that her husband-to-be was at least a hundred years old. He had white hair, a drooping forehead, mangy eyebrows, cropped ears, a dyed mustache and beard, red eyes, bleached and hollow cheeks, a flabby nose, overlapping teeth, loose lips like camel's kidneys, and a face like a cobbler's apron. In short, he was a terror, a horror, a monster. Indeed, he was the most frightful sight of his time. In contrast, the girl was the fairest and most graceful of her time, more elegant than the finest gazelle, more tender than the gentlest breeze, and certainly more beautiful than the brightest moon. She was made for love and walked with a graceful sway that captivated all those who saw her. In short, she was more beautiful and sweeter than her two sisters, who were splendid specimens themselves. So when she saw her suitor, she went to her room and strewed dust on her head, tore her clothes, slapped her face, and wept.

Now, her brother, Prince Kamar al-Akmar had just returned from a journey, and when he heard weeping like that he entered his sister's chamber (for he loved her with more affection than his other sisters) and said, "What's wrong with you? What's happened to you? Tell me everything, and don't hide a thing."

"My brother," she responded, "I have nothing to hide. Our father has decided to do something atrocious, and I intend to leave the palace. And I'll do this even if he doesn't consent, for the Lord will provide for me."

"What's the meaning of this talk?" her brother responded. "What's caused all this trouble and disturbed your heart?"

And the princess answered, "Our father has promised me in marriage to a wicked magician who has brought him a horse of black wood as a gift. This magician has bewitched our father with his craft and sorcery, but as for me, I don't want to have anything to do with him, and I wish I had never been born because of him."

After her brother comforted her, he went to his father and said, "Who is this wizard that you're going to wed to my youngest sister? What's so wonderful about his present that you don't care if your daughter is deeply distressed? Do you think what you're doing is right?"

Burton, Richard F., trans. *Arabian Nights: The Marvels and Wonders of the Thousand and One Nights.* Adapted by Jack Zipes. New York: Penguin Books USA, 1991.

HOW BRAVE WALTER
HUNTED WOLVES

A humorous European folktale about a little boy who claims he's a mighty wolf-hunter—until he goes hunting alone.

Walter was six years old, and he was soon to begin school. He could not read yet, but he could do many other things. He could turn cartwheels, stand on his head, ride a see-saw, and throw snowballs; but first of all I must tell you how brave he was and how he hunted wolves.

Once in the spring, a little before Midsummer, Walter heard that there were a great many wolves in the wood, and that pleased him. He was wonderfully brave when he was in the midst of his companions or at home with his brothers and sister. He used often to say, "One wolf is nothing, there ought to be at least four."

Indeed, some thought that the brave boy boasted a little; but one must indeed believe him since he said so himself. So Jonas and Lena used to say of him "Look, there goes Walter, who shoots the wolves." And other boys and girls would say "Look, there goes brave Walter, who is brave enough to fight with four."

There was no one so fully convinced of this as Walter himself, and one day he prepared himself for a real wolf hunt. He took with him his drum and his tin sabre. He did not forget to arm himself quite to the teeth with his pop-gun, his bow, and his air-pistol. He had a burnt cork in his pocket to blacken his moustache, and a red cock's feather to put in his cap to make himself look fierce.

Jonas was going with corn to the mill, and Walter got a seat on the load, while Caro, the dog, ran barking beside them. As soon as they came to the wood Walter looked cautiously around him to see perchance there was a wolf in the bushes, and he did not omit to ask Jonas if wolves were afraid of a drum.

"Of course they are," said Jonas. There upon Walter began to beat his drum with all his might while they were going through the wood.

When they came to the mill Walter immediately asked if there had been any wolves in the neighborhood lately.

"Alas! Yes," said the miller, "last night the wolves ate our fattest ram there by the kiln not far from here."

"Ah!" said Walter, "do you think that there were many?"

"We don't know," answered the miller.

"Oh, it is all the same," said Walter. "I only asked so that I should know if I should take Jonas with me. I could manage very well alone with three, but if there were more, I might not have time to kill them all before they ran away."

"In your place I should go quite alone, it is more manly," said Jonas.

"No, it is better for you to come too," said Walter. "Perhaps there are many."

"No, I have not time," said Jonas, "and besides, there are sure not to be more than three. You can manage them very well alone."

"Yes," said Walter, "certainly I could; but, you see, Jonas, it might happen that one of them might bite me in the back, and I should have more trouble in killing them. If I only knew that there were not more than two I should not mind, for then I should take one in each hand and give them a good shaking."

"I certainly think that there will not be more than two," said Jonas, "there are never more than two when they slay children and rams; you can very well shake them without me."

"But, you see, Jonas," said Walter, "if there are two, it might still happen that one of them escaped and bites me in the leg, for you see I am not so strong in the left hand as in the right. You can very well come with me, and take a good stick in case there are really two. Look, if there is only one, I shall take him so with both my hands and throw him living on to his back, and he can kick as much as he likes. I shall hold him fast."

"Now, when I really think over the thing," said Jonas, "I am almost sure there will not be more than one. What would two do with one ram? There will certainly not be more than one."

"But you should come with me all the same, Jonas," said Walter. "you see I can very well manage one, but I am not quite accustomed to wolves yet, and he might tear holes in my new trousers."

"Well, just listen," said Jonas, "I am beginning to think that Walter is not so brave as people say. First of all you would fight against four, and then against three, then two, and then one, and now Walter wants help with one. Now I see quite well that you are frightened!"

This touched Walter's pride very near. "I shall show that I am not frightened," he said; and so he took his drum, sabre, cock's feather, pop-gun and air-pistol, and went off quite alone to the wood to hunt wolves.

It was a beautiful evening, and the birds were singing in all the branches. Walter went very slowly and cautiously. He quite thought something moved away there in the ditch. Perhaps it was a wolf.

"Shall I go back and say that I struck one wolf and it escaped?" thought Walter. "Fie!" said his conscience, "If you tell a lie today and say you struck a wolf, tomorrow surely it will eat you up."

"No, I will go the kiln," thought Walter, and so he went. But he did not go quite near. He went only so near that he could see the ram's blood which colored the grass red, and some tufts of wool which the wolves had torn from the back of the poor animal.

It looked dreadful.

"I wonder what the ram thought when they ate him up," thought Walter to himself; and just then a cold shiver ran through him from his collar right down to his boots.

"It is better for me to beat the drum," he thought to himself again, and so he began to beat it. But it sounded horrid, and an echo came out from the kiln that seemed almost like the howl of a wolf. The drumsticks stiffened in Walter's hands, and he thought now they are coming. . . !

Yes, sure enough, just then a shaggy, reddish-brown wolf's head looked out from under the kiln!

What did Walter do now? Yes, the brave Walter who alone could manage four, threw his drum away, took to his heels and ran, and ran as fast as he could back to the mill

But, alas! The wolf ran after him. Then Walter ran faster. He ran over sticks, stones, and ditches; he lost drum-sticks, saber, bow, and air-pistol, and in his terrible hurry he tripped over a tuft of grass. There he lay, and the wolf jumped on to him. . .

Now you may well believe that it was all over with Walter and all his adventures. But do not be surprised if it was not quite so bad as that, for the wolf was quite a friendly one. He certainly jumped on to Walter, but he only shook his coat and rubbed his nose against his face; and Walter shrieked.

Happily Jonas heard his cry of distress, for Walter was quite near the mill now, and he ran and helped him up.

"What has happened?" he asked. "Why did you scream so terribly?"

"A wolf! A wolf!" cried Walter, and that was all he could say.

"Where is the wolf?" said Jonas. "I don't see any wolf."

"Take care, he is here, he had bitten me to death," groaned Walter.

Then Jonas began to laugh; yes he laughed so that he nearly burst his belt.

Well, well, was that the wolf? Was that the wolf which Walter was to take by the neck and shake and throw down on its back, no matter how much it struggled?

"Down, Caro! You ought to be rather ashamed to have put such a great hero to flight!"

Walter got up feeling very foolish.

"It was only a dog, if it had been a wolf I certainly should have killed him. . ."

"Indeed!" laughed Jonas. "Are you at it again? Dear Walter, remember that it is only cowards who boast; a really brave man never talks of his bravery."

Lang, Andrew, ed., *The Lilac Fairy Book*. New York: Dover Publications, Inc., 1968.

AT THE BACK OF THE NORTH WIND

George MacDonald

Young Diamond is the son of a coachman, and he and his wife sleep in a cozy hayloft above the stable. One evening the North Wind comes in through a hole in his wall. Diamond is surprised to find that the North Wind is actually a beautiful lady—and he follows her out on a strange journey through the night.

Chapter IV 'NORTH WIND

And as she stood looking toward London, Diamond saw that she was trembling. "Are you cold, North Wind?" he asked.

"No, Diamond," she answered, looking down upon him with a smile, "I am only getting ready to sweep one of my rooms."

As she spoke he could have told by her voice, if he had not seen with his eyes, that she was growing larger and larger. Her head went up and up towards the stars; and as she grew, still trembling through all her body, her hair also grew—longer and longer, and lifted itself from her head, and went out in black waves. Then she put her hands behind her head, and gathered some of her hair, and began weaving and knotting it together. When she had done, she bent down her beautiful face close to his, and said—

"Diamond, I am afraid you would not keep hold of me, and if I were to drop you, I don't know what might happen; so I have been making a place for you in my hair. Come."

Diamond held out his arms, for with that grand face looking at him, he believed like a baby. She took him in her hands, threw him over her shoulder, and said, "Get in, Diamond."

And Diamond parted her hair with his hands, crept between, and feeling about, soon found the woven nest. It was just like a pocket, or like the shawl in which gypsy women carry their children. North Wind put her hands to her back, felt all about the nest, and finding it safe, said—

"Are you comfortable, Diamond?"

"Yes, indeed," answered Diamond.

The next moment, he was rising in the air. North Wind grew towering up to the place of the clouds. Her hair went streaming out from her, till it spread like a mist over the stars. She flung herself abroad in space.

Diamond held on by two of the twisted ropes which, parted and interwoven, formed his shelter, for he could not help being a little afraid. As soon as he had come to himself, he peeped through the woven meshes, for he did not dare to look over the top of the nest. The earth was rushing past like a river or a sea below him. Trees, and water, and green grass hurried away beneath. A great roar of wild animals rose as they rushed over the Zoological Gardens, mixed with a chattering of monkeys and a screaming of birds; but it died away in a moment behind them. And now, there was nothing but the roofs of houses, sweeping along like a great torrent of stones and rocks. Chimney pots fell, and tiles flew from the roofs; but it looked to him as if they were left behind by the roofs and the chimneys as they scudded away. There was a great roaring, for the wind was dashing against London like a sea; but at North Wind's back Diamond, of course, felt nothing of it all. He was in a perfect calm. He could hear the sound of it, that was all.

By and by he raised himself and looked over the edge of his nest. There were the houses rushing up and shooting away below him, like a fierce torrent of rocks instead of water. Then he looked up to the sky but could see no stars; they were hidden by the blinding masses of the lady's hair which swept between. He began to wonder whether she would hear him if he spoke. He would try.

"Please, North Wind," he said, "what is that noise?"

From high over his head came the voice of North Wind, answering him gently—

"The noise of my broom. I am the old woman that sweeps the cobwebs from the sky; only I'm busy with the floor now."

"What makes the houses look as if they were running away?"

"I am sweeping so fast over them."

"Please, would you mind going a little slower, for I want to see the streets?"

"You won't see much now."

"Why?"

"Because I have nearly swept all the people home."

"Oh! I forgot," said Diamond, and was quiet after that, for he did not want to be troublesome.

But she dropped a little towards the roofs of the houses, and Diamond could see down into the streets. There were very few people about, though. The lamps flickered and flared again, but nobody seemed to want them.

Suddenly Diamond espied a little girl coming along a street. She was dreadfully blown by the wind, and a broom she was trailing behind her was very troublesome. It seemed as if the wind had a spite at her—it kept worrying her like a wild beast and tearing at her rags. She was so lonely there!

"Oh! Please, North Wind," he cried, "won't you help that little girl?"

"No, Diamond; I mustn't leave my work."

"But why shouldn't you be kind to her?"

"I am kind to her: I am sweeping the wicked smells away."

"But you're kinder to me, dear North Wind. Why shouldn't you be as kind to her as you are to me?"

"There are reasons, Diamond. Everybody can't be done to all the same. Everybody is not ready for the same thing."

"But I don't see why I should be kinder used than she."

"Do you think nothing's to be done but what you can see, Diamond, you silly! It's all right. Of course you can help her if you like. You've got nothing particular to do at this moment; I have."

"Oh! Do let me help her, then. But you won't be able to wait, perhaps?"

"No, I can't wait; you must do it yourself. And, mind, the wind will get a hold of you, too."

"I want to go," said Diamond. "Only there's just one thing—how am I to get home?"

"If you're anxious about that, perhaps you had better go with me. I am bound to take you home again, if you do."

"There!" cried Diamond, who was still looking after the little girl; "I'm sure the wind will blow her over, and perhaps kill her. Do let me go."

They had been sweeping more slowly along the line of the street. There was a lull in the roaring.

"Well, though I cannot promise to take you home," said North Wind, as she sank nearer and nearer to the tops of the houses, "I can promise you it will be all right in the end. You will get home somehow. Have you made up your mind what to do?"

"Yes; to help the little girl," said Diamond firmly.

The same moment, North Wind dropt into the street and stood, only tall lady, but with her hair flying up over the housetops. She put her hands to her back, took Diamond, and set him down in the street. The same moment, he was caught in the fierce coils of the blast, and all but blown away. North Wind stepped back a pace and, at once, towered in stature to the height of the houses. A chimney pot clashed at Diamond's feet. He turned in terror, but it was to look for the little girl, and when he turned again the lady had vanished, and the wind was roaring along the street as if it had been the bed of an invisible torrent.

MacDonald, George. *At the Back of the North Wind.* New York: Books of Wonder, William Morrow and Co., 1875, 1964.

THE NUTCRACKER

E.T.A. Hoffmann

Of all her wonderful Christmas gifts, Marie is most charmed by an exquisite little man in uniform who cracks nuts between his jaws. Her brother Fritz doesn't see how special the nutcracker is and plays with it roughly enough to break it. Claire stays up late Christmas night putting the broken toy to bed in the cupboard with the rest of the childrens' toys, when something extraordinary begins happening.

WONDERFUL EVENTS

Don't be too long, Marie, or you'll be tired in the morning," her mother called as she started up the stairs. As soon as her mother was out of sight, Marie unwrapped the Nutcracker, who had been resting in her handkerchief, and examined his wounds. He was very pale, but he still had a kind, melancholy smile that pierced Marie's heart.

"Oh, Nutcracker," she whispered, "please don't be angry with Fritz.

"He didn't mean to hurt you. It's just that all his soldiering has left its mark. Underneath, he's really a very nice boy. Don't worry. I'll take care of you. We'll get your teeth fixed and your shoulder set right. Godpapa Drosselmeier will see to that and—"

Marie stopped short and blinked. She could have sworn that at the mention of Godpapa Drosselmeier, the Nutcracker had made a horrible face. His blue eyes had flashed, and his mouth and nose had twisted with revulsion. It had been only for an instant, and just as Marie started to feel afraid, she saw that her dear Nutcracker had the same kind expression he always had. Marie looked up at the ceiling lamp and decided there had been a draft that the light flicker and her eyes play tricks on her.

"How silly of me!" she said, glancing around the room and then back at the Nutcracker. "Wooden dolls can't make faces. Why should I be frightened of my dear friend?" She adjusted his bandage and went over to the shelf where her dolls were. "As I was saying—in order to get better, you have to rest." Then she looked at her new doll, who was all ready to be placed in her big, comfortable bed, and said, "Won't you do me a favor,

Miss Clara, and give your bed to poor, sick Nutcracker? A lady with cheeks as rosy and plump as yours should have no problem sleeping on the sofa."

Miss Clara, however, looked quite superior and made no response. "Well," Marie said, "I was only being polite." And with that, she took the bed, moved it closer, and laid the Nutcracker tenderly down on the lace pillow. Taking another ribbon from her dress, she wrapped it around his damaged shoulder and pulled the covers up to tuck him in. Miss Clara looked more disdainful than ever, so Marie picked up the bed.

"We can't have that nasty Clara scowling at you," she said, and moved him to the upper shelf near the village where Fritz had his army barracks. With the Nutcracker settled down for the night, Marie closed the cabinet and turned to go to bed. She hadn't taken two steps when—reader, do listen carefully—a low rustling and rattling and the sound of whispering came from behind the drapes, under the chairs, from every corner of the room!

The clock on the wall ground and whirred but couldn't strike the hour. Marie looked up and saw that the big golden owl that usually sat straight on top of the clock was hunched forward, its long beak jutting way out, its wings completely covering the hands and face. The clock's noisy gears continued to work until Marie could hear words in the pattern of the grinding:

> *Clocks, clocks, stop your ticking!*
> *Strike not, but sound this warning!*
> *The Mouse King hears you all.*
> *Prr prr, poom poom!*
> *He sings the age-old song of doom.*
> *Prr prr, poom poom!*
> *Bells, now chime!*
> *And so ring out the fated time!*

Then she heard the hoarse, smothered "poom" of the clock strike twelve.

Suddenly Marie heard a shrill squeaking and legions of tiny feet scurrying, while thousands of pinpoint lights glittered out through the cracks in the walls. It took Marie a moment to realize that the tiny lights were really eyes! Everywhere mice were peeping and squeezing themselves out through cracks all around the room.

It was a good thing Marie was not afraid of mice, as many children are, for once the shock had passed, she found all their running around quite funny. But then a sound from somewhere close by sent a chill down her back. The ground erupted at her feet, heaving up sand, lime, and broken stone. Out of the earth rose seven mouse heads with seven shiny crowns, all growing out of one large mouse body. Each head was hissing and squeaking in unison, calling the mouse army to gather before it. Marie's heart had been beating so fiercely that she thought she would die of fright, but now she felt as if her heart had stopped. Half-fainting, she fell back against the cupboard. Her elbow hit the glass front and one of the panes shattered, falling to the floor in splinters. There was a stinging in Marie's arm, but she didn't mind it, because the awful squeaking had stopped. She thought that perhaps she had frightened the mice away—but still, she dared not look.

Meanwhile, right behind her, a great commotion started on the shelves of the cupboard, and small voices could be heard saying:

> *Awake and fight*
> *For what is right!*
> *Up now, away—*
> *This is the night!*

Glass harmonica bells tinkled so cheerfully that Marie found herself turning around to see who played them. Inside the cupboard, the tiny lamps were lit, and dolls, along with other little figures, hurried about, waving their arms. The Nutcracker threw off his blanket and leaped out of bed, shouting:

> *Knack knack knack,*
> *Stupid mousey pack!*
> *All their skulls we'll crack*
> *Mousey pack, crick and crack—*
> *Cowardly lot of schnack!*

He drew his sword and held it in the air. "My loyal subjects and friends," he cried, "are you ready to stand beside me in this great battle?" Immediately, a clown named Scaramouche, one comical old man, four chimney sweeps, two zither players, and a drummer cried, "Yes, Your Highness! We, your loyal servants, will follow you to victory or death, come what may!" One after the other, they jumped down to the bottom shelf, their cotton insides and soft clothing affording them a safe landing. The fragile Nutcracker, however, would have broken something in the perilous leap if Miss Clara had not opened her arms and received the hero, drawn sword and all, in her tender embrace.

"Oh, Clara!" Marie cried. "How I misjudged you! You wanted to give your bed up to Nutcracker all along."

Miss Clara hugged the Nutcracker close and pleaded, "My lord, please do not fight this battle! You are wounded and sick, and your many followers are only too willing to fight in your place. Stay here with me and plan your victory from a safe distance." The Nutcracker, however, kicked impatiently until Clara let him go. When she released him,

320

he sank down gracefully on one knee and said to her, "My lady, the kindness you have shown me will strengthen my heart for the battle to come." Clara bowed and, taking the Nutcracker by the arm, brought him to his feet.

When the Nutcracker hit the floor of the living room, the squeaking and piping started up louder than before. Hordes of mice formed huge battalions, awaiting orders from the terrible, seven-headed Mouse King. Where would it all end?

Hoffman, E.T.A., *The Nutcracker*. New York: Crown Publishers, 1984.

MADSCHUN

A Turkish folktale of baldness, determination, and one magic word.

nce upon a time, there lived, in a small cottage among some hills, a woman with her son, and to her great grief, the young man, though hardly more than twenty years of age, had not as much hair on his head as a baby. But old as he looked, the youth was very idle, and whatever trade his mother put him to, he refused to work.

On a fine summer morning, he was lying as usual half asleep in the little garden in front of the cottage when the sultan's daughter came riding by. The youth lazily raised himself on his elbow to look at her, and that one glance changed his whole nature.

"I will marry her and nobody else," he thought. And jumping up, he went to find his mother.

"You must go at once to the sultan, and tell him that I want his daughter for my wife," he said.

"What?" shouted the old woman, shrinking back into a corner, for nothing but sudden madness could explain such an amazing errand.

"Go at once to the sultan and tell him," repeated the youth impatiently.

"Can you really expect that the sultan would give his daughter to a penniless baldy like you?"

"Do as I bid you." And neither day nor night did her son cease tormenting her till, in despair, she put on her best clothes and went over the hill to the palace.

It was the day that the sultan set apart for hearing the complaints and petitions of his people, so the woman found no difficulty in gaining admission to his presence.

"Do not think me mad, O Excellency," she began, "though I know I must seem like it. But I have a son who, since his eyes have rested on the veiled face of the princess, has not left me in peace day or night till I consented to come to the palace and to ask your Excellency for your daughter's hand."

Now the sultan always loved anything out of the common, and this situation was new indeed. So, instead of ordering the trembling creature to be flogged or cast into prison, as some other sovereigns might have done, he merely said: "Bid your son come hither."

The old woman stared in astonishment at such a reply. But when the sultan repeated his words even more gently than before, and did not look in anywise angered, she took courage, and bowing again, she hastened homeward.

"Well, how have you sped?" asked her son eagerly as she crossed the threshold.

"You are to go up to the palace without delay and speak to the sultan himself," replied the mother.

"Ah, the lightning will not fly more swiftly," cried he. And in another instant he was out of her sight.

When the sultan beheld the bald head of his daughter's wooer, he no longer felt in the mood for joking, and resolved that he must somehow or other shake himself free of such an unwelcome lover. But as he had summoned the young man to the palace, he could hardly dismiss him without a reason, so he hastily said: "I hear you wish to marry my daughter? Well and good. But the man who is to be her husband must first collect all the birds in the world, and bring them into the gardens of the palace; for hitherto, no birds have made their homes in the trees."

The young man was filled with despair at the sultan's words. How was he to snare all these birds? And even if he did succeed in catching them, it would take years to carry them

Love at first sight

How the BIRDS were brought to the SULTAN

to them palace! Still, he was too proud to let the sultan think that he had given up the princess without a struggle, so he took a road that led past the palace and walked on, not noticing whither he went.

In this manner a week slipped by, and he found himself crossing a desert with great rocks scattered here and there. In the shadow cast by one of these was seated a holy man, or dervish, as he was called, who motioned to the youth to sit beside him.

"Something is troubling you, my son," said the holy man; "tell me what it is, as I may be able to help you."

"O, my father," answered the youth, "I wish to marry the princess of my country; but the sultan refuses to give her to me unless I can collect all the birds in the world and bring them into his garden."

"Do not despair," replied the dervish, "it is not so difficult as it sounds. Two days' journey from here, in the path of the setting sun, there stands a cypress tree, larger than any other cypress that grows upon the earth. Sit down where the shadow is darkest, close to the trunk, and keep very still. By and by, you will hear a mighty rushing of wings, and all the birds in the world will come and nestle in the branches. Be careful not to make a sound till everything is quiet again, and then say, 'Madschun!' At that the birds will be forced to remain where they are—not one can move from its perch; and you will be able to place them all over your head and arms and body, and in this way, you must carry them to the sultan."

The young man thanked the dervish and paid such close heed to his directions that, a few days later, a strange figure covered with soft feathers walked into the presence of the sultan. The princess's father was filled with surprise, for never had he seen such a sight before. Soon a gentle stirring was heard, and what a multitude of wings unfolded themselves: blue wings, yellow wings, red wings, green wings. And when the young man whispered "Go," they first flew in circles round the sultan's head, and then disappeared through the open window, to choose homes in the garden.

"I have done your bidding, O Sultan, and now give me the princess," said the youth. And the sultan answered hurriedly: "Yes? Oh, yes! you have pleased me well! Only one thing remains to turn you into a husband that any girl might desire. That head of yours, you know—it is so very bald! Get it covered with nice thick curly hair, and then I will give you my daughter. You are so clever that I am sure this will give you no trouble at all."

Silently the young man listened to the sultan's words, and silently he sat in his mother's kitchen for many days to come till, one morning, the news reached him that the sultan had betrothed his daughter and that the wedding was to celebrated without delay in the palace. With that he arose in wrath, and made his way quickly and secretly to a side door, and unseen by anyone, he made his way into the palace. Here the bride and bridegroom and two or three friends were assembled, waiting for the appearance of the sultan for the contract to be signed.

"Madschun!" whispered the youth. And instantly, everyone remained rooted to the ground, and some messengers whom the sultan had sent to see that all was ready shared the same fate.

At length, angry and impatient, the sultan went down to behold with his own eyes what had happened, but as nobody could give him any explanation, he bade one of his attendants to fetch a magician to remove the spell which had been cast by some evil genius.

"It is your own fault," said the magician when he had heard the sultan's story. "If you had not broken your promise to the young man, your daughter would not have had this ill befall her. Now there is only one remedy, and the bridegroom you have chosen must yield his place to the bald-headed youth."

So a fresh contract was prepared and the youth was led to the big hall, where everyone was standing exactly as they were when the young man had uttered the fatal word.

"Can you remove the spell?" asked the sultan anxiously.

"I think so," replied the young man (who, to say the truth, was a little anxious himself), and stepping forward, he cried: "Let the victims of Madschun be free!"

No sooner were the words uttered than the statues returned to life, and the bride placed her hand joyfully in that of her new bridegroom. As for the old one, he vanished completely, and no one ever knew what became of him.

Lang, Andrew, ed. *The Olive Fairy Book.* New York: Dover Publications, Inc., 1907.

PECOS BILL

ADRIEN STOUTENBERG

Pecos Bill, inventor of the lasso and the cowboy song, was the first real cowboy. Raised by coyotes, and mean as a rattler, this legendary American hero was as wild and untamed as the West itself.

ecos Bill's father was one of the first settlers in the West. There was lots of room in Texas, with so much sky that it seemed as if there couldn't be any sky left over for the rest of the United States.

Bill was a little over one year old when another family of pioneers moved into the country. The new family settled about fifty miles from where Bill's folks had built their homestead.

"The country's getting too crowded," said Bill's father. "We've got to move farther west."

So the family scrambled back into their big wagon and set out, the oxen puffing and snorting as they pulled the wagon toward the Pecos River. Bill was sitting in the rear of the wagon when it hit some rocks in a dry stream bed. There was a jolt, and Bill went flying out of the wagon. He landed so hard that the wind was knocked out of him, and he couldn't even cry out to let his folks know.

Young Bill sat there in the dry stream bed a while, wondering what to do. Then, suddenly, he saw a pack of coyotes off in the distance, eating the remains of a dead deer. These coyotes had never seen a human baby before, and they didn't know quite what to think. Apparently, they decided Bill was some new kind of hairless animal, for one of the female coyotes took a hunk of deer meat in her teeth and trotted over to Bill with it.

Bill had not eaten much raw meat before, but he knew that the female coyote meant well, and he didn't want to hurt her feelings. So he picked the meat up and began chewing. It tasted so good that he walked over and joined the other coyotes.

From that time on, Bill lived with the coyotes, going wherever they went, joining in their hunts, and even learning their language. By the time Bill was ten years old, he could outrun and outhowl any coyote in the Southwest. And since he had not seen any other human beings in all that time, he thought he was a coyote himself.

He might have gone on believing this forever if one day a cowboy hadn't come riding through the sagebrush. The cowboy stopped, stared, and rubbed his eyes, because he could scarcely believe what he saw. There in front of him stood a ten-year-old boy, as naked as a cow's hoof, wrestling with a giant grizzly bear. Before the cowboy could say, "Yipee yi-yo!" the boy had hugged the bear to death.

The cowboy tossed Bill a plug of tobacco. Bill ate it and decided it tasted pretty good, so when the cowboy came up close, Bill didn't bite him.

The cowboy stayed there for three days, teaching Bill to talk like a human. Then he tried to prove to Bill that Bill wasn't a coyote.

"I must be a coyote," Bill said. "I've got fleas, haven't I? And I can howl the moon out of the sky."

"All Texans have got fleas and can howl," the cowboy said. "In order to be a true coyote, you have to have a bushy tail."

Bill looked around and realized for the first time that he didn't have a nice bushy, waving tail like his coyote friends. "Maybe I lost it somewhere."

"No siree," the cowboy said. "You're a human being, sure as shooting. You'd better come along with me."

Being human was a hard thing for Bill to face up to, but he realized that the cowboy must be right. He told his coyote friends good-by and thanked them for all that they had taught him. Then he straddled a mountain lion he had tamed and rode with the cowboy toward the cowboy's ranch. On the way to the ranch, a big rattlesnake reared up in front of them. The cowboy galloped off, but Bill jumped from his mount and faced the snake.

"I'll let you have the first three bites, Mister Rattler, just to be fair. Then I'm going to beat the poison out of you until you behave yourself!"

That is just what Bill did. He whipped the snake around until it stretched out like a thirty-foot rope. Bill looped the rattler-rope in one hand, got back on his lion, and caught up with the cowboy. To entertain himself, he made a loop out of the snake and tossed it over the head of an armadillo plodding along through the cactus.

"I never saw anybody do anything like that before," said the cowboy.

"That's because nobody invented the lasso before," said Pecos Bill.

Before Pecos Bill came along, cowboys didn't know much about their job. They didn't know anything about rounding up cattle, or branding them, or even about ten-gallon hats. The only way they knew to catch a steer was to hide behind a bush, lay a looped rope on the ground, and wait for the steer to step into the loop.

Pecos Bill changed all that the minute he reached the Dusty Dipped Ranch. He slid off his mountain lion and marched up to the biggest cowboy there.

"Who's the boss here?" he asked.

The man took one look at Bill's lion and at the rattlesnake rope, and said, "I was."

Young though he was, Bill took over. At the Dusty Dipper and at other ranches, Bill taught the cowboys almost everything they know today. He invented spurs for them to wear on their boots. He taught them how to round up the cattle and drive the herds to railroad stations where they could be shipped to market. One of the finest things Bill did was to teach the cowboys to sing cowboy songs.

Bill made himself a guitar. On a night when the moon was as reddish yellow as a ripe peach, though fifty times as large, he led some of the fellows at the ranch out to the corral and set himself down on the top rail.

"I don't want to brag," he told the cowhands, "but I learned my singing from the coyotes, and that's about the best singing there is."

He sang a tune the coyotes had taught him and made up his own words:

"My seat is in the saddle, and my sadle's in the sky,

and I'll quit punchin' cows in the sweet by and by."

He made up many more verses and sang many other songs. When Bill was through, the roughest cowboy of all, Hardnose Hal, sat wiping tears from his eyes because of the beauty of Bill's singing. Lefty Lightning, the smallest cowboy, put his head down on his arms and wept. All the cowboys there vowed they would learn to sing and make up songs. And they did make up hundreds of songs about the lone prairie, and the Texas sky, and the wind blowing over the plains. That's why we have so many cowboy songs today.

Stoutenberg, Adrien. *American Tall Tales*. New York: The Viking Press, Inc., 1966

THE ADVENTURES OF PINOCCHIO

CARLO COLLODI

In the original story of Pinocchio by Carlo Collodi, the famous wooden boy, though he often means well, is very selfish and disobedient, and takes advantage of Geppetto's generosity. The following chapters begin with Pinocchio making typically false promises to Geppetto in order to get him to replace his wooden feet, which he has lost in a fire.

CHAPTER 8

Geppetto makes Pinocchio new feet, and sells his own coat to buy him a primer

I promise to go to school, and study, and do my best as a good boy should—"

"All children, when they want something, say the same thing."

"But I'm not like other children! I'm better than all of them, and I always tell the truth. I promise you, Daddy, that I shall learn a trade, and be the staff and comfort of your old age."

Geppetto tried to look very severe; but his eyes were full of tears, and his heart was full of sadness when he saw his poor Pinocchio in such a dreadful state. He did not say another word, but, taking his tools and two little pieces of seasoned wood, he set to work as hard as he could.

In less than an hour the feet were ready—two well-shaped, nimble, swift little feet that might have been carved by a great artist.

Then Geppetto said to Pinocchio, "Shut your eyes and go to sleep."

Pinocchio shut his eyes, and pretended to be asleep. And while he did so Geppetto, with some glue melted in an eggshell, fastened the feet in place; and he did it so neatly that no one could even see where they were joined together. As soon as Pinocchio discovered he had his feet again, he jumped down from the table where he was lying and began to gambol and dance around the room, nearly mad with joy.

"Now, to prove to you how grateful I am," said Pinocchio to his father, "I want to go to school at once."

"What a good boy!"

"But if I'm going to school, I must have some clothes."

Geppetto, who was poor and had not a farthing in his pocket, made Pinocchio a suit out of flowered paper, a pair of shoes out of bark from a tree, and a hat out of bread.

Pinocchio ran to look at himself in a basin of water; and he was so pleased with himself that he said, as he strutted about, "I look exactly like a gentleman!"

"By the way, speaking of school," added Pinocchio, "there's still something I must have—the most necessary of all."

"And that is. . .?"

"I have no primer."

"That's right. But how shall I get one?"

"That's easy! Go to the bookseller and buy one."

"And the money?"

"I haven't any."

"Neither have I," added the good old man, sadly.

"Wait," Geppetto cried suddenly and, jumping up, he put on his old coat, full of holes and patches, and ran out of the shop.

In a little while he was back again, with a primer in his hand for Pinocchio. But the poor man was in his shirt-sleeves, and it was snowing outside.

"Where is your coat, Daddy?"

"I have sold it."

"Why did you sell it?"

"Because it made me too warm."

Pinocchio understood this answer instantly; and he was so overcome by the feeling of his good heart, that he threw his arms around Geppetto's neck and kissed him again and again.

CHAPTER 9

Pinocchio sells his primer that he may go and see the marionettes

When it stopped snowing, Pinocchio started for school with his fine new primer under his arm. On the way, he never stopped imagining all sorts of fine plans. He began by saying to himself, "At school today I shall learn to read in no time; tomorrow I shall learn to write, and the day after tomorrow I shall learn all the figures. Then I shall be clever enough to earn lots of money; and with the very first money I get I shall buy my father the nicest, new coat."

While he was saying this more and more excitedly, he thought he heard music in the distance that sounded like fife and drum: fi-fi-fi. . . zum, zum, zum, zum.

He stopped and listened. The sounds came from the end of the street that crossed the one which led to school, at the end of the little village near the sea.

"What can that music be? What a pity I have to go school! Otherwise . . ." He hesitated, deciding whether to go to school or listen to the fifes.

"Today I shall listen to the fifes, and tomorrow I shall go to school," this naughty boy said finally, shrugging his shoulders.

No sooner said than done. He ran, and the farther he ran the more distinctly he heard the tune of the fifes and the beating of the big drum: fi-fi-fi, fi-fi-fi,. . . zum, zum, zum.

At last he came to a little square full of people who were gathered around a great building of boards and cloth, painted in all colors of the rainbow.

"What is that big building?" Pinocchio asked a boy who seemed to live there.

"Read the poster—it is all written there—and then you'll know."

"I'll gladly read it, but I don't know how to read today."

"Bravo, nincompoop! I'll read it for you. Know, then, that on that big poster, in fiery red letters, is written: GREAT PUPPET SHOW."

"How much does it cost to go in?"

"Twopence."

Pinocchio was in such a fever of curiosity that he lost his self-control and without any shame, he said to the little boy, "Will you lend me twopence until tomorrow?"

"I'd simply love to," said the boy, laughing at him, "but I can't today."

"I shall sell you my jacket for twopence," said the puppet.

"What could I do with a jacket of flowered paper? If it should rain or get wet, I couldn't take it off."

"Will you buy my shoes?"

"They're only good for lighting a fire."

He hesitated, but at last he said, "Will you buy this new primer for twopence?"

"I am only a boy, and I do not buy anything from other boys," said the other, having more sense than the puppet.

"I'll give you twopence for the primer," cried an old-clothes dealer who had overheard the conversation.

The book was sold at once. And to think that poor Geppetto stayed at home shivering in his shirt sleeves because he had to sell his coat to buy that primer for his son!

CHAPTER 10

The puppets recognize Pinocchio as one of them, and are pleased to see him, but Fire-eater, the Showman, appears in the midst of their joy, and Pinocchio almost comes to a bad end

hen Pinocchio entered the puppet show, he nearly caused a revolution. Harlequin and Punchinello were on the stage, quarreling as usual threatening every moment to come to blows. But all at once Harlequin stopped and, turning to the public, pointed to the pit of the theatre, and shouted dramatically:

"Heavens above! Am I dreaming? That must be Pinocchio there!"

"Yes, it's indeed Pinocchio!" cried Punchinello.

"Here's Pinocchio! Here's Pinocchio!" shouted all the puppets in chorus, running to the stage from every wing. "Here's our brother Pinocchio! Hurrah for Pinocchio!"

"Come up here to me, Pinocchio!" cried Harlequin. "Come and throw yourself into the arms of your wooden brothers!"

At this affectionate invitation, Pinocchio made one jump from the back of the pit to the front sets. Another jump, and he landed on the head of the orchestra leader, and from there he jumped to the stage.

It is impossible to describe the hugging and kissing that followed the friendly pinches, the brotherly taps that Pinocchio received from the actors and actresses of that puppet company.

It was a very spectacular sight, but the audience, when they saw that the play had stopped, grew impatient and began shouting, "The play! We want the play! Go on with the play!"

However, their breath was wasted, for the puppets, instead of continuing the play, redoubled their noise and, placing Pinocchio on their shoulders, carried him in triumph before the footlights.

Suddenly the Showman appeared. He was very tall, and so ugly that he frightened anyone who looked at him. His beard was like black ink, and it was so long that it reached the ground. His mouth was as big as an oven, and his eyes were like two burning red lanterns.

When the Showman appeared so unexpectedly, everybody was speechless. No one breathed. Even the poor puppets trembled like so many leaves.

"Why have you come here to disturb my theatre?" he asked Pinocchio, in a voice like that of a spook with a bad cold in his head.

"Believe me, Your Honor, it was not my fault."

"Not another word! We shall settle our accounts tonight."

As soon as the show was over, the Showman went into the kitchen, where the whole sheep, which he was preparing for his supper, was roasting on the slowly turning spit.

When he saw that there was not enough wood to finish roasting it, he called Harlequin and Punchinello and said, "Bring me in Pinocchio! He is made of nice, dry wood, and I am sure he will make a good fire for my roast."

At first Harlequin and Punchinello hesitated; but, when the Showman glanced at them menacingly, they obeyed. In a few moments they returned carrying poor Pinocchio, who was wriggling like an eel out of water, and shouting desperately.

CHAPTER 11

Fire-eater sneezes and pardons Pinocchio, who later saves the life of his friend Harlequin

Fire-eater, for that was the Showman's name, looked a horrid man, there can be no doubt about it, particularly with his black beard hanging down like an apron, covering his chest and legs. Yet at heart, he was really not so bad. When he saw poor Pinocchio struggling and crying he felt sorry for him and, although he tried to, at last he could not help it and sneezed violently.

Harlequin, who had been sad and downhearted, and looking like a weeping willow, when he heard that sneeze, became cheerful, and bending towards Pinocchio, whispered, "Good news, brother! The Showman sneezed. That's a sign that he's pitying you, and you are saved."

For you must know that, whilst other men weep, or at least pretend to wipe their eyes, when they pity somebody, whenever Fire-eater really pitied anyone, he had the habit of sneezing.

After the Showman had sneezed, he continued speaking gruffly, and shouted at Pinocchio, "Can't you stop crying? It gives me a nasty feeling in my stomach. I feel such a pain that. . . that. . . Atchoo! Atchoo!"—and this time he sneezed twice.

"God bless you!" said Pinocchio.

"Thank you. And your father and mother, are they alive?" asked Fire-eater.

"My father is, but I never knew my mother."

"Who knows how sorry your old father would be if I threw you on the fire! Poor old man! A-tchoo! A-tchoo! A-tchoo!"—and he sneezed three times.

"Bless you!" cried Pinocchio.

"Thank you. But on the other hand, you must be sorry for me, too, because, as you see, I haven't enough wood to finish roasting my mutton—and believe me, you certainly would have been very useful. But now I have spared you, and I must not complain. Instead of you, I shall burn some puppet of my company. Come on, gendarmes!"

Two wooden gendarmes appeared immediately at this command. They were very tall, and very thin. They wore tricorne hats, and carried drawn swords in their hands.

The Showman ordered them hoarsely, "Take that Harlequin, bind him strongly and throw him on the fire."

Imagine poor Harlequin! He was so frightened that his legs bent under him, and he fell on his face.

At this heart-breaking sight, Pinocchio knelt down at the Showman's feet and, weeping, he soused with tears the whole length of his long beard. Then he pleaded, "I implore you to pardon poor Harlequin!"

"It cannot be done. As I pardoned you, I must put him on the fire, for my mutton must be well roasted."

"In that case," cried Pinocchio, rising and throwing away his hat of bread, "I know my duty. Forward, gendarmes! Bind me and throw me in the fire! It is not just that poor Harlequin, my truest friend, should die for me."

These words, shouted in a loud, heroic voice caused all the marionettes present to weep. Even the gendarmes, although made of wood, cried like newborn babies.

At first Fire-eater remained as hard and cold as ice: slowly he began to melt and to sneeze. When he sneezed four or five times, he opened his arms affectionately to Pinocchio, saying, "You are a good, brave boy. Come here, and give me a kiss."

Pinocchio ran quickly and, climbing up the Showman's beard like a squirrel, gave him a loud kiss on the tip of his nose.

"And is my life spared?" asked poor Harlequin, in a trembling voice that could hardly be heard.

"Your life is spared," replied Fire-eater. Then he added shaking his head, "Very well, then! This evening I must eat my mutton half done; but another time, woe to him who. . .!"

When they knew that their brothers were pardoned, all the puppets ran back to the stage, lit the lights as for a festive performance, and began to jump and dance. They were still dancing at dawn.

Collodi, Carlo. *The Adventures of Pinocchio.* New York: Alfred A. Knopf, 1988.

THE RETURN OF THE KING: BEING THE THIRD PART OF THE LORD OF THE RINGS

J.R.R. Tolkien

In the third part of the Lord of the Rings trilogy, the original group that set out to destroy the ring has been separated. In this chapter, Pippin (or Peregrin) and Gandalf the wizard venture toward the city of Gondor and Minas Tirith. Pippin is very proud of being a hobbit and is quite insulted when he and Gandalf are stopped by a group of horsemen who mistake Pippin for a dwarf. Gandalf tells them that Pippin is a man, at which point the hobbit feels that he must speak up and defend his name.

Chapter 1 MINAS TIRITH

Pippin looked out from the shelter of Gandalf's cloak. He wondered if he was awake or still sleeping, till in the swift-moving dream in which he had been wrapped so long since the great ride began. The dark world was rushing by, and the wind sang loudly in his ears. He could see nothing but the wheeling stars, and away to his right, vast shadows against the sky where the mountains of the South marched past. Sleepily he tried to reckon the times and stages of their journey, but his memory was drowsy and uncertain.

There had been the first ride at terrible speed without a halt and then in the dawn he had seen a pale gleam of gold and they had come to the silent town and the great empty house on the hill. And hardly had they reached its shelter, when the winged shadow had passed over once agian, and men wilted with fear. But Gandalf had spoken soft words to him, and he had slept in a corner, tired but uneasy, dimly aware of comings and goings and of men talking and Gandalf giving orders. And then again riding, riding in the night. This was the second, no, the third night since he had looked in the Stone. And with that hideous memory he woke fully, and shivered, and the noise of the wind became filled with menacing voices.

A light kindled in the sky, a blaze of yellow fire behind dark barriers. Pippin cowered back, afraid for a moment, wondering into what dreadful country Gandalf was bearing him. He rubbed his eyes, and then he saw that it was the moon rising above the eastern shadows, now almost at the full. So the night was not yet old and for hours the dark journey would go on. He stirred and spoke.

"Where are we, Gandalf?" he asked.

"In the realm of gondor," the wizard answered. "The land of Anórien is still passing by."

There was a silence again for a while. Then, "What is that?" cried Pippin suddenly, clutching at Gandalf's cloak. "Look! Fire, red fire! Are there dragons in this land? Look, there is another!"

For answer Gandalf cried aloud to his horse. "On Shadowfax! We must hasten. Time is short. See! The beacons of Gondor are alight, calling for aid. War is kindled. See, there is the fire on Amon Dîn, and flame on Eilenach; and there they go seeding west: Nardol, Erelas, Min-Rimmon, Calehad, and the Halifirien on the borders of Rohan."

But Shadowfax paused in his stride, slowing to a walk, and then he lifted up his head and neighed. And out of the darkness, the answering neigh of other horses came; and presently the thudding hoofs were heard, and three riders swept up and passed like flying ghosts in the moon and vanished into the West. Then Shadowfax gathered himself together and sprang away, and the night flowed over him like a roaring wind.

Pippin became drowsy again and paid little attention to Gandalf, telling him of the customs of Gondor, and how the Lord of the City had beacons built on the tops of outlying hills along both borders of the great range, and maintained posts at these points where fresh horses were always in readiness to bear his errand-riders to Rohan in the North, or to Belfalas in the South. "It is long since the beacons of the North were lit," he said; "and in the ancient days of Gondor they were not needed, for they had the Seven Stone." Pippin stirred uneasily.

"Sleep again, and do not be afraid!" said Gandalf. "'For you are not going like Frodo to Mordor, but to Minas Tirith, and there you will be as safe as you can be anywere in these days. If Gondor falls, or the Ring is taken, then the Shire will be no refuge."

"You do not comfort me," said Pippin, but nonetheless, sleep crept over him. The last thing that he remembered before he fell into deep dream was a glimpse of high white peaks, glimmering like floating isles above the clouds, as they caught the light of the westering moon. He wondered where Frodo was, and if he was already in Mordor, or if he was dead; and he did not know that Frodo, from far away, looked on that same moon as it set beyond Gondor ere the coming of the day.

⋙⋘

Pippin woke to the sound of voices. Another day of hiding and a night of journey had fleeted by. It was twilight: the cold dawn was at hand again, and hill grey mists were about them. Shadowfax stood steaming with sweat, but he held his neck proudly and showed no sign of weariness. Many tall men heavily cloaked stood beside him, and behind them in the mist loomed a wall of stone. Partly ruinous it seemed, but already before the night was passed the sound of hurried labor could be heard: beat of hammers, clink of trowels, and the creak of wheels. Torches and flares glowed dully here and there in the fog. Gandalf was speaking to the men that barred his way, and as he listened, Pippin became aware that he himself was being discussed.

"Yea truly, we know you, Mithrandir," said the leader of the men, "and you know the passwords of the Seven Gates and are free to go forward. But we do not know your companion. What is he? A dwarf out of the mountains in the North? We wish for no strangers in the land at this time, unless they be mighty men of arms in whose faith and help we can trust."

"I will vouch for him before the seat of Denethor," said Gandalf. "And as for valor, that cannot be computed by stature. He has passed through more battles and perils than you have, Ingold, though you be twice his height; and he comes now from the storming of Isengard, of which we bear tidings, and great weariness is on him, or I would wake him. His name is Peregrin, a very valiant man."

"Man?" said Ingold dubiously, and the others laughed.

"Man!" cried Pippin, now thoroughly roused. "Man! Indeed not! I am a hobbit and no more valiant than I am a man, save perhaps now and again by necessity. Do not let Gandalf deceive you!"

"Many a doer of great deeds might say no more," said Ingold. "But what is a hobbit?"

"A Halfling," answered Gandalf. "Nay, not the one that was spoken of," he added seeing the wonder in the men's faces. "Not he, yet one of his kindred."

"Yes, and one who journeyed with him," said Pippin. "And Boromir of your city was with us, and he saved me in the snows of the North, and at the last he was slain defending me from many foes."

Tolkien, J.R.R. *The Return of the King: Being the Third Part of The Lord of The Rings.* New York: Ballantine Books, 1955.

MISTRESS MASHAM'S REPOSE

T.H. WHITE

Maria is a spirited orphan who lives a very strange life on the ramshackle, though formerly grand, estate of her ancestors, with only a governess, a cook, and a tutor. One day she explores an island which lies in the middle of a small pond on the grounds of her estate. Once a serene resting spot for the late Mistress Masham, the abandoned cupola on the island, as Maria soon discovers, is now home to an entire community of tiny people!

CHAPTER II

The island on which she found herself was about the size of a tennis court. It had been carried there on boats, when the first duke had been beautifying his park, and it had risen from the water two hundred years before, an artificial emerald of green grass, crowned by the white dome of its cupola. There, perhaps, the Mistress Hill who was to become Mistress Masham—had sat in silks and laces, in the summer weather, drinking tay.

But now the island was tangled with every kind of briar. There seemed to be no way of reaching the little temple without pain, for the nettles were ready to sting and the briars were ready to prick, and what she really needed was a machete—or any similar instrument used by Indians, in cutting their trackways through the bush.

If she had been a gamekeeper with thick clothes and leather leggings, she might have been able to push her way through; if she had been a farm laborer, she could have cleared a path with her brush hook; as she was neither of these, but a determined person all the same, she bashed her way with the boat's oar. When she had beaten down a bramble, she trod on it reluctantly; when they caught in her dress, she stopped and took them out—sometimes; when they scratched her face, she swore the appropriate oath; and so, slowly but surely, she burrowed her way into the forest belt. She tore her skirt in three places, and scratched the brown legs horribly, until she had to go back for the shoes.

The tanglewood stopped suddenly, several yards from the steps of the temple, and the intruder came to a halt with a blackberry branch in her hair.

Where the brambles ended, the grass began: the same neat, artificial grass which Lady Masham must have known. It was still kept as short, or even shorter. It was as smooth as a bowling green.

In the middle, there was the beautiful, sun-drenched temple, rising airily on its pillars.

But what was strange—and here Maria's heart went pat, she knew not why—the strange thing was that everything was neat.

She looked everywhere, but not a soul was to be seen. Not a leaf stirred in the little amphitheater, nor was there any trace of a hut to live in. There was not shed to hold a lawn mower, nor any mower standing on the lawn.

Yet somebody had mowed the grass.

Maria took the bramble out of her hair, disentangled herself from the last branches, and went forward to her doom.

The plaster inside the dome had fallen in some places; but the wooden slats, which were visible in most of the ruined ceilings of her home, were not exposed in this one. It looked as if the roof had been repaired from inside, with clay or paper, as if it had been done by wasps.

Everything was so clean, so different from the wasteland which she had come through—so square and round and geometrical, just as it had been when first erected—that her eye was drawn to details.

She saw: first, a square opening, about eight inches wide, in the lowest step, which she took to be the ventilator of a damp course—but there was a path leading to it, trodden in the fine grass, a path for mice; next she saw a seven-inch door in the base of each pillar —but, and this she did not notice because they were nearly as small as match heads, these doors had handles; finally, she saw that there was a walnut shell, or half one, outside the nearest door. Several walnuts grew in the park, though none were very close. She went to look at the shell—but looked with the greatest astonishment.

There was a baby in it.

She bent down to pick up the cradle, which she took to be some kind of toy, a toy made more beautifully than any she had ever seen. When the shadow of her hand fell across the baby, which was nearly an inch long, it wagged its head on the minute cushion of moss, put out its fists in both directions, pulled up its knees as if it were bicycling, and gave a thin mew, which she could hear.

She did not snatch away her hand when the creature mewed. On the contrary, she grabbed the walnut. It there were one thing now in all the world which Maria was inclined to snatch, it was the baby.

She held it tenderly in the palm of her hand, not breathing for fear of spoiling it, and examined its wonderful perfection as well as she could. Its eyes, which were as small as shrimp's, seemed to have the proper marble-blue for babies; its skin was slightly mauve, so that it must have been a new one; it was not skinny, but beautifully plump, and she was

just able to distinguish the creases round its fat wrists—crease which looked as if the thinnest hair had been tied round in a tight bracelet, or as if the hands had been fitted, on the ball-and socket principle, by the most cunning of all the dollmakers there had ever been.

It was truly alive and seemed to be fairly pleased at being picked up, for it held out one hand toward her nose and chuckled. At least, by listening to it like a watch, with her head on one side, she was certain that it made a noise.

While Maria was in a rapture with this windfall, she felt a sharp pain in her left ankle, as bad as if she had been stung by a bee.

Like most people whose ankles are stung, she stamped her foot and hopped about on one leg—a useless procedure, so far as bees are concerned, because it only annoys the others, and the first one cannot sting again.

She held the cradle with greatest care while she hopped, clapped her spare hand to the hurt ankle, and confronted her assailant from a safe distance, standing on one leg.

There was a fat woman, about five inches high, standing on the marble pavement of the temple, and brandishing a sort of harpoon. She was dressed in rust-colored stuff, like the breast of a robin, and she was wild with rage or terror. Her little eyes were flashing, her hair had come down at the back, her bosom was heaving, and she was shouting in an unknown language something about Quinba Flestrina. The harpoon, which was as sharp as a needle, had a steel head half as long as the baby. Some blood was trickling between the fingers of Maria's spare hand.

Maria was not the kind of person who bore malice for injuries, and she was certainly not the kind of kidnapper who habitually stole babies from their heartbroken mothers, for the mere cynical pleasure of hearing them scream. She guessed immediately that this was the mother of the baby, and instead of feeling angry about the harpoon, she began to feel guilty about the baby. She began to have an awful suspicion that she would have to give it back.

Yet the temptation to keep it was severe. She would never drop on another find like this, she knew, not if she lived to be a thousand.

Think to yourself, truly, whether you would have returned a live one-inch baby to its relatives, if caught fairly in the open field?

But Maria did her best.

She said: "I am sorry if this is your baby. Please, I have not done it any harm. Look, you can have it safe.

"And really," she added, almost tearfully, "it is a beauty."

She leaned forward to put the cradle at the mother's feet.

The fierce woman was either too hysterical to listen, or else she did not understand English, for she slashed at the huge hand with her weapon as soon as it came within reach, and cut it across the thumb.

"Oh, you would, would you?" cried Maria. "You little viper!"

So, instead of giving up the baby, she wrapped it in her handkerchief, cradle and all, and put the bundle in the pocket of her skirt. Then she took a second handkerchief out of the other pocket, waved it in the face of the mother so that she fell on her back, dropped it over head, flicked away the fallen harpoon, and gathered her as well.

Stuffing the larger bundle into the other pocket—it was kicking as hard as it could— she made for her passage through the brambles. When she got there she turned round for a last look at the temple. She saw a group of three men struggling at the pillar door. Two of them were holding the third by the arms, to keep him back, and he was fighting them to follow her. He was a splendid fellow in a fur tunic, made of moleskin, and well over six inches high.

White, T.H. *Mistress Masham's Repose*. New York: G.P. Putnam's Son's, 1946.

THE GOLDEN KEY

George MacDonald

A boy living on the edge of Fairyland learns of a golden key which is said to lie beneath the rainbow's end. Without even knowing what the magical key will unlock, he follows the rainbow into the forest.

here was a boy who used to sit in the twilight and listen to his great-aunt's stories. She told him that if he could reach the place where the end of the rainbow stands, he would find there a golden key.

"And what is the key for?" the boy would ask. "What is it the key of? What will it open?"

"That nobody knows," his aunt would reply. "He has to find that out."

"I suppose, being gold," the boy once said, thoughtfully, "that I could get a good deal of money for it if I sold it."

"Better never find it than sell it," returned his aunt.

And then the boy went to bed and dreamed about the golden key.

Now all that his great-aunt told the boy about the golden key would have been nonsense, had it not been that their little house stood on the borders of Fairyland. For it is perfectly well known that out of Fairyland nobody ever can find where the rainbow stands. The creature takes such good care of its golden key, always flitting from place to place, lest anyone should find it! But in Fairyland, it is quite different. Things that look real in this country look very thin indeed in Fairyland, while some of the things that here cannot stand still for a moment, will not move there. So it was not in the least absurd of the old lady to tell her nephew such things about the golden key.

"Did you ever know anybody find it?" he asked, one evening.

"Yes. Your father, I believe, found it."

"And what did he do with it, can you tell me?"

"He never told me."

"What was it like?"

"He never showed it to me."

"How does a new key come there always?"

"I don't know. There it is."

"Perhaps it is the rainbow's egg."

"Perhaps it is. You will be a happy boy if you find the nest."

"Perhaps it comes tumbling down the rainbow from the sky."

"Perhaps it does."

One evening, in summer, he went into his own room, and stood at the lattice-window, and gazed into the forest which fringed the outskirts of Fairyland. It came close up to his great-aunt's garden, and indeed, sent some straggling trees into it. The forest lay to the east, and the sun, which was setting behind the cottage, looked straight into the dark wood with his level red eye. The trees were all old and had few branches below, so that the sun could see a great way into the forest, and the boy, being keen sighted, could see almost as far as the sun. The trunks stood like rows of red columns in the shine of the red sun, and he could see down aisle after aisle in the vanishing distance. And as he gazed into the forest, he began to feel as if the trees were all waiting for him, and had something they could not go on with till he came to them. But he was hungry, and wanted his supper. So he lingered.

Suddenly, far among the trees, as far as the sun could shine, he saw a glorious thing. It was the end of a rainbow, large and brilliant. He could count all the seven colors, and could see shade after shade beyond the violet; while before the red stood a color more gorgeous and mysterious still. It was a color he had never seen before. Only the spring of the rainbow arch was visible. He could see nothing of it above the trees.

"The golden key!" he said to himself, and darted out of the house, and into the wood.

He had not gone far before the sun set. But the rainbow only glowed the brighter. For the rainbow of Fairyland is not dependent upon the sun, as ours is. It was a grand sight, burning away there in silence, with its gorgeous, its lovely, its delicate colors, each distinct, all combining. He could now see a great deal more of it.

He stood gazing at it till he forgot himself with delight—even forgot the key which he had come to seek. And as he stood, it grew more wonderful still. For in each of the colors, which was as large as the column of a church, he could faintly see beautiful forms slowly ascending as if by the steps of winding stair. The forms appeared irregularly—men and women and children—all different, all beautiful.

He drew nearer to the rainbow. It vanished. He started back a step in dismay. It was there again, as beautiful as ever. So he contented himself with standing as near it as he might, and watching the forms that ascended the glorious colors towards the unknown height of the arch, which did not end abruptly but faded away in the blue air, so gradually that he could not say where it ceased.

When the thought of the golden key returned, the boy very wisely proceeded to mark out in his mind the space covered by the foundation of the rainbow, in order that he might know where to search, should the rainbow disappear. It was based chiefly upon a bed of moss.

Meantime, it had grown quite dark in the wood. The rainbow alone was visible by its own light. But the moment the moon rose the rainbow vanished. Nor could any change of place restore the vision to the boy's eyes. So he threw himself down upon the mossy bed to wait till the sunlight would give him a chance of finding the key. There he fell fast asleep.

When he woke in the morning the sun was looking straight into his eyes. He turned away from it, and the same moment saw a brilliant little thing lying on the moss within a foot of his face. It was the golden key. The pipe of it was of plain gold, as bright as gold could be. The handle was curiously wrought and set with sapphires. In a terror of delight, he put out his hand and took it, and had it.

MacDonald, George. *The Golden Key*. New York: Farrar, Straus and Giroux, 1967.

THE TEMPEST

WILLIAM SHAKESPEARE

AS RETOLD BY CHARLES AND MARY LAMB

Prospero is an exiled nobleman, who studies the "magical arts." Now living on an island with his young daughter Miranda and the spirits he has in his service, he conjures up a terrible storm to strand the ship of those that have deposed him so that he may regain his former position, and his beautiful daughter may meet and marry the son of the king.

here was a certain island in the sea, the only inhabitants of which were an old man, whose name was Prospero, and his daughter Miranda, a very beautiful young lady. She came to this island so young, that she had no memory of having seen any other human face than her father's.

They lived in a cave or cell, made out of a rock; it was divided into several apartments, one of which Prospero called his study; there he kept his books, which chiefly treated of magic, a study at that time much affected by all learned men: and the knowledge of this art he found very useful to him; for being thrown by a strange chance upon this island, which had been enchanted by a witch called Sycorax, who died there a short time before his arrival, Prospero, by virtue of his art, released many good spirits that Sycorax had imprisoned in the bodies of large trees because they had refused to execute her wicked commands. These gentle spirits were ever after obedient of the will of Prospero. Of these Ariel was the chief.

The lively little sprite Ariel had nothing mischievous in his nature, except that he took rather too much pleasure in tormenting an ugly monster called Caliban, for he owed him a grudge because he was the son of his old enemy Sycorax. This Caliban Prospero found in the woods, a strange misshapen thing, far less human in form than an ape: he took him home to his cell and taught him to speak. And Prospero would have been very kind to him, but the bad nature which Caliban inherited from his mother, Sycorax, would not let him learn anything good or useful: therefore he was employed like a slave, to fetch wood, and do the most laborious offices; and Ariel had the charge of compelling him to these services.

Having these powerful spirits obedient at his will, Prospero could by their means command the winds, and the waves of the sea. By his orders they raised a violent storm, in the midst of which, and struggling with the wild sea waves that every moment threatened to swallow it up, he showed his daughter a fine large ship, which he told her was full of living beings like themselves. "O my dear father," said she, "if by your art you have raised this dreadful storm, have pity on their sad distress. See! the vessel will be dashed to pieces. Poor souls! they will all perish."

"Be not so amazed, daughter Miranda," said Prospero; "there is no harm done. I have so ordered it, that no person in the ship shall receive any hurt. What I have done has been in care of you, my dear child. You are ignorant who you are or where you came from, and you know no more of me, but that I am you father and live in this poor cave. Can you remember a time before you came to this cell? I think you cannot, for you were not then three years of age."

"Certainly I can, sir," replied Miranda.

"By what?" asked Prospero; "by any other house or person. Tell me what you can remember my child."

Miranda said: "It seems to me like the recollection of a dream. But had I not once four or five women who attended upon me?"

Prospero answered: "You had, and more. How is it that this still lives in your mind? Do you remember how you came here?"

"No, sir," said Miranda, "I remember nothing more."

"Twelve years ago, Miranda," continued Prospero, "I was duke of Milan, and you were a princess, and my only heir. I had a younger brother, whose name was Antonio, to whom I trusted everything: and as I was fond of retirement and deep study, I commonly left the management of my state affairs to your uncle, my false brother (for so indeed he proved). I, neglecting all worldly ends, buried among my books, did dedicate my whole time to the bettering of my mind. My brother Antonio being thus in possession of my power, began to think himself the duke indeed. The opportunity I gave him of making himself popular among my subjects awakened in his bad nature a proud ambition to deprive me of my dukedom: this he soon effected with the aid of the king of Naples, a powerful prince, who was my enemy."

"Wherefore," said Miranda, "did they not that hour destroy us?"

"My child," answered her father, "they durst not, so dear was the love that my people bore me. Antonio carried us on board a ship, and when we were some leagues out at sea, he forced us into a small boat, without either tackle, sail, or mast: there he left us, as he thought, to perish. But a kind lord of my court, one Gonzalo, who loved me, had privately placed in the boat, water, provisions, apparel, and some books which I prize above my dukedom."

"O my father," said Miranda, "what a trouble must I have been to you then!"

"No, my love," said Prospero, "you were a little cherub that did preserve me. Your innocent smiles made me bear up against my misfortunes. Our food lasted till we landed on this desert island, since when my chief delight had been in teaching you, Miranda, and well have you profited by my instructions."

"Heaven thank you, my dear father," said Miranda. "Now pray tell me, sir, your reason for raising this sea storm?"

"Know then," said her father, "that by means of this storm, my enemies, the king of Naples, and my cruel brother, are cast ashore upon this island."

Having so said, Prospero gently touched his daughter with his magic wand, and she fell fast asleep; for the spirit Ariel just then presented himself before his master, to give an account of the tempest, and how he had disposed of the ship's company, and though the spirits were always invisible to Miranda, Prospero did not choose she should hear him holding converse (as would seem to her) with the empty air.

"Well, my brave spirit," said Prospero to Ariel, "how have you performed your task?"

Ariel gave a lively description of the storm, and of the terrors of the mariner; and how the king's son, Ferdinand, was the first who leaped into the sea; and his father thought he saw his dear son swallowed up by the waves and lost. "But he is safe," said Ariel, "in a corner of the isle, sitting with his arms folded, sadly lamenting the loss of the king, his father, whom he concludes drowned. Not a hair of his head in injured, and his princely garments, though drenched in the sea waves, look fresher than before."

"That's my delicate Ariel," said Prospero. "Bring him hither: my daughter must see this young prince. Where is the king, and my brother?"

"I left them," answered Ariel, "searching for Ferdinand, whom they have little hopes of finding, thinking they saw him perish. Of the ship's crew not one is missing; though each one thinks himself the only one saved: and the ship, though invisible to them, is safe in the harbor."

Lamb, Charles and Mary. *Tales from Shakespeare.* New York: Puffin Books, Penguin Books USA Inc., 1994.

THE STEADFAST TIN SOLDIER

Hans Christian Andersen

The Tin Soldier is unlike other toy soldiers—he only has one leg—but he is very proud in any case. And he is in love with a beautiful dancing doll. One night, he falls out of the children's nursery window and the next thing he knows, two boys make a paper boat and sail him down the street.

There were once five-and-twenty tin soldiers; they were brothers, for they had all been cast from an old tin spoon. They shouldered their muskets and looked straight before them; and their uniforms were splendid in red and blue. The first thing they heard in the world, when the lid was taken off the box in which they lay, were the words "Tin Soldiers!" shouted by a little boy, as he clapped his hands in glee. The soldiers had been given to him on his birthday, and now, he joyfully set them out on the table. Each soldier was exactly like every other, except one, and he had but one leg. He had been cast last of all, and there had not been enough tin to finish him, but he stood as firm on his one leg as the others on their two; and he is the very one that became remarkable.

On the table on which the soldiers had been placed stood many other playthings, but the toy that attracted most attention was a delightful castle of cardboard. Through the little windows one could look straight into the rooms. Before the castle stood a number of little trees, round a little looking glass which was to represent a lake. Wax swans swam on this lake and were mirrored in it. All this was very pretty, but the prettiest of all was a little lady who stood in the open doorway of the castle. She, too, was cut out of paper, but she had a dress of the clearest gauze, and a little narrow blue ribbon, that looked like a scarf, over her shoulders; and in the middle of this ribbon was a shining tinsel rose as large as her whole face. The little lady stretched out both her arms, for she was a dancer; and she lifted one leg so high that the Tin Soldier could not see it at all, and thought that, like himself, she had but one.

That would be just the wife for me! thought he; but she is very grand. She lives in a castle, while I have only a box, and there are five-and-twenty of us about that. It is no place for her! But still, I must try and make her acquaintance!

Then he lay down at full length behind a snuff box which stood on the table; there he could easily watch the dainty little lady, who continued to stand on one leg without losing her balance.

Along in the evening, all the other tin soldiers were put into their box, and the people in the house went to bed. Now the toys began to play at "visiting," and at "war," and at "having dances." The tin soldiers rattled in their box, for they wanted to join the fun; but they could not lift the lid. The nutcracker threw somersaults, and the pencil amused itself on the slate; there was so much noise that the canary awoke, and began to take part in the conversation, and that in verse. The only two who did not stir from their places were the Tin Soldier and the Dancing Lady; she stood straight up on the points of her toes, and stretched out both her arms; he was equally steady on his one leg; and he never turned his eyes away from her a single moment.

The clock struck twelve—and, pop! The lid flew off the snuff box. There was no snuff in it, Oh, no! but there was a little black Goblin. It was a Jack-in-the-box, you see.

"Tin Soldier!" said the Goblin. "Keep your eyes to yourself, will you!"

But the Tin Soldier pretended not to hear him.

"Just you wait till tomorrow!" said the Goblin.

When the morning came and the children were out of bed, the Tin Soldier was placed in the window; and whether it was the Goblin or a draft that did it, all at once the window flew open, and the Soldier fell head over heels down from the third story. That was a terrible fall! His leg stuck up in the air, and thus he remained standing, with helmet downward and his bayonet between the paving stones.

The servant girl and the little boy came down directly to look for him, but though they almost trod upon him, they could not see him. If the Soldier had shouted, "Here I am!" they would surely have found him; but he did not think it fitting that a soldier dressed in full uniform as he was should cry out loudly.

It now began to rain; the drops fell faster and faster, and soon it was streaming down. When the shower was over, two street boys came by.

"Look!" said one of them, "there lies a tin soldier. He must have a boat ride."

So they made a boat out of a newspaper, put the Tin Soldier in the middle of it, and away he sailed down the gutter. The two boys ran along beside him and clapped their hands. Goodness preserve us! how the waves rose in that gutter, and what a current! You see it had been a very heavy shower. The paper boat rocked up and down, and sometimes spun round so quickly that the Tin Soldier trembled; but he didn't move, and never changed countenance; he looked straight before him, holding his musket.

All at once, the boat went into a long drain, and it became as dark as it had been in his box.

"Where am I going now?" he thought. "Yes, yes, it is all the Goblin's fault! Ah! If the little lady were only sitting here in the boat with me, it might be twice as dark for all I should care."

Just then a great Water Rat, which lived in the drain, came up to the boat.

"Have you a passport?" asked the Rat. "Out with your passport!"

But the Tin Soldier kept silence, and held his musket tighter than ever.

The boat rushed on, and the Rat after it. My! how he gnashed his teeth and shouted to the straws and bits of wood:

"Stop him! Stop him! He hasn't paid toll—he hasn't shown his passport!"

But the current ran faster and faster. The Tin Soldier could already see the bright daylight where the drain ended; but he heard a terrible roaring noise that was indeed enough to frighten the bravest of men. Just think, where the tunnel ended, the drain dropped into a great canal; and for him that was as dangerous as for us to be carried down a great waterfall.

He was already so near it that he could not stop. The boat rushed out, the poor Tin Soldier stiffening himself as much as he could, and no one could say that he had as much as blinked. The boat whirled round three or four times, and was full of water to the very edge. It would surely sink.

Andersen, Hans Christian. *Hans Christian Andersen Fairy Tales.* Translated by Reginald Spink. New York: Everyman's Library Children's Classics, Alfred A. Knopf, 1992.

FINN FAMILY MOOMINTROLL

TOVE JANSSON

The Valley of the Moomins is home to lots of silly creatures, and strange and magical things happen there every day. In these two excerpts, Moomintroll, Snufkin, Sniff, and their friends discover that the black top hat that they found in the Hobgoblin's cave has some mysterious powers.

CHAPTER II

PART I

One warm summer day it was raining softly in the Valley of the Moomins, so they all decided to play hide-and-seek indoors. Sniff stood in the corner with his nose in his paws and counted up to ten before he turned round and began hunting—first in the ordinary hiding-places and then in the extraordinary ones.

Moomintroll lay under the veranda table feeling rather worried—it wasn't a good place. Sniff would be sure to lift the table cloth, and there he would be stuck. He looked about and then caught sight of the tall, black hat which stood in a corner. That would be a brilliant idea! Sniff would never think of looking under the hat. Moomintroll stole quietly to the corner and pulled the hat over his head. It didn't reach further than his middle, but if he made himself very small and tucked in his tail, he would be quite invisible. He giggled to himself when he heard all the others being found, one after another. The Hemulen had obviously hidden himself under the sofa again — he could never find a better place. And now they were all running about searching for Moomintroll.

He waited until he was afraid they would get bored with the search, and then he crept out of the hat, stuck his head through the door and said: "Look at me!"

Sniff stared at him for a long time, then he said rather unkindly: "Look at yourself!"

"Who's that?" whispered the Snork, but the others only shook their heads and continued to stare at Moomintroll.

Poor little chap! He had been turned into a very strange animal indeed under the Hobgoblin's Hat. All his fat parts had become thin, and everything that was small had

353

grown big. And the strangest thing about it was that he himself didn't realize what was the matter.

"I thought I'd surprise you all," he said taking an uncertain step forward on his long, spindly legs. "You've no idea where I've been!"

"It doesn't interest us," said the Snork, "but you're certainly ugly enough to surprise anybody."

"You are unkind," said Moomintroll sadly. "I suppose you got tired of hunting. What shall we do now?"

"First of all perhaps you should introduce yourself," said the Snork Maiden, stiffly.

Moomintroll looked at her incredulously, but then it dawned on him that perhaps this was a new game. He laughed delightedly and said: "I'm the King of California!"

"And I'm the Snork Maiden," said the Snork Maiden. "This is my brother."

"I'm called Sniff," said Sniff.

"I'm Snufkin," said Snufkin.

"Oh, dear! How boring you all are," said Moomintroll. "Couldn't you have thought of something more original! Now let's go out—I think the weather's clearing." And he went down the steps into the garden, followed by a rather surprised and suspicious little trio.

"Who's that?" asked the Hemulen, who was sitting in front of the house counting the stamens of a sunflower.

"It's the King of California, I think," said the Snork Maiden.

"Is he going to live here?" asked the Hemulen.

"That's for Moomintroll to decide," said Sniff. "I wonder where he's got to."

Moomintroll laughed. "You really are quite funny at times," he said. "Shall we go and look for Moomintroll?"

"Do you know him?" asked Snufkin.

"Ye-es," said Moomintroll. "Rather well as a matter of fact." He was thoroughly enjoying the new game and thought he was doing rather well at it.

"How did you come to know him?" asked the Snork Maiden.

"We were born at the same time," said Moomintroll, still bursting with laughter. "But he's an impossible fellow, you know! You simply can't have him in the house!"

"How dare you talk about Moomintroll like that!" said the Snork Maiden fiercely. "He's the best Moomin in the world, and we think a great deal of him."

This was almost too much for Moomintroll. "Really?" he said "Personally, I think he's an absolute pest."

Then the Snork Maiden began to cry.

"Go away!" said the Snork to Moomintroll. "Otherwise we shall have to sit on your head."

"All right, all right," Moomintroll said, soothingly. "It's only a game, isn't it? I'm awfully glad you think so much of me."

"But we don't," screamed Sniff, shrilly. "Take away this ugly king who runs down our Moomintroll."

And they threw themselves onto poor Moomintroll. He was much too surprised to defend himself, and when he began to get angry it was too late. So when Moominmamma came out on the steps he was lying underneath a large pile of flailing paws and tails.

"What are you doing there, children?" she cried. "Stop fighting at once!"

"They're walloping the King of California," sniffed the Snork Maiden. "And it serves him right."

Moomintroll crawled out of the scrum, tired out and angry.

"Mother," he cried. "They started it. Three against one! It's not fair!"

"I quite agree," said Moominmamma seriously. "However, I expect you had teased them. But who are you, my little beast?"

"Oh, please stop this awful game," wailed Moomintroll. "It isn't funny anymore. I am Moomintroll, and you are my Mother. And that's that!"

"You aren't Moomintroll," said the Snork Maiden scornfully. "He has beautiful little ears, but yours look like kettle-holders!"

Moomintroll felt quite confused and took hold of a pair of enormous crinkly ears. "But I am Moomintroll!" he burst out in despair. "Don't you believe me?"

"Moomintroll has a nice little tail, just about the right size, but yours is like a chimney sweep's brush," said the Snork.

And, oh dear, it was true! Moomintroll felt behind him with a trembling paw.

"Your eyes are like soup plates," said Sniff. Moomintroll's are small and kind!"

"Yes, exactly," Snufkin agreed.

"You are an imposter!" decided the Hemulen.

"Isn't there anyone who believes me?" Moomintroll pleaded. "Look carefully at me, Mother. You must know your own Moomintroll."

Moominmamma looked carefully. She looked into his frightened eyes for a very long time, and then she said quietly: "Yes, you are my Moomintroll."

And at the same moment he began to change. His ears, eyes and tail began to shrink, and his nose and tummy grew, until at last he was his old self again.

"It's all right now, my dear," said Moominmamma. "You see, I shall always know you, whatever happens."

PART II

 little later on, Moomintroll and the Snork were sitting in one of their secret hiding places—the one under the jasmine-bush which was hidden by a curtain of green leaves.

"Yes, but you must have done something to change you," the Snork was saying.

Moomintroll shook his head. "I didn't notice anything unusual," he said. "And I didn't say any dangerous words either."

"But perhaps you stepped into a fairy ring," suggested the Snork.

"Not that I know of," said Moomintroll. "I sat the whole time under that black hat that we use as a waste paper basket."

"In the hat?" asked the Snork, suspiciously.

Moomintroll nodded, and they both thought for a long time. Then suddenly they burst out together: "It must be." and stared at each other.

"Come on!" said the Snork

They went onto the veranda and crept up to the hat very cautiously.

"It looks rather ordinary," said the Snork. "Unless you consider that a top hat is always somewhat extraordinary, of course."

"But how can we find out if it was that?" asked Moomintroll. "I'm not going to get into it again!"

"Perhaps we could lure somebody else into it," suggested the Snork.

"But that would be a low-down trick," said Moomintroll "How should we know that he would be all right again?"

"What about an enemy?" suggested the Snork.

"Hm," said Moomintroll. "Do you know of one?"

"The Pig-Swine," said the Snork.

Moomintroll shook his head. "He's too big."

"Well, the Ant-lion then?" the Snork suggested.

"That's a good idea," Moomintroll agreed. "He once pulled my mother down into a hole and sprayed sand into her eyes."

So they set out to look for the Ant-lion and took a big jar with them. You should look for ant-lions' holes in a sandy place, so they wandered down to the beach, and it wasn't long before the Snork discovered a big, round hole and signaled eagerly to Moomintroll.

"Here he is!" whispered the Snork. "But how shall we lure him into the jar?"

"Leave it to me," whispered Moomintroll. He took the jar and buried it in the sand a little distance away, with the opening on top. Then he said loudly: "They are very weak creatures these ant-lions!" He signed to the Snork, and they both looked expectantly down at the hole, but although the sand moved a bit nothing was to be seen.

"Very weak," repeated Moomintroll. "It takes several hours for them to dig themselves down into the sand, you know!"

At that moment a threatening head with staring eyes popped up from the hole in the sand.

"Did you say weak?" hissed the Ant-lion. "I can dig myself down in exactly three seconds!"

"You should really show us how it's done, so that we can believe such a wonderful feat is possible," said Moomintroll, persuasively.

"I shall spray sand on you," replied the Ant-lion very crossly, "and when I have sprayed you down into my hole I shall gobble you up!"

"Oh, no," pleaded the Snork. "Couldn't you show us how to dig down backwards in three seconds instead?"

"Do it up here so that we can see better how it's done," said Moomintroll, and pointed to the spot where the jar was buried.

"Do you think I am going to bother myself with showing tricks to babies?" said the Ant-lion, huffily. But all the same he simply could not resist the temptation to show them how strong and quick he was, so, with scornful sniffings, he scrambled up out of his hole and asked haughtily.

"Now, where shall I dig myself in?"

"There," said Moomintroll pointing.

The Ant-lion drew up his shoulders and raised his mane in a terrifying manner.

"Out of my way!" he cried. "Now I'm going underground, but when I come back I shall gobble you up! One, two, three!" And he backed down into the sand like a whirling propeller, right into the jar which was hidden under him. It certainly did only take three seconds, or perhaps two and a half, because he was so awfully angry.

"Quick with the lid," cried Moomintroll, and scraping away the sand they screwed it on very tightly. Then they both heaved up the jar and began to roll it home, with the Ant-lion inside screaming and cursing and choking with sand.

"It's frightful how angry he is," said the Snork. "I daren't think what will happen when he comes out!"

"He won't come out now," said Moomintroll, quietly, "and when he does I hope he will be changed into someting horrible."

When they arrived at Momminhouse Moomintroll summoned everyone with three long whistles. (Which means: Something quite extraordinary had happened.)

The others arrived from all directions and collected round the jar with the screw-top.

"What have you got there?" asked Sniff.

"An ant-lion," said Moomintroll proudly. "A genuine, furiously angry ant-lion that we have taken prisoner!"

"Fancy you daring!" said the Snork Maiden admiringly.

"And now I think we'll pour him into the hat," said the Snork.

"So that he will be changed like I was," said Moomintroll.

"B-But he could turn into absolutely anything!" squeaked Sniff. "He could turn into something still more dangerous than an ant-lion and gobble us all up in a minute." They stood in terrified silence looking at the pot and listening to the muffled sounds coming from inside.

Snufkin suggested they should all hide under the table while the change took place and put a big book on top of the hat. "You must always take risks when experimenting," he said. "Tip him in now at once."

Sniff scrambled under the table while Moomintroll, Snufkin, and the Hemulen held the jar over the Hobgoblin's Hat and the Snork gingerly unscrewed the lid. In a cloud of sand the Ant-lion tumbled out, and quick as lightning, the Snork popped a Dictionary of Outlandish Words on top. Then they all dived under the table and waited.

At first nothing happened.

They peeped out from under the tablecloth, getting more and more agitated. Still there was not change.

"It was all rot," said Sniff, but at that moment the big dictionary began to wrinkle up, and in his excitement, Sniff bit the Hemulen's thumb thinking it was his own.

Now the dictionary was curling up more and more. The pages began to look like withered leaves, and between them the Outlandish Words came out and began crawling around on the floor.

"Goodness, gracious me," said Moomintroll.

But there was more to come. Water began to drip from the brim of the hat and then to overflow and to splash down onto the carpet so that the Words had to climb up the wall to save themselves.

"The Ant-lion had only turned into water," said Snufkin in disappointment.

"I think it's the sand," whispered the Snork. "The Ant-lion is sure to come soon."

They waited again for an unbearably long time. Then suddenly on the edge of the hat appeared the world's smallest hedgehog. He sniffed the air and blinked, and he was very tangled and wet.

There was dead silence for a couple of seconds. Then Snufkin began to laugh, and in a very short time they were all howling and rolling about under the table in pure delight.

Meanwhile, the little hedgehog had wandered solemnly and a little sadly to the door and out down the steps. The water had stopped flowing and now filled the veranda like a lake. And the whole ceiling was covered with Outlandish Words.

Jansson, Tove, *Finn Family Moomintroll*. New York: Farrar, Straus and Giroux, 1948.

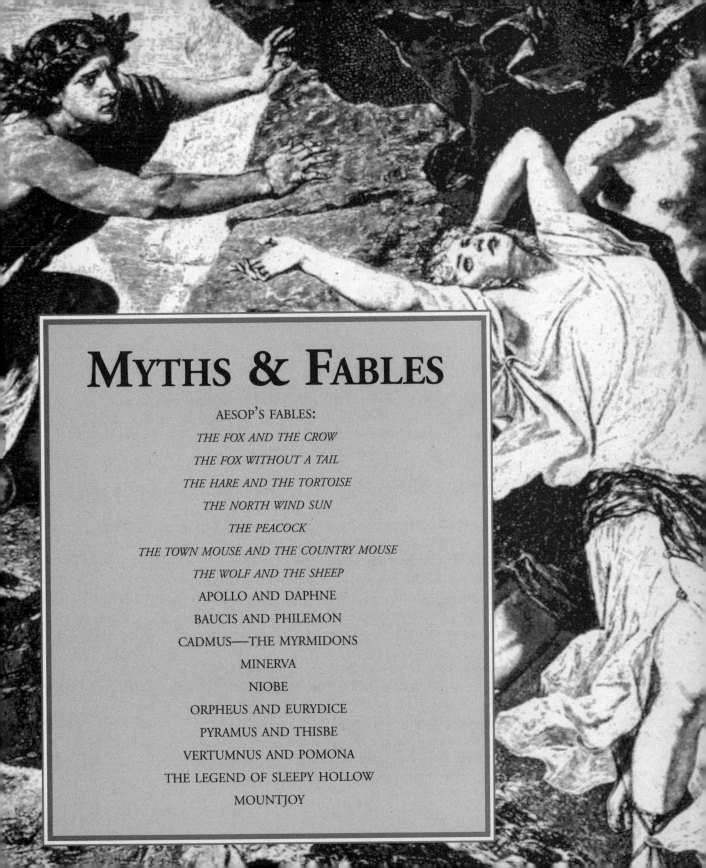

MYTHS & FABLES

AESOP'S FABLES

Aesop's Fables are a collection of short tales that entertain and also teach basic truths or morals. The animals and forces of nature in these fables often speak, think, and act like human beings. Some of these stories are now collected for you to enjoy.

THE FOX AND THE CROW

A crow falls for a fox's flattery.

ne bright morning as the Fox was following his sharp nose through the wood in search of a bite to eat, he saw a Crow on the limb of a tree overhead. This was by no means the first Crow the Fox had ever seen. What caught his attention this time and made him stop for a second look, was that the lucky Crow held a bit of cheese in her beak.

"No need to search any farther," thought the sly Master Fox. "Here is a dainty bite for my breakfast."

Up he trotted to the foot of the tree in which the Crow was sitting, and looking up admiringly, he cried, "Good-morning, beautiful creature!"

The Crow, her head cocked on one side, watched the Fox suspiciously. But she kept her beak tightly closed on the cheese and did not return his greeting.

"What a charming creature she is!" said the Fox. "How her feathers shine! What a beautiful form and what splendid wings! Such a wonderful Bird should have a very lovely voice, since everything else about her is so perfect. Could she sing just one song, I know I should hail her Queen of Birds."

Listening to these flattering words, the Crow forgot all her suspicion, and also her breakfast. She wanted very much to be called Queen of Birds.

So she opened her beak wide to utter her loudest caw, and down fell the cheese straight into the Fox's open mouth.

"Thank you," said Master Fox sweetly, as he walked off. "Though it is cracked, you have a voice sure enough. But where are your wits?"

The flatterer lives at the expense of those who will listen to him.

THE FOX WITHOUT A TAIL

A Fox tries to hoodwink the other foxes and fails.

A fox that had been caught in a trap succeeded at last, after much painful tugging, in getting away. But he had to leave his beautiful bushy tail behind him.

For a long time he kept away from the other Foxes, for he knew well enough that they would all make fun of him and crack jokes and laugh behind his back. But it was hard for him to live alone, and at last he thought of a plan that would perhaps help him out of his trouble.

He called a meeting of all the Foxes, saying that he had something of great importance to tell the tribe.

When they were all gathered together, the fox Without a Tail got up and made a long speech about those Foxes who had come to harm because of their tails.

This one had been caught by hounds when his tail had become entangled in the hedge. That one had not been able to run fast enough because of the weight of his brush. Besides, it was well known, he said, that men hunt Foxes simply for their tails, which they cut off as prizes of the hunt. With such proof of the danger and uselessness of having a tail, said Master Fox, he would advise every Fox to cut it off, if he valued life and safety.

When he had finished talking, an old Fox arose, and said smiling:

"Master Fox, kindly turn around for a moment, and you shall have your answer."

When the poor Fox Without a Tail turned around, there arose such a storm of jeers and hooting, that he saw how useless it was to try any longer to persuade the Foxes to part with their tails.

Do not listen to the advice of him who seeks to lower you to his own level.

THE HARE AND THE TORTOISE

A conceited Hare races a tortoise and is taught a lesson.

A Hare was making fun of the Tortoise one day for being so slow.

"Do you ever get anywhere?" he asked with a mocking laugh.

"Yes," replied the Tortoise, "and I get there sooner than you think. I'll run you a race and prove it."

The Hare was much amused at the idea of running a race with the Tortoise, but for the fun of the thing he agreed. So the Fox, who had consented to act as judge, marked the distance and started the runners off.

The Hare was soon far out of sight, and to make the Tortoise feel very deeply how ridiculous it was for him to try a race with a Hare, he lay down beside the course to take a nap until the Tortoise should catch up.

The Tortoise meanwhile kept going slowly but steadily, and after a time, passed the place where the Hare was sleeping. But the Hare slept on very peacefully; and when at last he did wake up, the Tortoise was near the goal. The Hare now ran his swiftest, but he could not overtake the Tortoise in time.

The race is not always to the swift.

THE NORTH WIND AND THE SUN

The North Wind and the Sun fight to see whose power is greater.

he North Wind and the Sun had a quarrel about which one of them was the stronger. While they were disputing with much heat and bluster, a Traveler passed along the road wrapped in a cloak.

"Let us agree," said the Sun, "that he is the stronger who can strip that Traveler of his cloak."

"Very well," growled the North Wind and at once sent a cold, howling blast against the Traveler.

With the first gust of wind the ends of the cloak whipped about the Traveler's body. But he immediately wrapped it closely around him, and the harder the Wind blew, the tighter he held it to him. The North Wind tore angrily at the cloak, but all his efforts were in vain.

Then the Sun began to shine. At first his beams were gentle, and in the pleasant warmth after the bitter cold of the North Wind, the Traveler unfastened his cloak and let it hang loosely from his shoulders. The Sun's rays grew warmer and warmer. The man took off his cap and mopped his brow. At last he became so heated that he pulled off his cloak and, to escape the blazing sunshine, threw himself down in the welcome shade of a tree by the roadside.

Gentleness and kind persuasion win where force and bluster fail.

THE PEACOCK

The Peacock discovers that what he thought he wanted, is not really so great after all.

The Peacock, they say, did not at first have the beautiful feathers in which he now takes so much pride. These, Juno, whose favorite he was, granted to him one day when he begged her for a train of feathers to distinguish him from the other birds. Then, decked in his finery, gleaming with emerald, gold, purple, and azure, he strutted proudly among the birds. All regarded him with envy. Even the most beautiful pheasant could see that his beauty was surpassed.

Presently the Peacock saw an Eagle soaring high up in the blue sky and felt a desire to fly, as he had been accustomed to do. Lifting his wings he tried to rise from the ground. But the weight of his magnificent train held him down. Instead of flying up to greet the first rays of the morning sun or to bathe in the rosy light among the floating clouds at sunset, he would have to walk the ground more encumbered and oppressed than any common barnyard fowl.

Do not sacrifice your freedom for the sake of pomp and show.

THE TOWN MOUSE AND THE COUNTRY MOUSE

A country mouse discovers what she truly values after visiting with her friend, the Town Mouse.

A Town Mouse once visited a relative who lived in the country. For lunch, the Country Mouse served stalks, roots, and acorns, with a dash of cold water for drink. The Town Mouse ate very sparingly, nibbling a little of this and a little of that, and by her manner, making it very plain that she ate the simple food only to be polite.

After the meal the friends had a long talk, or rather the Town Mouse talked about her life in the city while the Country Mouse listened. They then went to bed in a cozy nest in the hedgerow and slept in quiet and comfort until morning. In her sleep the Country Mouse dreamed she was a Town Mouse with all the luxuries and delights of city life that her friend had described for her. So the next day when the Town Mouse asked the Country Mouse to go home with her to the city, she gladly said yes.

When they reached the mansion in which the Town Mouse lived, they found on the table in the dining room the leavings of a very fine banquet. There were sweetmeats and jellies, pastries, delicious cheeses, indeed, the most tempting foods that a Mouse can imagine. But just as the Country Mouse was about to nibble a dainty bit of pastry, she heard a Cat mew loudly and scratch at the door. In great fear the Mice scurried to a hiding place, where they lay quite still for a long time, hardly daring to breathe. When at last they ventured back to the feast, the door opened suddenly and in came the servants to clear the table, followed by the House Dog.

The Country Mouse stopped in the Town Mouse's den only long enough to pick up her carpet bag and umbrella.

"You may have luxuries and dainties that I have not," she said as she hurried away, "but I prefer my plain food and simple life in the country with the peace and security that go with it."

Poverty with security is better than plenty in the midst of fear and uncertainty.

THE WOLF AND THE SHEEP

A clever sheep figures out why a wolf asks for her help.

 wolf had been hurt in a fight with a bear. He was unable to move and could not satisfy his hunger and thirst. A Sheep passed by near his hiding place, and the Wolf called to him,

"Please fetch me a drink of water," he begged; "that might give me strength enough so I can get me some solid food."

"Solid food!" said the Sheep. "That means me, I suppose. If I should bring you a drink, it would only serve to wash me down your throat. Don't talk to me about a drink!"

A knave's hypocrisy is easily seen through.

Aesop's Fables. New York: Checkerboard Press, 1919.

THE AGE OF FABLE

Thomas Bulfinch

The fables included here are all ancient, well-loved Greek myths. Some of the tales concern gods and mortals who compete for power. When the mortals challenge the gods' position or authority, the gods get angry and seek to punish them. Sometimes the gods are very violent and their revenge is harsh. These tales are battles of good against evil. Other myths are more like fairytales. The gods and goddesses and young women and men in them are very beautiful, talented and brave. And they fall in love a lot. All of these myths show a broad range of emotions and are full of adventure.

APOLLO AND DAPHNE

Cupid, the god of love, is taunted by Apollo one day and decides to get even with him. So, Cupid shoots a golden arrow into Apollo, who falls hopelessly in love with Daphne. Then Cupid shoots a leaden arrow into Daphne which makes her immune to love.

Daphne was Apollo's first love. It was not brought about by accident, but by the malice of Cupid. Apollo saw the boy playing with his bow and arrows; and being himself elated with his recent victory over Python, he said to him, "What have you to do with warlike weapons, saucy boy? Leave them for hands worthy of them. Behold the conquest I have won by means of them over the vast serpant who stretched his poisonous body over acres of the plain! Be content with your torch, child, and kindle up your flames, as you call them, where you will, but presume not to meddle with my weapons."

Venus's boy heard these words, and rejoined, "Your arrows may strike all things else, Apollo, but mine shall strike you."

So saying, he took his stand on the rock of Parnassus, and drew up from his quiver two arrows of different workmanship, one to excite love, the other to repel it. The former was gold and sharp pointed, the latter, blunt and tipped with lead. With the leaden shaft he struck the nymph Daphne, the daughter of the river god Peneus, and with the golden one Apollo, through the heart. Forthwith the god was seized with love for the maiden, and she abhorred the thought of loving. Her delight was in woodland sports and in the spoils of the chase. Many lovers sought her, but she spurned them all, ranging the woods, and taking no though of Cupid nor of Hymen.

Her father often said to her, "Daughter, you owe me a son-in-law; you owe me gran-children."

She, hating the thought of marriage as a crime, with her beautiful face tinged all over with blushes, threw her arms around her father's neck, and said, "Dearest father, grant me this favor, that I may always remain unmarried, like Diana."

He consented, but at the same time said, "Your own face will forbid it."

Apollo loved her, and longed to obtain her; and he who gives oracles to all the world was not wise enough to look into his own fortunes. He saw her hair flung loose over her shoulders, and said, "If so charming in disorder, what would it be if arranged?"

He saw her eyes bright as stars; he saw her lips, and was not satisfied with only seeing them. He admired her hands and arms, naked to the shoulder, and whatever was hidden from view he imagined more beautiful still. He followed her; she fled, swifter than the wind, and delayed not a moment at his entreaties.

"Stay," said he, "daughter of Peneus; I am not a foe. Do not fly me the way as a lamb flies the wolf or a dove the hawk. It is for love I pursue you. You make me miserable for fear you should fall and hurt yourself on these stones, and I should be the cause. Pray run slower, and I will follow slower. I am no clown, no rude peasant. Jupiter is my father and I am lord of Delphos and Tenedos, and know all things, present and future. I am the god of song and the lyre. My arrows fly true to the mark; but, alas! an arrow more fatal than mine has pierced my heart! I am the god of medicine, and know the virtues of all healing plants. Alas! I suffer a malady that no balm can cure!"

The nymph continued her flight, and left his plea half uttered. And even as she fled, she charmed him. The wind blew her garments, and her unbound hair streamed loose behind her. The god grew impatient to find his wooings thrown away, and, sped by Cupid, gained upon her in the race. It was like a hound pursuing a hare, with open jaws ready to seize, while the feebler animal darts forward, slipping from the very grasp. So flew the god and the virgin—he on the wings of love, and she on those of fear. The pursuer is the more rapid, however, and gains upon her, and his panting breath blows upon her hair. Her strengh begins to fail, and ready to sink, she calls upon her father, the river god: "Help me Peneus! Open the earth to enclose me, or change my form, which has brought me into this danger!"

Scarcely had she spoken when a stiffness seized all her limbs; her bosom began to be enclosed in a tender bark; her hair became leaves; her arms became branches; her foot stuck fast in the ground, as a root; her face became a tree-top; retaining nothing of its for-mer self but its beauty. Apollo stood amazed. He touched the stem, and felt the flesh trem-ble under the new bark. He embraced the branches, and lavished kisses on the wood. The branches shrank from his lips. "Since you cannot be my wife," said he, "you shall assured-ly be my tree. I will wear you for my crown; I will decorate with you my harp and my quiver; and when the great Roman conquerors lead up the triumphal pomp to the capitol, you shall be woven into wreaths of their brows. And, as eternal youth is mine, you also shall be always green, and your leaf know no decay."

The nymph, now changed into a laurel tree, bowed its head in grateful acknowledgement.

BAUCIS AND PHILEMON

When a god and his son decide to visit the mortal world disguised in a human shape, some very strange things happen.

n a certain hill in Phrygia stands a linden tree and an oak, enclosed by a low wall. Not far from the spot is a marsh, formerly good habitable land, but now indented with pools, the resort of fen-birds and cormorants. Once upon a time Jupiter, in human shape, visited this country, and with him his son Mercury (he of the caduceus), without his wings. They presented themselves, as weary travelers, at many a door, seeking rest and shelter, but found all closed, for it was late, and the inhospitable inhabitants would not rouse themselves to open for their reception.

At last a humble mansion received them, a small thatched cottage, where Baucis, a pious old dame, and her husband Philemon, united when young, had grown old together. Not ashamed of their poverty, they made it endurable by moderate desires and kind dispositions. One need not look there for master or for servant alike. When the two heavenly guests crossed the humble threshold, and bowed their heads to pass under the low door, the old man placed a seat, on which Baucis, bustling and attentive, spread a cloth, and begged them to sit down. Then she raked out the coals from the ashes, and kindled up a fire, fed it with leaves and dry bark, and with her scanty breath blew it into a flame.

She brought out of a corner split sticks and dry branches, broke them up, and placed them under the small kettle. Her husband collected some pot-herbs in the garden, and she shred them from the stalks, and prepared them for the pot. He reached down with a forked stick a flitch of bacon hanging in the chimney, cut a small piece, and put it in the pot to boil with the herbs, setting away the rest for another time. A beechen bowl was filled with warm water, that their guest might wash. While all was doing, they beguiled the time with conversation.

On the bench designed for the guests was laid a cushion stuffed with seaweed; and a cloth, only produced on great occasions, but ancient and coarse enough, was spread over that. The old lady, with her apron on, with trembling hand set the table. One leg was shorter than the rest, but a piece of slate put under restored the level. When fixed, she rubbed the table down with some sweet-smelling herbs. Upon it she set some of chaste Minerva's olives, some cornel berries preserved in vinegar, and added radishes and cheese, with eggs lightly cooked in the ashes. All were served in earthen dishes, and an earthenware pitcher, with wooden cups, stood beside them. When all was ready, the stew, smoking hot, was set on the table. Some wine, not of the oldest, was added; and for dessert, apples and wild honey; and over and above all, friendly faces, and simple but hearty welcome.

Now while the repast proceeded, the old folks were astonished to see that the wine, as fast as it was poured out, renewed itself in the pitcher, of its own accord. Struck with terror, Baucis and Philemon recognized their heavenly guests, fell on their knees, and with clasped hands implored forgiveness for their poor entertainment. There was an old goose, which they kept as the guardian of their humble cottage; and they bethought them to make this a sacrifice in honor of their guests. But the goose, too nimble, with the aid of feet and wings, for the old folks, eluded their pursuit, and at last took shelter between the gods themselves. They forbade it to be slain; and spoke in these words:

"We are gods. This inhospitable village shall pay the penalty of its impiety; you alone shall go free from the chastisement. Quit your house, and come with us to the top of yonder hill."

They hastened to obey, and, staff in hand, labored up the steep ascent. They had reached to within an arrow's flight of the top, when turning their eyes below, they beheld all the country sunk in a lake, only their own house left standing. While they gazed with wonder at the sight, and lamented the fate of their neighbors, that old house of theirs was changed into a temple. Columns took the place of the corner posts, the thatch grew yellow and appeared a gilded roof, the floors became marble, the doors were enriched with carving and ornaments of gold. Then spoke Jupiter in benignant accents:

"Excellent old man, and woman worthy of such a husband, speak, tell us your wishes; what favor have you to ask of us?"

Philemon took counsel with Baucis a few moments; then declared to the gods their united wish. "We ask to be priests and guardians of this your temple; and since here we have passed our lives in love and concord, we wish that one and the same hour may take us both from life, that I may not live to see her grave, nor be laid in my own by her."

Their prayer was granted. They were the keepers of the temple as long as they lived. When grown very old, as they stood one day before the steps of the sacred edifice, and were telling the story of the place, Baucis saw Philemon begin to put forth leaves, and old Philemon saw Baucis changing in like manner. And now a leafy crown had grown over their heads, while exchanging parting words, as long as they could speak.

"Farewell, dear spouse," they said, together, and at the same moment the bark closed over their mouths. The Tyanean shepherd still shows the two trees, standing side by side, made out of the two good old people.

Chapter XII CADMUS—THE MYRMIDONS

Cadmus, while in search of his sister who was carried away by a god, must do battle with a venomous serpent.

Jupiter, under the disguise of a bull, had carried away Europa, the daughter of Agenor, king of Phoenicia. Agenor commanded his son Cadmus to go in search of his sister, and not to return without her. Cadmus went and sought long and far for his sister, but could not find her, and not daring to return unsuccessful, consulted the oracle of Apollo to know what country he should settle in. The oracle informed him that he should find a cow in the field, and should follow her wherever she might wander, and where she stopped, should build a city and call it Thebes.

Cadmus had hardly left the Castalian cave, from which the oracle was delivered, when he saw a young cow slowly walking before him. He followed her close, offering at the same time his prayers to Phoebus. The cow went on till she passed the shallow channel of Cephisus and came out into the plain of Panope. There she stood still, and raising her broad forehead to the sky, filled the air with her lowings. Cadmus gave thanks, and stooping down kissed the foreign soil, then lifted his eyes, greeted the surrounding mountains.

Wishing to offer a sacrifice to Jupiter, he sent his servants to seek pure water for a libation. Near by there stood an ancient grove which had never been profaned by the axe, in the midst of which was a cave, thick covered with the growth of bushes, its roof forming a low arch, from beneath which burst forth a fountain of purest water. In the cave lurked a horrid serpent with a crested head and scales glittering like gold. His eyes shone like fire, his body was swollen with venom, he vibrated a triple tongue, and showed a triple row of teeth. No sooner had the Tyrians dipped their pitchers in the fountain, and the ingushing waters made a sound, than the glittering serpent raised his head out of the cave and uttered a fearful hiss.

The vessels fell from their hands, the blood left their cheeks, they trembled in every limb. The serpent, twisting his scaly body in a huge coil, raised his head so as to overtop the tallest trees, and while the Tyrians from terror could neither fight nor fly, slew some with his fangs, others in his folds, and others with his poisonous breath.

Cadmus, having waited for the return of his men till midday, went in search of them. His covering was a lion's hide, and besides his javelin he carried in his hand a lance, and in his breast a bold heart, a surer reliance than either. When he entered the wood, and saw the lifeless bodies of his men, and the monster with his bloody jaws, he exclaimed, "O faithful friends, I will avenge you, or share your death."

So saying he lifted a huge stone and threw it with all his force at the serpent. Such a block would have shaken the wall of a fortress, but it made no impression on the monster. Cadmus next threw his javelin, which met with better success, for it penetrated the serpent's scales, and pierced through to his entrails. Fierce with pain, the monster turned back his head to view the wound, and attempted to draw out the weapon with his mouth, but broke it off, leaving the iron point rankling in his flesh. His neck swelled with rage, bloody foam covered his jaws, and the breath of his nostrils poisoned the air around.

Now he twisted himself into a circle, then stretched himself out on the ground like the trunk of a fallen tree. As he moved onward, Cadmus retreated before him, holding his spear opposite to the monster's open jaws. The serpent snapped at the weapon and attempted to bite its iron point. At last Cadmus, watching his chance, thrust the spear at a moment when the animal's head thrown back came against the trunk of a tree, and so succeeded in pinning him to its side. His weight bent the tree as he struggled in the agonies of death.

While Cadmus stood over his conquered foe, contemplating its vast size, a voice was heard (from whence he knew not, but he heard it distinctly) commanding him to take the dragon's teeth and sow them in the earth. He obeyed. He made a furrow in the ground, and planted the teeth, destined to produce a crop of men. Scarce had he done so when the clods began to move, and the points of spears to appear above the surface. Next helmets with their nodding plumes came up, and next the shoulders and breasts and limbs of men with weapons, and in time a harvest of armed warriors. Cadmus, alarmed, prepared to encounter a new enemy, but one of them said to him, "Meddle not with our civil war."

With that he who had spoken smote one of his earth-born brothers with a sword, and he himself fell pierced with an arrow from another. The latter fell victim to a fourth, and in like manner the whole crowd dealt with each other till all fell, slain with mutual wounds, except for five survivors. One of these cast away his weapons and said, "Brothers, let us live in peace!" These five joined Cadmus in building his city, to which they gave the name Thebes.

Cadmus obtained in marriage Harmonia, the daughter of Venus. The gods left Olympus to honour the occasion with their presence, and Vulcan presented the bride with a necklace of surpassing brilliancy, his own workmanship. But a fatality hung over the the family of Cadmus in consequence of his killing the serpent sacred to Mars. Semele and Ino, his daughters, and Actaeon and Pentheus, his grandchildren, all perished unhappily, and Cadmus and Harmonia quitted Thebes, now grown odious to them, and emigrated to the country of the Enchelians, who received them with honor and made Cadmus their king.

But the misfortunes of their children still weighed upon their minds; and one day Cadmus exclaimed, "If a serpent's life is so dear to the gods, I would if I were myself a serpent."

No sooner had he uttered the words than he began to change his form. Harmonia beheld it and prayed to the gods to let her share his fate. Both became serpents. They live in the woods, but mindful of their origin, they neither avoid the presence of man nor do they ever injure any one.

Chapter XIV MINERVA

Arachne is super at weaving and embroidery and is very proud of her skills. She challenges the goddess, Minerva, to a contest.

inerva, the goddess of wisdom, was the daughter of Jupiter. She was said to have leaped forth from his brain, mature, and in complete armor. She presided over the useful and ornamental arts, both those of men—such as agriculture and navigation—and those of women—spinning, weaving, and needlework.

She was also a warlike divinity; but it was defensive war only that she patronized, and she had no sympathy with Mars's savage love of violence and bloodshed. Athens was her chosen seat, her own city, awarded to her as the prize of a contest with Neptune, who also aspired to it.

The tale ran that, in the reign of Cecrops, the first king of Athens, the two deities contended for the possession of the city. The gods decreed that it should be awarded to that one who produced the gift most useful to mortals. Neptune gave the horse; Minerva produced the olive. The gods gave judgment that the olive was the more useful of the two, and awarded the city to the goddess; and it was named after her, Athens, her name in Greek being Athene.

There was another contest, in which a mortal dared to come in competition with Minerva. That mortal was Arachne, a maiden who had attained such skill in the arts of weaving and embroidery that the nymphs themselves would leave their groves and fountains to come and gaze upon her work.

It was not only beautiful when it was done, but beautiful also in the doing. To watch her, as she took the wool in its rude state and formed it into rolls, or separated it with her fingers and carded it till it looked as light and soft as a cloud, or twirled the spindle with skillful touch, or wove the web, or, after it was woven, adorned it with her needle, one would have said that Minerva herself had taught her. But this she denied, and could not bear to be thought a pupil even of a goddess.

"Let Minerva try her skill with mine," said she; "if beaten I will pay the penalty." Minerva heard this and was displeased. She assumed the form of an old woman and went and gave Arachne some friendly advice. "I have had much experience," said she, "and I hope you will not despise my counsel. Challenge your fellow-mortals as you will, but do not compete with a goddess. On the contrary, I advise you to ask her forgiveness for what you have said, and as she is merciful perhaps she will pardon you."

Arachne stopped her spinning and looked at the old dame with anger in her countenance. "Keep your counsel," said she, "for your daughters and handmaids; for my part I know what I say, and I stand to it. I am not afraid of the goddess; let her try her skill, if she dare venture."

"She comes," said Minerva; and dropping her disguise stood confessed.

The nymphs bent low in homage, and all the bystanders paid reverence. Arachne alone was unterrified. She blushed, indeed; a sudden color dyed her cheek, and then she grew pale. But she stood to her resolve, and with a foolish conceit of her own skill rushed on to her fate. Minerva forbore no longer nor interposed any further advice.

They proceed to the contest. Each takes her station and attaches the web to the beam. Then the slender shuttle is passed in and out among the threads. The reed with its fine teeth strikes up the woof into its place and compacts the web. Both work with speed; their skillful hands move rapidly, and the excitement of the contest makes the labor light. Wool of Tyrian dye is contrasted with that of other colors, shaded off into one another so adroitly that the joining deceives the eye. Like the bow, whose long arch tinges the heavens, formed by sunbeams reflected from the shower, in which, where the colors meet they seem as one, but at a little distance from the point of contact are wholly different.

Minerva wrought on her web the scene of her contest with Neptune. Twelve of the heavenly powers are represented, Jupiter, with august gravity, sitting in the midst. Neptune, the ruler of the sea, holds his trident, and appears to have just smitten the earth, from which a horse had leaped forth. Minerva depicted herself with helmeted head, her Aegis covering her breast. Such was the central circle; and in the four corners were represented incidents illustrating the displeasure of the gods at such presumptuous mortals as had dared to contend with them. These were meant as warnings to her rival to give up the contest before it was too late.

Arachne filled her web with subjects designedly chosen to exhibit the failings and errors of gods. One scene represented Leda caressing the swan, under which form Jupiter had disguised himself; and another, Danae, in the brazen tower in which her father had imprisoned her, but where god effected his entrance in the form of a golden shower. Still another depicted Europa deceived by Jupiter under the disguise of a bull. Encouraged by the tameness of the animal Europa ventured to mount his back, whereupon Jupiter advanced into the sea and swam with her to Crete. You would have thought it was a real bull, so naturally was it wrought, and so natural the water in which it swam. She seemed to look with longing eyes back upon the shore she was leaving, and to call to her companions for help. She appeared to shudder with terror at the sight of the heaving waves, and to draw back her feet from the water.

Arachne filled her canvas with similar subjects, wonderfully well done, but strongly marking her presumption and impiety. Minerva could not forbear to admire, yet felt indignant at the insult. She struck the web with her shuttle and rent it in pieces; she then touched the forehead of Arachne and made her feel her guilt and shame. She could not endure it and went and hanged herself.

Minerva pitied her as she saw her suspended by a rope. "Live," she said, "guilty woman! And that you may preserve the memory of this lesson, continue to hang, both you and your descendants, to all future times."

She sprinkled her with juices of aconite, and immediately her hair came off, and her nose and ears likewise. Her form shrank up, and her head grew smaller yet; her fingers cleaved to her side and served for legs. All the rest of her is body, out of which she spins her thread, often hanging suspended by it, in the same attitude as when Minerva touched her and transformed her into a spider.

NIOBE

Niobe, like Arachne, is so proud that she decides to challenge a goddess' authority. The goddess, Latona, is not pleased.

The fate of Arachne was noised abroad through all the country, and served as a warning to all presumptuous mortals not to compare themselves with the divinities. But one, and she a matron too, failed to learn the lesson of humility. It was Niobe, the queen of Thebes. She had indeed much to be proud of; but it was not her husband's fame, nor her own beauty, nor their great descent, nor the power of their kingdom that elated her; it was her children; and truly the happiest of mothers would Niobe have been if only she had not claimed to be so.

It was on occasion of the annual celebration in honor of Latona and her offspring, Apollo and Diana, when the people of Thebes were assembled, their brows crowned with laurel, bearing frankincense to the altars and paying their vows, that Niobe appeared among the crowd. Her attire was splendid with gold and gems, and her aspect beautiful as the face of an angry woman can be. She stood and surveyed the people with haughty looks.

"What folly," said she, "is this!—to prefer beings whom you never saw to those who stand before your eyes! Why should Latona be honored with worship, and none be paid to me? My father was Tantalus, who was received as a guest at the table of the gods; my mother was a goddess. My husband built and rules this city, Thebes, and Phrygia is my paternal inheritance. Wherever I turn my eyes I survey the elements of my power; nor is my form and presence unworthy of a goddess.

"To all this let me add I have seven sons and seven daughters, and look for sons-in-law and daughters-in-law of pretensions worthy of my alliance. Have I not cause for pride? Will you prefer to me this Latona, the Titan's daughter, with her two children? I have seven times as many. Fortunate indeed am I, and fortunate I shall remain! Will any deny this? My abundance is my security. I feel myself too strong for fortune to subdue. She may take from me much; I shall still have much left. Were I to lose some of my children, I should hardly be left as poor as Latona with her two only. Away with you from these solemnities —put off the laurel from your brows—have done with this worship!" The people obeyed, and left the sacred services uncompleted.

The goddess was indignant. On the Cynthian mountain top where she dwelt she thus addressed her son and daughter:

"My children, I who have been so proud of you both, and have been used to hold myself second to none of the goddesses except Juno alone, begin now to doubt whether I am indeed a goddess. I shall be deprived of my worship altogether unless you protect me."

She was proceeding in this strain, but Apollo interrupted her. "Say no more," said he; "speech only delays punishment."

So said Diana also. Darting through the air, veiled in clouds, they alighted on the towers of the city. Spread out before the gates was a broad plain, where the youth of the city pursued their warlike sports. The sons of Niobe were there with the rest, some mounted on spirited horses richly caparisoned, some driving gay chariots.

Ismenos, the firstborn, as he guided his foaming steeds, struck with an arrow from a bow, cried out, "Ah me!" He dropped the reins, and fell lifeless.

Another, hearing the sound of the bow, like a boatman who sees the storm gathering and makes all sail for the port, gave the reins to his horses and attempted to escape. The inevitable arrow overtook him as he fled. Two others, younger boys, just from their tasks, had gone to the playground to have a game of wrestling. As they stood breast to breast, one arrow pierced them both. They uttered a cry together, together cast a parting look around them, and together breathed their last.

Alphenor, an elder brother, seeing them fall, hastened to the spot to render assistance, and fell stricken in the act of brotherly duty. One only was left, Ilioneus. He raised his arms to heaven to try whether prayer might not avail.

"Spare me, ye gods!" he cried, addressing all, in his ignorance that all needed not his intercessions; and Apollo would have spared him, but the arrow had already left the string, and it was too late.

The terror of the people and grief of the attendants soon made Niobe acquainted with what had taken place. She could hardly think it possible; she was indignant that the gods had dared, and amazed that they had been able to do it. Her husband, Amphion, overwhelmed with the blow, destroyed himself. Alas! how different was this Niobe from her who had so lately driven away the people from the sacred rites, and held her stately course through the city, the envy of her friends, now the pity even of her foes!

She knelt over the lifeless bodies, and kissed now one, now another of her dead sons. Raising her pallid arms to heaven, "Cruel Latona," said she, "feed full your rage with my anguish! Satiate your hard heart, while I follow to the grave my seven sons. Yet where is your triumph? Bereaved as I am, I am still richer than you, my conqueror."

Scarce had she spoken, when the bow sounded and struck terror into all hearts except Niobe's alone. She was brave from excess of grief. The sisters stood in garments of mourning over the biers of their dead brothers. One fell, struck by an arrow, and died on the corpse she was bewailing. Another, attempting to console her mother, suddenly ceased to speak, and sank lifeless to the earth. A third tried to escape by flight, a fourth by concealment, another stood trembling, uncertain what course to take. Six were now dead, and only one remained, whom the mother held clasped in her arms, and covered as it were with her whole body. "Spare me one, and that the youngest! O spare me one of so many!" she cried; and while she spoke, that one fell dead.

Desolate she sat, among sons, daughters, husband, all dead, and seemed torpid with grief. The breeze moved not her hair, no color was on her cheek, her eyes glared fixed and immovable, there was no sign of life about her. Her very tongue cleaved to the roof of her mouth, and her veins ceased to convey the tide of life. Her neck bent not, her arms made no gesture, her foot no step. She was changed to stone, within and without. Yet tears continued to flow; and born on a whirlwind to her native mountain, she still remains, a mass of rock, from which a trickling stream flows, the tribute of her neverending grief.

Chapter XXIV ORPHEUS AND EURYDICE

Orpheus, a god, and Eurydice, a goddess, marry. When Eurydice accidentally steps on a poisonous snake and dies, Orpheus travels to the underworld to find her.

Orpheus was the son of Apollo and the Muse Calliope. He was presented by his father with a lyre and taught to play upon it, which he did to such perfection that nothing could withstand the charm of his music. Not only his fellow-mortals, but wild beasts were softened by his strains, and gathering round him laid by their fierceness, and stood entranced with his lay. Nay, the very trees and rocks were sensible to the charm. The former crowded round him and the latter relaxed somewhat of their hardness, softened by his notes.

Hymen had been called to bless with his presence the nuptials of Orpheus with Eurydice; but though he attended, he brought no happy omens with him. His very torch smoked and brought tears into their eyes. In coincidence with such prognostics, Eurydice, shortly after her marriage, while wandering with the nymphs, her companions, was seen by the shepherd Aristaeus, who was struck with her beauty and made advances to her.

She fled, and in flying trod upon a snake in the grass, was bitten in the foot, and died. Orpheus sang his grief to all who breathed the upper air, both gods and men, and finding it all unavailing resolved to seek his wife in the regions of the dead. He descended by a cave situated on the side of the promontory of Taenarus and arrived at the Stygian realm. He passed through crowds of ghosts and presented himself before the throne of Pluto and Proserpine.

Accompanying the words with the lyre, he sung,

> "O deities of the under-world,
> to whom all we who live must come,
> hear my words, for they are true.
> I come not to spy out the secrets of Tartarus,
> nor to try my strength against the

three-headed dog with snaky hair
who guards the entrance. I come to seek my wife,
whose opening years the poisonous
viper's fang has brought to an
untimely end.

Love has led me here,
Love, a god all powerful with us
who dwell on earth, and, if
old traditions say true,
not less so here.

I implore you by these abodes
full of terror, these realms of silence
and uncreated things,
unite again the thread of Eurydice's life.
We all are destined to you,
and sooner or later must pass to your domain.
She too, when she shall have
filled her term of life, will rightly be yours.
But till then grant her to me,
I beseech you.

If you deny me I cannot return alone;
you shall triumph in the death of us both."

As he sang these tender strains, the very ghosts shed tears. Tantalus, in spite of his thirst, stopped for a moment his efforts for water, Ixion's wheel stood still, the vulture ceased to tear the giant's liver, the daughters of Danaus rested from their task of drawing water in a sieve, and Sisyphus sat on his rock to listen.

Then for the first time, it is said, the cheeks of the Furies were wet with tears. Proserpine could not resist, and Pluto himself gave way. Eurydice was called. She came from among the newly arrived ghosts, limping with her wounded foot. Orpheus was permitted to take her away with him on one condition, that he should not turn around to look at her till they should have reached the upper air.

Under this condition they proceeded on their way, he leading, she following, through the passages dark and steep, in total silence, till they had nearly reached the outlet into the cheerful upper world, when Orpheus, in a moment of forgetfulness, to assure himself that she was still following, cast a glance behind him, when instantly she was borne away.

Stretching out their arms to embrace each other, they grasped only the air! Dying now a second time, she yet cannot reproach her husband, for how can she blame him his impatience to behold her?

"Farewell," she said, "a last farewell," and was hurried away, so fast that the sound hardly reached his ears.

Orpheus endeavored to follow her, and besought permission to return and try once more for her release but the stern ferryman repulsed him and refused passage. Seven days he lingered about the brink, without food or sleep; then bitterly accusing of cruelty the powers of Erebus, he sang his complaints to the rocks and mountains, melting the hearts of tigers and moving the oaks from their stations. He held himself aloof from womankind, dwelling constantly on the recollection of his sad mischance.

The Thracian maidens tried their best to captivate him, but he repulsed their advances. They bore with him as long as they could; but finding him insensible one day, excited by the rites of Bacchus, one of them exclaimed, "See yonder our despiser!" and threw at him her javelin. The weapon, as soon as it came within the sound of his lyre, fell harmless at his feet. So did also the stones that they threw at him. But the women raised a scream and drowned the voice of the music, and then the missiles reached him and soon were stained with his blood. The maniacs tore him limb from limb, and threw his head and his lyre into the river Hebrus, down which they floated, murmuring sad music, to which the shores responded a plaintive symphony.

The Muses gathered up the fragments of his body and buried them at Libethra, where the nightingale is said to sing over his grave more sweetly than in any other part of Greece. His lyre was placed by Jupiter among the stars. His shade passed a second time to Tartarus, where he sought out his Eurydice and embraced her with eager arms. They roam the happy fields together now, sometimes he leading, sometimes she; and Orpheus gazes as much as he will upon her, no longer incurring a penalty for a thoughtless glance.

PYRAMUS AND THISBE

Pyramus and Thisbe are young lovers whose families forbid them to see eacho ther. So they communicate through a chink in the wall between their two buildings.

 yramus was the handsomest youth, and Thisbe the fairest maiden, in all Babylonia, where Semiramis reigned. Their parents occupied adjoining houses; and neighborhood brought the young people together, and acquaintance ripened into love. They would gladly have married, but their parents forbade.

One thing, however, could not be forbid—that love should glow with equal ardor in the bosoms of both. They conversed by signs and glances, and the fire burned more intensely for being covered up. In the wall that parted the two houses there was a crack, caused by some fault in the structure. No one had remarked it before, but the lovers discovered it. What will no love discover! It afforded a passage to the voice; and tender messages used to pass backward and forward through the gap. As they stood, Pyramus on this side, Thisbe on that, their breaths would mingle.

"Cruel wall," they said, "why do you keep two lovers apart? But we will not be ungrateful. We owe you, we confess, the privilege of transmitting loving words to willing ears."

Such words they uttered on different sides of the wall; and when night came and they must say farewell, they pressed their lips upon the wall, she on her side, he on his, as they could come no nearer.

Next morning, when Aurora had put out the stars, and the sun had melted the frost form the grass, they met at the accustomed spot. Then, after lamenting their hard fate, they agreed that next night, when all was still, they would slip away from watchful eyes, leave their dwellings and walk out into the fields; and to insure a meeting, repair to a well-known edifice of Ninus, and that the one who came first should await the other at the foot of a certain tree.

It was a white mulberry tree, and stood near a cool spring. All was agreed on, and they waited impatiently for the sun to go down beneath the waters and night to rise up from them. Then cautiously Thisbe stole forth, unobserved by the family, her head covered with a veil, made her way to the monument and sat down under the tree. As she sat alone in the dim light of the evening she descried a lioness, her jaw reeking with recent slaughter, approaching the fountain to slake her thirst. Thisbe fled at the sight, and sought refuge in the hollow of a rock. As she fled she dropped her veil. The lioness after drinking at the spring turned to retreat to the woods, and seeing the veil on the ground, tossed and rent it with her bloody mouth.

Pyramus, having been delayed, now approached the place of meeting. He saw in the sand the footsteps of the lion and the color fled from his cheeks at the sight. Presently he found the veil all rent and bloody.

"O hapless girl," said he, "I have been the cause of thy death! Thou, more worthy of life than I, hast fallen the first victim. I will follow. I am the guilty cause, in tempting thee forth to a place of such peril, and not being myself on the spot to guard thee. Come forth, ye lions, from the rocks, and tear this guilty body with your teeth."

He took up the veil, carried it with him to the appointed tree, and covered it with kisses and with tears. "My blood also shall stain your texture," said he, and drawing his sword plunged it into his heart.

The blood spurted from the wound, and tinged the white mulberries of the tree all red; and sinking into the earth reached the roots, so that the red color mounted through the trunk to the fruit.

By this time Thisbe, still trembling with fear, yet wishing not to disappoint her lover, stepped cautiously forth, looking anxiously for the youth, eager to tell him the danger she had escaped. When she came to the spot and saw the changed color of the mulberries she doubted whether it was the same place. While she hesitated she saw the form of one struggling in the agonies of death. She started back, a shudder ran through her frame as a ripple on the face of the still water when a sudden breeze sweeps over it.

But as soon as she recognized her lover, she screamed and beat her breast, embracing the lifeless body, pouring tears into its wounds, and imprinting kisses on the cold lips. "O Pyramus," she cried, "what has done this? Answer me, Pyramus; it is your own Thisbe that speaks. Hear me, dearest, and lift that drooping head!"

At the name of Thisbe, Pyramus opened his eyes, then closed them again. She saw her veil stained with blood and the scabbard empty of its sword. "Thy own hand has slain thee, and for my sake," she said. "I too can be brave for once, and my love is as strong as thine. I will follow thee in death, for I have been the cause; and death which alone could part us shall not prevent my joining thee. And ye, unhappy parents of us both, deny us not our united request. As love and death have joined us, let one tomb contain us. And thou, tree, retain the marks of slaughter. Let thy berries still serve for memorials of our blood."

So saying she plunged the sword into her breast. Her parents ratified her wish, the gods also ratified it. The two bodies were buried in one sepulchre, and the tree ever after brought forth purple berries, as it does to this day.

Chapter X VERTUMNUS AND POMONA

Pomona is a wood-nymph and loves the garden more than anything else. Vertumnus loves Pomona and decides that to woo her, he will disguise himself as an old woman and convince Pomona to give him a chance.

The Hamadryads were Wood-nymphs. Pomona was of this class, and no one excelled her in love of the garden and the culture of fruit. She cared not for forests and rivers, but loved the cultivated country, and trees that bear delicious apples. Her right hand bore for its weapon not a javelin, but a pruning-knife. Armed with this, she busied herself at one time to repress the too luxuriant growths, and curtail the branches that straggled out of place; at another, to split the twig and insert therein a graft, making the branch adopt a nursling not its own. She took care, too, that her favorites should not suffer from drought, and led streams of water by them, that the thirsty roots might drink.

This occupation was her pursuit, her passion; and she was free from that which Venus inspires. She was not without fear of the country people, and kept her orchard locked, and allowed not men to enter. The Fauns and Satyrs would have given all they possessed to win her, and so would old Sylvanus, who looks young for his years, and Pan, who wears a garland of pine leaves around his head. But Vertumnus loved her best of all; yet he sped no better than the rest. O how often, in the disguise of a reaper, did he bring her corn in a basket, and looked the very image of a reaper! With a hay band tied round him, one would think he had just come from turning over the grass. Sometimes he would have an ox-goad in his hand, and you would have said he had just unyoked his weary oxen. Now he bore a pruning hook, and personated a vine dresser; and again, with a ladder on his shoulder, he seemed as if he was going to gather apples. Sometimes he trudged along as a discharged soldier, and again he bore a fishing rod, as if going to fish. In this way he gained admission to her again and again, and fed his passion with the sight of her.

One day he came in the guise of an old woman, her grey hair surmounted by a cap, and a staff in her hand. She entered the garden and admired the fruit.

"It does you credit, my dear," she said, and kissed her, not exactly with an old woman's kiss. She sat down on a bank, and looked up at the branches laden with fruit which hung over her. Opposite was an elm entwined with a vine loaded with swelling grapes. She praised the tree and its associated vine, equally.

"But," said she, "if the tree stood alone, and had no vine clinging to it, it would have nothing to attract or offer us but its useless leaves. And equally the vine, if it were not twined round the elm, would lie prostrate on the ground. Why will you not take a lesson from the tree and the vine, and consent to unite yourself with some one?

"I wish you would. Helen herself had not more numerous suitors, nor Penelope, the wife of shrewd Ulysses. Even while you spurn them, they court you—rural deities and others of every kind that frequent these mountains. But if you are prudent and want to make a good alliance, and will let an old woman advise you—who loves you better than you have any idea of—dismiss all the rest and accept Vertumnus, on my recommendation. I know him as well as he knows himself. He is not a wandering deity, but belongs to these mountains. Nor is he like too many of the lovers nowadays, who love any one they happen to see; he loves you, and you only. Add to this, he is young and handsome, and has the art of assuming any shape he pleases, and can make himself just what you command him.

"Moreover, he loves the same things that you do, delights in gardening, and handles your apples with admiration. But now he cares nothing for fruits nor flowers, nor anything else, but only yourself. Take pity on him, and fancy him speaking now with my mouth. Remember that the gods punish cruelty, and that Venus hates a hard heart, and will visit such offenses sooner or later. To prove this, let me tell you a story, which is well known in Cyprus to be a fact; and I hope it will have the effect to make you more merciful.

"Iphis was a young man of humble parentage, who saw and loved Anaxarete, a noble lady of the ancient family of Teucer. He struggled long with this passion, but when he found he could not subdue it, he came a suppliant to her mansion. First he told his passion to her nurse, and begged her as she loved her foster-child to favor his suit. And then he tried to win her domestics to his side. Sometimes he committed his vows to written tablets, and often hung at her door garlands which he had moistened with his tears. He stretched himself on her threshold, and uttered his complaints to the cruel bolts and bars. She was deafer than the surges which rise in the November gale; harder than steel from the German forges, or a rock that still clings to its native cliff. She mocked and laughed at him, adding cruel words to her ungentle treatment, and gave not the slightest gleam of hope.

"Iphis could not any longer endure the torments of hopeless love, and, standing before your doors, he spake these last words: 'Anaxarete, you have conquered, and shall no longer have to bear my importunities. Enjoy your triumph! Sing songs of joy, and bind your forehead with laurel,—you have conquered! I die; stony heart, rejoice! This at least I can do to gratify you, and force you to praise me; and thus shall I prove that the love of you left me but with life. Nor will I leave it to rumor to tell you of my death. I will come myself, and you shall see me die, and feast your eyes on the spectacle. Yet, O ye Gods, who look down on mortal woes, observe my fate! I ask but this: let me be remembered in coming ages, and add those years to my fame which you have reft from my life.'

"Thus he said, and, turning his pale face and weeping eyes towards her mansion, he fastened a rope to the gate-post, on which he had often hung garlands, and putting his head into the noose, he murmured, 'This garland at least will please you, cruel girl!' and falling hung suspended with his neck broken. As he fell he struck against the gate, and the sound was as the sound of a groan. The servants opened the door and found him dead, and with explanations of pity raised him and carried him home to his mother, for his father was not living. She received the dead body of her son, and folded the cold form to her bosom, while she poured forth the sad words which bereaved mothers utter.

"The mournful funeral passed through the town, and the pale corpse was born on a bier to the place of the funeral pile. By chance the home of Anaxarete was on the street where the procession passed, and the lamentations of the mourners met the ears of her whom the avenging deity had already marked for punishment.

"'Let us see this sad procession,' said she, and mounted to a turret, whence through an open window she looked upon the funeral. Scarce had her eyes rested upon the form of Iphis stretched on the bier, when they began to stiffen, and the warm blood in her body to become cold. Endeavoring to step back, she found she could not move her feet; trying to turn away her face, she tried in vain; and by degrees all her limbs became stony like her heart. That you may not doubt the fact, the statue still remains, and stands in the temple of Venus at Salamis, in the exact form of the lady. Now think of these things, my dear, and

385

lay aside your scorn and your delays, and accept a lover. So may neither the vernal frosts blight your young fruits, nor furious winds scatter your blossoms!"

When Vertumnus had spoken thus, he dropped the disguise of an old woman, and stood before her in his proper person, as a comely youth. It appeared to her like the sun bursting through a cloud. He would have renewed his entreaties, but there was no need; his arguments and the sight of his true form prevailed, and the Nymph no longer resisted, but owned a mutual flame.

Bulfinch, Thomas. *The Age of Fable.* New York: E. P. Dutton & Co., 1910.

THE LEGEND OF SLEEPY HOLLOW

WASHINGTON IRVING

Many superstitions surround Sleepy Hollow. Some say that a magic spell was cast on it long ago and as a result, all of its inhabitants go about as if in a dream state. These same people also say that there's a ghost that rides on horseback in search of his head which was blown off during the revolutionary war. Ichabod Crane, is the singing master as well as the schoolmaster for the children of the region.

The schoolmaster is generally a man of some importance in the female circle of a rural neighbourhood, being considered a kind of idle gentlemanlike personage, of vastly superior taste and accomplishments to the rough country swains, and, indeed, inferior in learning only to the parson. His appearance, therefore, is apt to occasion some little stir at the tea table of a farmhouse, and the addition of a supernumerary dish of cakes or sweetmeats, or, peradventure, the parade of a silver teapot. Our man of letters, therefore, was peculiarly happy in the smiles of the country damsels. How he would figure among them in the churchyard, between services on Sundays! Gathering grapes for them from the wild vines that overrun the surrounding trees, reciting for their amusement all the epitaphs on the tombstones, or sauntering, with a whole bevy of them, along the banks of the adjacent millpond, while the more bashful country bumpkins hung sheepishly back, envying his superior elegance and address.

From his half-itinerant life, also, he was a kind of travelling gazette, carrying the whole budget of local gossip from house to house, so that his appearance was always greeted with satisfaction. He was, moreover, esteemed by the women as a man of great erudition, for he had read several books quite through, and was a perfect master of Cotton Mather's History of New England Witchcraft, in which, by the way, he most firmly and potently believed.

He was, in fact, an odd mixture of small shrewdness and simple credulity. His appetite for the marvelous, and his powers of digesting it, were equally extraordinary; and both had been increased by his residence in this spellbound region. No tale was too gross or monstrous for his capacious swallow. It was often his delight, after his school was dismissed in the afternoon, to stretch himself on the rich bed of clover, bordering the little brook that whimpered by his schoolhouse, and there con over old Mather's dire tales, until the gathering dusk of the evening made the printed page a mere mist before his eyes. Then, as he wended his way, by swamp and stream and awful woodland, to the farmhouse where he happened to be quartered, every sound of nature, at that watching hour, fluttered his excited imagination: the moan of the whippoorwill from the hillside; the boding cry of the tree toad, that harbinger of storm; the dreary hooting of the screech owl, or the sudden rustling in the thicket of birds frightened from their roost. The fireflies, too, which sparkled most vividly in the darkest places, now and then startled him, as one of uncommon brightness would stream across his path; and if, by chance, a huge blockhead of a beetle came winging his blundering flight against him, the poor varlet was ready to give up the ghost, with the idea that he was struck with a witch's token. His only resource on such occasions, either to drown thought or drive away evil spirits, was to sing psalm tunes; and the good people of Sleepy Hollow, as they sat by their doors of an evening, were often filled with awe, at hearing his nasal melody, 'in linked sweetness long drawn out', floating from the distant hill or along the dusky road.

Another of his sources of fearful pleasure was to pass long winter evenings with the old Dutch wives as they sat spinning by the fire, with a row of apples roasting and sputtering along the hearth, and listen to their marvelous tales of ghosts and goblins, and haunted fields, and haunted brooks, and haunted bridges, and haunted houses, and particularly of the headless horseman, or the galloping Hessian of the Hollow, as they sometimes called him. He would delight them equally by his anecdotes of witchcraft, and of the direful omens and portentous sights and sounds in the air, which prevailed in the earlier times of Connecticut; and would frighten them woefully with speculations upon comets and shooting stars, and with the alarming fact that the world did absolutely turn around, and that they were half the time topsy-turvy!

But if there was a pleasure in all this, while snugly cuddling in the chimney corner of a chamber that was all a ruddy glow from the crackling wood fire, and where, of course, no spectre dared to show his face, it was nearly purchased by the terrors of his subsequent walk homewards. What fearful shapes and shadows beset his path amidst the dim and ghastly glare of a snowy night! With what wistful look did he eye every trembling ray of light streaming across the waste fields from some distant window! How often was he appalled by some shrub covered with snow, which, like a sheeted spectre, beset his every path! How often did he shrink with curdling awe at the sound of his own steps on the frosty crust beneath his feet; and dread to look over his shoulder, lest he should behold some uncouth being tramping close behind him! And how often was he thrown into complete dismay by some rushing blast, howling among the trees, in the idea that it was the Galloping Hessian on one of his nightly scourings!

All these, however, were mere terrors of the night, phantoms of the mind that walk in darkness; and though he had seen many spectres in his time, and been more than once beset by Satan in diverse shapes, in his lonely perambulations, yet daylight put an end to all these evils, and he would have passed a pleasant life of it, in despite of the devil and all his works, if his path had not been crossed by a being that causes more perplexity to mortal man than ghosts, goblins, and the whole race of witches put together, and that was—a woman.

Among the musical disciples who assembled, one evening in each week, to receive his instructions in psalmody, was Katrina Van Tassel, the daughter and only child of a substantial Dutch farmer. She was a blooming lass of fresh eighteen, plump as a partridge, ripe and melting and rosy-cheeked as one of her father's peaches, and universally famed, not merely for her beauty, but her vast expectations. She was withal a little of a coquette, as might be perceived even in her dress, which was a mixture of ancient and modern fashions, as most suited to set off her charms. She wore the ornaments of pure yellow gold, which her great-grandmother had brought over from Saardam; the tempting stomacher of the olden time; and withal a provokingly short petticoat, to display the prettiest foot and ankle in the country around.

Irving, Washington. *Rip Van Winkle and Other Stories.* New York: Puffin Books, a division of Penguin Books USA Ltd., 1986.

MOUNTJOY:
OR SOME PASSAGES
OUT OF THE LIFE OF
A CASTLE-BUILDER

Washington Irving

The narrator of this tale likes to build castles in the air and weave stories out of his imagination. He grows up in a mansion with his sister Sophy and the characters in their story-books become their friends.

I was born among romantic scenery in one of the wildest parts of the Hudson, which at that time was not so thickly settled as at present. My father was descended from one of the old Huguenot families, that came over to this country on the revocation of the Edict of Nantes. He lived in a style of easy, rural independence, on a patrimonial estate that had been for two or three generations who took the world as it went, and had a kind of laughing philosophy, that parried all rubs and mishaps, and served him in the place of wisdom. This was the part of his character least to my taste; for I was of an enthusiastic, excitable temperament, prone to kindle up with new enthusiasm by some unlucky joke; so that whenever I was in a glow with any sudden excitement, I stood in mortal dread of his good-humour.

Yet he indulged me in every vagary; for I was an only son, and of course a personage of importance in the household. I had two sisters older than myself, and one younger. The former were educated at New York, under the eye of a maiden aunt; the latter remained at home, and was my cherished playmate, the companion of my thoughts. We were two imaginative little beings, of quick susceptibility, and prone to see wonders and mysteries in everything around us. Scarce had we learned to read, when our mother made us holiday presents of all the nursery literature of the day; which at that time consisted of little books covered with gilt paper, adorned with 'cuts', and filled with tales of fairies, giants, and enchanters. What draughts of delightful fiction did we then inhale! My sister Sophy was of a soft and tender nature. She would weep over the woes of the Children in the Wood, or quake at the dark romance of Blue-Beard, and the terrible mysteries of the blue chamber.

But I was all for enterprise and adventure. I burned to emulate the deeds of that heroic prince who delivered the white at from her enchantment; o he of no less royal blood, and doughty emprise, who broke the charmed slumber of the Beauty in the Wood!

The house in which we lived was just the kind of place to foster such propensities. It was a venerable old mansion, half villa, half farmhouse. The oldest part was of stone, with loop-holes for musketry, having served as a family fortress in the time of the Indians. To this there had been made various additions, some of brick, some of wood, according to the exigencies of the moment; so that it was full of nooks and crook, and chambers of all sorts and sizes. It was buried among willows, elms, and cherry trees, and surrounded with roses and hollyhocks with honeysuckle and sweet-briar clambering about every window. A brood of hereditary pigeons sunned themselves upon the roof; hereditary swallow and martins built about the eaves and chimneys; and hereditary bees hummed about the flower-beds.

Under the influenced of our story-books every object around us now assumed a new character, and a charmed interest. The wild flowers were no longer the mere ornaments of the fields, or the resorts of the toilful bee; they were the lurking places of fairies. We would watch the humming-bird, as it hovered around the trumpet creeper at our porch, and the butterfly as it flitted up into the blue air, above the sunny tree tops, and fancy them some of the tiny beings from fairyland. I would call to mind all that I had read of Robin good-fellow and his power of transformation. Oh, how I envied him that power! How I longed to be able to compress my form into utter littleness; to ride the bold dragon-fly; swing on the tall bearded grass; follow the ant into his subterraneous habitation, or dive into the cavernous depths of the honeysuckle!

While I was a mere child I was sent to a daily school, about two miles distant. The schoolhouse was on the edge of the wood, close by a brook overhung with birches, alders, and dwarf willows. We of the school who lived at some distance came with our dinners put up in little baskets. In the intervals of school hours we would gather round a spring, under a tuft of hazel-bushes, and have a kind of picnic; interchanging the rustic dainties with which our provident mothers had fitted us out. Then when our joyous repast was over, and my companions were disposed for play, I would draw forth one of my cherished story-books, stretch myself on the greensward, and soon lose myself in its bewitching contents.

I became an oracle among my schoolmates on account of my superior erudition, and soon imparted to them the contagion of my infected fancy. Often in the evening, after school hours, we would sit on the trunk of some fallen tree in the woods, and vie with each other in telling extravagant stories, until the whippoorwill began his nightly moaning, and the fire-flies sparkled in the gloom. Then came the perilous journey homeward. What delight we would take in getting up wanton panics in some dusky part of the wood;

scampering like frightened deer; pausing to take breath; renewing the panic, and whimpering off again, wild with fictitious terror!

Our greatest trial was to pass a dark, lonely pool, covered with pond-lilies, peopled with bull-frogs and water snakes, and haunted by two white cranes. Oh! the terrors of that pond! How our little hearts would beat as we approached it; what fearful glances we would throw around! And if by chance a plash of a wild duck, or the guttural twang of a bull-frog, struck our ears, as we stole quietly by—away we sped, nor paused until completely out of the woods. Then, when I reached home, what a world of adventures and imaginary terrors would I have to relate to my sister Sophy!

As I advanced in years, this turn of mind increased upon me, and became more confirmed. I abandoned myself to the impulses of a romantic imagination, which controlled my studies, and gave a bias to all my habits. My father observed me continually with a book in my hand, and satisfied himself that I was a profound student; but what were my studies? works of fiction; tales of chivalry; voyages of discovery; travels in the East; everything, in short, that partook of adventure and romance.

Irving, Washington. *Rip Van Winkle and Other Stories.* New York: Puffin Books, a division of Penguin Books USA, Ltd., 1986

Acknowledgments

"Veruca in the Nut Room" from *Charlie and the Chocolate Factory* by Roald Dahl, illustrated by Joseph Schindelman. Copyright © 1964 and renewed 1992 by Roald Dahl. Illustrations copyright © 1964 and renewed 1992 by Alfred A. Knopf, Inc. Reprinted by permission of Alfred A. Knopf, Inc.

"The Humbug Volunteers" from *The Phantom Tollbooth* by Norton Juster, illustrated by Jules Feiffer. Text copyright © 1961 and renewed 1989 by Norton Juster. Illustrations copyright © 1961 and renewed 1989 by Jules Feiffer. Reprinted by permission of Random House, Inc.

Chapters 14, 15 & 16 from *James and the Giant Peach* by Roald Dahl, illustrated by Nancy Ekholm Burkert. Copyright ©1961 and renewed 1989 by Roald Dahl. Illustrations copyright © 1961 and renewed 1989 by Alfred A. Knopf, Inc. Reprinted by permission of Alfred A. Knopf, Inc.

Excerpt and illustrations from *Mary Poppins*, copyright © 1934 and renewed 1962 by P.L. Travers, illustrations by Mary Shepard, reprinted by permission of Harcourt Brace & Company.

"Edmund and the Wardrobe" from *The Chronicles of Narnia: The Lion, the Witch and the Wardrobe* by C.S. Lewis. Copyright © 1950 by C.S. Lewis. Used by permission of HarperCollins Publishers Limited.

From *Incredible Journey* by Sheila Burnford. Copyright © 1960, 1961 by Sheila Burnford. Used by permission of Bantam Books, a division of Bantam Doubleday Dell Publishing Group, Inc.

The selection from *All-of-a-Kind Family* by Sydney Taylor is reprinted by permission of GRM Associates, Inc., Agents for the Estate of Ralph Taylor; Copyright © 1951 by Follett Publishing Company; Copyright © renewed 1979 by Ralph Taylor.

Excerpt from *. . . and now Miguel* by Joseph Krumgold. Copyright © 1953 by Joseph Krumgold. Used by permission of HarperCollins Publishers.

Excerpt from *The Black Pearl*. Copyright © 1967 by Scott O'Dell. Reprinted by permission of Houghton Miflin Co. All rights reserved.

Excerpt from *The Endless Steppe* by Esther Hautzig. Copyright © 1968 by Esther Hautzig. Used by permission of HarperCollins Publishers.

From *The Gold Cadillac* by Mildred D. Taylor. Copyright © 1987 by Mildred D. Taylor. Used by permission of Penguin Books USA, Inc.

Excerpt from *Harriet the Spy* by Louise Fitzhugh. Copyright © 1964, 1984 by Louise Fitzhugh. Used by permission of HarperCollins Publishers.

Excerpt from *Otherwise Known As Sheila the Great* by Judy Blume. Copyright © 1972 by Judy Blume. Used by permission of Penguin Books USA, Inc.

Excerpt from *Over Sea, Under Stone*, copyright © 1965 by Susan Cooper and renewed 1993 by Susan Cooper Grant, reprinted by permission of Harcourt Brace & Company.

Excerpt from *Philip Hall likes me. I reckon maybe.* by Bette Greene. Copyright © 1974 by Bette Greene. Used by permission of Penguin Books USA, Inc.

Text excerpt from chapter 3, and illustration from *Ramona and Her Mother* by Beverly Cleary. Illustrated by Alan Tiegreen. Copyright © 1979 by Beverly Cleary. Used by permission of Morrow Junior Books, a division of William Morrow & Company, Inc.

Excerpt from *Roll of Thunder, Hear My Cry* by Mildred D. Taylor. Copyright © 1976 by Mildred D. Taylor. Used by permission of Penguin Books USA, Inc.

"The First Shlemiel" from *Zlateh the Goat and Other Stories* by Isaac Bashevis Singer. Copyright © 1966 by Isaac Bashevis Singer. Used by permission of HarperCollins Publishers.

Excerpt and illustration from *The Moffats* by Eleanor Estes with illustrations by Louis Slobodkin, copyright © 1941 by Harcourt Brace & Company and renewed 1969 by Eleanor Estes, reprinted by permission of the publisher.

Excerpt from *The Cricket in Times Square* by George Selden. Illustrations by Garth Williams. Copyright © 1960 by George Selden Thompson and Garth Williams. Used by permission of Farrar, Straus and Giroux.

Excerpt from *Crow and Weasel* by Barry Lopez. Copyright © 1990 by Barry Lopez. Used by permission of Farrar, Straus and Giroux.

Excerpt from *Freddy the Cowboy* by Walter R. Brooks. Published by Alfred A. Knopf. Copyright © 1950 by Walter R. Brooks. Copyright renewed © 1977 by Dorothy Brooks. Reprinted by permission of Brandt & Brandt Literary Agents, Inc.

Excerpt from *Frog and Toad are Friends* by Arnold Lobel. Copyright © 1970 by Arnold Lobel. Used by permission of HarperCollins Publishers.

Excerpt from *Redwall* by Brian Jacques, copyright © 1987 by Brian Jacques. Reprinted by permission of Philomel Books.

Excerpt from *The Trumpet of the Swan* by E. B. White. Copyright © 1970 by E. B. White. Used by permission of HarperCollins Publishers.

"Zlateh the Goat" from *Zlateh the Goat and Other Stories* by Isaac Bashevis Singer. Copyright © 1966 by Isaac Bashevis Singer. Used by permission of HarperCollins Publishers.

"The Gravitty-Bitties" from *Centerburg Tales* by Robert McCloskey. Copyright © 1951 by Robert McCloskey. Copyright © renewed 1979 by Robert McCloskey. Used by permission of Penguin Books USA, Inc.

"Harvest" from *Little House in the Big Woods* by Laura Ingalls Wilder. Copyright © 1932 by Laura Ingalls Wilder. Copyright © renewed 1963 by Roger L. Macbride. Reprinted by permission of HarperCollins Publishers.

Excerpt from *The Return of the King*. Copyright © 1955, 1965 by J.R.R. Tolkien, renewed 1983 by Christopher R. Tolkien, Michael H.R. Tolkien, John F.R. Tolkien and M.A.R. Tolkien. Reprinted by permission of Houghton Miflin Co. All rights reserved.

Reprinted by permission of The Putnam Publishing Group from *Mistress Masham's Repose* by T. H. White. Copyright © 1946 by T. H. White; Renewed © 1974 by Lloyd's Bank.

Excerpt from *Finn Family Moomintroll* by Tove Jansson. English translation copyright © 1958 by Ernest Benn Ltd. Text and illustrations copyright © 1948 by Tove Jansson. Used by permission of Farrar, Straus and Giroux.